She hadn't expected to hear that ~~admi~~ ... ~~s~~ quiet statement held more power than if he'd yelled it. "Um . . ." She swallowed. *Um, what?* She wasn't about to apologize for saving her own life. "I didn't mean to."

"I know, you can't help it." He watched her closely, the low light enough to cast a gleam on his eyes, giving them an intensity she hadn't noticed earlier. "You don't panic in a crisis, and you don't wait for someone to save you." His gaze roamed her face, as if memorizing the details of each feature. "Last year, when I first listened to you tell us about how you escaped the drug dealers in Colombia, I admired your self-reliance and determination."

"You did?"

He nodded slightly, almost to himself. "I don't anymore."

"What?" She set her fork aside, forgetting about her risotto. "Why not?"

"Because it's hard to admire what scares me to death. You're risking your life." His voice was low, almost grave. "I need you to stop it."

Her gaze kept drifting to his mouth, distracting her with the memory of what it felt like to be kissed by those lips. His gaze wandered, too, lingering on her mouth, her hair, even her breasts, leaving tingling sensations everywhere it touched. Shadows moved along his jaw as muscles tensed. "Stop making me crazy, Janet."

She shook her head as if she were confused about what he meant. But she knew. She was starting to feel a little crazy herself. . . .

This title is also available as an eBook

Also by Starr Ambrose

Lie to Me
Our Little Secret

Available from Pocket Books

Thieves LIKE US

STARR AMBROSE

Pocket Books

New York London Toronto Sydney

Pocket Books
A Division of Simon & Schuster, Inc.
1230 Avenue of the Americas
New York, NY 10020

This book is a work of fiction. Names, characters, places, and incidents either are products of the author's imagination or are used fictitiously. Any resemblance to actual events or locales or persons, living or dead, is entirely coincidental.

First Pocket Books paperback edition December 2010

POCKET and colophon are registered trademarks of Simon & Schuster, Inc.

For information about special discounts for bulk purchases, please contact Simon & Schuster Special Sales at 1-866-506-1949 or business@simonandschuster.com.

The Simon & Schuster Speakers Bureau can bring authors to your live event. For more information or to book an event contact the Simon & Schuster Speakers Bureau at 1-866-248-3049 or visit our website at www.simonspeakers.com.

Cover illustration by Craig White

Manufactured in the United States of America

10 9 8 7 6 5 4 3 2 1

ISBN 978-1-4391-8129-4
ISBN 978-1-4391-8130-0 (ebook)

To Stevie,
who gave me the idea

Acknowledgments

For advice on things I didn't know and couldn't get away with making up, thanks to Patti Shenberger and Nick Anderson.

Thanks to Jim and Ariana for reading early drafts.

As always, thanks to my agent, Kevan Lyon, for unending patience and support, and to the wonderful people at Pocket Books, especially Danielle Poiesz, who does her best to make me look good.

Chapter One

Dumping the world's worst husband called for more than a celebration. It required a symbolic act. Like hocking her engagement ring.

"You know what this is? It's poetic justice." Janet Aims admired the tasteful display of diamonds twinkling in the window of Portman's Jewelers as if she were buying, not selling. "This is where Banner bought the stupid thing in the first place. I found the receipt."

"That doesn't mean they'll buy it back," Ellie pointed out. "I don't think jewelry stores do that, Jan, especially high-class places like Portman's."

"They buy estate jewelry. This ring is now part of the Westfield *estate,* which ought to be enough to impress anyone in this town. I just have to suck it up and be a Westfield one last time."

She shifted to get a better view of her reflection and finger combed the hairs that barely covered her ears. She wasn't used to the short haircut yet, but she liked it. It was all part of the new Janet. New haircut, new condo, and new marital status—single, with no dazzling diamond ring to remind her of the biggest mistake of her life.

"Do I look rich and influential enough?"

Her friend laughed. "You were born rich and influential. You can do rich and influential in jammies and bunny slippers."

"Not Westfield rich. It's a whole different class of wealth." She gave Ellie a significant eyebrow wiggle. "One you'd better get used to."

"Jack's a Payton, not a Westfield."

"Payton, Westfield, what's the difference? They all connect to Elizabeth Payton Westfield, and it doesn't get any richer than that, at least not in Bloomfield Hills, Michigan." She pulled a white box out of her purse. "Come on, I'll take advantage of my status one last time and show you how the rich folk throw their weight around."

Ellie snickered. "You demonstrate. I'll take notes. You know, it would almost be worth telling Banner what you did with his big, expensive ring—just to ruin his day."

"Since that would require speaking to him, no way. But I like the sentiment." She paused to give her friend a quick hug. "This whole mess has been easier having your support. You're the best." Taking Ellie's hand, she pulled her inside the store. "Let's do this."

Ellie walked fast to keep up. "I'm glad you're in such a good mood. I have to ask you a favor."

"Anything."

"It involves Rocky."

Damn! That was *not* what Janet wanted to hear. She turned, ready to accuse Ellie of taking advantage of her excitement, when a voice behind her said, "Mrs.

Westfield! Welcome to Portman's. How may I help you?"

"We'll discuss this later," Janet hissed to Ellie before replacing her glare with a smile. She turned toward the man behind the counter. She didn't know him, so he must have recognized her from newspaper photos—the wife of the accused. One more reason to hate Banner.

"Hello, Mr. . . ."

"Portman. William Portman."

"Mr. Portman. I'm Miss Aims now."

He flushed. "Of course, I'm sorry."

Letting him feel a little embarrassed might work in her favor. She placed the small box on the glass countertop and opened the white silk lid. "Do you remember this ring, Mr. Portman?"

He smiled as soon as he saw the large diamond flanked by two smaller stones. "Oh, yes. A beautiful piece. We designed the setting exclusively for—" his smile slipped and he cleared his throat. "For Mr. Westfield."

"Yes, you did. So you can understand why, as beautiful as it is, I don't want it anymore."

"Hmm, yes." He pursed his lips and frowned, apparently unsure of the protocol when acknowledging one's association with a known criminal.

"How much can you give me for it?"

Portman looked even more uncomfortable. "Miss Aims, Portman's doesn't accept returns on used jewelry."

"*Used?*" She arched an eyebrow. "Mr. Portman, this jewelry belongs to the Westfield estate. Do you, or do you not, deal in estate jewelry?"

Janet saw his gaze dart across the room to a tall

display case labeled, "Estate Jewelry," then shift quickly away. "Yes, but those are heirloom pieces, crafted by well-known artists. They have historic value in addition to their intrinsic worth."

"I see." She smiled sweetly. "And my ring was crafted by—whom did you say?"

"By, um, us."

"By Portman's Jewelers. A name with a long-standing reputation for fine jewelry. One would hope it was well deserved." She nearly winced at her own arrogance, and reminded herself it was for a good cause—getting rid of the last trace of Banner Westfield. "As for its value, well, I am in possession of the original receipt for this ring. The price was quite impressive. I would hope that a diamond ring costing as much as my BMW would be worth what my husband paid." *Whoops*—the BMW had been Banner's idea, too. The car would have to go. Maybe she should make a list.

Portman turned an interesting shade of dusky purple. "Portman's Jewelers is competitively priced. The price on your ring was fair. Your diamond is of exceptional quality, Miss Aims."

"Of course it is. Heirloom quality, you might say. And it does come with a rather interesting history, doesn't it?" If one were interested in high-profile criminals charged with drug running, money laundering, and attempted murder.

Janet picked up the ring box, admiring the brilliance of the stones. "I had many compliments on the ring. I'm sure you could sell it again. Or even reset the stones. The large one must be quite valuable on its own."

Portman took the ring from the box, allowing the

diamond's facets to catch the bright overhead lights. Tiny arrows of color shot from its surface as the smaller diamonds twinkled beside it. "I don't know." He spoke quietly, almost to himself. "It would be highly irregular and against store policy."

Janet felt a surge of excitement. If he was waffling, she had him.

"My father still owns the store, you know," Portman continued. "Going strong at seventy-six. He doesn't care to make exceptions to the rules."

She knew just how to handle this final hurdle. "Oh yes, Lewis Portman. I believe my mother-in-law, Elizabeth Westfield, knows him well." Janet inserted herself back into the Westfield family temporarily, hoping Elizabeth wouldn't mind. She seemed to like Janet better than her own son these days, anyway. "She's purchased so many lovely pieces of jewelry from your store over the years." She paused deliberately. "The Westfields have always been good customers."

"That's true."

She waited while he thought about the possibility of offending a long-term customer. A *wealthy* long-term customer.

"I couldn't give you anything near what Mr. Westfield paid for the ring."

Warm relief coursed through her, spreading heat to her cold limbs. "I understand completely, Mr. Portman, and I trust whatever you think is fair. Oh, and I wonder if you could include this in the purchase." Before he could object, she pulled a crinkled wad of tissue from her purse and set it on the counter. Inside the thin wrapping, metal rattled against glass. "It was a gift from Mr. Westfield, and I would rather not keep it."

Portman frowned at the tiny bundle as if she'd placed a toad on his immaculate display case. "I really don't think—"

Sensing rejection, Janet rushed to remove the tissue. A double-strand pearl necklace slithered out, followed by a clunk from the attached pendant. Portman stopped talking.

Janet angled the pendant toward Portman. Inside an ornate, filigreed circle of gold, a large red stone glowed beneath the store's strong lights. "If you don't want it, I'll take it somewhere else. I just want to get rid of it." No sense blowing the whole deal because he didn't want her ugly necklace.

Portman leaned closer. So did Ellie, showing the first glimmer of interest in the proceedings. "When did you get that?" Ellie asked. "It's kind of gaudy, isn't it?"

Janet nodded. "Banner bought it for my birthday. I didn't want to offend him by not wearing it, but it's awfully heavy and definitely not my style."

Portman touched the pearl chain and spread it across the glass, giving him a better view of the pendant. Janet said nothing, watching his expression grow thoughtful. He lifted the necklace and let the pendant dangle. Areas of solid gold were decorated with curlicues and raised gold beads. In Janet's opinion, it missed being pretty and went straight to tacky.

"Where did your husband buy this?" he asked without looking away from the necklace.

She was tempted to correct her marital status, but decided not to distract Portman from his obvious fascination with the necklace. If she'd known it would get this sort of reaction, she would have shown it to him first.

"I don't know where he bought it. I've never seen anything like it."

"I have," Portman murmured, lost in his examination. "Somewhere. The style is quite old; it might be a copy of a museum piece. Quality workmanship . . ." His voice faded out as he fumbled beneath his collar and then pulled out a chain with a gold hexagon on the end. He opened it like a jackknife, revealing a jeweler's loupe. Portman held it to his eye and peered closely at the stone. Seconds passed. He tilted the pendant at different angles, still saying nothing. Janet wondered if he'd forgotten about her.

Portman finally looked up, dropping the loupe to let it hang over his tie. "Fifteen thousand."

Her mouth opened, but it took a couple more seconds for words to come out. "Sorry, what?"

"Five for the ring, and ten for the necklace. You understand, I'm taking a big chance on the ring. It's possible no one will want it—with its shady history." He didn't even look embarrassed when he said it.

Janet stared. The ring was worth ten times what he offered, but she hadn't expected more. It was the offer for the necklace that threw her. It had been an afterthought to bring it along, and she would have been thrilled if he'd offered even a few hundred dollars for it.

"Ten thousand dollars for the necklace?"

"Again, a risk on my part."

He didn't strike her as the type to take risks with money. "Then the stone is real?"

"Real? Yes, it's a gemstone."

"A ruby?"

The corner of his mouth gave an arrogant twitch

upward. "No. Quality rubies don't come that large. I'm sure it's a spinel."

His expression was unreadable. She had a feeling he wasn't lying to her, but he also wasn't offering information. "Is that good?"

"Depends. Historically, they were often mistaken for rubies and used in fine pieces of jewelry, most notably in England's Imperial State Crown. Today, they are less common but smaller ones are quite affordable."

She tried to sort out the pertinent facts. "Are you saying this could be a historic piece?"

He shifted from one foot to the other, looking suddenly uncomfortable. "Possibly. It could also be a modern knockoff and relatively worthless." He pursed his lips as he took her measure, probably weighing how far he could push her. "My father is the expert on antique jewelry. If you'd like to wait a couple days for him to look at it—"

And risk having him reduce the price to two hundred dollars? "No need. I accept your offer."

Portman gave a brisk nod and moved quickly to the back of the store.

Ellie grabbed her arm. "Are you crazy? What's the hurry? You should have Rocky look at the necklace. No one knows more about precious gems than he does, and he wouldn't lie to you."

"I don't think Mr. Portman is lying."

"And he's not telling you the whole truth, either. That necklace could be worth a fortune. Rocky would know. Why don't you let me call him?"

Rocky again. Just the thought of him made her insides jumpy.

Trying to keep her voice level, she said, "I'll take the

opinion of a professional over an ex-con jewel thief."
She almost winced at her own words; they sounded so
harsh and unfair, but she really didn't want to discuss
Rocky.

"Jack's an ex-con," Ellie said, unoffended.

"That's different. Banner framed him; he was innocent." Janet could never think of Jack as an ex-con,
and she knew Ellie couldn't, either.

Unfortunately, it wasn't helping her argument against
Rocky. "Rocky was framed, too," Ellie pointed out.

She knew. She'd never asked for the details, but she
believed Ellie, and deep down she knew Rocky was a
good person. He also stirred other feelings inside her—
feelings that she wasn't ready to have yet.

"It's not fair to think of him as a jewel thief," Ellie
said, still stuck on defending the man who'd become
her business partner and her husband's best friend.

"I don't want to think of him at all."

Ellie narrowed her eyes at Janet's stubborn expression, which made Janet nervous. No one knew her
better than Ellie and eventually, she'd figure it out.
Thankfully, Portman reappeared with a check, giving
her an excuse to change the subject. She thanked him,
tucked it into her purse, and motioned Ellie toward the
door.

But Ellie wasn't ready to drop the subject. Once
back in the June sunlight, she said, "*Everyone* likes
Rocky. I can't believe you don't."

Probably because she *did* like him, far more than
she wanted to.

Janet sighed dramatically. "Okay, let's skip the
setup. I can see you're determined to make me like
Rocky. What does he have to do with this favor you

want? Because I'm sure I can continue to dislike the man while doing whatever it is you want me to do." Or at least pretend to dislike him.

Ellie frowned. "Probably. But you can't let it show, because you'll be in public. I need you to cover for me and help Rocky with a demonstration we scheduled for tomorrow night."

"For Red Rose Security? But I don't know anything about your business."

"You don't have to. You just have to be Rocky's assistant. He'll show you everything you need to know."

"Uh-huh." She bet he would. "You know, you look so innocent with those big blue eyes and your hair in a cute little ponytail. Almost like you *aren't* trying to set me up."

"I'm not." At Janet's skeptical look, she threw up her hands. "Honest. Jack and I just finally want to take our delayed honeymoon. But I had the brilliant idea to have Rocky speak to some women's groups about home security. He's so charming they fall all over themselves making appointments for personal consultations. We get a ton of business that way."

It was true. Women ate up that big, lopsided grin, especially when it was combined with his former bad boy life of crime, which Rocky always admitted to. His burglary skills were his credentials. Between his expertise at advising clients on the best security systems and Ellie's skills at planning and organization, their fledgling security business was booming.

Janet pointed toward her car, parked a couple spaces away, to keep Ellie talking as they walked. "It's not hard; you just need to be an extra set of hands, then set up any appointments. I'd ask Lisa, but she can't get a sitter at night. I canceled everything else for the next two weeks, but I can't get out of this one. I know you're busy trying to reestablish Aims Air Freight, but—"

"Okay, okay, okay," Janet relented with a groan. She started the car. "I'm not going to keep my best friend from her honeymoon."

Her racing heart sounded louder than the engine.

Five minutes later, Janet could feel Ellie studying her as she drove. "You know, he doesn't feel the same way about you. He thinks you're great," Ellie said.

Oh, she knew. Better than she'd ever let on. He hadn't made it a secret, and resisting a devilishly cute, smooth-talking hunk of man went against some basic instinct that she had to stomp down every time she saw him.

"If you didn't already know him, I'd introduce you, because I think you two would be great together. Did you know he's nearly at the top of his class in law school? Smart guy. Plus he's cute, and funny, and he loves kids. Like you."

Another perfect man. Although Rocky was possibly the real thing—unlike her ex-husband, who had hidden a psychopath's personality behind the guise of perfection. She'd paid a big price for her little lapse in judgment, so big that she didn't know if she could ever trust her gut again. If only Banner had come with the warning, "Willing to screw you over to get what I want," she could have saved herself a lot of time and heartache.

Ellie was still watching her with a bemused expression.

"Stop matchmaking, El. You found the only perfect

guy out there, and I'm willing to settle for watching from the sidelines."

"Jack *is* perfect," she agreed. "And no, you aren't."

Trust a best friend to point out when you're lying. "Stop being a pain in the butt and tell me about this honeymoon of yours. Where are you going to go?"

Ellie took the hint and started talking about her trip. It kept them occupied until they got to Ellie's house.

Janet pulled in the driveway behind Jack, who was standing beside his car with a well-built, tanned man in a Hawaiian shirt and cutoff shorts. Rocky.

"Crap."

Ellie laughed.

Not saying hello would be rude. Janet was willing to tarnish her reputation and bolt, but Ellie took her sweet time getting out of the car, long enough for Rocky to stroll over to the driver's side. Not opening the window would be beyond rude, and it would make Ellie mad. *Crap again.*

She hit the power switch and ordered herself to relax. Rocky waited for the glass to lower all the way, then folded his arms on the open window and leaned down. His dark eyes were level with hers, and he was close enough for her to appreciate the thick lashes that any woman would have envied.

"Hey, Janet." His mouth curved into the lopsided smile she'd prepared for, but something still tripped in her chest.

"Hi."

"Still avoiding me?"

Heat threatened to creep up her neck to her face.

"Still deluding yourself that everything I do revolves around you?"

"Interesting fantasy." His gaze wandered over her for several seconds while she tried not to squirm. "Nice haircut. It looks good on you."

"Thanks," she mumbled, unable to stop the automatic response good manners demanded. Damn her proper upbringing. "I thought you liked long hair." It was the only defiant thought that came to mind.

His smile grew. "Is that why you cut it?"

"No!" This time she felt the blush reach her cheeks and was furious at her own reaction. The idea that cutting her hair had anything to do with him was absurd, but he always seemed to keep her off balance. She needed to take the lead instead of letting him manipulate the conversation. "I just learned I'm filling in for Ellie at some demonstration you're doing tomorrow night. Can you give me the time and place?"

"I'll pick you up at seven."

"I'll meet you there," she protested. But when Rocky moved his hand and she felt his fingers brush her cheek, her words faltered.

"A mosquito," he explained. "If we use one car we'll save gas. It's ecologically responsible."

He knew her well enough to throw out the one reason she wouldn't argue with. No doubt Ellie had been talking about her. "Fine." She looked pointedly at his shirt. "Are you dressing like that?"

He feigned surprise. Glancing at the shirt, one of several that made up what Ellie called his "surfer dude" look, he asked, "Is there something wrong with pineapples and palm fronds?"

She considered the loud yellow-and-green pattern. "I'm gonna go with yes."

He looked amused. "Don't worry, tomorrow night I will wear what proper Bloomfield Hills ladies expect me to wear."

That meant something conservative and expensive. She had a wardrobe full of that. "Okay, I'll be ready."

"I can come early if you'd like. We can practice."

She recognized the unspoken meaning, but was annoyed that she didn't flush at the thought. "No, thanks. I don't need practice."

He winked. "Good to know. See you tomorrow."

Arrogant jerk. He stepped back as she jammed the car into reverse. She barely remembered to wave at Ellie and Jack before speeding off.

Rocky strolled back up the driveway. Jack watched his wife's rear end appreciatively as she walked to the house before turning his attention back to the matter at hand. Digging into his pocket, he handed the house keys to Rocky. "Ellie said you only have to water the plants once."

Uh-huh. That wasn't the thought behind that carefully neutral expression. "And what did she say about Janet?"

Jack's mouth quirked upward, obviously unperturbed at relaying his wife's message. "That you shouldn't rush her."

"Who's rushing? I've known her a year."

Jack leaned against the car and folded his arms. "Yeah, I was there when you met. You decided you wanted her after knowing her two whole hours. You don't call that rushing?"

"This from the man who got engaged after knowing a woman—what? Two minutes?"

Jack's composure slipped into a slight frown. "That doesn't count. It wasn't real for at least a week." Seeing Rocky's smile, he apparently thought better of using the details of his impromptu engagement to Ellie as a shining example of restraint. "Come on, Rocky. Ellie has a point. I know you're putting your life back together. You've done a good job of it, too, starting the business with Ellie and going to law school. But you don't have to have everything all at once. You can't just go out and get an instant wife and family."

"What family? Janet doesn't have kids. And I'm not looking to marry her, just *be* with her. Minus her clothes." Crude guy humor was safer than admitting the truth, that he just might want something more with this woman.

Jack snorted. "It doesn't all happen that fast just because you want it to. And you can't expect her to accommodate your accelerated schedule."

"Overlooking the fact that it happened exactly that fast for *you*, I have to repeat, I've known Janet for a year. Hell, I knew her six months before I even kissed her. That's beyond patient for me. I've never even had a relationship that lasted that long."

Jack's brow lifted. "You kissed her?"

"You mean it wasn't a household news flash? She didn't tell Ellie? Those two talk about everything."

Jack waved it off. "I'm sure she told Ellie. But no one told me. When did this happen?"

He didn't even question his friend's intrusion on what he might normally consider private business. He'd met Jack in jail, where privacy was nearly impossible and personal issues were discussed openly. Jack Payton was closer to him than his own brother. "Here, at your New Year's Eve party."

Jack made a scoffing noise. "New Year's kisses don't count."

"It wasn't like that. And believe me, this one counted."

Jack gave it a moment's consideration. "Still, I gotta trust Ellie on this. You might be moving too fast. If she's not ready, you'll blow it."

It was a valid point. Janet had been uncertain and scared after her disastrous marriage to Banner. But her confidence was back now: She laughed a lot and had plans for her future. He needed her to know he wanted to be part of that future.

"I think she likes me."

"Right. That's why she acts like she wants nothing to do with you."

He looked down the street toward where Janet's car had disappeared, smiling as he thought about it. "That's what I'm hoping."

Chapter Two

It was unusual for her doorbell to ring on a Tuesday morning while she was getting ready for work. It was even more unusual to find two uniformed police officers on her front porch.

"Are you Janet Aims?"

She glanced at their photo IDs and blinked in confusion. "Yes, I am. What can I do for you?"

"May we come in?"

Her gaze automatically flicked past them to the lawn outside her condo. Sprinklers swished across green lawns, and someone walked by with a dog, glancing curiously at the patrol car, then at the officers in her doorway. "Sure." She stood aside and closed the door behind them, suddenly filled with dread. Didn't the police always want to talk to you in private when they delivered bad news?

"Did something happen? Was there an accident?" Her mind raced through the possibilities before they could answer. Her parents lived in Arizona—could there have been a medical emergency? Her pulse shot up. Or Elizabeth, who seemed perfectly healthy, but was getting to that age when . . . Oh, God! Ellie and Jack were getting on a plane today. But it wouldn't have left yet, would it? Her mind whirled and her stomach tightened, bracing for bad news. One of them spoke, but her frantic pulse was so loud in her ears she didn't catch what he said.

"I'm sorry, what did you say?" She gripped her hands together to keep them from shaking.

The officer—Furley, according to his name badge— spoke more slowly. "Miss Aims, did you sell some pieces of jewelry yesterday at Portman's Jewelers?"

"What?" She must have looked as dumbfounded as she sounded. Relief washed through her like a cool wave as she tried to concentrate on what he'd said. "Yes. Yes, I did. Why?"

He pulled a piece of paper from an inner pocket in his jacket, unfolding it to reveal a picture. "Do you recognize this?"

One corner of the white paper showed a computer-generated digital picture. But not that of the diamond ring she expected to see. Instead, it was the pearl-studded chain and the ugly gold pendant with the embedded red stone. Curiosity was overcoming surprise as she met the officers' expressionless gazes. "Yes, that's my necklace. I mean, it was. I sold it to Mr. Portman."

Furley shot a quick glance at the other policeman, making Janet tense up. "What's wrong? Has there been a robbery or something?" Not that it should involve her, but maybe Mr. Portman needed her to verify his inventory.

Something flickered in Furley's eyes and he looked more alert. "Why do you say that?"

"Because I don't know why you would ask me to identify the necklace, unless to verify that Portman's had it."

But that wasn't it, she could tell from his blank expression. Another thought struck her—what if Mr. Portman had discovered that it wasn't nearly as valuable as he'd thought, and wanted his money back? Would he call the police for that?

No, of course not. But the thought did nothing to allay her heart-pounding panic. There was still something wrong, and the police had come to *her* house, looking stern and implacable. That couldn't be good.

When Furley didn't say anything, she tried a direct approach. "Why are you asking me about the necklace?"

"Miss Aims, how did you acquire the necklace?"

The same thing Portman had asked.

"My ex-husband gave it to me for my birthday. I don't know where he bought it. I already told Mr. Portman all this." If she knew what they were getting at, she could be more helpful, not to mention a whole lot less nervous. It was amazing how being questioned by the police had a way of making a simple transaction sound terrifying.

"Do you have a sales receipt for it?"

"No, it was a gift."

"Do you usually sell expensive gifts from family members?"

Nerves gave way to annoyance. He'd just hit what was still a very sensitive spot. "No, I don't. Officer, do you know who my ex-husband is?"

"Yes, ma'am, I do. Banner Westfield, currently

awaiting trial on charges of drug running and money laundering."

"And attempted murder. Of *me*." She let it sink in. "And you wonder why I don't want to keep a memento of our wonderful time together?" She nodded at the picture. "Besides the fact that it's ugly. Just look at it. Frankly, I don't know if Portman's can find a market for it. No one makes necklaces like that anymore."

"No ma'am, they don't. Not for the past several hundred years, since the time this one was made." He held the photo out again.

She gave the picture a careless glance. So it really was an heirloom. Old, but probably cheap, being so unattractive. It wouldn't be fair to keep the ten thousand dollars, but right now she felt like she deserved something, if only because her breakfast was now a hard lump in her stomach. Maybe fifty dollars. Portman *had* agreed to buy the thing, after all. "It's old. So what?"

"The senior Mr. Portman identified it as soon as he saw it. He showed us a detailed drawing of it in a book. The necklace is part of a jewelry collection that was owned by a museum in Germany until it was stolen in"—he looked at something scribbled on the back of the photo—"1788."

Her uncharitable thoughts about Portman came screeching to a halt. "Wait. It was stolen? From a museum?" She had no idea how Banner ended up buying it more than two hundred years later, but that wasn't her problem. If it had been stolen, that meant it had to be returned. No one got to keep the necklace. Which meant she couldn't keep the money. She sighed, prepared to deal with yet another piece of debris from her disastrous marriage.

"It's not a problem, officer. I'm quite willing to give Mr. Portman his money back. I'll just rip up the check."

"Ma'am, you can work that out with Portman's later. Right now we'd like you to come to the station with us for a talk."

She nodded, willing to cooperate, but unsure what more she could tell them. "About what?"

"About why you were in possession of priceless stolen jewelry. And why you were so anxious to sell it." He raised an eyebrow, the first change in his expression. "Just to clear things up."

Priceless? Janet swallowed, and wasn't surprised to feel a lump in her throat. "Do I need a lawyer?"

"No, ma'am. But you can call one if you'd like. We'll wait."

She reminded herself that innocent people providing information didn't need lawyers. But she'd seen too much TV to think the facts couldn't get twisted. "Just give me a couple minutes to make that call."

But not to her lawyer. The woman had done an excellent job of protecting her against Banner's legal sharks during their divorce, but had no experience with criminal cases. There was only one person she knew of who understood the ins and outs of the legal system and knew something about stolen jewelry—Rocky Hernandez.

With no windows to let in fresh air, the interview room smelled of body odor and stale coffee.

And criminals. She couldn't help the irrational thought. Her ex-husband had probably sat in this very room with one or two of his high-priced attorneys. This was where they brought their suspects.

They could have talked with her in that bright office she'd passed, but they'd brought her here. Maybe they thought the privacy would make her more relaxed, but it just reminded her that murderers and rapists had sat in this spot before her. Edging forward, she put the smallest possible part of her in contact with her chair.

She nearly jumped up when Rocky came in, followed by Furley and his partner. She half stood, barely having enough time to register her surprise at Rocky's neatly tailored three-piece suit before he surprised her again by leaning down to give her a brief hug. She realized just how nervous she'd been when she felt herself relax. As they sat, he kept his arm slung across the back of her chair.

"Thanks for coming," she said.

"No problem." His hand came up to touch her shoulder and his dark brown eyes crinkled with a reassuring smile before he turned to face the officers across from them. "Let's just tell them what they want to know, and we'll be out of here."

She nodded. The sooner the better.

Furley and his partner were distant but polite as she gave a detailed story of receiving the necklace from Banner, then selling it to Portman's along with her engagement ring. But it was Rocky's hand resting lightly on her shoulder that kept her calm and steady. She never realized how much trust and confidence she had in him. Maybe it was the suit. She'd rarely seen him in anything but the ubiquitous Hawaiian shirts and jeans. She barely recognized him.

Unfortunately, it seemed Sergeant Furley did. When she finished talking, it was Rocky who captured his attention. Furley gave him a hard stare that made her shift uncomfortably in her chair again, but Rocky seemed unaffected. "What did you say your name was?"

"Roberto Hernandez."

"Huh. I've heard of you before."

"Really? I'm sorry I can't say I've heard of you."

Furley's brow puckered as he thought. "I've seen your picture."

Rocky gave a modest shrug. "I'm quite photogenic."

Beckman, Furley's partner, had said nothing while Janet spoke, and he didn't move now as he regarded Rocky from his tipped-back chair. After several seconds the stony facade cracked, and a smile that was more like a sneer crossed his face. He whacked his partner in the shoulder. "Rocky Hernandez. Spent some time as a guest of the county."

Furley brightened. "Right. Now I remember. Burglary, wasn't it?"

"No." Rocky corrected him with a tight smile. "Breaking and entering. But it's nice to be remembered."

He cocked an eyebrow. "Thought you said you were a law student."

"I am."

"They let criminals become lawyers?"

"With good character references." He flashed a smile. "I have an exemplary character."

Furley smirked. "Ya don't say."

Janet gave Rocky a worried glance. He looked unconcerned, even though his steady gaze seemed to hide a touch of annoyance at the line of questioning. Furley, on the other hand, was beginning to look like a lion stalking a zebra. "Rumor has it you're a pro."

"You can't believe everything you hear. And I'll be glad to chat with you about it later, but my past has nothing to do with Janet."

Furley ignored the hint. "Jewelry, isn't it? That's your thing." He looked between Janet and Rocky. "And your pretty little friend here was selling a hot necklace. Wouldn't you call that interesting?"

"I'd say it's more ironic," Rocky answered.

Janet didn't know how Rocky could remain so calm when Furley's smile had become so predatory. Feeling uneasy, she shifted her gaze to Beckman. He stared back with the same intensity her cat had while watching birds, unflinching and ready to pounce. A tiny whiplash of panic sent her heart racing. "Rocky?"

He squeezed her shoulder. "It's all right, Janet. These nice officers are right to be concerned, but you haven't done anything wrong. You didn't know the necklace was stolen, you went to a respected jeweler, and you didn't try to hide your identity or deny what you did." He looked at Furley. "Just like any innocent person would do."

Furley gave him an emotionless glance, then focused on Janet. "This friend of yours," he consulted his notes, "Ellie. She heard the whole transaction?"

"Yes."

"I'd like her address and phone number so we can verify your story."

Janet wiggled on the edge of her chair. "I can give it to you, but she's not there. She left on vacation this morning, and she's probably halfway over the Atlantic right now."

Furley raised an eyebrow. "She left the country?"

Janet could almost hear alarm bells ring and fought

to stay calm. "It's a delayed honeymoon. She went with her husband."

"So the trip was planned for some time?"

Damn. "Uh, no, I don't think so. It was a spontaneous thing." She widened her eyes at Rocky in an appeal for help.

"Newlyweds," he said with a happy smile, as if that explained everything. "They didn't leave their itinerary, but I believe they're flying to Heathrow, then Frankfurt. Perhaps you can find a way to leave a message for them."

They had a staring contest for several seconds. Since Rocky looked unperturbed, Janet sat quietly and waited it out. Finally, Furley turned back to her. "Did your husband give you any other pieces of jewelry?"

"Ex-husband." She and Rocky said it together.

"No," she told Furley.

"Perhaps you forgot."

"Not a chance. We weren't together that long, and he wasn't that generous."

Furley rubbed his upper lip while waiting for her to volunteer more information. When she didn't, he pulled out a business card and pushed it across the table. "If you find anything that indicates where your ex-husband bought the necklace"—he emphasized the *ex* part, as though indulging an unreasonable request—"give me a call."

He stood, and Janet breathed a sigh of relief. "I doubt I'll find anything," she told him. "Whatever I didn't give away or throw out, I dumped into a big pile and burned." She followed Rocky's lead and rose, conscious of his hand on her back as she left the room. He kept it there until they reached the front door of the police station, and he held it open for her. Once on the sidewalk, he grinned at her. "That wasn't so bad."

She shivered, even though the sun felt warm. "I felt like a suspect."

"You *were* a logical suspect."

He seemed too complacent about it. "It's not funny."

"Sorry." But he shook his head and chuckled. "I just never thought being questioned by the police was something we'd have in common."

That better be as far as it went; she had no desire to see the inside of a jail cell. She sighed. "Thank you for coming down here. I didn't know who else to call."

"My pleasure, even if I was your default choice for someone with criminal experience."

He was so amused by the whole thing, she decided she might be overdramatizing the incident. At least he'd gone to the trouble of wearing a power suit to impress the cops. She took a second to admire the look. "You know, for an ex-con, you clean up well." She fingered his jacket. "I didn't know you even owned a suit."

"There's a lot you don't know about me." He gave her a smile that made her think of a mischievous little boy, but one who was all grown up and interested in far more adult pursuits. The trippy feeling hit her chest again.

He didn't seem to notice the effect he had on her. "You should have called me before you went to Portman's. I could have saved you the embarrassment of being hauled down to the police station and treated like a criminal."

"I wasn't 'hauled' down anywhere, I went willingly."

But he was right, it was embarrassing. His grin defused her temper. "How could you have prevented that? Are you telling me you know more about jewelry than Mr. Portman and his father?"

"Apparently, I know more about stolen jewelry. I recognized the necklace."

"You did?" She couldn't keep the amazement out of her voice. "They said it was stolen over two hundred years ago, so I know you had nothing to do with it."

He put a hand to his chest. "You wound me. I really must clarify my criminal history for you sometime."

She gave him a sidelong glance, thinking that might be a good idea. And a dangerous one—if she found out he really wasn't the criminal she'd tried to pretend he was, she'd have fewer defenses against all that sexy charm. She needed to resist him. Rocky was the most tempting man she'd ever met, but she couldn't afford to make the same mistake she had with Banner.

"I really would like to hear what you know about the necklace."

"It'll be best if I can use the Internet."

That meant letting him in her house. "Okay," she agreed, telling herself it was for educational purposes only.

The laptop was where she'd left it on the coffee table. Beside it, her large black-and-white cat sprawled in a pool of sunlight. She shooed him away while Rocky stripped off his suit coat and adjusted his vest before sitting down and tapping at the keys. For a moment she let her mind go fuzzy. He did the corporate look so well, it was hard to picture him in his stupid Hawaiian shirts. The man was a chameleon. Probably a good quality in a thief, but not in a . . . whatever he was to her. Acquaintance.

After only ten seconds of searching, he turned the screen toward her. "There's your necklace."

She sat beside him, studying the picture on the screen. The ugly necklace was laid out on black velvet, twinkling from every gold link that showed between the small pearls. The pendant glowed with rich red tones.

"How can there be a picture of it if it disappeared before the invention of the camera?"

"It's a copy." He stroked the cat, who had settled on the couch beside him. "Most famous jewels and jewelry are copied. Now look at this."

He reached across her and clicked open another window. Now the necklace was the central piece in an arrangement of matching jewels—two earrings, a ring, and a brooch. Red stones shone on all the pearl-encrusted gold pieces, but none as large as the one in the necklace. "Have you ever seen any of those?"

She shook her head. "Were those stolen, too?"

"Yes, all at the same time. And they most likely went to the same collector."

"So where are they now?"

"No one knows. They could have been passed down through generations, but it's more likely that whoever stole them cared more for money than gems and sold them through underground connections. They could have traveled the world several times since their theft as they changed hands. How they popped up now is the million-dollar question. Or, I should say, millions of dollars."

He had to be kidding. "For those ugly things?"

"For the *Pellinni Jewels*. What's this guy's name?" He scratched a furry cheek in what the cat obviously thought was just the right spot.

"Jingles," she told him absently, looking at the computer screen.

He winced. "Sorry, man," he commiserated, scratching Jingles's other cheek. The cat purred while Janet hunched forward to examine the earrings. Passably pretty, she decided. The ring and brooch were downright ugly.

"Why is it so valuable?"

"Large spinels are rare. The Pellinni is thought to be forty-two carats, but it's only an estimate because accurate measurements weren't available until the early twentieth century, and by that time it was long gone."

She stared at the necklace that she'd shoved in the back of her lingerie drawer a year ago, not even bothering to put it in the safe as Banner had instructed. Millions of dollars? She turned to cast a curious look over her shoulder. "How do you know about some Italian jewelry collection that's a few hundred years old?"

"Over six hundred years. And it started out Italian, but it's actually considered German."

Janet sat back, waiting for the explanation.

Bending toward Jingles's furry head, he said, "He's pretending not to be impressed with my wealth of knowledge."

She tried not to smile, which was difficult while he massaged her cat into a purring, drooling state of bliss. Not that she'd let it influence her, but the cat had disliked Banner, with what she suspected was good reason.

Jingles flopped over, shamelessly begging for more attention as Rocky talked. "A rich Florentine bride, Giovanna Pellinni, brought it with her as part of her dowry when she married a German nobleman, Franz Konig. That was in 1465. It was passed down in the Konig family as the Pellinni Jewels, until they were donated to a museum in the eighteenth century."

"Probably when some smart Konig woman refused to wear them."

She wasn't kidding, but he smiled anyway. "Maybe. They were stolen soon after that, in 1788, and never seen again. That is, until Banner gave you the Pellinni necklace and you sold it."

"Very impressive. So how do you know all that? Did you expect to come across famous missing German jewelry while looting someone's safe in Bloomfield Hills?"

His smile grew wider and more lopsided. Cuter, too, damn it. "No. You could call it professional interest. I like to know my trade."

"So you know what to steal."

"So I'd know what *not* to steal. I was extremely selective. And that"—he indicated the picture on the screen—"is something I would have avoided. But I'll admit it would be nice to admire the workmanship up close."

The history of the necklace she'd temporarily owned was fascinating, but she was suddenly more interested in Rocky's career as a jewel thief. She only knew what Ellie had told her, and she hadn't been interested in hearing it back then.

"Ellie told me you only stole from other thieves."

He wiggled an eyebrow. "You were talking about me?"

Don't blush! "I wasn't, Ellie was."

"Ah." She was relieved he let it go. "Stealing from other thieves is simplifying it. But yes, every person I stole from had purchased the gems illegally. They bought stolen goods, and they knew it. You could say I reclaimed them."

"Nice euphemism. It's still stealing."

"Yes, it is."

She thought about it for another moment. "But they can't report it."

"That's right. They can't run to the police and say, this guy stole a hundred thousand dollars worth of diamonds from me, when coincidentally that was the value of the stones taken in a recent robbery. Even if they can't pin the robbery on the guy, he can't prove the stones are his, and he's drawn unwanted attention to himself. So he has to write it off as a loss."

"Or try to get even."

He winked at her. "You know, I always liked that about you, Janet. You think like a criminal."

She gave him a sour look. "Is that supposed to be a compliment?"

"Absolutely. That's how you stayed alive when Banner sent you off with Colombian drug dealers who were supposed to kill you—you knew what they intended to do, and you found a way out of it. Successful criminals have to be resourceful and think a step ahead or they get caught."

"You got caught."

He actually looked embarrassed. "A technicality. I was set up by someone who held a grudge and I was stupid enough to fall for it. But smart enough not to get caught with the gems he was hoping I'd take."

He seemed to be waiting for more questions, but she didn't want to ask them. If she knew his whole story she had a feeling he wouldn't look like an ordinary thief at all. She might even admire him.

"Thanks for telling me," she mumbled. She folded the laptop closed, hoping he got the message—lesson over, time to go.

He got up, receiving a surprised blink from Jingles, but made no move to leave. "You really have no idea where or how Banner got the necklace?"

"No. But I'm pretty sure he didn't steal it himself, if that's what you mean. His style is to let other people do the actual dirty work while he pockets the money."

He nodded in a distracted way, as if it wasn't pertinent. "Do you have any idea how long he had it?"

"No. I had the impression he'd just bought it, but I don't remember if he actually said that." She didn't like the concerned look on his face. "Why does it matter?"

"Because whoever owned the necklace most likely owned the rest of the collection. And whoever stole it most likely stole those other pieces, too."

"But I don't have them."

"No one knows that, Janet. And someone will be looking for them."

She knew he was right and felt the first prick of apprehension. "You know the jewelry trade. Will they be able to trace the necklace back to me?"

"All too easily. Portman's had it, and believe me, they'll be talking about it. You showing up at Portman's with that necklace is like someone walking into an art gallery with a missing Picasso. It's news. Word will travel through the legitimate people in the industry, to the slightly less legitimate, right down to the shady fences you don't want to meet. Everyone will know the Pellinni necklace has reappeared—and who had it."

She was afraid of that. "And you think someone will break in here, hoping to steal them from me."

His smile was forced. "Definitely. Whoever secretly owned that collection paid a lot for it. You'd better believe he wants it back before the FBI gets their hands on it and returns it to that museum in Germany, which is probably where the necklace will be going soon. Look at it this way: Most people think the necklace has been found. But someone out there thinks of it as lost. Missing from his private collection. And if he doesn't move fast, the rest of the pieces will be lost, too."

She wasn't ready to panic, but she knew the implications. "So I'm in danger."

"Let's just say not all jewel thieves are as charming and suave as the one you know."

She couldn't resist a sly comeback. "Or as filled with self-admiration?"

He flashed his killer smile again. "Well, they might be, but of course it's sadly misplaced."

"Of course." Things were starting to feel too friendly, considering her determination to keep him at a distance. "Look, all kidding aside—"

"I'm not kidding." He cut her off, his light tone suddenly sharp. "This is not a game, and the people who will be looking for the jewels are deadly serious. Emphasis on deadly."

"I understand." He'd stepped closer, and she crossed her arms over her chest. "I'm not helpless. You know I have an excellent security system, because you installed it yourself."

"Windows can be broken, wires can be cut, doors can be smashed in."

Irritation flickered. She knew what he wanted; he wanted her to move out. The ironic part was, if this had happened a year from now when she was more secure in her independence, she might not have argued. Logic told her he was right. But he'd touched on a purely emotional issue. She'd just rid herself of the last trace of her controlling ex-husband, and hearing another man tell her what to do aroused in her an irrational stubbornness.

"I've been held captive by drug lords and faced down a killer. You didn't know me well back then, but you were there, so you know I'm capable of handling myself."

"I know you're brave." His face softened. "But you're not bulletproof, Janet."

Damn, he could be pretty persuasive when he stood that close and looked that concerned. Also, when he was right. "I'll consider leaving," she said.

"Soon."

"Don't push." She said it quietly, needing him to understand.

He studied her, then gave a brief nod. "Okay. But one question. If it were someone else asking, would you move out now?"

She did a mental stumble. Would she? Or was she simply resisting him on principal, trying to push him away?

She *did* want to push him away. Having him near awoke a desire she thought Banner had killed, a desire she couldn't trust. It turned out that attempted murder was a good cure for following one's heart. She couldn't risk being with Rocky, not when he made her feel so confused and flushed and—what was the question?

She stuck her hands in her pockets, feeling suddenly awkward. "It has nothing to do with you. I keep telling you, not everything does."

His lips curved up slowly, as if the thought behind his smile kept getting better and better. "But some things do, don't they?" he said over his shoulder as he headed for the door.

Butterflies fluttered in her stomach. She watched him leave, staring at the closed door and wondering just how many of her thoughts he had read.

Seconds later she jumped at his sharp knock. "Lock it," Rocky called from the other side. "I'm waiting."

With new resolve, she marched over and gave the deadbolt a sharp twist. She'd work with him tonight because she'd promised Ellie, but that was it. Life was easier when she avoided Rocky.

Rocky sat in his car, studying Janet's condo, thinking of all the ways he could break in.

It was too easy. If he could think of them, so could a pro, and that's who would be coming. Someone who wouldn't be stopped by the best security systems because they would know, as Rocky did, that the easiest way around them was through the front door. If she was too cautious to let someone in, they only had to wait for her to go out. It would be easy enough to overpower her. No alarm, no forced entry. And no one else in the house to contend with.

He couldn't watch her all the time. He had work

to do, even more than usual with Ellie gone for two weeks. He shouldn't even be sitting here now; he had afternoon appointments waiting.

He started the car and pulled out, reassuring himself that she probably had a few days grace before anyone would track her down. But they would. He'd hinted only that it was possible, because he hadn't wanted to scare her. In truth, it was a *certainty*. If he had to, he'd insist she leave or he'd park in her driveway day and night. She was probably stubborn enough to make him do it, too.

He knew she needed to learn to trust herself again. But damn, he hoped they got past this stage soon. It was driving him crazy.

He'd felt the spark between them the day they'd met. He could tell she had, too, but she was confused and tried to deny it. He couldn't blame her. Her son of a bitch husband was still out to get her back then, and death threats could be a bit distracting. Even after Banner was in jail, Rocky had respected her need to let the emotional wounds heal. Something that happened sooner than he'd expected. By New Year's Eve, when he'd seen her efficiently handle several guys hitting on her at Jack and Ellie's party, he'd thought she was still hiding behind that wall she'd erected. But then she'd given him that look.

He smiled at the memory. She'd just deflected some poor guy's advances, then bent to get a can of pop out of the refrigerator. When she'd straightened to find him watching her from the kitchen doorway and realized he'd witnessed the blunt rejection, her cheeks turned pink. He hadn't determined yet if she just blushed easily, or if it was only when he was around.

The party noise was subdued in the kitchen, and he spoke without closing the distance between them, afraid to spook her. "Not ready to jump into the dating pool yet?"

She shrugged.

"What was wrong with him?" he asked, nodding toward the dining room where the guy had disappeared.

She popped the lid on her drink and took a sip. "He's not the right guy."

"Is there a right guy?" Hope made him ask.

That was when she'd lifted her gaze, letting it travel over him before settling with veiled intent on his face. "I'm not sure yet."

His heart jumped in his chest. He hadn't expected the opening, but he wasn't about to let it go by. The trick was to take it slowly.

She watched his approach as she took another sip, acting more nonchalant than he knew she felt, judging by the pulsing vein in her neck. He wondered if shooting down a few advances in one night had given her an unexpected spurt of confidence. He wished he felt it, too, because the last thing he wanted to do was come on too strong.

Sudden laughter rolled through the crowd in the living room, but it faded into background noise as he stood in front of her. The fizz from her can sounded unnaturally loud as he shut out everything but the two of them.

"Feel like giving it another try?"

She smiled, a heavy-lidded look that started a slow burn inside him. "I was thinking I might. Sort of a New Year's resolution."

"It's not midnight yet."

She lifted a shoulder. "I'm not a stickler for rules."

It was a clear invitation. Still, he moved carefully, watching her reaction as he raised a hand to cup her cheek. She pushed against his palm the tiniest bit, molding her face against his hand, her eyes never leaving his.

Like touching a live wire, electricity shot up his arm, awakening every nerve in his body. He wondered if his touch had the same effect on her, because her mouth opened, emitting a tiny mew of surprise.

It was irresistible. While her lips were still parted, he leaned in and kissed her—one long, gentle kiss that melted away the tension and started a low hum through him. Her free hand slid up his shoulder, fingertips pressing into him as she made a satisfied sound in her throat, her tongue finding his for one brief, teasing moment, dancing an invitation to go deeper.

She pulled back suddenly, alarm flashing through her eyes. He knew somehow he'd crossed a line, that the flare of desire he'd welcomed had been more than she'd expected, more than she was ready to handle.

"Too much too soon," he murmured.

She wouldn't admit it but didn't deny it, either.

Reluctantly, he lowered his hand. "I won't push, Janet. But—" he brushed a kiss on her cheek, feeling her shiver in response. "We'd be good together," he whispered before taking a step back. She watched him, her eyes large and blinking anxiously. "Let me know when you're ready, because I'll be waiting. The next move is up to you."

He'd left her there. Later, when the year counted down to zero and several couples kissed amid the cheers and laughter, her gaze had wandered around the room and found his. He saw heat touch her cheeks again before she turned away.

She'd been avoiding him for the six months since. But she hadn't dated anyone else. He understood her problem was not with dating; it was with her attraction to him. He intended to change that, but he'd have to be patient.

He hoped she'd make a move soon. What they were missing was too good to ignore.

Chapter Three

Janet opened the door and stared at Rocky incredulously. "You're wearing *that*?"

He looked at his black jeans and black T-shirt, then back at her. "What's wrong with it?"

Not a thing. He looked sexy as hell, in a cat burglar sort of way. But that was a different problem. "You said to dress how Bloomfield Hills ladies would expect. I assumed that meant like this." She indicated her linen pant suit, pumps, and smart little matching handbag.

"Nice," he said, giving her an appreciative look. "But that's not what I said. I said I'd wear what they expect *me* to. I'm an ex-burglar talking about personal and home security. This is what they'll expect."

She pursed her lips and considered his clothes while trying not to consider the extremely fit body filling them out. "You're right, that's what they'll expect." They'd probably have fantasies about being burglarized by him, too.

"And as gorgeous as you look, I think you'd better change into jeans and tennis shoes. Those heels will be slippery, and I wouldn't want to get that nice suit dirty."

"How would you do that?" She narrowed her eyes. "Exactly what is it I'm helping you demonstrate?"

"Self-defense. I thought Ellie told you."

Ellie would pay for this. "She said you were demonstrating security systems. I thought I'd be doing a Vanna White, holding up dead bolt locks while you explained why they weren't secure enough."

He grinned. "We'll do that, too. But mostly I need you so I don't have to pick some little old lady out of the audience, grab her around the neck, and teach her how to defend herself from an attacker."

She had a feeling none of the ladies, even the little old ones, would mind having Rocky wrap his arms around their neck and hold them close. *She* was the only one who would feel uncomfortable doing that.

She might have to kill Ellie.

"Have a seat. I won't be long," she muttered, and left to change her clothes. Thanks to her divorce, she had a closet full of jeans. Banner hated them so naturally, she'd bought at least a dozen pairs as part of her celebration when she was free of the rotten prick. With a white T-shirt and blue jeans she didn't look like a cat burglar, but at least she was properly dressed for a scuffle with an assailant. A scuffle with Rocky. The thought of being pinned against his chest made her body flush with heat, then go cold with nerves.

"Idiot," she told herself, pushing it out of her mind. This was business. If she didn't think and just did it, she'd be okay.

She returned to find Rocky having a one-sided conversation with Jingles. A smile started to curve across her mouth, but she squashed it flat, refusing to be suckered in just because he was gorgeous and liked her cat.

He stopped talking when he heard her.

"What were you telling my cat?"

"We were just talking about my cat. He wants a play date with my cat, Fluff."

"Fine with me, as soon as he gets his driver's license. You're getting white hairs all over your shirt."

"I'm a cat owner, I have a lint brush in the car. Ready?"

She was never going to be ready for this. "Let's go."

She sat off to the side of the room, expecting to be bored. Despite what she thought was a good performance of looking indifferent, she was fascinated.

So were the Lady Sparks. The women's group was dedicated to bettering themselves and their community, and Janet had no doubt they were learning a lot about security tonight. But despite their open notepads and ready pens, no one had written a word. They didn't need to; with the sort of rapt attention they were giving Rocky, she was sure they'd remember everything he said.

He was right about his clothes. As soon as he introduced himself as a reformed cat burglar-slash-jewel thief, the Sparks had perked up, appraising him with interest. When he told them how he and Ellie had started from nothing and made a success of Red Rose Security, he could have gotten dates with at least three of them immediately. Of course, he'd flashed his crooked smile, and who could resist that? Most of them were old enough to be his mother, but charm was charm.

She should have guessed that a man with his gift for smooth talking would be able to keep an audience interested, even in the nuts and bolts of security systems. Somehow thinking of him as an ex-con had prevented her from seeing that he was just as instrumental as Ellie in turning Red Rose into a profitable and respected business. Damn, another point in his favor.

Rocky's talk was so absorbing she nearly forgot she had a part to play until he shoved a table aside, clearing a large area of floor at the front of the room. "I promised to teach you some basic self-defense techniques," he said. Standing there in those snug jeans and a T-shirt that molded to the muscular contours of his chest, he looked like someone who could threaten their safety in more ways than one. He put his hands on his hips, looking more authoritative. "But I have to warn you about something first."

In the few seconds while he paused, Janet could feel a slight tension in the room. She had to hand it to him, he was good at this.

"I will not show you how to protect yourself from someone with a gun." He scanned the audience with a serious look, ensuring he had everyone's attention. "If you are ever in that situation, your options depend on the circumstances. He would want you to be quiet and he might want to take you someplace safer. Safer for him means more dangerous for you, so you don't want to go. First, if anyone can hear you, scream. And second, if he's not holding onto you, run. That's it. Thinking you can disarm your attacker is foolhardy. I've practiced martial arts for fifteen years, but I'm still not faster than a bullet."

His self-deprecating smile allowed them to relax.

There was a lot more to this guy than she'd ever suspected.

"Okay, time to show you ladies how to protect yourselves." Rocky rubbed his hands together. "Normally my business partner, Ellie, would play the victim, but since she couldn't be here her friend Janet has agreed to help out."

Janet got a smattering of polite applause as she stepped to the center of the floor beside Rocky. He grinned at her before addressing the audience, and she felt the usual self-conscious heat begin to spread inside her. *Boy, was she in trouble; he hadn't even touched her yet.*

"Our scenario takes place in the park. Janet will be the pretty, unsuspecting victim. I'll be the creepy, albeit devilishly handsome, stranger who attacks her." Warm hands landed on her shoulders and nudged her back. "Start over there, Janet, and walk toward me. We're just two people passing on the hiking trail."

He could have just pointed. Obviously, he was going to use any excuse torture her.

She followed directions, walking the few steps forward that brought her to the center of the room. Not sure what to expect, she was half braced for an attack, but he walked past her with barely a glance. The hairs on the back of her neck seemed to sense him behind her, straining toward him. The Sparks might not see him as creepy, but it was a good description of what he was doing to her.

Two steps past him she was suddenly jerked from behind and hauled against him. Rocky's right arm encircled her neck, while the other crossed just beneath her breasts, holding her close. Her gasp might have sounded like a dramatic effect to the entranced women, but it was as real as her thundering heartbeat.

Her head was against Rocky's cheek, and she felt his breath on her forehead. He was so close she could smell his shampoo or soap—something fresh and vaguely spicy. It was almost enough to make her forget she was supposed to resist him, not melt into him.

"In this situation, Janet's instinctive reaction is panic and fear," he told the women.

Her instincts must be a little off. Her heart was pounding hard enough, but the energy surging through her felt more like excitement.

"Most women would struggle to get away, which would be completely ineffective. Show them, Janet."

Obediently, she twisted and fought against his hold. Finding her right hand free, she pulled at the rock-hard muscles of his arm where it circled her neck, accomplishing nothing. He still held her fast against his chest. She tried to look upset about it.

"Now, this is what I want you all to remember. Even though she seems helpless, she has weapons. Men call it fighting dirty, but really it's fighting smart. I'm not following the rules by attacking her, so neither should she. She can bite, and if her hands are free, she can scratch." He turned his head toward her and lowered his voice. "Bite me."

It sounded so intimate she nearly blushed. Instead, she closed her teeth on his arm, meeting corded muscle. Her tongue registered a faint taste of salt and the tickle of coarse hairs. She knew her actions were supposed to look desperate and violent, and couldn't figure out why she felt suddenly shy. It's not like it was some kind of love bite. She bit down harder.

Rocky didn't react. "You might find this distasteful, especially since muggers aren't known for their good hygiene." He waited for the laughter to stop. "But I want you to bite into his arm hard, like it's filet mignon and you haven't eaten in two days. You're trying to tear out a chunk, not make dainty dental impressions. And don't stop there. You have fingernails—use them like claws. Janet . . ."

His lips brushed the top of her head as he spoke, and she went weak all over. It seemed he had a few unorthodox weapons himself.

"She can reach for my face," he told the women. She followed his direction, reaching back over her head. Her fingers touched his nose and cheek. "Don't hesitate," he stressed to the audience, adding, "I'm not talking to you, Janet. You can hesitate."

She held her hand up to his face and watched thirty women grin at Rocky as he told them how to gouge and rip at an attacker's face. They looked eager to try it. When he instructed them to inflict vicious pinches on whatever body parts they could reach, she saw avid interest in the gazes that followed her hand down to his thigh, where she clutched a handful of denim-clad muscle.

"Your feet are weapons, too," he told them. "Especially if you're wearing heels. Stomping a three-inch heel into someone's toes can be pretty effective if he isn't expecting it."

This part she already knew. Ever since the horror of seeing Ellie held tightly against Banner with a gun in her side, she'd wondered what she would have done if it had been her. Along with her teeth, her feet had seemed the strongest weapons. She was ready for Rocky's next move.

"If you're wearing something soft, like Janet's tennis shoes, you can always bash away at his shin. But no tentative moves, make it a good hard kick."

She did. Not enough to hurt him, but she didn't aim at his shin, either. That was for old ladies with limited range. Lifting her leg, she sent a sharp jab sideways, hitting the side of Rocky's knee.

Taken by surprise, he stumbled, giving her enough room to duck out of his grip, and push him off balance. She turned with a triumphant look, just in time to see him land on his butt.

His startled expression turned into a rueful grin as the audience laughed and clapped at her success. "That works, too," he acknowledged.

She covered her smile with one hand. "I'm sorry! I thought you were ready for that."

"No, I wasn't. But I guess that makes my point, doesn't it?"

She was afraid he might be embarrassed, but his eyes sparkled as he got to his feet. "I think Janet's ready for more advanced lessons," he told the ladies.

They laughed again. A few gave her envious glances.

A warm feeling spread through her, along with a bit of apprehension; it was becoming far too easy to like Rocky Hernandez.

She shoved the feeling aside and played her part as he showed them how to deal with an assault from the front, demonstrating both a choke hold and a bear hug that pinned her arms to her sides. She figured out one valuable hint on her own—don't look your attacker directly in the eyes. It could distract you to the point that you forget what you are supposed to be doing.

The only advantage this time was that it seemed to be a bit distracting to him, too.

By the time the lesson ended, Rocky had the Sparks asking if he did martial arts demonstrations, too. While he mingled with his new fans and passed out business cards, Janet wrote down a couple appointments for home security assessments for the following week. More promised to call over the next few days. It was nearly ten thirty, forty minutes after the meeting ended, when they finally hauled his sample alarms and motion detectors out to the car.

She took a deep breath of the cool, night air. It had gotten a little warm in there. Twenty-nine was too young for hot flashes, but she could have sworn she'd had a few during the self-defense demonstration.

Rocky slid the sun roof back as soon as he started the car, and she relaxed in the passenger seat, content to watch the stars.

"Thanks for your help tonight."

Her smile was sincere. "It was fun. I think you and Ellie have stumbled into a gold mine. Those women loved you, and they'll be talking about it to their friends. Red Rose Security is going to be busy."

"It did seem to go well. They're interested in martial arts demonstrations now, but I don't think I want to get into that."

"It's you they're interested in."

"I've always liked public speaking," he said, surprising her by downplaying his ability. "I was the class clown in school."

"I'll bet you were." She laughed, having no trouble seeing Rocky as a shaggy-haired imp, irritating teachers and amusing classmates. "But tonight was informative, too. I even learned a few things."

"About self-defense?"

She started to answer yes, because what else would she be talking about, burglar alarms? But he glanced at her with a hint of mischief, taking his eyes off the road for longer than he should. She realized he was talking about himself. About them. About what she might have learned by having his arms around her and their bodies pressed together. Turning an innocent comment into a sly innuendo.

She gave him an exasperated look. "Don't you ever give up?"

"Nope. I can last as long as I have to, but you do test my patience. I'm just about ready to—what the hell?"

She was dying to know what he was just about ready to do, but then she saw it, too. Caught in his headlights as he turned onto her cul-de-sac, her car sat by the curb in front of her condo, a jagged scrape showing as a bright silvery line against the dark blue paint. The line followed the whole length of the driver's side. "Oh, no!"

He pulled in the driveway, but held her back when she rounded his car and hurried toward hers. "Don't touch anything."

"Why? This isn't a crime scene. Someone sideswiped me." The car had lost its appeal ever since she'd remembered the purchase had been Banner's idea.

"No one sideswiped it, Janet. It was keyed. See how the line wavers? Another car would leave a straight line in the surface, or an even curve. Someone did this by scraping it with a piece of metal. Intentionally."

His eyes scanned the car, front to back. "Damn." Walking to the trunk, he poked one finger under the lid and lifted. The trunk opened. "What did you have in here?"

"Nothing." She peered inside along with Rocky. Still nothing, except for a long gash in the carpet.

"They were looking for something. Did you have anything inside the car?"

She shook her head. "Just a few CDs."

They moved to the side windows and peered in. The leather upholstery was slashed in long, diagonal slices.

Janet put her hand to her mouth. "Oh, my God," she groaned. "Why?" As soon as she said it, an answer occurred to her. "The necklace."

Rocky's mouth was a tight line. "Yeah, I think so."

"But why would they look in my car? It makes more sense to—" she drew in a sharp breath and darted toward her condo, but was stopped by a strong grasp on her wrist.

"Don't."

She wasn't going to take time to discuss it, so she said the words that were most important. "Jingles! I have to go!"

"Stay here, I'll look." He held her by both arms, forcing her to look at him. She scowled, suddenly impatient with his domineering attitude. "I mean it, Janet. You stay right here beside my car. If anyone went in there, someone could still be inside."

That stopped her cold.

"Do you have your cell phone?"

She nodded.

"Call nine-one-one. And give me your keys."

She fumbled in her purse, pulling out both the cell

and her keys. "Here, this one's the front door. And the code is two-one-six-zero."

"I remember; I programmed it."

She dialed 9-1-1, but her gaze stayed on Rocky as he examined the lock on her front door, then inserted the key. All she cared about was knowing that her cat and her belongings were safe. No, forget the belongings. If they'd hurt her cat, she'd hunt them down.

The two minutes he was inside felt like an eternity. She gave her name and address to the emergency operator, told them about the car and a possible break-in, then hung up. It wasn't the most accurate report, but she was too preoccupied to think, torn between running into her house to find Jingles and obeying Rocky's order to stay by his car. It went against her instincts to stand by passively and do what she was told. Still, after he'd told her about the necklace, she'd started to trust Rocky when it came to her own safety. It was a strange feeling, one she'd never had with anyone else, but she listened to it. Like it or not, this was his territory. He was an expert. Leaning on the car, she chewed a fingernail and watched her front door.

When he appeared again she jerked upright. "It's all right," he called. "No one's been inside and the cat's fine."

That was all she needed to hear as she rushed past him to see for herself.

Jingles was finishing a leisurely stretch, claws firmly embedded in the living room carpet, no doubt preparing to wrap himself around Rocky's ankles. She looked around, reassuring herself that nothing had changed.

"Everything's fine upstairs, too." Rocky ignored the cat and talked to her. "I don't think anyone even touched the lock on the front door. Whatever they wanted, they only looked in the car."

It could be a coincidence—random robberies happened, especially to people dumb enough to leave an expensive car parked on the street instead of in the garage. She wouldn't do that again. Still . . . "It must have something to do with the necklace, right?"

"I agree. Which is why you can't stay here."

She winced. "I wish you'd quit saying that. After Banner, I have this irrational need to resist when a man tells me what to do."

He nodded. "Understandable. However, I have this irrational need to make sure you're safe. You can think of it as professional advice if it makes you feel better."

It might. "Is that what it is, professional advice?"

"Hell, no. It's personal." It could have come out sounding irritated and angry, but he lowered his voice and held her eyes with his, and it was sexy as sin.

She felt caught by the tension that was always there between them, the unspoken but ever-present knowledge that he wanted a relationship with her, vying with her fear of giving in to her emotions. The air itself felt strained, and she was glad when the silence was broken by slamming car doors outside. "Excuse me," she mumbled, brushing by Rocky to open the door for the police officers.

It was the second time today she'd had police officers at her door. The neighbors in her quiet development were going to have a lot to talk about.

She spent the next hour talking with officers. They wanted Rocky's version of events, too, so he stayed. By the time the officer was preparing to leave, the adrenaline high had worn off and Janet was exhausted. As soon as the last detective was out the door, she was going to make sure Rocky was right behind him.

She had her hand on the doorknob as the officer paused on the threshold. "Miss Aims, do you have a friend you could stay with for a day or two?"

She avoided looking at Rocky in case he was smirking. Putting on a polite smile, she answered, "Yes, I'll be calling her as soon as you leave. Thanks for your concern."

"Good night, ma'am. Take care." The door closed on his final word. She turned to find Rocky watching her with arms folded. No smirk, thank goodness.

He waited several seconds before asking, "So what's the real plan?"

She shook her head and smiled, impressed that he'd known she was just telling the policeman what he wanted to hear. "I keep having this argument with you in my head, you telling me to go, and me insisting I want to stay."

"Who's winning?"

She sighed. "You are. I guess I have to pack a bag."

He was smart enough not to look triumphant. "Take your time, I'll wait."

She couldn't drive her own car, not in that condition, but she didn't want him to get the wrong idea. "I'm not staying at your place."

"I'm not taking you there, nice as that sounds. I'm taking you to the Westfield's."

Make an unexpected, uninvited visit to her ex-mother-in-law? "That's not necessary. I can get a motel room."

His expression was soft, but his voice was firm. "Janet, let's not argue about this. There is no place safer than Elizabeth's house. I know it's late, and I know there's an uncomfortable history there."

Only the fact that she was responsible for sending Elizabeth's lying, thieving, doublecrossing son to jail.

"But I also know she loves you like a daughter and would be justifiably furious if I took you anyplace else." As Janet opened her mouth to respond, he added, "And I'm prepared to go to Ben if I have to."

Ben Thatcher was one of the nicest guys she knew. He was also the chief of police and the great love of Elizabeth Westfield's life. Both of those positions gave him an advantage he wouldn't hesitate to use if he thought it would help keep Janet safe.

She raised her eyebrows. "I was just going to say, okay."

"Oh." He recouped gracefully, pulling out his cell phone. "Great. I'll call to let her know we're coming."

She went upstairs to pack, trying not to think about how Ben would get involved anyway once the police report was filed, and then she'd have two well-meaning men telling her what to do.

And no car. This just got better and better.

She was back in minutes, a small duffel bag slung over her shoulder. "Did you make my reservations at the Westfield Hilton?"

His sense of humor seemed to come back now that she was cooperating, because he actually smiled. "Elizabeth said she's thrilled to have you back in her house."

"I'll bet. She agrees to keep her granddaughter so her son can take his wife to Europe for thier honey-moon, and now she gets her ex–daughter-in-law, too. The poor woman never gets any time to herself."

She talked as she headed for the front door, but Rocky hung back. "Don't you have a cat carrier for Jingles?"

She bit her lip; it hadn't been an easy decision. "I wasn't going to take Jingles. Do you think he's in danger here?"

"Frankly, no. They aren't going to bother with a cat, and he'll most likely hide. But I thought you'd want him with you."

"I do. But Elizabeth isn't a pet person. He has lots of food and water, a comfy couch, and no competition for the TV remote. He'll have a ball," she said, more to convince herself than Rocky. There wasn't much choice. She couldn't find a kennel that would take him at this time of night. If she was lucky, this would all be over in a day or two and she'd be back in her condo.

She felt self-conscious in the car, like a little kid being taken home to mommy's. Mommy's gated and guarded mansion. Still, she was touched by Elizabeth's warm hug at the front door.

"I'm sorry to intrude," Janet said.

"Nonsense. You were right to come here. You're family." From anyone else it would have sounded like a generous gesture; from Elizabeth Payton Westfield, it was irrefutable fact, a royal decree that allowed no argument. Elizabeth stepped back, her sharp gaze running over Janet from head to toe. "You look exhausted, dear. Why don't you head upstairs? Roberto can tell me about this horrible event."

Janet cast a sideways glance at Rocky. "Roberto exaggerates. But I am tired." She looked at the graceful sweep of stairs, thinking of the warm whirlpool tub and huge canopied bed in the suite of rooms she had once shared with Banner. "Same room?"

"It's always yours."

She smiled. "Thank you." It came out as a soft sigh. She was crashing fast. Starting toward the stairs, she turned for one final comment. "Elizabeth, please don't worry. This isn't nearly as dangerous as Rocky makes it sound."

Elizabeth gave her a serene smile. "Then we'll use it as a chance to visit. We can talk in the morning."

That sounded good. With a wave to Rocky, Janet climbed the stairs, looking forward to the whirlpool bath and huge, soft bed.

Rocky watched her go, but made no move to leave. Elizabeth turned to him, hands folded in front of her, as composed as always. Rocky thought if she were standing on the deck of the *Titanic* as it went down, she would have looked the same.

"I know you well enough to realize you did not bring Janet here because of some exaggerated hunch."

"No, ma'am."

"Is she in danger?"

"Yes." He looked up the long curve of stairs where Janet had disappeared. "More than she knows." His gaze went back to Elizabeth. "I know it's late, but could you call Ben for me? I need to talk to him."

"Tonight?"

He hated to confirm the worry in her eyes, but had no choice. "Yes. As soon as possible."

Chapter Four

Rocky hadn't been to Ben Thatcher's small house before, but wasn't surprised at its immaculate, barely lived-in look. How else could it be, when Ben spent most of his time at the Westfield mansion? Stubborn pride was all that kept him from moving in there, or so Elizabeth claimed. Rocky kept his mouth shut, but sympathized with Ben. The man probably didn't want to look like he was living off his rich lady friend, especially with his position in this town. Rocky assumed Ben was holding out for marriage. Rocky would be, if it were him. Some guys just preferred the traditional family life of marriage and children, even if it happened in reverse order.

Ben met him at the side door, barefoot and bare-chested, wearing only rumpled jeans. Running a hand through sleep-tousled hair, he grunted and motioned for Rocky to come in.

He entered into a small kitchen and took a chair at the table. Ben followed, sat down and hooked his foot around another chair to angle it closer. Propping his feet up on the second chair, he looked at Rocky. "Okay, shoot."

Rocky hesitated, distracted by the fact that Elizabeth's call had gotten Ben out of bed. "I'm sorry to wake you, I guess I lost track of the time."

Ben waved his concerns aside. "Liz said there was a problem with Janet. That ex-husband of hers might not be my son, but he is Liz's son, and Janet was Liz's daughter-in-law. Still is, by her reckoning. The way I look at it, that makes her my family, too. If she's in danger, I want to know about it."

"There's a chance I'm overreacting."

"I trust your instincts, kid. If you're worried, I'm worried. Now tell me."

Ben's fingers intertwined above an abdomen that looked washboard hard, even as relaxed as he was. Rocky reminded himself that Ben had only been eighteen when he'd met Elizabeth Payton, fallen in love with the pretty college freshman, and gotten her pregnant. His military service and Elizabeth's marriage to Leonard Westfield had kept them apart for more than thirty years, and had kept Elizabeth from acknowledging that Jack was Ben's son. It was only years later, with Elizabeth widowed and Ben single, that they had resumed their relationship.

Rocky understood how disoriented Jack must have been to find out the local police chief who had harassed him through his teen years was actually his father. Rocky felt a bit disoriented himself. Not many ex-convicts could claim the unquestioned loyalty of the local police chief, but thanks to his friendship with Jack, that's exactly what he had. He would never take advantage of that relationship for his own benefit, but he wouldn't hesitate to use it to help Janet.

As Rocky outlined the day's events, Ben listened, concern showing in the deepening creases on the older man's brow and the tightening around his mouth.

Ben raised a hand to his face, stroking the stubble above his upper lip as he regarded Rocky thoughtfully.

"You're right. We're not talking about ordinary vandalism. Someone's pretty damn desperate to find something, most likely the rest of that jewelry. And desperate people are dangerous."

Rocky nodded and delivered the punch line. "These people might be more dangerous than most." It was this fear that had brought him here, and he waited to see if Ben had been thinking along the same lines.

Recognition sparked in Ben's eyes. "You're talking about the gangs that prey on jewelry couriers."

"They aren't usually so destructive, but hitting the car first is how they think. It's their trademark."

"You think they'd be interested in the Pellinni Jewels?"

That was the part that bothered Rocky, too. "Not usually. But it's possible they saw it as an easy snatch if they moved fast. The industry has wised up and made it harder for them to stage successful grabs, so it might have looked like easy money. Safer than a smash and grab at a jewelry store."

"But it wasn't successful," Ben pointed out.

"No. And that worries me. That scratch down the side of the car had nothing to do with a search for the Pellinni Jewels. It was for shock effect, intimidation."

"Meaning what? Turn over the jewels or else?"

"Basically. And if it is one of these gangs and they try the condo next, Janet's in real trouble. They're a whole lot more dangerous than a solitary jewel thief who wants to get in and out as quietly as possible. These guys aren't subtle, and all they care about is the final result, getting the jewelry." The thought of them even putting a finger on Janet made his gut twist.

The frown on Ben's face showed he trusted Rocky's analysis and shared his concern. "You sure she's okay tonight? She's not gonna do something foolish like call a cab and go home?"

"I told both Elizabeth and her butler, Mr. Peters, that she shouldn't be allowed to leave. I don't think we have to worry."

Ben nodded his satisfaction. "I'll find out who's working her case and make sure I'm kept updated. And I'll talk to Janet in the morning, see if I can convince her to listen to your advice and stay with Liz for a while."

He pulled a grimace. "I don't recommend calling it my advice, not if you want her to take it."

"Huh." Ben studied him. "What's she got against you?"

"Nothing. She's just doesn't like me telling her what to do."

Ben mulled it over. Rocky squirmed under the scrutiny, regretting that he'd said anything.

"The girl knows her own mind. Maybe she just doesn't like you."

He didn't want to discuss it. "Maybe." Standing, he pushed his chair in. "Forget I mentioned it."

Ben didn't move. "Janet has a right to be gun-shy after what that bastard put her through."

"You're right." Rocky started for the door. "Thanks for looking out for her."

Ben still hadn't made any move to get up. "You know, her parents moved to Arizona."

He didn't like the feel of this. "Yeah, I heard they retired there."

"So the only family she has around here is Liz. And me."

"And Jack and Ellie."

Ben ignored him. "So I have to step in sometimes, since her dad can't be here."

Rocky sighed; he wasn't going to get out of this, so he might as well face it. "Look, Ben, Janet's twenty-nine years old. So am I. I'm not asking your permission to date her. But if it makes you feel any better, I know what she's been through and I'm not rushing her. That's all you'll get. Anything else is between me and Janet. It has nothing to do with you."

Ben cocked his head, pinning him with a hard look. "That so?"

If the comment was calculated to irritate Rocky, it couldn't have worked better. He'd finally made some progress with Janet tonight, then nearly ruined it by insisting she follow his orders. Even if it had been the safest course of action, he wasn't happy with the results. The proverbial "one step forward, two steps back." The last thing he needed now was someone else's opinion about their prickly relationship.

Staring back with an expression every bit as hard as Ben's, he said, "Damn right that's so. I'd say the same thing even if you were her father, and you're not. And for your information, Janet's not made of glass. She's tough and smart and capable of making her own decisions. One bad choice hasn't changed that. But she might be in over her head here, and all I'm asking is that you keep an eye on the legal end of things. I can handle whatever else comes up."

A smile played at the corner of Ben's mouth. "I believe you can, kid."

Rocky frowned, as irritated with himself as with Ben for baiting him. "Are you just jerking me around for fun, or are you going to help keep Janet safe?"

"I'll help. Jerking you around is just a bonus."

It was probably better if Rocky kept his mouth shut. Settling for a curt nod, he left. Driving home, the wry thought occurred to him that at least someone was getting a laugh out of his relationship with Janet. Too bad it wasn't him.

Janet sat halfway up the imposing cement and brick stairway to the Westfield's front door, hoping the morning humidity didn't send her short hair into mad ringlets. At the base of the steps, Jack's thirteen-year-old daughter sat astride one of the life-sized cement lions that guarded the entry. Libby bent backward like a circus performer, chin pointed to the sky and hair falling over the lion's rump, fixing an innocent look on Janet. "Is Rocky picking you up?"

"Yup."

"I like him."

"That's nice." She was careful not to say *me, too,* in front of Jack and Ellie's frighteningly perceptive daughter.

Rising up in a smooth move that made Janet's back hurt just watching, Libby turned around and sat backward, knees drawn up to her chin. "My friend Tanya likes him, too. She said Rocky's cute in a really bad way."

The teen was obviously digging for gossip Janet had no intention of providing. But Libby had caught her interest with that last bit. "What does that mean, cute in a bad way?"

"*Really* bad," Libby corrected. "It means he's cute, but not, you know, safe. Like he'd be good at doing bad things."

Janet instantly thought of a few bad things Rocky might do that made her mouth go dry. She knew exactly what Tanya meant. She squinted at Libby. "How old is Tanya?"

"Thirteen, same as me." She stretched out her legs and flexed her toes, balancing delicately. "She knows a lot of stuff about boys that they don't teach us in school."

A year ago Janet might have been thrown by the statement, but she'd gotten to know Jack's daughter since then. Before Jack had known of her existence, Libby had been abandoned by her drug addict mother and lived with her overwhelmed maternal grandparents. If not for the girl's own intelligence and her young aunt's valiant efforts at parenting, Janet imagined she wouldn't have come out of the experience as well adjusted as she had. As it was, Libby was a master manipulator, who practiced her skills at every turn.

Janet was determined not to fall for it. "What a thought-provoking comment."

Libby stuck out her lower lip in a deliberate pout and tried the direct approach. "What do *you* think about Rocky? Don't you think he'd make a good boyfriend?"

"Can't say. I really don't know him well enough."
What was taking Rocky so long?

"No one around here wants to talk about boys. How am I supposed to learn anything?"

"Try books. Or have you already exhausted that section at the public library?"

Libby slid off the lion and skipped up the steps to sit beside Janet. Leaning back on her elbows, she sighed heavily. "It's tough being precocious."

Janet laughed. As much as she dreaded being the target of Libby's overactive mind, Janet was crazy about Ellie's stepdaughter. With Jack and Ellie married for barely a year, the three of them had been feeling their way through family life, learning as they went. Despite the occasional hair-ripping and profanity-laced stories from Ellie about life with a teenager, they managed to make it sound like the best adventure life had ever thrown their way. And according to Ellie, they hoped to soon add a baby to the happy turmoil of the Payton family. Janet couldn't think of a better life, and despite the occasional twinge of jealousy, she was extremely happy for Ellie and honored to be included in their extended family.

A silver Lexus turned into the driveway, keying the gate open and following the half-moon curve that led up to the house.

Leaning over to plant a quick kiss on top of Libby's forehead, Janet said, "Stick to watching the guys your own age, kiddo. And especially avoid the ones who are cute in a really bad way."

Libby watched Rocky's car as she pondered Janet's comment. "Tanya and I were thinking that the cute in a bad way guys seem like they'd be a lot more fun to be with."

Janet would have loved to brush it off, but Libby's

voice had become hesitant and her expression was serious. She honestly wanted advice. A frisson of panic slid through Janet's chest at the thought that Libby might be pondering a relationship with a tempting bad boy. She might even already have one. Whatever Janet said could have a big impact.

Damn, this was supposed to be Ellie's job.

She took a deep breath and tried to give a serious answer without making it sound like a sermon. "Cute in a bad way also means dangerous. A guy who overwhelms your senses keeps you from thinking straight. That'll get you into trouble every time. Trust me. It's best to just avoid those guys for now." Or forever. Janet stood, anxious to meet Rocky at the bottom of the steps before Libby had a chance to ask more uncomfortable questions.

"Is that what you do?"

"Definitely," she called out. Halfway down the steps she turned to give Libby a sharp look. "And don't say it. Not that it's any of your business, but he's just giving me a ride."

Libby didn't say anything, but she didn't have to. Janet could clearly read the pity on the girl's expressive face. Great.

Slipping into Rocky's car, she slammed the door and grumbled, "Hi."

He smiled, steering around the paved loop that sent them back down the driveway. "Good morning to you, too, sunshine."

She squeezed her eyes shut. "Sorry. I just had my love life reviewed by a teenage girl and it was found lacking."

"Sad but true," he said with a nod. "By the way, I can fix that for you anytime you want."

She ignored the intriguing tickle in her mind and shot him an evil look. "That wasn't an invitation, Romeo. I happen to like my life the way it is."

He winked. "Tempt not a desperate man." The glance he slid her way held a flash of heat.

Her brow creased as she repeated the phrase to herself, testing its familiarity. *It couldn't be.* "Was that Shakespeare?"

"*Romeo and Juliet.* I thought we had a theme going."

She stared at him as he drove. "You're full of surprises, aren't you?"

When he turned toward her, that devilish look was back in full force. "You have no idea, sweetheart."

Her breath caught as desire slammed into her chest, then shot down to her pelvis with such weight that she wiggled in her seat. Naturally, he noticed. She saw his glance fall to her lap and an amused twitch touch the corner of his mouth. Cheeks flaming, she slunk down and faced out the window. Celibacy must really be taking its toll, because something about Rocky Hernandez had awakened hormones that had been slumbering peacefully in her for over a year. She had to get control of her body's reactions to those sexy smiles and searing looks.

She said nothing for a while, then decided the silence was too uncomfortable. "I got a call from Ellie last night."

He raised his eyebrows. "Why? Is something wrong?"

"Not really, but it scared Ellie. Authorities detained them at the Frankfurt airport until they contacted the Bloomfield Hills police. Seems Furley and Beckman took your advice and questioned her about our visit to Portman's."

"Huh. Good for them."

"What do you mean? Do the police really think this is some sort of international conspiracy, with Ellie spiriting the rest of the loot out of the country?"

Her outrage seemed to amuse him. "I doubt it, but it's good to know the detectives are looking into all possibilities and questioning everyone involved, even though I don't have much faith in their ability to find the rest of the jewels. They don't have enough contacts in that world to even know where to start."

She considered his answer. "And you do?"

"I did." He paused. "Yeah, I suppose I still do. But it's not my job to investigate robberies and find stolen jewels. Let the FBI do it."

She felt strangely relieved to hear that he had no interest in contacting people from his former life.

He pulled into her driveway, and she winced at the sight of her damaged car. The first thing on her agenda today was to get it to a repair shop and arrange for a rental car. "Thanks for the ride," she said, grabbing her overnight bag as she got out of the car. Rocky met her at the front bumper.

She stopped. "Where are you going?"

"Into your condo. Give me the key. You're not going inside until I check it out." He held out his hand.

It had been so long since a man had tried to look out for her instead of putting her in harm's way that it took her by surprise. Wordlessly, she handed over the key.

She stayed on his heels as he climbed the steps and unlocked the door. As soon as he pushed it open, she stepped forward, following him in. One step put her on the threshold; the second step made her run smack into his back.

"Hey! What are you do—" her complaint stopped when she noticed the alarm box on the wall beside her. The cover was dangling from the only wire that wasn't cut. Peeking around Rocky, she saw what had made him stop.

"Holy shit," she whispered.

Sofa cushions had been flung to the floor and slit open. So had the exposed back of the sofa. And the chairs. Janet stared, eyes wide and mouth gaping, barely able to comprehend the destruction. Paintings off the walls, furniture overturned, books scattered everywhere. Nothing seemed to have been spared, even the carpet, which had been sliced and pulled back in places, revealing the subfloor.

The scene hit with a visceral blow that left her gasping for breath. Strangers had been here, searching her home, handling her things, destroying whatever they touched. Violating her. Deep inside, something primitive and territorial screamed, "My stuff! My home!" They had no right. They'd probably even gone through her drawers, touching her most intimate possessions. Anger churned, building energy and seeking release.

Rocky forced her backward, out the door, and she turned on him, unleashing the outrage that had nowhere else to go. "Let me go!" She tried to push past him, but he grabbed her arm. "It's my house!"

"You're not going in there until the police go through it." He caught her struggling arms, holding her away from the door and absorbing a few flailing jabs in the process.

"I have to go in! Where's Jingles? Damn it, Rocky, what if they hurt him? Let go of me!"

"Janet, stop." When fighting him didn't work, she stood and glared. "Your cat's all right. He's probably hiding under the bed or on top of the refrigerator."

She aimed a vicious look at him for patronizing her. "You don't know that."

"I know whoever broke in doesn't care about your cat, and they wouldn't waste time catching him. They had only one thing in mind. Believe me, Jingles is fine."

She broke free with one final twist, still reluctant to back down. "He'd better be. How did this even happen? I thought the alarm system was supposed to go off if the wires were cut."

Her anger seemed to bounce off him without effect. He pulled his cell phone out but kept his eyes on her and didn't move away from the door, obviously not trusting her to stay out of her own home.

"Alarm systems work fine, and I'm sure this one went off as it should have. But I told you there are always ways to get around alarms. The guys who did this are pros, and nothing would keep them out."

He would know.

It was probably best not to throw his past in his face. After all, he was on her side. But the frustration boiled over, and she kicked the front door.

"I don't blame you for being mad," Rocky said. "But I'm sorry to say, this was bound to happen. It's why you stayed with Elizabeth last night, and I'm glad you did. Nothing can keep a determined thief out. This was probably the work of two or three men. They probably posed as employees of a security company. They could have told your neighbors they were testing your system, or working on it, and to ignore any alarms they might hear for the next ten minutes. Then they broke in, disabled the alarm—which went off for all of five seconds—and went through your house while the neighbors ignored the fact that you were being burglarized. But you can't blame them. The guys probably had uniforms and a van with a company name on the side. This was a professional job."

Her anger had died down during his speech until she was simply standing in thoughtful silence, amazed at how easily someone could bypass her security system. He took advantage of her subdued attitude, pointing at the wrought-iron bench beside the door. "Sit down. The sooner I call nine-one-one, the sooner you can go find Jingles, and a cat carrier, and whatever else you need to stay with Elizabeth until these guys are caught."

She sat. He was right. Right that she shouldn't go inside until the police arrived, right that she would have to move out, and right that breaking in had probably been a whole lot easier than she imagined. "What do you think they would have done if I'd been home?" she asked.

His jaw tightened and his tanned skin seemed to go a few shades paler. "I don't know. I'm just glad we didn't find out."

"Me, too." She leaned back against the iron curlicues of the bench, thinking about how close she'd come to danger and how scared Rocky had looked at the very idea. "Thanks, by the way. You're the reason I wasn't here."

A hint of his crooked, mischievous smile came back. "You're welcome."

She sighed. She couldn't help it, she loved when he did that. And hated that it made her feel weak all over. Mentally, she went through the litany. She couldn't trust her instincts. After being taken in so easily by a slimy psychopath like Banner, she'd be better off *never* trusting them again.

It was probably best to divert the conversation to a subject Rocky would be less charming about. "So what are we going to do about whoever broke in here?"

It worked; the smile disappeared. "*We're* not going to do anything. *The police* are going to investigate the break-in while you stay safely tucked away at the Westfield mansion."

The irony didn't escape her—Rocky, the ex-thief, was following the law to the letter, while she was looking for ways to skirt the cops and handle it herself.

"We could at least find out who sold Banner the jewelry in the first place, couldn't we? He rarely traveled, other than a couple business trips to Colombia, so I'll bet he bought them around here."

"Good point. I'll tell the cops and they can take care of it."

She blew out an exasperated breath. "Rocky, if I've learned anything from my train wreck of a marriage, it's that no one can take care of me better than I can. I did it when Banner tried to have me killed, and I did it again when he wanted to take me hostage. Okay," she amended, "you helped with the last one. You can help this time, too."

He snorted a laugh and shook his head. "I admire your spirit, but this isn't the same, and the police are already involved. Besides, they have better resources."

But not better contacts among professional thieves.

She wouldn't say it, because it would be like asking him to slip back into that life in order to help her, and she really didn't want him to do that.

She sat back on the bench and folded her arms over her chest. To her surprise, she felt his arm slide around her shoulders and squeeze gently. She stilled, not sure where this was going.

"I know you've gotten used to taking care of everything yourself."

She gave him a cautious look, but said nothing.

"That's what your life has been for a year now. You had to defend yourself against Banner, both physically and emotionally. You put in ridiculously long hours going over Aims's accounts with the IRS, trying to save the air freight division when Westfield-Benton would have written it off as a loss. Aims Air Freight only exists because of your efforts."

Ellie must have told him about that. "A lot of families depended on that company for jobs."

"And you saved them because you took charge when no one else would. That's fantastic. I can only imagine how you had to fight for every personal asset against Banner's rabid pack of divorce lawyers."

She raised an eyebrow, conceding his point. "They *were* vicious." She hadn't even asked for much. The car he'd bought for her and enough money to buy her condo. Even though Banner's own mother had encouraged her to demand more, it had all felt tainted by association with Banner. "How do you know about that?"

"I heard some things from Ellie, plus I could see the strain on your face. You've had a lot going on this past year."

"Oh good, I looked haggard and tense for a whole year. You sure know what a girl likes to hear."

She'd said it lightly, but his expression was serious, almost sad. "I didn't say you looked haggard. You looked like a beautiful woman with far too much stress in her life."

She hadn't been fishing for compliments. Suddenly self-conscious, she lowered her eyes, but he moved his arm off her shoulders and curved his finger beneath her chin, lifting it until she met his gaze again. He was a little too close, close enough for her to see that his eyes were a deep chocolate brown, and his lips had a sensual curve even when tightened by concern. Something inside her squirmed as she flicked her gaze from his eyes to his mouth and back to his eyes. She didn't know where to look when everything about him made her nervous.

He didn't seem to have the same problem; his gaze was unwavering. "I'm not trying to flirt with you, so don't get defensive. I'm only saying that taking care of everything by yourself has become a habit, and you don't need to do it anymore. You can actually depend on the authorities to take care of this one for you."

Despite that zinger about looking beautiful, which might not be flirting but was damned unsettling, he was right. His little speech wasn't a revelation, but she'd needed to hear it. It felt like someone had finally given her permission to relax, to quit trying to regain control of every aspect of her life.

She sighed and nodded, using the opportunity to pull away from his hand and quiet the fluttering in her chest. "Okay," she promised. "No chasing after jewel thieves."

He grinned, which made the whole lecture worthwhile. "Good. Besides, this might be the last you see of them. They did a thorough search, and didn't find anything. Maybe they'll figure out you don't have the other pieces." He cocked his head in a mild warning. "But just in case, you stay with Elizabeth for now. Agreed?"

Janet nodded. Since she didn't have a clue how to track down burglars, letting the police do it would be a relief. And staying with her ex–mother-in-law was better than staying at a hotel. From what she'd seen of her condo, it was a sure bet she wouldn't be living there again until the insurance company paid to replace her furniture, and that could take some time.

She hoped Elizabeth Westfield wasn't allergic to cats.

Rocky rescheduled the day's appointments while he waited for Janet. She spent the first fifteen minutes sobbing over slashed furniture and broken knickknacks, while nursing a rising panic when she couldn't find Jingles. They finally heard his plaintive meow from beneath her bed, and she gathered him in her arms. Both Janet and the cat calmed as she buried her face in his fur. With her worst fear eased, she spent the next half hour reviving her outrage as she packed a suitcase.

Selecting clothes was complicated; drawers had been dumped and their contents strewn about the room. She rose from her hands-and-knees search on the bedroom floor, clutching a handful of lacy undergarments, lip curling in distaste. "Ick. I can't stand the thought that they touched these. I'll have to wash every single thing before I can wear it again."

Rocky looked at the flimsy scraps of satin and lace. "I'll help," he offered.

She gave him an exasperated look. "No, thanks. I can handle it."

He watched her select a couple of bras from a tangle of lingerie and couldn't help forming a few ideas about handling some other things. He was only torturing himself. "Where did you say that cat carrier was? I'll go find it." It was better not to think about her bras and panties if he was going to keep picturing them on her body. Then taking them off her body.

Two hours later he deposited Janet, Jingles, and a car full of luggage at Elizabeth's door. As he walked back to the car, Janet called, "Aren't you coming in?"

After waiting nearly a year for that kind of invitation, he couldn't believe he was turning it down. "I have to talk to Ben about the break-in. I might have a few contacts who know something."

She frowned. "I can't get involved, but you can?"

"I'm not getting involved. I'm offering information. That's all."

Even as he said it, he was afraid that wouldn't be all. His former world was reaching out its dirty fingers to touch the woman he—what? Wanted? Belonged with? He was hoping to work that one out, but he needed to keep her safe in order to do it. That might mean dealing with some shady characters he'd sworn to never see again. It already meant dealing with the cops. In his experience, that was only marginally better. At least there was one cop he could trust.

Ben brought Rocky back to his office, settling behind his desk and indicating the chair on the other side.

Rocky was too restless to sit, though. He paced the room, pausing to look at pictures or handle objects without really seeing them.

Ben watched for several seconds before speaking. "I don't have anything new yet. It was a professional job, which you already know. At least two men, posing as security company employees." He rocked back in his chair. "The most we can tell, they weren't there more than a half hour, probably less. My guys will be asking questions, talking to contacts, coordinating with the FBI."

"You won't learn anything."

Ben pursed his lips, looking unhappy with the truth. "Maybe not. We don't usually see this kind of thing, but the FBI has experience with it on an international level."

Rocky shook his head as he paced. "This was someone local, I'll put money on it. It would have taken several days for news to get around and for the right people to fly here and start sniffing around. This happened within a day. I'm betting it's someone in the area."

Ben's eyebrows drew together in a look of disbelief. "And you think you can figure out who?"

"I'm not sure it even matters. If you catch them, someone else will just come looking for the Pellinni Jewels." He stopped in front of Ben's desk and braced his hands on the scarred top, leaning forward to emphasize the importance of what he was about to say. "This is going to get worse. These guys won't stop until they know Janet doesn't have the rest of the jewelry. You need to prove she doesn't."

Ben rubbed the crease between his eyebrows. "Should I even ask how I'm supposed to do that?"

"By finding out who does. Find out who sold Banner the necklace, and that person can tell you where the rest of the jewelry went."

"Sure, simple," Ben deadpanned.

"Maybe not. But it's possible. According to Janet, chances are good that Banner bought them around here, which means they were probably fenced around here. Damn it, Ben, the rest of that jewelry could be right in this area. Finding it is the only way to remove the bull's-eye from Janet's back."

Ben rocked forward, matching Rocky's intensity with a hard look. "My job is to find whoever slashed the hell out of Janet's condo and car. I don't have the resources to go running around solving international jewelry heists. But I'm sure the FBI would be interested in hearing about who might have fenced the necklace. You want to give me some names?"

He stepped back with a bitter laugh. "They wouldn't talk to the FBI."

"Who will they talk to? You?" Suspicion puckered Ben's brows. "You wouldn't be thinking of contacting some old friends, would you?"

"I don't have any friends in that business. In fact, there are plenty of people who'd be happy to show me just how much they *don't* miss me." But there were a few guys he'd never crossed who had no reason to dislike him. And if it meant saving Janet from some very determined thieves . . .

His thoughts must have shown on his face. "Rocky." Ben waited for him to meet his stern gaze. "You know I have a lot of respect for you. Plus, you're my son's best friend. I would be very disappointed if you stuck your foot back in that cesspool."

Rather than lie to Ben, he skirted the issue. "You know why I did it, and you know I'm done with it. There's no more reason to go back to that life."

"Because you took care of all the reasons. But maybe now you think you've got a new one."

"This isn't the same thing." But Janet was just as important to him as the crime that had initially drawn him into that life. No, he realized with a start. More important.

"Then why do I have the funny feeling that the line between legal and illegal just became very blurry for you?"

He smiled, forcing himself to look unconcerned. "Because you're cynical and jaded." And the best cop he knew. "But let me remind you that we're talking about Janet. If you're concerned about someone jumping into this mess who has no business mucking around in it, I'm not the one you should be worried about."

Ben groaned. "Damn it, whatever happened to women who sat back and let the men take care of things?"

Rocky snorted back a laugh. "I don't know, but Janet's sure not one of them. And frankly, if she were, I wouldn't find her as attractive as—" He cleared his throat. "Just keep in mind that if you don't act fast, you'll have Janet going after these guys herself. You know it as well as I do. And these guys are far too dangerous for her to tangle with."

"No argument there." Ben pinned Rocky with a sharp stare. "Just make sure you stay out of it, too."

Rocky held both hands up. "That's why I told you what I know, so you can handle it. For what it's worth, you have my opinion: I think the FBI should start looking for the rest of the Pellinni Jewels in the Detroit area." He started toward the door.

"Yeah, I'll pass that on." Ben raised his voice as Rocky reached for the doorknob. "And they better not get any unofficial help from you, Hernandez. I don't want to lock your ass up again."

At least they were in agreement on that. He raised a hand in acknowledgment without looking back. The sooner he got out of here, the sooner he could start looking for the person who had sold Banner the Pellinni necklace. Because he'd bet anything that the rest of the jewels had gone through those same hands. The FBI would never get a fence to rat out his customers, but Rocky might. Someone around here knew where the Pellinni Jewels had gone, and he wasn't going to rest until he found out who.

Chapter Five

"What is *that*?"

Janet cringed, cursing herself for not closing the door. She threw an "oh no, here it comes" grimace at Libby, who lowered her head and returned the look under the cover of her long hair. Then, pasting on a smile, Janet turned toward the bedroom door to face Elizabeth.

"That's my cat, Jingles." She made her voice light and happy. "Remember? I told you I sent him to live with my parents when I married Banner and moved in here, since Banner and Jingles didn't get along."

Elizabeth stared at the cat on the bed, who had paused in the middle of his bath, one hind leg pointed at the ceiling as he stared back at her. Neither moved.

"I'm sorry, I should have warned you I was bringing him. But don't worry, it's not permanent. I plan to take him to the kennel later today." She really didn't want to leave him caged up at some animal storage facility, though. They reminded her too much of the echoing corridors of the pound where she'd rescued him. It tore at her heart that he would think he'd been abandoned again. But she couldn't think of anyone who could take him.

"Banner didn't like your cat?" Elizabeth's voice was as cool as ever, her gaze still on Jingles.

"No. But the feeling was mutual."

A few more uncomfortable moments of silence ticked by. Libby took the opportunity to add her opinion. "He's really nice, Grandma. He always sits on my lap when Ellie and I visit Janet, and he never, ever scratches the furniture." Demonstrating Jingles's docile nature, she crawled onto the bed and stroked his back. Jingles lowered his leg, instantly regaining his dignity, and headbutted Libby's hand, his request to have his cheek scratched. Libby obliged while sneaking hopeful looks at her grandmother.

Elizabeth tilted her head, watching. "Banner never had a cat, you know. Or a dog. His father was allergic."

"He told me." She didn't think that had anything to do with her ex-husband's cold dislike of Jingles, but she didn't say so.

"I never had a cat, either." Elizabeth's right eyebrow rose, as if this startling fact had just occurred to her.

"Me, either," Libby was quick to add, looking as bereft as if she'd been deprived of an essential nutrient. The girl sure wasn't dumb.

Elizabeth shot a quick warning glance at her granddaughter. She wasn't dumb, either. Janet forced herself to stay quiet as Elizabeth studied Jingles again, finally asking, "Does he bite?"

"No!" Janet and Libby said together, Libby looking outraged at the very idea. She murmured reassurances to Jingles, who purred at high volume.

Elizabeth set her shoulders, a sure sign that a decision had been reached. "Then I don't see why he can't stay here. I'm sure something that small can't be much trouble."

Janet glanced at a few long black and white hairs that already clung to the pale yellow comforter and bit her cheek. "Thank you, Elizabeth."

"Thank you, Grandma!" Libby chorused, nearly bouncing with joy. "Janet, you can keep his food dish and litter box in my room, if you want to."

Janet laughed and started to explain that Jingles would probably be more comfortable staying with her, when Elizabeth interrupted. "Nonsense. A cat box doesn't belong in the bedroom. Peters will find a place for it in the laundry room. And his food bowl can go in the kitchen. Will that be okay, Janet?"

"Uh, sure." She hadn't expected to give Jingles the run of the house, but was certain he'd agree with the considerable expansion in territory.

"Excellent. I'll tell Peters." Elizabeth left with a purpose.

Janet grinned and shrugged at Libby. "Who'd have guessed?"

Libby gave a solemn nod, a miniature, blue-jean-clad sage. "I guess Rocky's right, you never know until you try."

Janet watched her stroke Jingles, her curiosity aroused. "When did Rocky say that?"

"Oh, a while ago. When I asked him about dancing."

"Why did you ask Rocky about dancing?"

"Grandma wanted me to take some classes in that old-fashioned ballroom stuff. I thought it sounded dorky, so I asked Rocky about it. He said I might like it, he did, and you never know until you try."

So many questions popped into her mind that it took awhile to sort through the confusion and pick one. She went for the big one, not sure she'd heard correctly. "Rocky knows how to ballroom dance?"

"I guess. I don't know. But he took lessons. He showed me some steps and spun me around. It was kind of fun."

She tried to picture Rocky swooping across a dance floor with a light-footed partner. It wasn't hard to imagine. He had an athletic grace about him that could translate easily into dance.

Intrigued with the idea, she nearly forgot to ask the obvious question. "So did you take the lessons?"

"Not yet. But I will when the juniors' class starts in the fall." She hauled Jingles into her lap and scratched both his cheeks at once while bending over and crooning, "You like that, don't you Jingle-Bingles? Yes, you do."

Jingles stretched his neck up, eyes closed blissfully, purr revving up to high. Janet's mind whirled with all the new things she'd learned about Rocky. The man who had seemed to be nothing more than a charming, small-time burglar was also a successful businessman, a martial arts expert, a charismatic public speaker, and a competent ballroom dancer. And an expert kisser. She hadn't forgotten that, even though her one experience with it had been half a year ago. If he did everything else as well as he did that, he was a very accomplished man indeed.

And apparently this thirteen-year-old girl knew more about him than she did. She studied Libby thoughtfully. "So do you usually consult Rocky when you need advice?"

"Sometimes. He's the coolest guy I know."

Rocky would seem cool to a teenage girl. "Jack's pretty cool. Ellie, too. Why not ask them for advice?"

"'Cause, duh, they're my parents." She looked at Janet as if her IQ had suddenly plummeted fifty points. "Besides, Rocky just looks like he knows about stuff like dancing and boys and—" she paused and Janet thought she blushed a little. "Other stuff. You know what I mean?"

She nodded. Oh, yeah. Especially the other stuff. He looked like he knew a lot about that. And God help her, Janet was starting to get curious about just how extensive his knowledge was, and how interesting it would be to find out.

Rocky slouched behind the wheel, staring at the small shop across the street. It was a narrow strip of crumbling brown brick tucked between an equally decrepit bail bondsman's office and a bar with blacked-out windows. The sign over the door said "Detroit Barber Shop," which explained the three barber's chairs inside. It had nothing to do with the real business transacted in the back room, where nearly every major piece of stolen jewelry in the Detroit Metro area was fenced. The owner was a middle-aged Russian immigrant with acne scars, lumbago, and seriously skewed ethics. The last time he was here, Rocky swore he'd never be back.

In the half hour he'd spent watching the shop, only one customer had entered. He'd left ten minutes ago with a buzz cut that looked more Russian army than *GQ*.

Jaywalking across the street, Rocky entered the shop. The two large men lounging in barber's chairs didn't have to look up at the bell; they'd been watching him through the front window since he'd stepped out of his car. Rocky recognized them both but didn't know their names. For all he knew, they didn't have names. He nodded a greeting, getting nothing in return but level gazes. He couldn't recall ever seeing a smile from either man and decided they were congenitally incapable of it.

"Is Vasili here?" he asked.

"In back. You wait."

Rocky nodded, knowing better than to ask how long. Vasili knew he was here and would come out when he was ready.

"Nice car."

Rocky focused on the first man, a bodybuilder in a white barber jacket. Rocky had never seen him cut hair; his jacket barely hid a holstered Sig Sauer.

"Thanks." The car *was* nice, a reward to himself for all the jobs he'd done for Vasili. The Russian was demanding but paid well.

"Bad neighborhood. You use club?"

"LoJack."

The man gave a solemn nod. "Good, very good."

Having dispensed with small talk, they resorted to form and simply watched him. Sticking his hands in his pockets, Rocky leaned against the wall, keeping his eyes on them. Vasili's goons had always reminded him of a pack of wild dogs—if he showed fear he'd be dead.

The staring contest lasted several minutes before a door opened at the back of the shop and an overweight man in a business suit appeared.

"Rocky!" Arms outstretched, the man hurried across the shop. Rocky barely had time to pull his hands from his pockets before being caught in a bear hug.

"Hey, Vasili." He spoke into the man's neck, inhaling a heavy dose of aftershave. "How have you been?"

"Awful! Lumbago is curse from devil." Unfortunately, it didn't keep him from squeezing his friends breathless. He released Rocky after adding a couple sound shoulder thumps. "Same shit, but I manage, as always. How about you? I hear you have honest business now."

"Yes, a security company."

Vasili looked at his associates and threw up his hands. "He keeps burglars out!" He laughed heartily, but the irony seemed to escape the others. Their flat stares didn't waver.

"You come to sell me security system?" He chuckled some more at the thought that he might not have enough security. The happy twins didn't find it funny.

"No security systems. I came to talk to you about a necklace."

Vasili cocked his head, studying him. "Ah. I have maybe heard. That one?"

"That one." Unless there was another hot priceless necklace floating around, and Rocky didn't think there was.

The Russian looked surprised. "It was yours?"

Rocky knew he meant it in a finders keepers sort of way—*your* burglary job, *your* necklace. "No, not mine. It's complicated. Can we talk?" Privately, where the two goons wouldn't overhear.

Vasili rubbed his chin thoughtfully, obviously too

interested to refuse. Putting an arm around Rocky's shoulder, he said, "Sure. We talk in my office. You tell why you not come see Vasili in two years." He started guiding Rocky toward the back room, then turned to rattle off something in Russian to the beefier of his two associates. The man nodded and eased his body out of the barber's chair. When the back door closed behind them, the man was sorting through a drawer of long, pointy scissors. Rocky hoped one of them was not intended for his tires as punishment for not keeping in touch with the overbearing Russian fence.

Vasili's office was a claustrophobic room containing a countertop work area with a track of spotlights above it, only one of which was currently on, and a tall stool. In the shadows behind the counter was a floor safe and an ancient wooden cabinet with dozens of tiny drawers. In the many times Rocky had been here, he'd never asked what was in the drawers, but imagined an assortment of watches and bracelets and whatever else wasn't expensive enough to rate inclusion in the safe. All Rocky's pieces went into the safe.

Vasili rounded the counter and settled his bulk on the barstool with a groan, holding his lower back. "This work, sitting like this, is bad for spine. But I see chiropractor now, like you tell me. He helps."

Rocky smiled from the other side of the countertop. "Told you he would."

"So why you give me this good advice, then never come see me?"

"Things came up. Like jail."

"*Pfft.*" Vasili waved off his jail term like the year

had been two weeks at day camp. "A few months. No excuse."

Rocky nodded. "I finished what I had to do, Vasili. I'm straight now, a law-abiding citizen."

"And you have no friends here anymore?"

He shifted uncomfortably but didn't look away. He'd never lied to Vasili, and wouldn't now. "You're a friend," he said, stretching the definition to its limits. "But not the kind I can afford to have right now. The police still remember who I was and what I did. If they see me here, it's not good for either one of us."

Vasili shrugged. "Police don't bother me. I'm law-abiding citizen, too. I'm struggling small businessman." He grinned, enjoying his own joke. "Like you, eh?"

"My business doesn't have a back room, Vasili."

The Russian nodded. "So why you here now? What you have to do with Pellinni Jewels? That what we talk about, right? Not your type job."

He ignored the fact that he no longer had a type of job. "The woman who sold the necklace is a friend of mine. She didn't know it was stolen. Her ex-husband had given it to her as a gift when they were married."

Bushy eyebrows rose. "Nice gift."

"She didn't think so. Especially now that someone is looking for the rest of the collection. They tore apart her house and her car, and I'm not sure they'll stop there. They want the other pieces and they think she has them."

"Maybe she does."

"No." He shook his head, keeping his eye contact as strong as his voice, making sure the Russian believed him. "She doesn't. I'm sure."

Vasili shrugged. "Neither do I."

"I didn't think so. Anyway, if you'd had them, they'd be in Russia by now." Vasili's connection to the Russian Mafia and their lucrative export business was not the best kept secret in town.

Vasili laughed and reached over to punch Rocky's shoulder. "You're right!"

"But maybe you heard something about the collection being fenced."

He shook his head. "Lot of stuff being pawned—recession good for business. But not that. I would know."

"It wouldn't have been recent." Mentally, he counted back the months to Janet's brief marriage to Banner. "Probably early last year."

Vasili gave it some thought. "You sure they fence in Detroit? All good stuff here comes to me, but I don't see Pellinni Jewels."

He should have realized the Russian would take it as a personal affront that he hadn't been chosen to fence the jewelry. "I'm not sure where they came from, just that it's likely they were bought around here. But I figure they were very hot and got dumped fast. Probably by someone who didn't know what he had, or else my friend's husband wouldn't have been able to afford it." Or, more likely, the greedy bastard wouldn't have given it to his wife.

The Russian nodded slowly. "Maybe." His gaze sharpened. "So what you want do? Find fence, threaten poor man's life? How that help your lady friend? How that help me?"

Rocky took a deep breath, praying to pitch this right, or Vasili wouldn't tell him anything. "If I can find the fence, maybe I can convince him to tell me what happened to the other pieces. I know they're long gone by now, sold to some new owner, and I can keep the fence's name out of it. He should be glad, because I don't think our new thief's the type to leave witnesses. If he finds the fence first, the guy might not live to talk about it."

Vasili nodded. "True. Dangerous business."

Rocky didn't point out that Vasili's associates were responsible for a large percentage of that danger. "If I can convince him to tell me where the rest of the collection went, I can find it. And I'm still the best in the business. If I get the jewelry back, the fence is safe. There's no reason to connect me to him, or the guy who sold it last year. The bad guys stop looking for it, the fence lives, and my lady friend is out of danger."

"And you bring to me. I use international contacts, sell to highest bidder, split with you eighty-twenty."

Rocky smiled, only partly at the low percentage being offered him. "Not exactly. I take them to the FBI. Game over."

Vasili looked crushed, shaking his big head. "Dickhead move. No one make money."

"But everyone stays safe."

"*Pfft.*" He sulked over the loss of income for several seconds. "You not so good businessman, Rocky. Could make lots money. But . . . your loss. You want name of fence? No skin off my nose. They find him, less competition for me." Vasili rubbed his chin again, thinking. "Had to be someone not know business too good, or never would have sold necklace, right? Who not recognize Pellinni Jewels?" He rolled his eyes to the ceiling over such incomprehensible ignorance. Then squinted as inspiration struck. "I know guy like this on West Side. Stupid shit. Don't know name. Not important. Like mosquito, I only swat him if get in my way." He sketched a map on a piece of paper, marking a spot with an *X,* then indicating major roads with a blunt forefinger. "This Evergreen, this Fenkell. Store on side street here. Called "Treasures," or "Fortunes." Some shit like that."

Rocky folded the paper and tucked it in a pocket. "Thanks, Vasili."

"You tell me what happens."

"I will."

"And don't be stranger. Keep in touch."

Not if he could avoid it. "I might come by more often if you'd buy another damn stool to sit on."

Vasili laughed and came around the counter, opening the door for Rocky and waving good-bye, his usual routine. Rocky was sure if he walked out alone he'd never make it to the front door of the barber shop without being tackled. The escort was for Rocky's safety.

Leaving was a relief, and not just because he had a lead on the necklace. Stepping back into the world of petty thieves, crime cartels, and armed bodyguards felt like walking in deep muck, the stink clinging to his clothes and dirtying everything he touched. He strode across the street to the abandoned parking lot where he'd left the Lexus, intent on getting out of this crumbling section of Detroit as fast as he could.

The Lexus was no longer alone in the lot. A yellow corvette was parked nearby, a man leaning against it as he waited. Rocky took in the studied indifference as the man watched him, finally flicking his cigarette to the ground and straightening as Rocky reached the lot.

Shit. Easy Joey, the last person he ever wanted to see again.

"Thought this was your car." Easy strolled around it to the driver's side, obviously satisfied with his sharp memory.

"Figured that out, huh?" He pulled the keys from his pocket and jingled them impatiently.

Easy had never tuned in to subtleties. Or maybe he was ignoring this one. "Heard you were out."

Rocky lifted an eyebrow. "I've been out for more than a year. That news is a bit out of date."

"And yet I never get tired of remembering that you went to jail."

His jaw tightened. "I'll bet." Easy was the one responsible for putting him there.

"How was it? I've never been, myself."

He'd give anything to wring the bastard's neck. "Interesting place. I made lots of new friends." He allowed a cool smile.

Easy's expression hardened. "Are you threatening me, Hernandez?"

Rocky allowed a short laugh. "I'm not that interested in you, Easy. And I'm leaving." He hit the remote button to unlock the car, waiting for Easy to stand aside. The idiot stepped toward him instead.

"Well, I'm not done with you."

Was the twerp really confronting him? He knew Easy was prone to rash moves but was surprised his anger could blind him to the obvious fact that he was a marshmallow.

Easy put on his tough face, squinting and curling his upper lip. The glimpse of nicotine-stained teeth was the only actual intimidating factor. "You took something from me, Hernandez. I intend to get even."

"You made sure I went to jail. I'd say we're even."

"Well, you're wrong. A year in County, big deal. Those gold coins were my big score, and you took them."

Marshmallow or not, the guy had hit a tender spot. Rocky made a conscious effort to control his temper as he leaned close to Easy. "Those gold coins weren't yours."

"I don't agree, and I want them back."

"Too bad. I don't have them."

Easy sneered. "You expect me to believe you'd fence them for a tenth of their value? I'm not stupid."

"You might have to reevaluate that claim. I gave them away."

He scowled, anger changing to disbelief. "To who?"

"To 'whom,' dumb fuck," Rocky corrected, enunciating it the way Elizabeth Westfield would, just to irritate the little prick. "To their rightful owner, which is not you. Now move."

He did, sliding a short, jagged-edged knife from his waistband and standing between Rocky and the car door. Rocky sighed. Some guys just couldn't separate their brains from their balls.

Easy let the knife flash in the sun, admiring the shine. "You're a fuckin' idiot if you—" his sentence ended abruptly as Rocky delivered a fast punch to the gut that sent Easy staggering against the car. Before he could recover, Rocky kicked the knife away, eliciting a high squeal from Easy as his fingers tried to go with it. Grabbing a handful of his shirt before Easy could recover, Rocky pushed him out of the way.

Easy sat on the gritty pavement, cradling his fingers

against his injured stomach and gasping for air as Rocky got in his car. Starting the ignition, he lowered the window to offer a final piece of advice. "Stay out of my way, Easy, and I'll do you a huge favor and stay out of yours."

Easy stood painfully, straightening as much as he could. "No one gets away with stealing from me, Hernandez. If you don't have the coins, I'll take something else." He paused to draw a few raspy breaths. "I'm warning you right now, you just made yourself a target. And you know I can do it."

Rocky wasn't sure about that, but he had to admit the guy was good at what he did. Joey Korchak hadn't picked up his nickname from an easygoing manner or an effortless way with women. It came from his brash but accurate claim that he could break into almost anyplace, "easy."

Rocky doubted Easy's skills could overcome the security measures at his apartment, but it might be fun to see what the guy could do. He'd have to be awfully good to bypass both Rocky's vigilance and a Red Rose alarm system.

"I can't stop you from trying, Easy. But remember what happens if you get caught in the act." He put the car in gear and eased off the brake. "Maybe I can use my connections and get you a cell with a view."

"Fuck off," Easy grunted as the car backed up. He was standing straight, if shakily, as Rocky drove off, calling out, "We're not done, Hernandez!"

Great. He stepped back into the underworld for one measly hour, and came away with its most slimy specimen stuck to him like a piece of gum on the bottom of a shoe.

Chapter Six

The rental car company made it easy, delivering an environmentally friendly, inconspicuous compact car right to the Westfields' door. And since Elizabeth was at a steering committee meeting for the downtown development group and Rocky was at work, Janet knew she could sneak away easily. After all, what did they expect her to do all day, watch TV? It was either go to work or go crazy.

Janet walked down the corridor of the Westfield-Benton office as if she had every right to be there. She did—in the department that ran Aims Air Freight. But not in the basement storage area.

Listening for footsteps before stepping into the deserted hall, she hurried to a locked room at the far end. Using the key she'd taken from the custodian's desk, she slipped inside. The room housed a collection of unused furniture, accessories, and electronics, along with seven nondescript cardboard boxes containing the personal effects from Banner's office.

She'd seen what was in them. Heck, she even helped

pack them. But she'd been married to him at the time
and had had a right to handle his possessions, even if
she'd done it in the presence of his attorney. Now she
was his ex-wife and the future star witness in the gov-
ernment's case against him. Getting caught searching
through his personal belongings probably wouldn't be
a good thing.

She was also breaking Rocky's and Ben's stern
warnings to stay home. That part couldn't be helped—
she had a business to run and a crime to solve. If she
got back to Elizabeth's before six as planned, they'd
never even know.

That gave her an hour to go through the seven
boxes again. When they'd packed them away she'd
only made sure they didn't contain personal items like
photographs or credit cards. This time she was looking
for receipts or jewelry boxes, anything that might be
related to the Pellinni Jewels.

She dragged a chair to the boxes, opened the first
one, and dug in.

Forty minutes later Janet sighed with frustration as she
opened the last box. At least this one didn't have any
tedious stacks of paper or loose leaf binders. It also
didn't have any likely connections to the missing jewelry. One by one, she lifted out the knickknacks that
had decorated Banner's desk and shelves—a chunk of
polished stone littered with trilobite fossils, a broken
piece of Aztec pottery that probably belonged in a museum, a trophy won in a sailing race on Lake Michigan, and a half dozen other unsuspicious mementos.

She pulled out the last object—a wooden humidor,
inlaid with ivory. She'd seen it before, it was where

Banner kept his cigars. This time it rattled when she picked it up. She held it on her lap and yanked at the tight lid. It opened with a pop, spilling the contents into her lap—eight golden golf balls.

She picked one up. It was obviously gold plated; it felt too light to be solid. A tiny flat base allowed each ball to sit so that the black lettering across the top could be read: Westfield-Benton Charity Golf Classic. Souvenirs for the top players at the company-sponsored annual golf event.

Disappointed, she gathered the balls and put them back in the box. One dropped from her lap and rolled across the cement floor. Janet muttered a curse as she retrieved it from beneath a desk, blowing off dust and cobwebs. She rubbed her finger along a dirty line, but it wouldn't come off. Using her fingernail, she scraped it. Her nail caught in a groove.

Hope fluttered in her chest as she wedged her thumb nails into the groove and pried. The ball fell open in two halves, revealing a hollow interior. No secret prize, no hidden jewelry. She didn't know what she'd been expecting; it wasn't big enough to hold one of the ornate Pellinni Jewels, anyway. It was just another cheaply made promotional gift.

To remove any doubt, she opened each one. All empty.

Disappointed, she packed them away with the other items. Closing the last box, Janet sighed. Whatever had happened to the rest of the Pellinni Jewels, Banner didn't seem to be involved.

She returned the key and headed to her rental car. The Westfield-Benton parking lot had emptied considerably, and only one other car pulled out when she did—a black Escalade that turned in the same direction. When she stopped for gas, it kept going.

She filled her tank and got back on the road. She looked in her rearview mirror as she changed lanes and noticed a black Escalade a couple cars back. When she turned onto the I-75 entrance ramp, she watched the mirror again. The Escalade was still there.

That didn't mean it was following her, she told herself. I-75 was the major traffic corridor in Oakland County; a whole string of commuters had taken the same entrance ramp. Plus, her little rental car made her blend in while the BMW was at the shop. But the way the Escalade hung in her rearview mirror made the skin on the back of her neck quiver with apprehension.

Her fears eased a bit as she passed Chrysler's headquarters and the Escalade pulled into the second lane and sped up. If she stayed where she was in the right lane, she'd know soon enough if the driver was tailing her.

The man behind the wheel was drawing even when she moved into the long exit lane for Square Lake Road. He moved right, too, hanging in her blind spot. But he wasn't in the exit lane. She breathed a sigh of relief. Rocky's fears had her imagination working overtime.

The next second, a sharp jolt sent her car skidding toward the abutment of the upcoming overpass.

She jerked the wheel left, instinctively steering away from the cement wall. The little rental car fishtailed on grass and gravel, sliding toward the embankment and scrub growth beyond the expressway. In the slow motion she'd often heard accident victims relate, she saw the car ahead of her pull to the right, ready to aid the potentially injured, while the car slightly ahead in the next lane swerved even farther away, causing a sharp blare of horns that cascaded across the expressway in a chain reaction.

The Escalade was still in her blind spot, but probably close, waiting to send her down the slight embankment if she pulled out of the skid. Not a deadly drop, but at this speed, enough to cause significant injury. The car slid on weeds as she fought for control. She stepped on the gas and the car lurched, front wheels catching on asphalt, then shooting forward as she regained the road.

Speed seemed like a good idea. Her compact car was no match for the powerful Cadillac SUV, but she wasn't about to stick around to see what it would do next. Darting around the concerned citizen who had pulled over ahead of her, she hit the gas. Behind her, the Escalade gave chase.

For once, Janet was thankful for the congested traffic on Square Lake. Her car dodged nimbly between vehicles, but the Cadillac was closing the gap, roaring up the center lane behind her. Its driver had the advantage of not caring what he hit.

She couldn't outrun him. The light ahead at heavily traveled Woodward Avenue turned yellow, and she laid on the horn, while saying a silent prayer that the car ahead of her was aggressive enough to speed through. It was. She followed, cutting sharply left into the center turn lane. If she couldn't escape her pursuer, she might at least find safety in numbers.

The U-turn exchange across the divided highway took her back to the light at Woodward. With a screech of tires, she cut across lanes and took a sharp right south bound, tearing up flowers as she careened over the curb. Horns blared and cars swerved as she wedged into a gap between vehicles, pissing off drivers for a good fifty yards behind her. A quick glance in the mirror showed the black Escalade following, bouncing over the curb and plowing through traffic. Cars scattered, opening the center lane, giving the driver a clear path. Damn. The Escalade leapt forward, accelerating with a high-pitched whine as it tore toward her. She couldn't outrun it. Her only choice was to find someplace safe, and quickly.

A police station would have been ideal. No such luck—the next mile of Woodward was a tree-lined boulevard. The few quiet side streets offered nothing but palatial mansions. The only exception was the long drive ahead on her right, leading to Cranbrook Academy. Several cars were slowing in the right lane, turning into the school. There must be a function tonight.

A crowd of people would provide protection, but she didn't have time to follow a stately line of cars down a winding lane. There was only one option. With a sharp swerve, she cut the line, wedging the little rental between a Land Rover and the Volvo ahead of it. A cacophony of blaring horns arose, aimed both at her and the Escalade as it tried to follow, forcing its way between indignant drivers.

They were about to get even more indignant. As soon as she turned into the drive, she angled the car to block as much of the road as possible, and then stopped.

Cars braked behind her. Horns honked. The driver

of the Land Rover slammed out of his vehicle and stalked toward her. But most importantly, the Escalade backed out of the expanding traffic jam before it could get trapped, laying rubber as it sped off.

Relief was a cool wave sweeping over Janet from head to toe. Giving the furious Land Rover driver an apologetic wave, she put the car in gear and straightened out. Before she could find a way to turn around, the loud whoop of a siren sounded behind her and red and blue lights flashed in her mirror.

Pulling two wheels over the curb, she moved aside enough for traffic to pass her. Hopefully, flattening the immaculate Cranbrook lawn wouldn't be included on her long list of violations.

At least no one was hurt.

"What were you thinking?! You were supposed to stay here where you'd be safe!"

Janet narrowed her eyes at Rocky from across Elizabeth Westfield's living room. "I was thinking I have a job and it might be nice if I did it before the company tanked. I was thinking I wasn't going to work my butt off to save Aims Air Freight only to lose it because you want me to be a virtual prisoner in this house. *That's* what I was thinking."

Her answer did nothing to quiet the storm roiling across his face. "You knew people were after you!"

He hadn't lowered his voice, so she raised hers to match. "I knew they were after the jewelry! I don't *have* the jewelry!"

She would have used stronger language, but Libby was listening, watching the argument from the sofa with the attention she might give a championship tennis match. Janet saw her expectant gaze dart back to Rocky for the return volley, but Elizabeth interrupted the tirade.

"I'm sorry, Roberto. It's partly my fault. I should have stayed with her."

They all started to contradict her, but it was Ben who spoke first. "It's not your fault, Liz. Janet's a big girl."

"Thank you." At least someone didn't want to treat her like a child.

"She can take responsibility for her own stupid choices."

She shot Ben an angry glare, one that clearly demanded to know whose side he was on. He stared back in cop mode, arms crossed, implacable gaze drilling holes through her, making the answer clear. He was on Rocky's side.

She threw up her arms. "Doesn't anyone care that I stayed calm and got myself out of a very dangerous situation? And what do I get for it? Two traffic tickets and a lecture!"

In the hostile silence that followed, Libby finally offered, "I think what you did was way cool."

Janet gave her a halfhearted smile. "Thanks."

Elizabeth touched her arm, forcing her to meet the firm parental look. "We're all grateful that you were quick witted enough to survive, Janet. We care about you."

Elizabeth was as collected as ever, even though Janet knew she loved her like a daughter. At least she treated her like one. And she supposed her own father would react to her brush with death a lot like Ben had, with relief followed by barely restrained anger. The depth of his concern warmed her even as it made her feel guilty. But Rocky . . .

She raised her eyes under lowered brows, taking in the flushed complexion and firmly clenched jaw that revealed his simmering temper. She'd never seen him so furious. She knew he cared about her, but she hadn't realized just how much.

With an impatient sigh, she said what she knew she had to say, whether she meant it or not. "Sorry," she muttered. "I won't do it again."

"Damn right you won't," Rocky said.

She fixed him with a cool look, keeping her voice low. "Don't press your luck, Hernandez."

Ben interrupted their glaring contest. "Janet, part of the reason we're worried is the way they went about this. This was more than a warning. It was bold and daring, an attack in broad daylight that could have injured or even killed you. That's not what I would expect from some cat burglar looking to find the remaining Pellinni Jewels."

"Exactly," Rocky said with a fierce nod. "There's something else going on here."

They were the experts on crime and criminals, so she'd take their word for it. She turned to Ben, who seemed the friendlier of the two at the moment. "Like what?"

"I don't know." But the quick look he threw at Rocky said he had an idea, and Rocky knew about it. She darted suspicious glances at each of them, but both had their lips pressed into tight lines, obviously not willing to share with the others.

She gave a toss of her head, forgetting there was no hair left to swing in a haughty arc. Flipping her bangs probably reduced the dramatic effect. "I'm sure you won't mind if I leave. I missed dinner and I'm starving." She made sure Rocky received the brunt of her disdainful look before she stalked out.

Rocky left in the opposite direction, stomping outside where he stood in the dark beside his car, arms folded, fuming over Janet's stubborn attitude. He doubted all their lecturing had made any difference—she would still follow up on the next idea that popped into her head, no matter how dangerous.

She'd always been that way. It had worked for her—a risky, bold maneuver had saved her life when Banner had tried to have her killed. Another one had helped bring his illegal schemes to an end. There was no reason to think she'd change her ways now. Rocky would be better off keeping her close and watching out for her than trying to dissuade her from helping.

But damn it, she could get hurt. Or worse. And he couldn't live with that.

He also couldn't control her actions—Janet would never speak to him again if he tried. Besides, he wouldn't be nearly so attracted to her if she were the type to wait for guidance every time there was a crisis. He *liked* her initiative and courage. It's just that it was killing him.

Perhaps his only option was to admit it.

The kitchen was silent except for the low hum and swish of the dishwasher. Janet flipped on the low wattage lights that ran beneath a cabinet, enough to find a plate and silverware while still letting her stew in the gloom that suited her mood. Light reflected dully off stainless steel appliances and floated in a dim glow over the granite countertops. The semidark was a soothing balm after the tension in the brightly lit living room.

Knowing that Michael, Elizabeth's high-priced chef, would have saved leftovers for her, she rooted through the covered dishes in the refrigerator, coming out with something that looked like wild mushroom risotto with chicken. She lifted the lid and sniffed—finally, something good about her day. She spooned some onto a plate, nuked it, and poured herself a glass of white wine. The barstools at the island countertop seemed to suit solitary dining better than the dining room table. Settling in, she took a large forkful and closed her eyes, appreciating Michael's culinary artistry.

"Janet."

She nearly choked, and quickly gulped some wine before she could speak. "You scared me," she accused.

Rocky crossed the shadowy kitchen. The dim room matched his black hair, dark eyes, and generally pissy mood.

He stopped beside her, the tall barstool putting them at nearly the same eye level. She took another bite of risotto to hide her discomfort.

"You're mad at me," he observed.

"No shit, Sherlock."

The side of his mouth twitched, but she couldn't tell if it was amusement or irritation. She stabbed more food with her fork.

"You scared the hell out of me."

She stopped with the fork halfway to her mouth, then slowly lowered it. She hadn't expected to hear that admission, and his quiet statement held more power than if he'd yelled it. "Um . . ." She swallowed. *Um, what?* She wasn't about to apologize for saving her own life. "I didn't mean to."

"I know, you can't help it." He watched her closely, the low light enough to cast a gleam on his eyes, giving them an intensity she hadn't noticed earlier. It was slightly mesmerizing. "You don't panic in a crisis, and you don't wait for someone to save you. You take charge and save yourself. You always have." His gaze roamed her face, as if memorizing the details of each feature. She wanted to seem unimpressed by his attention, but she couldn't look away. "Last year, when I first listened to you tell us about how you escaped the drug dealers in Colombia, the ones who were supposed to kill you, I admired your self-reliance and determination."

"You did?"

He nodded slightly, almost to himself. "I don't anymore."

"What?" She set her fork aside, forgetting about the risotto. "Why not?"

"Because it's hard to admire what scares me to death. You're risking your life." His voice was low, almost grave. "I need you to stop it."

Her gaze kept drifting to his mouth, distracting her with the memory of what it felt like to be kissed by those lips. They were far more clever at scrambling her brain than she would have guessed. She wondered if they would have the same effect now, as irritated as he was with her. The thought distracted her from what he'd been saying. "Stop what?"

"Stop putting yourself in danger. Stop trying to

handle everything yourself instead of trusting me to help you." His gaze wandered, too, lingering on her mouth, her hair, even her breasts, leaving tingling sensations everywhere it touched. Shadows moved along his jaw as muscles tensed. "Stop making me crazy, Janet."

She shook her head as if she were confused about what he meant. But she knew. She was starting to feel a little crazy herself.

He held her eyes with his, a force too strong to look away. With a start of recognition, she knew what would happen next. She felt it growing between them like a volcanic eruption, building deep below the surface and getting stronger as it surged upward. The longer they waited, the stronger it got. She trembled, wanting him to do it now, wanting him . . .

But he wouldn't. He'd told her long ago that it had to be her move.

Someone had inched closer, maybe both of them. His face was nearer, his breaths faster and deeper than hers. In fact, she wasn't sure if she was breathing at all. But who needed air? The energy between them was more than enough to sustain her.

Closing her eyes and sucking in a slow breath, she leaned forward and laid her lips against his. For a moment, neither of them moved. Then, pressing gently with her mouth, Janet reached for his neck and let her tongue play against his lips.

His arms closed around her in a hungry embrace. One hand hauled her against him, while the other reached up to cup her head. His kiss opened her mouth, plunging past her gentle beginning, demanding more. She gave it eagerly, meeting his tongue with hers,

blending her delighted moan with his rumble of satisfaction. She would have slid off the stool, boneless and
limp, if he hadn't held her in place to better devour her.
Both hands moved to her hair, touching her cheeks,
tilting her head to provide a new angle for his kiss.

He was as good as she remembered. Maybe better.
She clung to his shoulders, taking whatever he gave.
She gasped when he pulled away, melted when he
kissed her cheeks and forehead, and sighed against his
lips when they touched her mouth again, softer this
time. When he finally broke the kiss she kept her eyes
closed, waiting for her heart to stop pounding against
her rib cage.

She hadn't expected to feel that needy, that vulnerable. What had happened to her defenses? "I still don't
like you," she whispered, trying to believe it.

His lip ticked up again. "Okay."

She looked away, suddenly self-conscious about
how quickly she'd come apart in his arms.

With the hand that still cupped her head, he tilted
her forward to place a kiss on top of her head. "Please
don't leave this house, Janet. Promise me."

She nodded.

"I'll call you tomorrow."

She watched him go, then stared at the plate of risotto, now merely the *second* best thing that had happened to her all day. She'd finish it in a minute. Right
now she wanted to savor the lingering taste of Rocky.
She had a feeling she was going to become much better
acquainted with it in the near future.

The Westfield mansion had felt more like a mausoleum
than a home when Janet had lived there with Banner.

Now, with her intimidating husband gone and Libby in temporary residence, the house took on an entirely different feel, reflecting the confidence Libby had gained during her time with Jack and Ellie. The girl's presence could not be ignored.

Janet's first impression of Ellie's stepdaughter had been one of introspection and shyness, but Libby had blossomed in her new setting in Bloomfield Hills. She lit up any room like a bright fountain, bubbling nonstop with conversation and energy. And when she was out of sight, the pounding of footsteps on the stairs, the blast of music from the media room, or the laughter from phone conversations filled the empty rooms. The difference in the Westfield home enchanted Janet, and it was obvious that Elizabeth enjoyed it even more. The woman had mellowed remarkably since the days when she lived with Banner, to the point where Janet suspected she was even warming to the unexpected addition of Jingles to the household.

Unfortunately, cats never knew where to draw the line. Janet watched him wrap around Elizabeth's ankles as her ex–mother-in-law stood at the stove, fixing a cup of tea. Janet bit her lip, waiting for the cat to get shoved aside and hoping it would be gentle.

"Good morning, Jingles." Elizabeth's dignified greeting carried no trace of the high-pitched, animated voice most people use with pets and babies. She might just as well have said, "Good morning, Peters," with the exception that her butler's likely response would not have been a regal strut around the kitchen island. Janet watched her cat with amusement, enjoying his confident assumption of power in the Westfield household.

Until he passed the barstool, and her mind slipped. Memories from last night flashed back with a suddenness that snatched her breath and pushed her pulse into overdrive. Images of touching her lips to Rocky's, pressing her breasts against the hardness of his chest, and melting into him in the most mindless and soul-searing kiss of her life flooded her senses.

Heat rushed over her. She lowered her face, shoving a forkful of food into her mouth and hoping Libby and Elizabeth wouldn't wonder how Belgian waffles with strawberries could cause such furious embarrassment. Damn, she might have kept her long hair if she'd known she'd be doing things that made her want to hide behind it.

Fortunately, Libby had her own pressing concerns and had stopped her grandmother before she could escape to the patio with her tea. "Can I spend the night at Ginny Anderson's?"

"No, dear. I'm afraid I don't know the Andersons."

"You don't have to. Dad and Ellie let me stay there all the time."

"Well, I can't call and ask them, so you'll have to wait until they get back."

"But that's two weeks! That's so unfair." Libby scowled at her breakfast. "It's like I'm a prisoner here."

"Yes, conditions are quite brutal," Elizabeth agreed, casting a look around the expansive kitchen and the sparkling pool visible through the French doors. "However, once you finish your tennis lesson, you may invite Ginny to spend the night here."

Libby thought it over. "Can I invite April, too?"

"No. One friend, nonnegotiable."

Libby sulked for two more seconds. "Okay. Right after tennis."

Elizabeth escaped outside, no doubt intending to enjoy some solitude while she could. Libby sighed, rolled her eyes, and gave Janet an exasperated look. "That's what blows about getting dumped here. No social life."

Libby's standards had changed since coming to live with her father and falling into the Payton-Westfield fortune. Her first twelve years of life, when Jack hadn't known she existed, had been spent with her financially strapped grandparents and aunt. Since leaving them, she'd had a crash course in every sport or talent she cared to try. She took more lessons than anyone Janet knew. Between that, school friends, and her grandmother's country club membership, it was a wonder Libby wasn't looking for a break from her hectic social life. "What's so special about staying at Ginny's house?"

Libby leaned forward. "She has a Wii *and* an Xbox! Almost *all* my friends have at least one of them."

"You don't?"

Her eyes widened at the horror. "No! Can you believe it?"

Knowing what conscientious parents Ellie and Jack were, she could. "I imagine your parents would rather have you do something better with your time."

Libby's suspicious look said Janet had just aligned herself with the enemy. "Yeah, that's what they say. But I think they have another motive."

Of course she did. The girl analyzed everything. "What's that?"

Libby gave her a sly look. "It's 'cause they want to be alone together."

The emphasis on "alone together" made it obvious Libby didn't think they were watching TV. Having to take the time to swallow her food meant Janet didn't blurt out the first thing that came to mind, which was *What do you know about their sex life?* Libby was probably fishing for information as much as showing off her sophistication. With admirable calm, Janet sipped her juice and said, "I don't see the connection."

"It's obvious. If I ask to go to my friends' houses all the time so I can play their Xbox, then Dad and Ellie have our house to themselves." She arched an eyebrow, trying to look coolly mature, but Janet saw a blush creep into her cheeks. "I'm thirteen and a half. I know what's going on when I'm not there."

Janet couldn't think of anything to say. The kid was probably right. Jack and Ellie had been married for less than a year, and it was obvious to everyone how madly in love they were. Plus, from what Ellie said, living with a teenager hadn't put a dent in her sex life. Libby might very well have discovered why.

Janet made a contemplative sound and refused to comment. She wasn't going to get pulled into another discussion about Libby's current favorite topic. Which probably meant she was going to have to avoid the girl. That could be a problem. Having agreed that the outside world was temporarily a dangerous place to be, she was effectively grounded, stuck in the house with Libby, who only had a tennis lesson to distract her. And her friend Ginny.

God, two of them. This could be bad.

"Excuse me, I have to make a call." Janet ran upstairs, dug into her purse, and found the slip of paper with Rocky's phone number. Pulling out her cell phone, she committed the number to speed dial as she called him.

"Red Rose Security." His voice was competent and businesslike. She was probably interrupting him at work.

"Rocky, you have to save me."

She heard noises as something was dropped or put down hastily. "What happened?" More clunking sounds. There was an edge of panic in his voice. "Where are you?"

"I'm right where I'm supposed to be, and nothing happened. Yet. But it will, if I have to stay here all day with Libby and her hormone-saturated friend. Get me out of here."

She heard an exasperated sigh. "Jesus, don't scare me like that. I thought there was a *real* problem. What's wrong with Libby? She's a great kid."

"She's obsessed with sex."

He chuckled. "She's thirteen, Janet."

"She's trying really hard to be thirty. And it's not funny. I don't care to answer questions about my sex life. Her parents are supposed to handle that subject."

"Yeah? What questions? And what did you tell her? In lurid detail, please."

"Screw you," she said mildly.

"Ahh . . ." He cleared his throat. "Please note that I am politely passing on that beautiful setup." She had time to blush before he went on. "I trust you weren't that blunt with Libby. Just relax. Teenagers often select adult mentors. It's normal. You should be flattered."

She lowered the phone long enough to give it a quizzical look, wondering when he would quit surprising her. "Since when do you know so much about teenagers?"

"I have six nieces and nephews, and three of them are teenagers."

"Oh."

There were several seconds of dead air. "So are we okay with leaving you at home with Libby?"

"No, we are not. And by the way, she thinks you're hot, and so does her friend."

"Libby's a bright girl."

"Uh-huh. Actually, she didn't say hot. She said you're cute in a really bad way, meaning you do bad things. I'm sure she means sexual things."

"Uh . . ."

"I expect that any second now she'll be speculating aloud about *your* sex life. That girl has quite an imagination. Being the anointed mentor, I suppose I'll have to try my best to answer, although I don't really *know* the answers, so I'll have to make some things up."

"I see. I'll pick you up when I finish this job."

"Thank you."

"Perhaps I can help you come to some conclusions. 'Bye."

She pocketed the phone, trying to pretend that the fluttery feeling in her stomach wasn't anticipation.

He worked as fast as he could, but it was nearly two hours before he made it to the Westfield mansion, and from the look on Janet's face he wasn't a moment too soon. Libby had just finished her tennis lesson and was walking off the court to greet her audience. Janet and Elizabeth were clapping at her performance when the trio caught sight of him strolling across the lawn. He could have sworn Janet heaved a sigh of relief. As he drew closer her smile grew wider and her eyes took on a new sparkle. A sharp kick of excitement hammered through his chest; he'd waited a long time for that sort of reaction from her.

Libby claimed his attention first. "Hi, Rocky! You missed my great serve."

"Hey, gorgeous. I'll bet it was terrific." He high-fived her. "How's the backhand coming along?"

"So-so. My playing is still uninspired." She said it without a trace of the crestfallen look most kids would have shown.

"Your coach is an idiot. Do you want me to have him mugged in a dark alley?"

She grinned. "No, stupid." She slapped at his arm playfully. "He's just doing his job. He wants me to be more aggressive."

"So why aren't you?"

She rolled her eyes. "It's just a game, hitting a ball back and forth."

"We obviously need to have a talk about the competitive spirit. Later. Right now I have to take Janet someplace."

"Where?" She asked automatically, as if there were no reason that anyone might keep something from her. But he couldn't tell her he was rescuing Janet from the attentions of two curious thirteen-year-olds.

"To see a friend," Janet supplied, stepping past Libby. "He won't let me go anywhere alone." She made a face to show how ridiculous she thought it was for him to be preoccupied with her safety.

"Good," Libby approved. Sensible as always. If the kid ever wanted to run away from home, he'd take her in any day.

They said good-bye and walked across the lawn to his car. Janet leaned closer. "No wonder she thinks you're so great," she said, keeping her voice low so it wouldn't carry. "You call her gorgeous and offer to beat up anyone who criticizes her."

"I'd do the same for you, beautiful. Who do you want me to kill?" She laughed, but no longer showed that slightly flustered blush she got whenever he flirted with her. He hoped that meant she was getting comfortable with his attentions, because he was more than ready to take it to the next level. And she finally seemed to be ready, too.

Chapter Seven

He hadn't started the car. "So where are we really going?" Janet asked. "I don't mind if you have another job, I just needed to get out of the house. I can tag along and stay out of the way."

His smile was oddly thoughtful. "You're not in the way."

"Okay." She had no idea what he was thinking, and he wasn't giving her any clues. A belated prick of guilt made her wonder what she'd taken him away from. "Did you need to go to class?"

"Summer break."

He still had that contemplative look, as if he was doing a mental assessment. Hair, check. Nose, check. Ears, check. With a worried frown she flipped the visor mirror down and peered closely. "Do I have something on my face?"

"There's not a thing wrong with your face." He gave her the charmingly cockeyed smile that sent hormones zipping through her system. Great, her body was tuning in to his signals whether her emotions were ready or not. Another minute of that and she'd be going for a repeat of last night's amazing kiss. Then they wouldn't be going anywhere.

Her glance fell on a slip of paper stuck in the cup holder. It looked like a crudely drawn map. "What's this? Is this where your next job is? I promise I don't mind if you take me along." She put a hand over her heart. "Home security has always been my secret passion."

"You really are desperate." He took the paper from her and stuffed it back in the cup holder. "It's just a lead I got on a guy who might have fenced your necklace. I haven't checked it out yet; it could be nothing."

"The necklace?" She couldn't keep the sudden excitement out of her voice. "You have a lead already? Why didn't you tell me? Let's go talk to the guy."

Rocky shook his head. "No way. I'm not taking you to some scuzzy pawnshop to meet some guy who may or may not be able to help us."

"Why? You think scuzzy is contagious? Besides, it sounds like you've never met him, so you don't even know what he's like. Maybe he eats truffles and listens to Beethoven while he lists his pawned items on eBay."

His lips pressed into a cynical smile. "Trust me, this guy is the lowest of the low. You don't want to meet him. I'm sure we can find something better to do."

Maybe the sexual innuendo was all in her imagination, but his frank look made her breath catch and her breasts tingle.

Unfortunately, the guilt he raised was even stronger than the lust. He wanted to help her, but doing it would put him back into the same criminal world he'd barely managed to escape a year and a half ago. She didn't know how he'd become a jewel thief in the first place, or what had made him turn from a life of crime to the honest business world. Which meant she didn't know how precarious his straight life was. If he were somehow drawn back into his criminal past because of her, she'd feel responsible. She'd hate herself. Ellie and Jack would hate her. Hell, even Elizabeth Westfield and Ben Thatcher would be furious.

Janet didn't know how to tell Rocky that without insulting him.

Apparently, her long pause had made him nervous. "Look, Janet, I know you don't want anything more to do with men who have a police record."

"I wasn't thinking about that! I mean, I know you aren't Banner."

He almost smiled. "I think we got past that last night. But I was talking about the kind of criminals this pawnbroker deals with. He's a fence. He knows what he's buying is hot, and he knows the men he deals with are criminals. He doesn't care. You don't belong in that world, Janet."

"Neither do you." She felt the heat in her face and knew she was blushing at bringing up his past. His history hadn't embarrassed her before, so it shouldn't now. Just because she'd kissed him . . .

He cocked his head, seeming intensely interested in her embarrassment—and amused. "There's a lot you don't know about my past, Janet. I'm not going back to that life."

That was good to hear. "Still, you're talking to these people on my behalf, and some of them might not be too happy to see you again."

He raised an eyebrow. "You're probably right. But I can handle it."

"But you shouldn't have to. This is about me, not you. I appreciate that you're willing to help me, but you can't expect me to stay home while you go out and risk your safety and your—" she struggled for the right word "—your legal status, all because of me."

"My legal status?" He smiled, and reached over to hold her face between his hands. She felt the scrape of calluses from his palms, evidence of the honest work he did every day. "Babe, I'd risk a lot for you, but trust me, my legal status isn't in danger. Nothing's going to pull me back into that world." His gaze held hers, gently demanding. "Do you believe me?"

She nodded, confident he was telling the truth, but finding it difficult to talk while caught in the depths of his brown eyes.

"Good." He leaned forward and placed a tender kiss on her lips. "So you understand why I want you to stay safely at home when I go see this pawnbroker?"

She found her focus again. "No."

"Janet—"

"No. It's my problem, and I'm not handing it over to you to take care of. You have to take me with you."

He sighed. "I don't want to argue with you—"

"Then don't."

"—but you can't make me take you, either."

She studied him for several seconds, then dug into her purse for the keys to her rental car. "Just in case I lose you, that was a side street just off Evergreen and Fenkell, right?"

Rocky's jaw muscle twitched as he clenched his teeth harder. "Okay, you win."

She smiled sweetly and put the keys away. "Thank you."

He shook his head. "I hope I don't regret this."

"Not a chance." She flashed a smile. "I'm good company."

He lifted one eyebrow. "Yes, you are. And just remember while we're visiting the sleazy, scuzzy fence that I had something way more fun in mind."

Desire shot through her again. The intense look he gave her before starting the car left no doubt about what sort of fun he'd had planned. If she hadn't guessed from his kiss last night, he'd just confirmed that she'd opened a door he'd been waiting behind for too long. There would be no more harmless flirting and cute allusions to sex; he meant to have the real thing.

She smiled to herself. Chances were good he was going to get it.

They passed the pawnshop, turned around, and parked halfway up the block on the opposite side of the street. Rocky made no move to get out of the car.

"What are we waiting for?"

"I don't like to walk in without knowing who might already be in there. So we watch for a bit."

She looked over at the door with the scratched gold lettering. "Lost and Found Treasures." Fancy name for a dull gray building. The barred front window showed an array of digital cameras, video recorders, and TVs, all looking surprisingly new. "Looks like a small-scale Radio Shack."

"It should. A lot of this stuff probably came from there. Or was meant to end up there, before it was stolen off the truck. I mean, before it was *lost*. Nice euphemism."

He was right; this was a world she knew nothing about.

A minute later a thin black woman walked out of the store. Five minutes after that a white teenager slouched through the door, stayed less than a minute, and slouched out again. They waited another seven minutes, but no one went in or out.

"Okay, let's go." He paused with his hand on the door handle. "Just so we're clear, I do the talking."

"No problem. I'm here to watch and learn."

He gave a cynical laugh. "There's a scary thought."

He took her hand as they crossed the street and held it as they walked into Lost and Found Treasures. It felt protective, something she was glad for when an angry buzzer sounded and the door closed behind her with a suspicious click.

They were in a jail cell. The next thing to it, anyway. The space was no bigger than her bedroom, maybe twelve feet on each side, with the barred front window at her back and another in front of her that looked like the betting window at a race track. Sudden claustrophobia made her chest ache with the effort to breathe. Or maybe it was just the heavy haze of cigarette smoke.

"Is this what all pawnshops are like?" she whispered to Rocky.

"No." His gaze was wandering as much as hers, skimming the merchandise. "This guy must deal with some crazy people."

Tall display cases covered the walls on each side, with more barred glass protecting shelves crowded with watches and small electronic items. There were more than a hundred watches, she guessed, and dozens of cell phones and MP3 players. Her gaze darted across the glittering array until a deep voice startled her.

"Help ya?"

Rocky stepped closer to the caged window where a young man stood. Janet stared at his narrow, pale face. His hair was pulled into a stringy ponytail at his collar, long enough that she couldn't see the end. His arms were heavily tattooed and nicotine-yellowed fingers held a burning cigarette. This open violation of the law against smoking in places of business was probably insignificant compared to what else went on here.

The man's light blue eyes scanned Rocky, then lingered on Janet with interest. She could almost feel shutters banging closed inside her, as if attempting to protect her from something dirty and unpleasant.

"I'm looking for some jewelry," Rocky said.

The young man's gaze dragged back to him. "Got lots of that. What kind?"

"Some particular pieces that you don't have. But you did. You sold one to a friend of mine, and I'm looking to buy the rest of them."

The man's face grew cautious. "If I don't have 'em, I don't have 'em. Why you asking me? You a cop?"

"Not even close. My name's Rocky Hernandez. Mean anything to you?"

"No." He took a long draw on the cigarette and let his gaze run over Janet again, long enough to make the back of her neck prickle. "Should it?"

"Ask around. I used to work this area."

When Rocky didn't say anything else, the guy squinted at him. "So? What do I care?"

"Go ahead. Do it now. I'll wait."

She knew it was a contest of wills. Rocky was unyielding and the guy was either curious or bored. After another lengthy look at her, he said, "Wait here." He disappeared around a corner.

Janet slipped her hand from Rocky's, more comfortable now that the sleazy guy was gone. She looked around the room as they waited. "Isn't he afraid we'll take something? Smash the glass and take off?"

"The door locked behind us and there are probably at least two cameras on you. He'll be watching the monitors while he makes his calls."

The casual way he said it made her look back at him, wondering how dangerous his other life had been. She knew the worry showed on her face and knew he was wishing he'd followed his instincts and never brought her here. In an attempt to lighten the mood, she said, "They didn't cover this job at career day."

He smiled, causing the happy skip in her chest that seemed to have become her conditioned response. "Life's full of missed opportunities."

"Isn't it?" Her words were drowned out by a keening whine.

They exchanged puzzled looks, then peered over the ledge into the caged-in area that the man had recently vacated. Another whine ended with a metallic rattle as a kenneled puppy caught their eyes, its tail banging against its cage in a happy wag.

Janet smiled at the German shepherd. It couldn't be more than ten weeks old, with one big ear standing up and the other flopped over. "Hey, pup. You're a cutie, aren't you?"

The puppy yipped and squirmed.

She laughed, then sobered as the pale man returned, scowling at her. "Don't talk to the dog. He ain't no pet."

She frowned at him, annoyed at the way the puppy slunk back when he passed. "Then what is he?"

"He's a guard dog. Will be, anyway, soon as he's trained. So don't go baby-talkin' him." Before she could respond, he looked at Rocky and said, "Show me your back."

To her surprise Rocky turned his back to the window and raised the white polo shirt that said "Red Rose Security" on the front, pulling it to shoulder level. On the back of his well-defined right shoulder, she saw what Sleazy had evidently been expecting—a tattoo of three jagged lines in red and black resembling claw marks. Deep ones. They were simultaneously chilling and compelling. Something tempted her to reach out and touch them, to stroke her hand over Rocky's broad back, to reassure herself with the flex and ripple of intact muscle beneath her hand.

"Okay," Sleazy grunted. "You're him."

Rocky lowered his shirt, tucking it into his pants as he turned back to face the window. Stepping closer, he nodded toward the door where they'd come in. "Is that door locked?"

"Yeah." Sleazy sounded cautious, but Janet didn't know if it was because of what he'd just learned on the phone, or because Rocky's voice had gone low and rough.

"Good. I'm going to tell you a story now, and I want you to just listen. Because it might save your life. You understand?"

Janet grew still, fascinated by the change in Rocky.

His voice had a hard edge, and even his stance looked tougher. He was tense and poised, a picture of barely restrained energy, ready to rip through the bars of the window if Sleazy answered incorrectly.

Even with the bars between them and the gun that undoubtedly lay within reach beneath the counter, the slight man looked intimidated by Rocky. The hand holding his cigarette trembled when he took a long drag, although that could have been from his general unhealthy condition. Smoke rose from his mouth and nose as he spoke, as if betraying a fire that slowly ate at his insides. "Why would you want to save my life?"

"I don't. It's just a benefit of following my advice, if you're smart enough to take it." He gave Sleazy a few seconds to contemplate life and death. "You sold a necklace to a man last year, part of a collection of jewelry called the Pellinni Jewels. I'm sure you didn't know that at the time. I'm also sure you've heard of it by now."

Janet knew Rocky hadn't been positive they'd come to the right fence, the one who had sold the necklace to Banner, but when Sleazy didn't deny the connection she released a shaky breath. It must be him.

"Someone's looking for those pieces now."

Sleazy shrugged. "Someone's always looking for the good pieces. To steal 'em, or buy 'em."

Rocky nodded. "These pieces were a little more important than other pieces. And the guy looking for them is anxious to find them. See, the guy you sold the necklace to gave it to this lady here." They both looked at Janet. "And now someone has torn up her house and her car, looking for the rest of the collection."

"Tough luck." It wasn't much as sympathy went.

"Yeah. For you, too, once they realize she doesn't have them. Because you did, and that means maybe you still do."

Anger touched his face, drawing his eyebrows down. "You better not be tellin' people that. 'Cause I don't have them, either."

"Like you said, tough luck. 'Cause I don't intend to let this lady get hurt for something she doesn't have. You can see why I need to find the rest of the jewelry."

He blew smoke forcefully to the side. "You ain't listenin'. I said I don't have them."

"Then tell me who does. I'll get them back, and if you checked me out you know that's not an empty promise. Then both you and the lady here avoid the not-so-nice people who are looking for them. I'd be doing you a favor."

Sleazy turned up the corner of his lip, giving them a glimpse of yellow teeth. "You can't do nothin' for me. I sold 'em all to the same guy."

Janet opened her mouth. Rocky made a small motion with his hand to shush whatever protest she was about to make. She bit her cheek and let him talk.

"He doesn't have them," he told Sleazy, keeping his cool better than she would have.

The guy shrugged. "Can't help you, then. Find out what bitch he gave them to. Or who he sold them to. Probably the same people he sold the diamonds to."

Rocky leaned close to the bars and gave the guy a hard look through narrowed eyes. Janet thought for sure he was going to jump all over the guy for implying that Banner gave the jewelry to another woman. "What diamonds?" His voice snapped with tension.

"The ones with the jewelry. That's what the guy wanted, mostly. Diamonds. No settings, ya know what I mean?" He took another disdainful puff while he waited to see if Rocky was too dumb to know what he meant.

Rocky's jaw muscle jumped so much she was surprised she couldn't hear his molars grinding. "How many diamonds?"

"That time? Not too many, 'cause of the jewelry. Sixty or seventy-K, maybe."

Seventy thousand dollars' worth of diamonds, in addition to the Pellinni Jewels? Janet knew her mouth had dropped open. Banner must have been in deeper shit than anyone realized if he was laundering that kind of money.

"That time?" Rocky repeated.

"Did business with him three or four times. Money for diamonds." He showed his teeth again. "It ain't illegal. You can't prove I did nothin' illegal."

"I don't have to, pal. The people who are after the jewelry don't care about laws. And the ones who got the diamonds . . . well, let's just hope they got everything they were supposed to get, or they'll be looking for the rest. You know what I mean?"

His harsh question purposely echoed Sleazy's sullen one, with a whole lot more menace implied. Sleazy didn't like it.

"I told you, I ain't got the jewelry. The guy bought all of it. You should be askin' him."

"Apparently you don't follow the news. He's in jail, most likely heading for prison, and he's not coming out in your lifetime."

"Shit." Janet didn't know which part Sleazy found

upsetting—that he might become a target for someone looking for the jewels, or that he'd lost any chance of future business deals with Banner. "But I still ain't got the rest."

Rocky didn't look like he believed him. "How many pieces did you have?"

"Five, including the necklace."

At least that part was right. Rocky glanced her way, a quick puzzled look. She shook her head to indicate she didn't know anything about the other pieces of jewelry. If he'd had the other pieces, Banner must have given them away.

Her mind snagged on the possibilities. If he hadn't given them to her, had they gone to the Colombians as part of the money laundering scheme? Or had there been someone else, as Sleazy implied? A mistress? She'd never had reason to think so, but their marriage had been brief and she really hadn't known him that well. She certainly hadn't seen the murdering, drug running, money laundering side of him. Why not a mistress?

The idea didn't even bother her, proving how little attachment she had to Banner. The only problem with that theory was that his sex drive hadn't been high, certainly not high enough to keep two young women satisfied. Heck, he hadn't even satisfied her all that well. Unless that *was* why, because two women were such a drain on his libido.

She gave herself a mental shake, scattering all speculation on Banner's sex life. She was getting sidetracked by something that didn't concern her anymore. All she cared about was finding the jewelry and getting whoever was after it off her trail.

"Here's a hot tip for you," Rocky told Sleazy. "Until the rest of the Pellinni Jewels show up, I'd suggest you watch your back."

"Yeah? I thought you were going to save my life."

"Turns out you're too dumb to save. If you can't tell me where the rest of the jewelry is, I can't help you."

"I told you—"

"Yeah, the guy bought all of them. And I'm telling you he doesn't have them. So I'm still looking. But in the meantime, I'd be careful if I were you, because someone else is looking, and they've got a real mean disposition." He nodded toward the dog kennel on the floor. "You'd better hope Bruno there grows up real fast."

Sleazy ground his butt out in an ashtray. "Thanks for nothin'. And his name's Adolf, as in Hitler."

Rocky gave him a sick smile. "Cute. Open the door, we're done."

A buzzer signaled that the front door was unlocked, and Rocky ushered Janet through. She stepped onto the sidewalk with relief. Even the noise and exhaust fumes of Detroit's streets felt clean after the unpleasant atmosphere inside Lost and Found Treasures. She felt dirty enough to take a scrub brush to her skin.

"Ick," she said, shuddering as she walked.

"That sums it up nicely." His frown lines eased away. "But at least we learned how Banner was laundering most of the drug money—he was exchanging it for diamonds. Makes sense. They're easy to transfer to his Colombian connection, and easy for them to smuggle out of the country."

"Oh!" She laughed abruptly as the facts clicked in her head. "I know how he did it!"

Rocky stopped. "How?"

"He had these souvenir golf balls, commemorating the Westfield-Benton Charity Tournament. I just found them yesterday when I was at the office. They're hollow. They're too small to hold ornate jewelry, but if you stuffed them with cotton, you could put a fortune in diamonds inside one of those and never even hear it rattle."

Rocky nodded. "Clever."

"It's just too bad they were all empty. I'll bet those Colombians are looking for a gold golf ball *full* of diamonds."

"Our sleazy pawnshop owner better hope they don't come here looking for them."

Talking about him made her feel dirty all over again. "I should call the ASPCA. That man has no business owning a puppy."

"I like the way you think." He put an arm around her, pulling her close as they walked back to the car. Even in the growing heat of the day, it felt good to be so close to him. He squeezed her shoulder. "And while we're on the subject, I like the way you smile, I like the way your nose wrinkles when you laugh, and I like the way you wear that little gold chain on your ankle all summer long."

She suddenly forgot all about the slimy pawnshop. She looked down to where the hem of her jeans brushed her foot just above her tennis shoe, wondering when he'd noticed the chain that didn't show right now. "You do?"

"Oh, yeah. And if it matters, I like that little blue top with the white flowers on it that you wore last summer. I'm looking forward to seeing that one again."

"Blue top?" She gave him a puzzled look as he opened the car door, waiting while she slid in. Even if he was one of those rare guys who noticed what women wore, they'd hardly seen each other last summer because he and Ellie were busy starting up Red Rose Security. He must have her mixed up with some other woman. "I don't remember—oh, wait, I know which one you mean. The halter top with the cute crisscross lacing in back." Amazed that he'd remembered it, she mused, "I wonder where I put that?"

"Well, I hope you remember soon, because it drove me crazy imagining how pulling one string would make all those laces come loose."

Heat shot through her, and she covered it up with a laugh. "Pervert. It doesn't work that way. The laces are for decoration; it has a couple hooks in front."

"Really?" His face lit with a whole new interest.

"You're weird." *In a really sexy way,* she thought.

Jeez, what was wrong with her? She sounded like Libby, like a thirteen-year-old girl, not a twenty-nine-year-old woman. She pulled the car door closed, hoping to distract him from the evidence on her T-shirt—two hard nubs poking through her flimsy bra. The man seriously turned her on, and she was dying to do something about it.

Rocky walked around the front of the car, got in, and started the engine, but left the car in park when his phone rang. She turned on the air as he talked, short sentences that ended quickly as he flipped the phone closed.

"That was Ben. Someone broke into your place again."

"Again? What was left to look through?"

"It wouldn't have been the same person. My guess is the Colombians were looking for diamonds the first time, judging by the thorough job and the fact there was more than one person. This time, I'm betting it's whoever wants the rest of the Pellinni Jewels."

She gave him a weak smile. "Seems I'm pretty popular."

"Forget it. Nothing's changed, and you're safe. That's all that counts." He ran his knuckles down her cheek, and just like that, she forgot all about her condo. She fiddled with the vents, desperately trying to cool down. The rising heat and humidity outside had little to do with the perspiration that made her T-shirt and jeans stick to her skin. The fact that his mesmerizing eyes and sexy smile reminded her of a hungry wolf had everything to do with it, and she blasted the cold air directly at her chest.

"Hungry?" he asked.

"What?" Her startled response probably destroyed any chance that she could pull off a cool and collected facade.

"Would you like to stop somewhere to eat? It's early, but I'm starving." Behind that intense gaze, he was doing cool and collected just fine. She was the one with her mind in the gutter.

"That sounds good." Not really, but she didn't want to go home, which seemed to be the only other option. And eating would give her something to do besides think about touching Rocky.

"What are you in the mood for?"

Several inappropriate responses came to mind, but she firmly shoved them out of her mind. She played it safe. "Anything. You decide."

"Italian?"

"Fine." If it was one of those cozy little restaurants with booths where they could sit close together. She would feel his thigh warm against her own, maybe let her hand stray . . .

She shut down the image and hoped she wasn't blushing.

She wasn't about to ask where they were going. With her hormones running amuck, she was better off saying nothing. Instead, she tried to cool her over-heated libido by reminding herself of all the reasons she'd resisted Rocky for the past year.

The biggest reason was herself. She had to consider her history of bad choices when it came to men. Well, a one-man history, but a doozy of a bad choice. Being taken in by Banner's smooth lies had shaken her to the core. It couldn't happen again. How much did she really know about Rocky?

Plenty: he was a reformed jewel thief; a law student and successful business owner; a charming, handsome, accomplished man. Helpful. Good with kids. Kind to animals. Janet rubbed her forehead as she watched the buildings pass by without really seeing them. This wasn't helping.

The man must have faults, but she was having a hard time finding them. She felt more attracted to him than to any man she'd ever known, including the man she'd married, back when she thought Banner was suave, sophisticated, and in love with her. He'd turned out to be none of those things. More like slick, slippery, and in love with her family's air freight company.

But not Rocky. He liked her boldness and independence, two things Banner had hated. He liked the way she kissed—that was obvious from the way he kissed her back. He liked her smile. He liked her ankle chain, for God's sake. He liked *her*.

She stole a look at him. She liked him, too. A lot. And this was doing nothing to suppress her wild sexual desire.

She had to stop thinking about him and concentrate on the present. Food.

She returned her attention to the scenery just as they turned onto a side street, then followed a drive to the back entrance of a condominium complex. He flashed a smile as he pulled into a garage. "Best place around for Italian food—my kitchen."

His place. Intimate. Private. Equipped with every comfort and convenience one could want for . . .

Eating dinner. Nothing more.

Rocky punched a code on a keypad by the door and led the way into a dim laundry room before locking the door behind them. Turning, he bumped into Janet.

"Sorry!" She stepped back, about to make some excuse about not paying attention, when he pulled her against his body.

"Not so fast," he murmured against her ear, sending shivers all the way to her toes. "Lasagna can wait another couple minutes. This is a better idea."

"I didn't mean to . . ." His mouth brushed a whisper-soft caress over her temple, then her cheek. Her bones went soft while other parts of her snapped to attention. "Oh, never mind."

"You seem jumpy. That's not conducive to a good meal. I think you need to relax first."

He stroked a hand down her back and over the curve of her bottom, coaxing her gently against the firm line of his thighs. She couldn't think of anything *less* conducive to relaxing—key parts of her body were suddenly zinging with erotic ideas that had nothing to do with dinner.

"You smell good enough to eat," he said against her hair. Raising his head, he gave her a feral smile. "Want to be the appetizer?"

"Oh, God," she moaned.

He backed her into the wall, and she slapped one hand against it for support as he pinned her with a deep kiss. Finding his waist with her other hand, she hooked her fingers in a belt loop and pulled him closer as she let the fire take her.

They were both breathing hard when he lifted his head. "I've wanted to do this for so long," he whispered. "I hope you don't mind if dinner is late." He reached back as he spoke, tossing the car keys on the washing machine with a sharp clang.

"A sacrifice I'm willing to—*eeek*!" she yelped. A white blur shot by Rocky's shoulder, thumped onto the dryer, and disappeared into the kitchen.

"My cat," he said. "She likes the view from the shelf up there." When she turned to look, he touched her head, turning it back toward him and placing a quick kiss on her mouth. "Uh-uh, no distractions. You might forget what we're doing."

Not likely. She could swear his touch had created an energy that traveled downward, flicking on nerve endings all over her body. Nerve endings that begged to be touched by him. Parts of her were coming alive that had been dormant for far too long; she practically squirmed with anticipation.

He seemed a bit eager himself. He pulled her into a

kitchen she barely glimpsed before backing her against the refrigerator and pinning her hands beside her head while he took her in a slow, deep kiss. She melted beneath him, as if she could absorb his hard body into hers. His pounding heart already felt like her own as it beat between them.

He looked at her from inches away. "I'm going to have fond memories every time I open this refrigerator."

"That's so romantic."

He grinned at her, not the least bit insulted. "You want romantic?" He teased his tongue across her lips then drew her into a lingering kiss while cupping her breast beneath her blouse and flicking his fingers across its sensitive nipple. A wet heat settled between her thighs. "Lasagna by candlelight, maybe?"

She framed his head in her hands, making sure she held his gaze with her own. "Rocky, I think we can skip the lasagna."

Heat flared in his eyes. He didn't say anything, but she understood things had just turned serious for him. If she'd had any doubts, the intensity of his gaze might have made her nervous, but it didn't. It excited her even more to know how important she was to him.

Without removing her top, his hands found the clasp of her bra and opened it. The next second she caught her breath as his mouth lowered first to one breast, then to the other, his warm suction creating an answering pull between her legs that left her flushed and panting.

If she hadn't had the refrigerator for support, her legs would have collapsed. As it was, her knees were shaky. She took a couple steadying breaths. "I don't suppose you have a bed?"

"Upstairs. But I don't think we're going to make it that far."

Fine with her, since she wasn't sure her legs were strong enough to climb the stairs. She would have settled for the floor, but he walked backward into the living room, pulling her along, tugging off her top and bra as they went. She removed his shirt, dropped it to the floor, and ran her hands over the smooth planes of his chest.

"*Mmm*," she hummed, and melted a little more.

He unzipped her jeans and reached inside with both hands, cupping her bottom. Warm, rough palms gripped her skin, igniting more flames. With a quick movement, he lifted her against him. Wrapping her legs around his hips, she closed her eyes and let the tiny shocks quiver through her.

Her breath came faster, responding to her urgency building inside. Clutching his shoulders, she arched back as his mouth sought her breast, suckling hard. She breathed his name, turning it into a plea, helpless against the desire racing through her.

He groaned against the swell of her breast. "God, Janet, I want you. Right now."

"Yes," she managed, because she didn't have enough breath to say: "Absolutely, take me, that's the best idea you've ever had, and if you don't hurry up I may just explode in your arms from sheer frustration."

"Yes" was enough. He passed by the stairs and entered a small room. It was an office, lit by muted beams of light that seeped through slatted blinds. He laid her on a leather couch and tugged her jeans off before working frantically at his own.

She licked her lips, watching as he dug through his

wallet for a condom and sheathed himself. He paused then, his hot gaze softening as he looked at her.

"God, you're beautiful."

Because she knew it wasn't just a line, her throat closed on a rush of emotion she didn't try to name. Her voice was barely a whisper as she held her hand out to him. "Come here."

Placing one knee on the couch, he hovered over her, touching her hair. "I'm sorry, I didn't want to rush this."

"You didn't." She raised a hand to his face, giving him a tremulous smile. "I want you, too."

She pulled him down, certain if he waited another minute she'd die. But he put his hand between them, stroking, then dipping inside her, assuring himself she was ready. She bit back a gasp. "Rocky, please . . ."

He sank into her. She thrust upward to meet him, watching his eyes as she undulated again. Each movement eased a yearning while creating another one. With one foot on the floor, he set the rhythm, slow then faster, holding them both at the brink. She panted, digging her nails into his shoulder, lost in the pulse that thrummed in her veins and rocked between her thighs.

Faster.

Harder.

The fiery, consuming explosion began, rolling outward in tight waves. She caught her breath, pressed against him, and held on. After a few more strokes, he rode it with her, until they both collapsed against the leather cushions, limp and exhausted.

She lay beneath him, breathing hard, mind racing. Wondering if it had been even half as incredible for him as it had been for her.

After a minute, he rolled to the tight space against the back cushions and threw his arm over his head. "Holy shit," he breathed softly.

She smiled. Maybe it had been.

She could have stayed there a long while, but some things couldn't wait. "Where's the bathroom?"

"Back toward the kitchen. Come on, I'll show you." He chuckled. "Then I'll fix us something to eat."

He watched as she stopped to pick up her scattered clothes. "If you put them on I'll just have to take them off all over again," he warned. Before she could respond, he perked up. "Never mind. Sounds like fun."

It did. But for a moment she felt oddly adrift, and realized it was because she no longer had to find a comeback, some smart remark that denied her mutual interest. She'd made that interest pretty clear a few minutes ago on his couch. She smiled. "Looking forward to it," she said, following him.

He was in the kitchen, bare-chested but wearing his jeans, when she came out. She didn't hesitate; walking up behind him, she ran her hands over the hard muscles of his back and arms, loving the strength she felt, then slid her hands around to the front. When her fingers encountered the button on his jeans, she flicked it open.

He spun her around so fast she gasped and laughed, finding herself trapped against the counter with his bare chest right in front of her. It looked as touchable as his back. She leaned into him, pressing a kiss above his heart, then trailing a line with her tongue up to his neck. He froze. She smiled to herself, feeling his skin shiver.

"Janet . . ."

"Hmm?"

Her tongue found his and she stood on tiptoe, molding her body to his in a long, slow kiss. When she finally pulled away, he swore under his breath.

"How do you feel about sex on a kitchen counter?"

She wasn't sure how that would work, but just the idea excited her. "I thought we were eating."

"Food can wait," he growled.

Barely controlling her excitement, she fed him the obvious straight line. "And I just put my clothes on."

"I can fix that." He grabbed a handful of shirt, prepared to tug it over her head when the doorbell rang.

They looked at each other. "Ignore it," he decided, lifting her shirt and molding her breasts with his hands. She closed her eyes.

The bell rang again and a woman's voice sang out, "Yoo-hoo, Mr. Hernandez! I have a package for you!"

She smiled at his look of irritation. "Girl next door?"

"Old lady next door. Mrs. Garfield."

"I think she knows you're here." She pulled her shirt down, determined to do this without interruptions. "Answer it. I'll be here when you get back."

He scowled. "Fine. But don't take anything off this time. I want to do that myself."

Pleasant shivers skittered down her back. "Promise."

Seconds later she heard him open the front door with a pleasant, "Hello, Mrs. Garfield." She hoped he'd remembered to fasten his pants.

The package had apparently only been part of Mrs. Garfield's news. When the woman's chattering hadn't died down a couple minutes later, she decided he needed rescuing. Grabbing a dish towel, she walked into the living room.

They stood just inside the door, the short, gray-haired lady rattling on about garbage pickup and Dumpster regulations while Rocky listened patiently, holding a box. Janet caught the lady's surprised look and smiled. "Hello, I'm sorry to interrupt. Where did you say you kept the flour, sweetie?"

Mrs. Garfield's face lit with curiosity. "Oh my, I'm sorry. I didn't know you had company." She made no move to leave.

"Mrs. Garfield, this is Janet."

Janet shook her hand and took the package from Rocky, a square box big enough to hold a basketball. "Here, let me take that." They exchanged grins. "The flour?" she reminded him.

"The cupboard beside the stove. I'll be right there to help, honey."

It was all very contrived, but she enjoyed the charade and being called honey. It felt almost natural around Rocky. In the pretense she'd invented she could easily see him returning to the kitchen to help her prepare dinner. He belonged in that sort of scenario.

He also belonged in bed, with her. That was an even better scenario, and one Mrs. Garfield was delaying with every word she spoke. Janet carried the package back to the kitchen and set it on the counter, waiting for Rocky to usher Mrs. Garfield out the door. She could hear him making excuses now, and smiled to herself while somehow still feeling sorry for poor Mrs. Garfield. Women naturally responded to Rocky's charm, and older women were no exception. She understood the attraction. Boy, did she ever. And as soon as she heard that door close behind Mrs. Garfield, they could get back to business.

Janet heard something coming from inside the box and frowned. Was it fizzing? She could have sworn it had made some sort of sound.

Approaching cautiously, she poked the box. Nothing happened. Could something inside have spilled? It hadn't felt too heavy, and she hadn't noticed a return address. Rocky would be here in a minute, but she could hear Mrs. Garfield going on about curbside recycling, and the box was definitely making a sound. And getting louder. She touched it. The cardboard was unnaturally warm.

Gingerly, she carried it to the sink. If they needed to contain a spill or put out flames, the box would at least be in the right place. She didn't know what else to do. Peering closely, she tried to find the return address.

A flash of light and a muffled explosion made her whirl away, raising a hand to her eyes. The world spun and she couldn't see. Blinking at the sudden pervasive whiteness, she covered her nose with her hand. Something smelled odd . . .

It was the last thing she remembered.

Chapter
Eight

Rocky heard it just as he closed the front door behind Mrs. Garfield, a small poof like starter fluid igniting on a charcoal grill. Not a sound he expected from his kitchen.

"Janet?"

She didn't answer, causing small tentacles of worry to clutch at his ribs and make him hurry to the kitchen. Their hold tightened when he saw her lying on the floor in front of the sink.

"Janet!" He dropped to her side. "Wake up!" Heart thundering and cold sweat gathering at every pore, he brushed her bangs aside and stroked her cheeks, repeating her name. Her eyelids fluttered. The roaring pulse in his ears eased a fraction, and he resisted the urge to yell and shake her. Leaning close, he held her pale face between his hands, slightly reassured by the warmth of her skin.

"Janet. Janet."

Her eyes opened, slowly focusing on him. Confusion drew her brows together. "Rocky?"

Her voice was groggy, but her eyes were clear. Sighing, he dropped a grateful kiss on her forehead. Controlling the nervous quiver that tried to grip his voice, he asked, "Do you remember what happened? I found you lying here on the floor. Did you trip?"

Her gaze drifted around the room as she thought, stopping at the sink. "I remember. The box. It made a sound and it started smelling funny. I put it in the sink." When he started to rise, she grabbed his hand. "Wait! Don't get too close. I think it exploded or something." She propped herself on her elbows.

"Just lie still. Don't get up yet." His order had no effect, as she propped herself against a cupboard door and massaged her temples. "Or just ignore me and take a chance on passing out again." He pushed her hand aside and lifted her chin, letting light from the window fall on her face. Color was returning to her cheeks. "Stubborn as usual. How are you feeling?"

"A little better." He must not have looked relieved because she clutched his hand and squeezed it. "Honest, I'm okay. You can check the box, Rocky. But if you smell something, hold your breath. Whatever it is, I think it's what got to me."

Cautiously, he stood and approached the sink. Tatters of cardboard flecked the countertop, and a blackened box sat in the stainless steel basin, its top flaps nothing but shredded edges. Inside, cushioned in ash-coated packing peanuts, wires connected a small box that looked like a kitchen timer to a broken glass jar. An acrid smell assaulted him, making him faintly dizzy, but it had dissipated enough to have lost its intended effect. Just to make sure, he bypassed the security system and opened the window above the sink, then ran water over the debris and threw a dish towel over the soggy ruins.

"It's some sort of bomb, isn't it," Janet said from the floor. It wasn't a question. Her eyes squinted and he was pretty sure she was feeling the beginnings of a nasty headache. "Why is someone sending you a bomb?"

Good question. But what really unnerved him was that Janet had been on the receiving end, not him. The only thing keeping him halfway calm was that she was all right.

He squatted in front of her and picked a couple flakes of cardboard out of her hair, wondering how much of an argument she was going to put up when he suggested she see a doctor. "You're right. It looks like it was rigged to blow open the box and release whatever gas knocked you out. It had some sort of timer."

"Why? Who have you been pissing off?"

"I don't know." Not for sure. The box had been sent to him with no return address—he'd seen that much before Janet had taken it from his hands. And he'd seen enough of its contents just now to know someone had intended to either knock him out or worse. He wasn't sure *why*, but he could make a good guess about *who*.

The obvious answer was one of the shady characters he'd been in touch with recently. Not the sleazy bottom-feeder at Lost and Found Treasures; the man couldn't have tracked him down that fast even if he had a reason, which he didn't. It would have to be from his visit to the Detroit Barber Shop. He'd given Vasili no reason to attack him; if anything, the local representative of the Russian Mafia was a little too fond of him. And his associates would never act without his approval. There'd been no potential for conflict in that visit, except for—

"Damn. Easy Joey."

She looked up from brushing off the shredded flakes clinging to her shirt. "Who?"

"A guy I ran into yesterday. Pretty good burglar, pretty lousy human being. He's invented some vendetta, and thinks he needs to steal something from me. He's all attitude and ego, but probably clever enough to rig a device like this. Except I don't see what good it would do him to knock me unconscious."

A second later, he did. A chill touched the back of his neck, like icy fingers tickling his skin. "Oh, shit," he whispered.

"What?" She'd picked up on his fear; her eyes wide and her voice low.

He listened for several seconds before answering. The house was silent. Far from reassured, he spoke so softly she had to lean forward to hear him. "He wants to break in here. I assumed it would be while I was gone. But the little bastard thinks he has something to prove. He might have the balls to try it when I'm here. In fact, that sounds exactly like his style—risky and overconfident."

She shrank back against the cabinet. "You mean he's trying to break in here *right now*?"

Instead of answering, Rocky put his finger to his lips and cocked his head.

Janet froze, biting her lip. The luscious lower lip he should be nibbling on right now. When he got his hands on Easy Joey, the little asshole was going to find burglary a bit more difficult with a couple broken limbs.

Rocky had to be right. Any second now Easy would trip an alarm. Both doors and windows had backup systems, a precaution the arrogant little twerp would never think to look for. And even if he got past them, Rocky would be there to catch him. In fact, catching him inside might be more rewarding than keeping him out. If he could just figure out the point of entry.

In the garage something metal clattered to the floor.

He smiled. Easy was going down.

Standing, he motioned for Janet to stay down, and he was mildly surprised when she did. That headache must be coming on strong; automatic obedience from her was something he'd learned not to take for granted.

He moved slowly, then paused with his back to the refrigerator, and tried not to think about how he'd pressed Janet to the same spot not long before, losing himself in her intoxicating taste and her soft skin. Instead, he thought about the giant error Easy had made when he was careless enough to get Janet involved in this feud. Rocky could tolerate teaching the guy a lesson in humility, if that's what he needed, but Easy had crossed the line.

Around the corner in the laundry room, a faint scraping came from the door. Someone was working the lock. With a quick move, Rocky killed the power on the keypad on the wall. Couldn't risk the backup alarm scaring Easy into running. He *wanted* the punk to walk into the condo. After that, Easy Joey would be breaking and entering, and the tools in his hand and the box in the sink clearly indicated his intention to do harm. A homeowner was entitled to defend himself. In another minute, Easy would be fair game.

With a barely audible click, the deadbolt slid open. Rocky plastered himself to the refrigerator. He couldn't hear him, but he could picture Easy creeping into the shadowy laundry room. A tiny metallic sound signaled the lock mechanism falling into place. Then nothing but silence. Easy was listening.

Rocky tensed, ready. *Come on, asshole, three more steps.*

He counted the seconds to himself, wondering how cautious the little prick would be.

With a soft thud, something hit the washing machine. A man's voice yelled a frightened profanity. Rocky understood instantly, and darted out, diving toward the laundry room in two quick strides, right into the path of his terrified cat.

A ball of white fur hit his ankle at the same moment he tried to widen his step to avoid the fast-moving animal. Losing his balance, he lunged forward, bouncing against the wall and falling to his knees. Three steps ahead of him, Easy Joey yanked the door open and ran into the garage.

Spitting a few profanities of his own, Rocky scrambled to his feet and followed. Easy was already through the side door, racing across Mrs. Garfield's drive. Three doors down, Rocky spotted the yellow Corvette idling by the curb, as if someone had left it for a moment while they dropped something off. Or stole something.

Easy vaulted the car door, slammed the vehicle into gear, and squealed his tires as he shot down the road. Rocky cleared the garage in time to inhale hot exhaust fumes and watch the car roar around the buildings, out of sight.

"Shit!"

He hadn't even had time to put a few dents in the shiny yellow car, much less its owner. And he couldn't chase him down, not with Janet sitting on his kitchen floor looking like she could use a half dozen Advil. Putting his anger aside for the moment, he hurried back inside.

Janet was on her feet, leaning against the counter. Her wobbly stance shot a fresh jolt of concern through him; he shouldn't have left her, even for a minute. He slung an arm around her and led her to a chair. "Sit. No standing. How are you feeling?"

She managed a weak smile. "My stomach's fine. My head, not so much."

"We'll get you to a doctor. Would you like a drink of water first?"

"I don't need a doctor, but water sounds good."

He bent down to look her in the eyes. "Janet, you're going to a doctor. For me, if not for you. Save the arguments."

He must have looked stern enough, or else her head was beginning to ache enough. "Fine," she grumbled. "Just get me a drink first."

He kissed the top of her head and fetched a glass of water along with a washcloth soaked in cold water. When he laid it on her forehead, she raised grateful eyes. "Thanks. I'm sorry I'm being difficult. You'd make a good mom."

He smiled. "That's not exactly the position I was looking to fill."

She tipped her head, squinting a warning look through her pain. "Are you still trying for something more permanent? 'Cause one session of hot sex doesn't constitute a relationship."

He cocked an eyebrow, willing to keep it light if that's what she wanted. "I was going for two when we got interrupted."

Beneath the washcloth, the edges of her eyes crinkled. "I know. But I don't think I'm up for it right now."

He grabbed her free hand, making sure she looked at him. Making sure he didn't laugh at her serious expression. "Babe, I didn't mean I was waiting to resume the action. We're taking you out of the game for the rest of the day. Maybe two. Okay?"

She sighed her disappointment. "Yeah."

He did smile then, and reached out to wipe a trail of water that dripped from the washcloth past her temple and down her jaw. He'd kissed those places just a short time ago and found himself tempted to kiss them again. To caress her skin with his lips, to massage the tension out of her neck before letting his hands skim down her sides. His fingers ached to touch her.

What kind of sick bastard would have erotic thoughts about a woman who was so obviously in pain? He stood, banishing all thoughts of sex. "Come on."

She let him help her without protest, and he tucked her against his body, supporting her weight. Putting his arm around her was beginning to feel right, which could be a very dangerous thing. He wondered how well he'd be able to hide his feelings from her. She probably thought this had been no-strings sex, but for once in his life he wanted a few strings. And stubborn, relationship-shy Janet Aims was not going to like that one bit.

Janet slumped in the passenger seat on the way back from the ER. Everything had gone to hell. Right now she should have been lying in Rocky's bed, exhausted and sexually sated. Or on his kitchen counter, equally sated. That one really would have been interesting. But instead she was nursing a toxic gas induced migraine while he drove her back to Elizabeth's house to sleep in her own bed. Alone.

His hand stroked her cheek in a way she was beginning to love. "Hey, babe, you awake? You're home."

She cracked an eyelid. "Yippee."

He came around the car and helped her out. "I know, it's been a long afternoon for you. Let's get you inside and into bed."

"If I could locate my sense of humor I'd make a saucy remark about that line."

He chuckled. "That's my girl."

She should have warned him to be careful with that phrase, but it sounded good right now, and having a deep conversation about relationships didn't. Her mind was fully occupied just watching the ground as she put one shaky foot ahead of the other.

He held her elbow as she negotiated the front steps in a terribly sweet gesture of concern. She turned her bleary gaze on him as he used her key to unlock the front door. "Just for the record, I think you're really nice," she said quietly.

"Thanks."

"Cute, too."

He grinned, ushering her inside. "I prefer handsome."

She nodded agreement. "That, too. I've had a lot of pain meds, haven't I?"

"Just enough. How's your head?"

"Still hurts."

He looked so upset at that she wished she'd lied and

said she could hardly feel it. She hated that he felt responsible for what had happened. But all his solicitous hand holding was what had gotten her through the afternoon at the ER without collapsing into a whimpering ball of pain. He hadn't left her side for a minute. And she hadn't wanted him to. No one she knew could have made her feel more reassured or cared for. Not Ellie, not Elizabeth, not even her parents. That was something she needed to examine further—when her head didn't hurt so much.

He guided her up the long, sweeping staircase to the second floor. They reached her bedroom just as Mr. Peters was leaving it.

The butler dipped his head in greeting. "I'm relieved to see you looking so well, Miss Aims. Nevertheless, I have drawn your blinds and turned down your bed, should you wish to relax a bit."

She had no idea how Elizabeth Westfield had found this living monument to British gentility in metropolitan Detroit, but she'd never appreciated him more. "You're such a liar, Mr. Peters, but I love you anyway. Thank you."

"Yes, ma'am. May I bring you anything? Tea, perhaps?"

"No, thanks. I just want to take a nap."

"A sensible plan."

Rocky jerked her aside as she stepped forward. "Watch out for Jingles," he warned. The big black-and-white cat had flopped onto the carpet in front of her, stretching to his full length with a playful meow.

Mr. Peters scooped him up with a startled vocal protest from Jingles. "I'll remove the cat until you feel better," he offered.

"No!" She smiled to offset the anxiety in her voice. "He can stay." Curling up with Jingles sounded as reassuring right now as her security blanket had when she was four years old.

"Very well." He deposited the cat on the carpet, where Jingles did his best to look regally offended. "Call if you need anything." She saw him pull a lint brush from his pocket and swipe at the stray cat hairs on his suit before closing the door behind him.

Pausing only long enough to remove her shoes, she crawled under the covers and sank onto the soft pillow with a sigh. Jingles jumped onto the bed, purring his pleasure that his owner had finally caught onto the obvious genius of sleeping during the day. She drew him against her, petting his back. "How's my big sexy boy?" she murmured into his ear.

"Hey! He's sexy and I'm just cute?"

She smiled at Rocky's indignant expression. "He's been the only man in my life for the past year."

"The competition, eh?" He gave Jingles a warning glare. "I'm calling you out, cat. Get ready."

An actual giggle burbled at the back of her throat, momentarily relieving the pain in her skull. Rocky could threaten her cat all day and it would never worry her, while one cold glance from Banner had convinced her to send Jingles to her parents' house.

The thought reminded her of something that had been bothering her since they left the pawnshop.

"Rocky, I think I should go see Banner."

His brows slammed together in a hard stare. "No, you shouldn't. And how the hell did he get into this discussion?"

She winced at the increased volume. "Relax. I was

just thinking that I should talk to him about the jewelry he bought from that guy. Maybe I can get some information out of him."

She gave him points for the obvious effort he made to remain calm, but if he clenched his jaw any tighter, he'd crack a molar. "Janet, Banner tried to have you killed. I don't want you anywhere near him, even if he is in jail. He's not powerless just because he's behind bars. He has money and contacts, and I'd rather he forgot about you."

"But what if he really did buy all of the Pellinni Jewels, like Sleazy said?"

"Sleazy? Perfect." He snorted in dry amusement at the name she'd given the owner of Lost and Found Treasures. "You said you searched everywhere and Banner didn't have them."

"He doesn't. Not in the safe here, not in the one at work, and not in the bank. But he doesn't appear to have the diamonds Sleazy said he bought, either. So what if he really did have the rest of the jewelry, and it went to whoever got the diamonds?"

He frowned, and she knew he'd followed her logic. To stop the attacks on her, they needed to find the rest of the jewelry, and Banner might know where it was. If Rocky looked that irritated, it must mean he agreed that she had to see Banner.

"We'll fight about this when you feel better."

"Fine, talking about Banner only makes my head hurt more. But I'm right."

He raised a cautionary eyebrow, and she decided not to tell him that he was far sexier than Jingles, even when he disagreed with her. Instead, she reached up to catch a handful of his shirt, pulling him toward her.

"Kiss me good-bye. Then go do something about your cat. Just don't take her back home; I don't trust that friend of yours not to hurt her, too."

"Easy isn't my friend. He isn't anyone's friend." But his expression softened as he leaned close to her and laid a hand against her face. "Feel better. And call me when you wake up."

"I will."

His mouth touched hers. The kiss was gentle, drawing a moan from her and making her clutch his shirt like a drowning woman hanging onto a life raft. When his tongue slid slowly against hers, she nearly forgot about the hammering in her head. He finally pulled away, and she sighed. "Or you could stay."

He chuckled. "Don't tempt me. Just sleep." He stroked his hand over her hair, then scratched Jingles on the cheek. "Take care of her, big guy."

Her heart melted a little more, and not just because she was such a big sap about her cat. She liked the man, damn it. She liked the way he stroked her cheek as if it was the softest velvet, and the way he kissed with enough passion to fuel a bonfire. Like the one smoldering between her thighs. Why had she waited so long to go after this?

Because she'd made such a bad choice with the last man. She needed to be cautious. But really, how much vetting did the guy need? Jack loved Rocky. Elizabeth Westfield respected him and treated him like family. Even Ben Thatcher, the chief of police, liked him.

Ellie trusted him, too, enough to form a partnership with him. But that was a business arrangement, not a personal one, with legal papers that specified the rules. He put up half the money and did half the work. It was all very neat and tidy.

Relationships had a way of being untidy, and no one knew that better than Janet. She should have been more cautious before falling for Banner's smooth talk and easy persuasion. Just because he'd fooled everyone else, too, didn't mean she could excuse herself. She'd seen what she'd wanted to see—the beautiful, successful exterior—not what was real. Maybe she was doing that with Rocky, purposely overlooking his shady past in favor of the charming man with the mischievous smile.

Oh, God, she hoped not. Long-dormant parts of her throbbed and burned in anticipation of his next touch. Every instinct said she could trust Rocky. But after choosing a man who turned out to be deceptive enough to marry for opportunity, greedy enough to smuggle drugs, and evil enough to try to murder whoever got in his way, including his wife . . . well, she would be crazy not to doubt her own judgment. Following her heart had nearly gotten her killed.

She needed to know why Rocky had done what he'd done, and why he quit doing it. If Ellie and Jack were here, she could ask them. But they weren't, so tomorrow she'd ask Rocky himself, and hope his answers didn't douse the fire he'd kindled inside her. Because she already knew how easily he could turn that flame into a roaring inferno. After a year of no sex—and six months before that of uninspired sex with Banner—she looked forward to being with someone who knew his way around a woman's body.

Rocky Hernandez seemed to be the perfect man for the job.

Rocky slowed as he approached his car. The hard-on he'd gotten just from helping Janet into bed had disappeared, but it seemed that now he had a different problem. He'd parked in his usual spot on the apron of asphalt beside the garage, right next to Ben Thatcher's unmarked police car. Now Elizabeth Westfield stood near the hood of his car, arguing with Ben. Dignified and imposing, even in a pert white tennis skirt and top, she stabbed a finger at Ben's chest as she made her point.

Great. The last thing he needed was to intrude on the private lives of the two most discreetly private people he knew.

He scraped his feet on the asphalt as he walked. Elizabeth either ignored him or didn't hear, folding her arms over her slender frame.

This could be embarrassing. Since he couldn't pretend to be heading anywhere else on the Westfield property, he added a tuneless whistle. Ben ignored his presence with the same indifference he showed Elizabeth's argument, shrugging his shoulders as he leaned against his car. Rocky was close enough now to hear him say, "You already know what I want."

Whatever it was, Elizabeth wasn't having any of it. "You're just being stubborn."

Ben nodded agreeably. "Yup."

Elizabeth straightened her already ramrod-straight back. Muscles tensed all the way down her well-toned thighs and calves. "We're too old to play these sorts of games, Ben."

"I'm not playing, Liz." With barely a change in expression, his eyes shifted toward Rocky. "Afternoon, Rocky. How's she doing?"

He'd called them from the hospital, but played down the incident, not wanting to cause unnecessary worry. With the panic over, they deserved the details. "She's fine now, probably sound asleep. They tested her blood levels at the hospital and gave her a ton of painkillers. They thought it might have been a small dose of sarin. Very small," he rushed to add as Ben stiffened, no doubt recognizing the favorite gas of terrorists. "She still has a headache, but they said there'd be no lasting effect."

A plaintive sound carried through the open window of his car. Elizabeth looked past him with a frown, seeming to notice his car for the first time. "Roberto. Why is there a cat in your car?"

Rocky's gaze went to the cat carrier in the back seat. He saw a bit of long, white fur, and heard the pitiful meows that sounded like, "Help. Help. Help." The typical cat aversion to riding in cars. "She exaggerates. She's fine; I left the window open."

"I realize that. Why are you transporting a cat in your car?" He knew he was getting a bit of the anger she'd shown Ben and was glad he didn't have to face her full fury. Everything about Elizabeth Westfield screamed breeding and elegance, traits he'd been raised to respect. He couldn't look as unconcerned as Ben in that intimidating presence.

"I'm taking her to a kennel. It's just a precaution. If that little practical joke with the gas was really meant for me and it happens again, I want my cat out of danger." The suggestion that the incident with the box was a poorly executed joke was weak; he couldn't believe Ben had bought it. The fight with Elizabeth must have put him off his game.

Good. Rocky didn't want the police getting involved; he intended to exact his own revenge on Easy.

Elizabeth pinned him with her stern gray eyes. "You mean you're going to make your cat live in a small cage in a strange place, with none of the people and things she's used to, until you decide it's safe to bring her home again? And how long will that be?"

"Uh . . . I'm not sure. But she'll be okay." Even though Elizabeth's description made him feel like a horribly mean owner.

"Of course she won't. How would you like being caged up all day?"

He couldn't help flashing back to a time when he had been caged up, days and weeks on end. He hadn't liked it at all. "Um . . ."

"Take her in the house and give her to Peters. She'll be much better off here."

His mouth opened in surprise. "I couldn't impose like that."

Ben brushed it off. "Oh, don't worry. She likes moving people and animals into her house. The more the merrier."

Elizabeth shot a furious look at him. "I have plenty of room."

"You do," Ben agreed. "Maybe you should go to the shelter and pick up a few more cats."

With a final glare, she whirled away and stomped across the lawn toward the tennis court. Ben looked at Rocky and smiled. "Temperamental."

Not in Rocky's experience. In the year he'd known

Elizabeth Westfield, he'd never seen her be anything but cool and collected. But there was definitely some tension around the subject of her taking in people and animals. And it had to do with Ben. "Do *you* have something against me leaving my cat here?"

"Nope. Doesn't affect me one way or the other. I don't live here."

It was the total disinterest on Ben's face that made him suspect he'd stumbled onto the crux of the argument, though he couldn't imagine how *not* living here could be a problem for Ben, since Elizabeth had extended an open invitation. There was more going on here than he knew.

Best to keep it that way. Elizabeth and Ben were two of those special people who made love look easy, but even the happiest lovers were entitled to disagreements now and then. He should take his cat and leave. But the way Elizabeth was smashing tennis balls across the court, anger driving each serve, made him hesitant to cross her just now. What the hell, Fluff was adaptable. The former street cat had spent her first two years living off scraps in Detroit alleys while dodging the assholes who found helpless animals fair game. She could handle a life of extreme privilege for a few days.

Hefting the cat carrier, he left Ben to brood over Elizabeth's foul mood and headed back toward the house. Jingles might not appreciate the company, but Fluff was scrappy enough to hold her own. He just hoped Mr. Peters had a couple more lint brushes.

Chapter Nine

Janet had been having a lot of sex dreams lately, so she wasn't surprised when it happened again.

But sitting on a countertop with a man standing between her open thighs was new. It was pure fantasy, of course, because countertops were too tall for that in real life—weren't they? She'd dug her fingernails into strong shoulders, muffled her low cry of joy in his neck, kissed her way toward his mouth—then recognized Banner's smooth as sin smile and woke with a scream.

She sat up in bed, her pelvis still pulsing with heat and her heart racing with terror. There was a logical explanation. Rocky had mentioned the countertop, and she'd decided to visit Banner in jail. But putting the two of them together was just plain freaky.

At least it reminded her of the first job on her to-do list for the day—the distasteful task of arranging to meet with Banner.

Visiting a prisoner at the county jail required following a lot of procedures. Inmates submitted names of allowed visitors; if you weren't on the list, you didn't get in. She was probably still on Banner's list from the one time she'd met with him to discuss their divorce. But even if she was on the list, it didn't mean he'd agree to see her just because she put in a request. Unless they were having snowball fights in hell while pigs flew overhead, his answer to her request would be no. She had to entice him into a meeting. Fortunately, she knew his Achilles's heel.

The fastest route was through his lawyers. Daily calls between Banner and his law firm probably weren't necessary, but from the fast response times during the divorce it was obvious they had regular contact. She looked up the number for the law firm and punched it into the phone.

"Sterling, Seabrook, and Holden," a woman answered. She had one of those smooth, amorphous voices like the ones in airports that announced, "The tram is approaching the station. Please exit to the right." It sounded soulless—just like the senior law partners.

"Mr. Seabrook, please." *The evil troll.* The senior partner was tall and imposing, with a voice that thundered in the courtroom. She would have been intimidated if she hadn't already learned that Banner's quiet composure was far more dangerous.

Still polite in case this impertinent request came from someone important, the receptionist asked, "Who's calling please?"

"This is Janet Aims, calling in regard to Mr. Seabrook's client, Banner Westfield."

"I'm sorry, Mr. Seabrook is unavailable." She didn't sound sorry—more like condescending. "May I take a message? Or would you care to make an appointment?"

Janet ignored the suggestions. "Please tell Mr. Seabrook that this involves an appallingly large amount of money and yet another potential criminal charge against his client. I'll hold."

After a few seconds of hesitation, the phone switched over to canned music interspersed with ads advising her that Sterling, Seabrook, and Holden did everything in their power to seek justice for victims of medical malpractice to dog bites.

It took him less than a minute. "Miss Aims. This is Bill Seabrook. How may I help you?"

Good old Bill. The man who claimed in a pretrial hearing that she had not only married Banner to get her hands on the Westfield millions, but had colluded with drug runners and faked her own attempted murder in order to destroy his reputation. A man with a vivid imagination and frightening lack of moral fiber.

"Hello, Bill. I need to meet with Banner as soon as possible."

She knew calling him by his first name followed by a demand would get her a flat denial. She did it just for the satisfaction of making him reverse his decision a minute later.

"Considering Banner's upcoming trial and your part in it, I don't think that's a wise decision, Miss Aims."

"Actually, it is, Bill. And I need to do it right away. This afternoon would be perfect." The sooner she could find out what he did with the diamonds and the Pellinni Jewels, the sooner people would stop targeting her.

She heard a derisive snort from Bill's end. "That's

impossible. There's a waiting list, and visiting days are in alphabetical rotation, as I'm sure you know. Banner's isn't until next Wednesday."

Examining a chip in her fingernail, she rubbed it on her jeans to smooth out the rough spot. "But you're such an influential man, Bill, I'm sure they'd make an exception if you asked." They had before, when Banner had met with his lawyers on an almost daily basis. Infamy had its privileges.

Janet could hear him grinding his teeth on the other end of the line. "Would you care to tell me what you find so important?"

Faking disappointment, she said, "I'm afraid I can't." Bill was good at down and dirty verbal battles, but she suspected nice people threw him off balance.

"Then *I'm* afraid the answer is no." Actually, like his secretary, he sounded quite pleased that the answer was no.

She continued as if he hadn't spoken. "But if Banner cares to tell you, he can pass the information on. I suspect he'll be in need of legal advice anyway. Or—" she drew it out, emphasizing the choice he had here "—I suppose you could advise him not to see me. I'm sure he'll trust whatever you say. Of course, when this little problem blows up . . ." She clicked her tongue in sympathy. "I'm afraid he'll fire you."

"Miss Aims, I don't take kindly to threats. Nor does my client."

"I know exactly how you feel, Bill." Thanks to all the threats from Banner and his slavering pack of lawyers.

He was quiet for several seconds. "As you know, Banner has expressed a desire to never see you again."

That would refer to her ex-husband's warning to "Stay the fuck out of his life" at their divorce proceedings.

"I remember." And she couldn't afford to waste time with repeated requests to talk with him. "Perhaps I could be a touch more specific. Tell him it involves diamonds. *Lots* of diamonds. I'm afraid anything else is confidential."

"Whose diamonds?" Bill's question was sharp with curiosity.

"You can reach me at this number to confirm the visit for this afternoon." She rattled off her cell number. "Good-bye, Bill." She hung up, feeling an unexpected sense of exhilaration. Power. Control. She wasn't used to experiencing them in relation to Banner, and it felt good.

It wouldn't last, though. She was certain she'd feel the familiar creepy shivers he always gave her when she was face-to-face with Banner. It would be nice to take Rocky along for support, but Banner would only be allowed one visitor. She'd have to face him alone.

Rocky wasn't sure if the silver Mercedes was following him. He'd noticed one yesterday evening outside his apartment when he'd picked up his mail, and he was pretty sure he'd seen one cruise by the Westfield place when he'd dropped Janet off from the ER. But the city was full of expensive foreign cars, and he'd probably seen a dozen Mercedes already today. Still, those smoke gray windows raised the hairs on the back of his neck, and he'd come to trust that intuition. He cut off Woodward onto a shaded side street, following a winding route. The Mercedes didn't follow.

So it was just a case of paranoia. Knowing that

Janet had been stalked spooked him. If they were still after her, it would make sense that they'd switch their attention to him. The only time she left the Westfield residence was with Rocky. And today would be no different.

On top of it all, Rocky was exhausted. He'd spent several fitful hours trying to sleep, but thoughts of Janet naked on his couch kept his mind—and his groin—fully alert. He hadn't been so persistently hard since he was a teenager.

But he wasn't a kid anymore, and he wouldn't rush Janet into bed as if she were an easy lay. He had a nice evening planned. *Then* bed. Or the kitchen counter, or the floor. Any one of those fantasies was enough to drive him mad with desire.

Damn. There was the Mercedes again. At least it was the same silver E-Class, coming toward him from the other direction as he pulled into Elizabeth's drive. He took his time at the gates, watching as it passed behind him. Two men were visible in the front seats before the car disappeared around a curve. This time Rocky didn't fool himself into believing that they were really gone.

This was bad. They'd known where he was going, and instead of falling for his ruse, they just waited for him to show up.

They wouldn't go far; they'd probably pull over up the street and wait for him to leave. He should call Ben, have him send out a squad car to hassle them a bit and get some ID. But Rocky couldn't prove the guys had done anything, and he was fairly certain the IDs would be phony and the car rented. All he'd be doing was showing them Janet had a layer of protection around her, something they already knew. He just needed to know why they were after her. Either they were early opportunists looking for the rest of the Pellinni Jewels, or they were with the Colombian cartel that had dealt with Banner. Based strictly on potential danger to Janet, he was rooting for the former. And he didn't need the cops to find out for sure.

He searched through the console between the seats, selecting a four-inch-long nail. It wouldn't work as well as a knife, but he wasn't going to chance some aggressive cop charging him with carrying a concealed weapon. One brush with the legal system had been more than enough. Nails weren't weapons—not technically.

Cutting across Elizabeth's yard, he pulled out his cell phone and hit four on his speed dial. The call was answered after two rings.

"Westfield residence."

"Hey, Mr. Peters, it's Rocky. Did Mrs. Westfield have you arrange for security patrols around the property?"

"Yes, sir. Chief Thatcher did."

"Well, I'm about to cut through the hedges on the west side, and I'd appreciate it if they didn't shoot me."

"Yes, sir. I'll let them know. Do you need assistance?"

"No, thanks. Just tell them the Hispanic man in the blue-and-green Hawaiian shirt isn't a prowler."

He pocketed the phone as he neared the dense hedge of rhododendrons and lilacs that screened the property from the street. From behind the house female voices floated on the humid breeze, punctuated by laughter and squeals. And splashing. Janet and Libby were obviously in the pool.

A peek over the low fieldstone wall confirmed his suspicions—the Mercedes was parked a few dozen feet into the neighbor's long driveway, out of sight of the house and inconspicuous from the street. From there they could wait for him to drive by without fear of arousing anyone's suspicion. If the homeowner showed up, they'd just claim to have the wrong address, apologize, and drive on.

He needed a stone. Searching beneath the lilacs, he cursed Elizabeth's dedicated lawn service for removing all the rocks from the area. After a couple of fruitless minutes, he gave up on the immaculate ground and used the nail to pry and wiggle a stone loose from the mortar of the old wall. Perfect.

The Mercedes had backed in, waiting for him to pass by on the street. He probably didn't even need the dense cover of spruce, maples, and oaks in the neighbor's yard that sheltered his approach from behind; the occupants were looking straight ahead. Both men jumped when Rocky tapped on the driver's door beneath the open window.

He leaned down to take a close look at the two startled faces. Black hair, white skin—he was betting on Spanish extraction, similar to his own. *Colombians. Shit.*

"Morning, gentlemen. Sorry to bother you, but I thought you might not be aware you have a flat tire."

Both men had stiffened, then looked confused when the information registered. "Flat tire?" the driver said.

Decent English, but a slight accent. He tried not to jump to conclusions, even though he already had.

"Yeah, back here." As the driver stepped out of the car to examine the tire, Rocky pulled the nail from his pocket, held it against the tire, and rapped it with the stone. It drove in nearly to the head.

"See, that's not gonna last long. Especially if I do this." Wrapping his fingers under the head, he pulled the nail out. A sharp hiss of air followed.

The man released a string of angry Spanish and lunged toward Rocky. He blocked the outstretched arm and whirled with one strategically placed kick, slamming the man just below the rib cage. He fell to the ground, clutching his midsection and gasping.

"Be glad I'm a nice guy and hit your diaphragm instead of your cojones," Rocky muttered.

The passenger had watched through the window, hesitating for the two seconds it took to dispatch the driver. Finally realizing what was happening, he jerked the door open. Through the tinted back window, Rocky saw him open the glove compartment. In another two seconds, he'd be facing a gun.

Dashing around the back of the car would take too long; he'd round the trunk just in time to meet a bullet head-on. Better to use the shortest distance between two points: a straight line over the roof. Using both hands, he vaulted himself onto the trunk. The second man opened the passenger door and stood, turning toward the rear of the car looking for Rocky. But the man never completed his turn. Rocky slammed into the back of his head, carrying them both into the open car door. The man's skull broke the impact.

Staggering and groaning, they both fell to the ground. Rocky rolled free, jumping to his feet. The other man didn't. In fact, it looked like he wouldn't be getting up for a while. Blood ran freely from his suddenly crooked nose, and a long "Ahhhh" died into a hoarse sob.

The gun lay several feet from the man's outstretched hands. Rocky picked it up, checked the safety, and tucked it into the back of his waistband.

"Hijo de puta!" The low, gravely words in Spanish made him look back. They matched the deadly look in the man's eyes. Or one eye rather, since one side of the man's face still lay against the cement.

"Yeah, yeah, tell it to the cops." Not that any one of them was going to report this little scuffle.

"Mataré tú," the man snarled, his words a little more distinct this time.

The words weren't even necessary; the hate in his narrowed eyes made the death threat perfectly clear. Rocky made sure to step on the man's outstretched fingers as he walked away.

Cutting through the overgrown and upward-sloping backyard, Rocky listened eagerly for shouts and laughter from the pool. The yard was quiet save for the rushing sound of the fountain in the koi pond.

Mr. Peters met him at the front door. "Problem taken care of, sir?"

"Yes, thanks. Where can I find the ladies?"

"They're waiting for you in the solarium."

A loud meow came from the floor near his feet and he looked down to see Fluff arching her back and rubbing on his leg. "Hey, there's my girl. How ya doin', Fluff? You miss me?" He bent down to offer the expected scratches and pets.

"She's adjusting quite well," Mr. Peters said, answering for the cat.

Fluff's purr turned into a hiss and Rocky followed her evil glare to where Jingles stalked behind a large potted fig tree.

Never one to back down, Fluff slunk forward, ears pinned and tail twitching. Before Rocky could scold her, Mr. Peters reached into his pocket, drew a small gun, and took aim at Fluff.

Rocky gave the gun a startled second glance but didn't have time to speak.

A thin stream of water shot out, hitting Fluff on her furry butt. With a yelp, she ran for the stairs. Jingles split just as quickly toward the kitchen.

Mr. Peters pocketed the squirt gun. "Except for a few territorial disputes," he amended.

Rocky lifted an eyebrow. "Nice shot," he muttered. "They teach that in butler school?"

"No, sir. I queried a private loop for butlers on the Internet and received several tips about dealing with multiple cats in the household."

He studied Mr. Peters's implacable expression. "You're kidding."

The proper look never altered, but Rocky thought he noted amusement in the way Peters cocked his head. "No, sir."

"Huh." Rocky supposed that level of resourcefulness was expected, but the man never ceased to amaze him.

With cat control covered, his thoughts returned to Janet. "Solarium," he repeated aloud, before he set off through the house.

Libby was nowhere to be found; she'd probably gone up to her bedroom. Janet greeted him as he approached the kitchen, hair toweled half dry and swimsuit concealed by a beach wrap covering her in a loose white material from neck to knees.

"You got out of the pool."

Janet looked confused at his comment. "Of course. Mr. Peters told us you called and said there might be a security problem. We thought it would be safer to wait inside."

Rocky started as Elizabeth got up from a chair. He hadn't even noticed her. "What's going on?"

"Nothing, now. Here," he said pulling the gun and holding it out to Elizabeth. "You can give this to Ben."

She stared it as if it were a snake. "Where did you get that?"

"Off one of the men in the car that was following me. I'm sure they have others, but maybe Ben can trace this one." Rocky held it out until she took it, two fingers gingerly gripping the barrel.

"Won't there be prints?"

"Hopefully." He doubted it mattered, though, and he cared even less. He had a good idea what the men wanted, and that was enough for him. No matter what he or Ben did to protect Janet, the thieves wouldn't give up until they got what they were looking for.

Janet scrunched her eyebrows and shot Rocky a suspicious look. "What happened?"

"I had a little confrontation with my lemmings. Probably the same ones who chased you and trashed your place. They weren't very friendly, and I think they're even less inclined to be after our talk."

"They were *here*?" Elizabeth looked outside, scanning the yard as if men might be hiding in the shrubbery. "On this property?"

"At the neighbor's. You should have Ben send a patrol car around, make sure they've left the area. Tell him it's two men in a silver E-Class Mercedes. And they might be changing a flat tire."

Elizabeth's mouth had tightened into a thin line and Rocky had a feeling he'd crossed into hostile territory. "Or I could call Ben," he suggested.

For a few seconds he felt anger radiating from her hot gaze. Then her features set with determination. "I'll have Peters relay the message." With a dignified turn, she left.

Rocky looked at Janet. "What'd the poor sucker do to her?"

"He wants her to sell the house." At his confused look, she dismissed the topic with a wave of her hand. "Later. Forget Ben for now. I'm more worried about you. Did they hurt you?"

He smiled, relieved to have the conversation back where he wanted it. "No. But just to be sure, you can kiss me and make it better."

"Good idea." She stepped forward without hesitation, her arms circling his neck in a move that felt so natural he couldn't believe he could still count the number of times he'd kissed her. He needed to work harder at losing track, starting now. He pulled her hips against his while she kissed him, feeling her damp bikini bottom through her cover-up. When her lips finally parted from his, he murmured, "What color is your bathing suit?"

She gave him a sly look. "Subtle, Hernandez. I'll show you if you tell me what happened."

"I already did. I confronted them, warned them off. Your turn."

"Not yet. You took their gun. Does that mean you went all macho on them?"

He squinted one eye, trying to calculate her reaction. She was tough, but he knew women often favored talking over using force. "Something like that."

He was afraid she was going to lecture him about not using violence to solve problems, but she just nodded.

He didn't want to scare her, but she had to know what was going on. It looked like kissing time was over. He led her to a wicker love seat and pulled her down beside him on the vine-patterned cushion. "Janet, these guys are not professional thieves, at least not in the way you think of it. They're Colombians."

"You mean Banner's Colombians?" He saw understanding flare in the depths of her eyes. "They're after the diamonds, aren't they? Not the ones Banner bought with the Pellinni Jewels, but one of those other deals Sleazy told us about. Payment for the drugs they smuggled. Except maybe he didn't pay off the last shipment before he was arrested."

"That's what I think, too. The Pellinni Jewels were probably part of his money laundering as well. When word of the necklace got out, I think these guys figured that you had their diamonds, too."

She wrinkled her nose in disgust. "Yeah, like I might have found a bag of diamonds laying around and kept them. There were federal agents crawling all over my house and the Westfield-Benton offices. They didn't leave a paperclip if they thought it might somehow be connected to the case. I think they would have found diamonds if there were any."

Rocky shrugged. "Even inside golf balls?"

She paused to think about it. "I'm pretty sure there weren't any others besides the empty ones I found. I watched the FBI go through the house. If there was a gold golf ball ready to be delivered to his Colombian contacts, I never saw it." One eyebrow rose. "But you can be sure I'll ask him about it this afternoon."

"What?"

Her sly look was definitely a smirk. "I just got a confirmation from his lawyer; I'm on the visitor's list."

He hadn't expected her to act that fast. "Janet, I don't want you seeing him alone. Hell, I don't want you to see him at all."

"I know." How could she be so calm when he felt like he was going to explode? "I appreciate your concern, but we have no choice. Banner is the only one who might have the answers we need, and only one person can see him at a time. I'm going."

She was right, though it still didn't make him feel any better. What did help was the fact that he was familiar with the visitation process at the Oakland County Jail: Banner wouldn't be able to touch her, and she wouldn't be alone with him.

He had to admire her determination and guts. The man was evil personified and had gone to great lengths to arrange her death; it couldn't be easy to look him in the eye and ask for information.

I'll go with you. I don't like the idea of you driving there alone, especially after I just pissed off your Colombian tail."

"Thanks, but Ben already arranged for a security guy to go with me."

He bit back any further objections. "Call me when you get back."

She smiled. "I will. Thanks for being so understanding."

"I'm faking it."

Her smile widened. "I know."

It was impossible to stay upset when she looked at him with that mixture of amusement and affection.

"So what happened when you talked to the Colombians?"

He shrugged. "We didn't have much to say to each other, outside of what sounded like some nasty threats."

"What do you mean? What did they say?"

"Just what you'd expect, something about killing me."

"What! What about killing you?"

Rocky smiled. He liked that she was concerned for his safety.

"I don't know exactly. It was in Spanish, but I got the point."

She blinked and gave him an odd look. "Are you telling me you don't speak Spanish? You, Roberto Hernandez?"

"Hey, I'm like, fifth-generation American. I know how to order burritos at the drive-through. I think my grandmother speaks a little Spanish."

She stared, then laughed. "Sorry, I know it's a stereotype. You're right, I have a lot to learn about you." The smile lingered, then faded a bit while she bit her lip, thinking. Her blue eyes took his measure. "And I think I'd like to."

The soft, innocuous words drove into his heart like an arrow.

Her carefully erected defenses had dropped, allowing

him in. It meant more than her willingness to jump into bed with him—far, far more—and he had to be careful not to scare her back behind her barricades.

"Whatever you want to know." He hadn't meant for it to come out so low and rough, but his voice was suddenly gone. Great, he beats up the bad guys and a wisp of a girl knocks him speechless.

He felt an urge to touch her, to remind himself of their connection. But she was still learning to open up, so he had to be careful. Lifting his hand slowly, he touched the tendrils behind her ear. He fingered the short strands, winding them absently around his finger and delighting when it made her eyes go hazy and her lips open slightly. It was good to know he could have that effect on her, especially since she seemed to have a greater effect on his emotional balance than he'd expected.

"That's not a commitment or anything." Her voice didn't seem that strong, either, despite her defiant words.

"I know. You want to get to know me better, that's all."

"Right. I mean, if we're still going to keep sleeping together."

"Damn right we are." He was practically growling now. He cleared his throat. "As soon as we give the cops time to either pick up those two SOBs or scare them off. We don't need them tailing us and parking outside while we—" his voice stopped as another thought clicked into place. They'd been tailing him because they were watching Janet, to either threaten her or see where she went. To see if she might lead them to the diamonds.

He stood abruptly. "Shit, shit, shit!"

She stopped in the middle of licking her tongue across her full lower lip, and rose beside him. He must have looked alarmed, because she'd picked up his expression. "What?"

"Sleazy. They were probably following us when we went there. We led them right to the pawnbroker who sold Banner the jewelry and the diamonds. Shit!"

Her eyes widened as she realized the ramifications faster than he could explain them. "They'll hurt him, won't they? They want information. He's dumb enough to refuse to give it."

"Exactly." He held her shoulders, kissing her more briefly than he wanted to. "I have to go."

"I'll go with you."

"Not this time." He held up his hand as her brows drew together. "No. He's either okay and I'll warn him, or they've already gotten to him. Either way, you don't need to be there. And I need to know that you're safe." He paused. "Besides, you have an appointment to see Banner." For once he was grateful to have Banner come between them.

After several seconds of clenched teeth and pressed lips, she conceded. "All right. But you call me. I mean *immediately*. I know how long it takes to get there, and I'm going to worry about you for every second you make me wait after that." Moisture gathered in her eyes and she slapped his chest. "Damn it. Look what you're doing to me. I hate you."

Warmth surged in his chest. He grabbed her, cupped her face in both hands, and kissed her hard, giving them both a few furious seconds' taste of desire. He stepped back, then stopped at a sudden memory. "Show me," he ordered, motioning at the wrap that covered her swim suit.

A tiny smile curved her lips as she opened three buttons and shrugged the thing off her shoulders. It fell at her feet. Rocky drank in the black bikini with gold swirls that followed the swell of each breast and dipped low between them. His eyes moved down her flat stomach to the gold-and-black triangle that smoothed across her lower abdomen and stretched into little more than strings across her hips. Following the long, tan line of her legs, his eyes caught the shine of gold around her ankle.

He skimmed his gaze back up, slowly, grinning. "Thank you, God," he murmured, and ran out the door.

The humidity felt like a blanket under overcast skies as Rocky drove to Detroit's West Side. Thunder was rumbling by the time he walked through the door of Lost and Found Treasures.

"Hello!" he called. No one came to the window. He couldn't imagine what would make Sleazy leave the front door open and the cash window untended. Prickles touched his neck, and he glanced around the ceiling for cameras. He spotted two at opposite corners of the room; a red light flashing beneath each one indicated that they were working. He wasn't reassured.

Leaning over the chest-high counter, Rocky peered into the small area behind the window. Papers, a computer terminal, stacked boxes. No sign of a scuffle, which was only mildly encouraging. The stillness of the place wasn't a good sign.

Access to the space behind the window was through

a door to his right. Knowing the security Sleazy employed on the outer room, he expected it to be locked with at least a couple deadbolts. He turned the knob. The door opened smoothly.

"Hey! Anybody here?" Utter silence. A narrow hallway led to the dim back area of the store, probably the main storeroom. No lights were on, shrouding the hallway in blackness. The silence was unnatural, so thick it buzzed in his ears. Every sense was on full alert.

He was worried about the Colombians, but in Sleazy's business, anyone could be a potential problem. The man obviously bought stolen goods, and it wasn't hard to imagine that some rejected, desperate druggie, unable to pawn his items, might try to rob him. Anyone could be standing back there right now, hand muffling Sleazy's mouth, waiting to see what Rocky would do. He had to go back there and find out what was going on.

But he needed a gun. Unfortunately, with his criminal record he'd never get a permit to carry one. Sleazy had to have one around somewhere, though.

Rocky looked under the window that divided the business area from the customers' and found a pump action 12-gauge with both barrels loaded. He tried to be reassured by the fact that it was there, that Sleazy hadn't felt he needed it. But its presence meant nothing except that Rocky didn't have to walk down that long hall without protection. Tucking the shotgun into a comfortable position at his side, he started toward the back of the store. He didn't call out anymore; he'd given the man plenty of opportunity to respond. Either Sleazy wasn't here, or he couldn't answer.

Slowly, Rocky felt inside the door at the end of the hall until he found the light switch. He hit it, sending a half dozen fluorescent tubes into a flickering fit. It took at least ten seconds for the lights to steady, illuminating several rows of metal shelves stacked with cardboard boxes. He made a careful sweep of the room, looking down empty row after empty row. No Sleazy. Turning all the way to the right, he saw a partially open door. Leading with his shotgun, he stepped toward the door, nudging it with the barrel. It moved two inches and stopped. He pushed harder, and it bounced back this time, hitting something resistant behind it.

He looked around the door into a small bathroom: a sink, a mirror, a toilet. And a body. Sleazy lay crumpled beside the toilet, a neat bullet hole in the back of his head.

Goddamn it. Rocky muttered it aloud several times, unable to think of anything more appropriate. He hadn't liked a single thing about the guy, but felt bad for the way he'd died. Not to mention he felt guilty, despite the fact that he'd warned Sleazy. Desperate addicts weren't noted for neat, execution-style slayings; this death was cold and deliberate.

Sleazy died because Rocky had led a killer to the shop.

Trudging back to the front desk, he wiped the shotgun clean of prints and put it back where he'd found it. Using the phone beside the window, he called 9-1-1, promising to wait for the officers to arrive. Then he pulled out his own cell phone and called Janet.

"I expected to hear from you fifteen minutes ago."

It was nervous relief he heard, not accusation. He felt some of his tension slip away, knowing she cared more than she'd admit. "Sorry, had to call the cops first. He's dead."

She was silent for several seconds. "I'm sorry." Her voice was quiet and not entirely steady.

"Yeah, me, too."

"Do you think it was the Colombians?"

He wanted to tell her that it absolutely was them, to at least put a name to her fears. But that might be minimizing the danger. "I don't know, babe. They're probably trying to track down the diamonds Banner bought, so it's possible that's what they were after. But that's not all Sleazy dealt in, so it also could be someone who followed us in an effort to trace the Pellinni Jewels. The jewels won't interest our Colombian friends. They're worth a fortune, but only if they remain in their original settings. Pry the stones out, and you've got a handful of ordinary pearls and one big spinel. Not something drug runners would use to move money offshore."

"You mean someone besides the Colombians might have killed Sleazy?"

"If they were after the Pellinni Jewels, yes. I'll call Ben and have him contact the cops here to see if that gun I confiscated earlier could have been the murder weapon. Maybe we'll get lucky and solve this quickly." When she didn't answer, he imagined her fear building, wondering if the same fate awaited her. He rushed to reassure her. "You're not like Sleazy, Janet. You're in a safe place, and you don't go anywhere alone. And that's the way it's going to stay until we catch whoever did this."

"I'm on my way to see Banner, Rocky. But I'm with Ben's guard, I'll be surrounded by police officers, and I'll go directly home afterward."

He gritted his teeth. "Once you're home, stay there. It's safer."

He heard a deep sigh. "I suppose you're right."

Maybe she finally trusted him. But maybe it didn't make any difference, because no matter how much they protected her, she would feel like a prisoner. He ached inside, wanting to make her feel better and knowing there wasn't much he could do. "Look, this could take a while. I'll have to talk to the officers, probably a homicide detective, too. I'll come see you when I'm done."

"You better." She sounded as emotionally drained as he felt. "It's not your fault, Rocky. You tried to warn him."

She was trying to make him feel better? God, he needed to see her, to just hold her. "I'll talk to you soon, babe. 'Bye." He flipped the phone closed and leaned against the wall, suddenly exhausted. It had been three days since he'd stepped back into his former life, and the contrast between his two worlds had been even more staggering than he'd expected.

When he'd begun his criminal career, he hadn't thought twice about what he had to do. It had been necessary, and so he'd become as skilled as possible until he'd accomplished what he'd set out to do. The jail stint at the end was a fluke, but a lucky one since there he'd met Jack Payton, his best friend. And through Jack he'd met Ellie, who'd become his business partner. And through Ellie he'd met Janet, who'd become—well, he suspected she might become even more important to him than Jack. It would have been a perfect transition, except that it had led him full-circle to his previous life, and he'd stepped back into a fetid swamp of thieves, pawnbrokers, and killers.

He closed his eyes, shutting out his surroundings while he waited, hearing nothing but the sound of traffic outside and the occasional clicks and hums from the computer on the counter. And a tiny scratching sound.

He cracked his eyes open. The noise had come from his left, in the small space where Sleazy had once sat, smoking. Rocky stepped past the computer and looked around.

It came again, one little shuffling sound. This time he knew what it was, and turned with the first sense of relief he'd had since entering the shop.

"Adolf. How ya doin', little guy?"

The pup wiggled, his paws making the same soft sound on the cage floor. He didn't move from the back of his cage but one ear cocked toward Rocky, oversized and too big for his puppy head. The other ear flopped over, still not strong enough to stand up. The dog gave Rocky a confused look, like he couldn't choose between happy and sad. He whined.

"Bad day, huh?" He could only imagine what had gone on in the shop to cause the puppy to slink to the back of his cage and stay there. Things would only get worse for the poor guy—he'd be confiscated and sent to the pound. Or if he was lucky, a shelter. Either way, he'd just become homeless.

Rocky didn't give his impulse a second thought. Grabbing the nylon leash beside the cage, he opened the door. "Come on, pup. Let's get you out of here. You're making a break for it before the cops come." Whatever the dog had witnessed, he couldn't testify to, and Rocky needed to salvage one good thing from this mess.

"Come on," he coaxed again, patting the floor. The puppy crept forward, wriggling at Rocky's feet. "Some watchdog you are. First thing we do is get you out of here. The second thing will be changing your stupid name."

Adolf stuck by Rocky's side as they walked to the car. The dog's submissive demeanor made him feel a little less upset about Sleazy. He cracked the windows, even though it had started to rain. "Sorry, fella, you have to stay here for now. It can't be any worse than that kennel." He locked the doors and hoped his carpet and leather seats were stain-proof.

It was nearly an hour before the police allowed him to leave the pawnshop. The puppy hadn't done more than track wet paw prints along the seats. Rocky walked him to the sidewalk where Adolpf piddled on a sorry scrap of grass, then put the pup in the car and called Janet.

"I'm on my way, but I have a few stops to make first." He needed to buy food for Adolf, and a new cage. He hadn't wanted to risk removing the pup's old cage, since it was now part of a crime scene.

"Okay. I'm about to go inside the jail, so I'll meet you at Elizabeth's." She paused. "You know, I was beginning to feel inadequate. I flash you in my sexiest bikini, and you disappear for hours."

"Not because I wanted to, believe me."

"Good, because I wasn't done with you."

He liked the sound of that. "I'm sorry, babe, but we may have to stick around the house for a while. I have someone with me."

He listened through the tense silence, until she said one terse word. "Who?"

"A friend. I think you'll like him."

"I already don't."

"Now, now. You're just being grouchy because you want to ravish my body."

"Yes. Is your friend listening to this?"

"Yeah, but don't worry, he's kind of young and not too bright." He didn't give her a chance to call him on that. "Hey, is Elizabeth home today?"

"Yes, why?" She was beginning to sound suspicious.

He reached out and scratched the pup's floppy ear. "I have a present for her."

"For Elizabeth?" He could almost see confusion, swimming in those beautiful eyes.

"Yup. See ya soon." He clicked the phone off before she could ask more questions.

If he was lucky, Elizabeth would be in a better mood. He suspected he'd picked up some residual anger earlier just by benefit of being a male of the same species as Ben. Adolf was male, but a different species. It might be enough of a difference to get him through the massive Westfield front door.

Chapter Ten

Janet wanted to see Banner as much as she wanted a pelvic exam. No, make that a lobotomy, because that's what she should get for putting herself through this torture again.

The private security guards who Elizabeth had insisted escort her to the jail had been forced to wait outside. Janet sat in the bare waiting room with eight other people. Ten chairs sat in a row facing a clock on the wall, the room's only adornment. She'd been there for an hour and seventeen minutes already and was rethinking her visit when a uniformed woman with a gun on her hip opened the door, followed by a male officer.

"Men over there," the woman barked, pointing to the far wall. "Women over here."

Janet lined up with the five other women. She'd been through this once before, but knowing what was coming didn't make it any easier.

The fact that the guards had been through it hundreds of times showed in the female guard's stern expression as she planted herself in front of the line and gestured with her handheld metal detector. "Take your shoes off."

They complied, most of them quickly.

"Arms out," she told Janet.

The guard ran a wand over her body, then patted her down. The procedure made her feel like a prisoner herself.

"Turn around, hands on the wall. Spread your legs."

Janet obeyed, studiously counting ceiling tiles as she was patted down in places only recently explored by Rocky and her gynecologist. The woman straightened and stepped back. "Shoes on."

She slipped her feet into her shoes, keeping her eyes to the front until the guard was done patting down the last woman in line. She didn't care to watch anyone else go through the same dehumanizing process.

A minute later they were herded through a metal detector, then a door locked behind them with an audible click. An elevator took them up to the third floor, then released them through another locked doorway where a guard waited at a desk. Another *armed* guard, she noted, wondering if it was ever necessary to draw his weapon—and if it would be for a prisoner or a visitor.

Janet presented her key card and was directed to a position in front of a screened dividing wall. A ledge—it could hardly be called a desk—ran across the length of it, and she watched a man and woman lay papers on it. Lawyers, perhaps, visiting their clients. She'd come with nothing but questions and would have thirty minutes to get answers. She stood patiently for another ten minutes, and stared into the empty room on the other side.

A loud click signaled the opening door. Prisoners filed through, dressed in orange jumpsuits. One young man broke into a grin and rushed up to a pregnant young woman from her group, who beamed on the other side of the screen. Others sauntered indifferently to meet their visitors. Banner was the last to enter.

His icy blue gaze latched onto hers in a way she'd once thought was magnetic. Now it was just creepy. It pinned her as effectively as if she were a specimen displayed for his observation, even though it was Banner who should have been the oddity on display here—the wealthy businessman and community leader reduced to a lowly prisoner. But instead his posture was as erect as ever, his expression arrogant and aloof, and the body that should have looked soft and pale was even more toned after months behind bars. He had *thrived* in jail. It seemed logical in a way. The man was finally in his natural element, surrounded by other criminals, even if they weren't as vicious and cold as he was.

He stood at the screen looking composed and slightly amused. "Hello, Janet." His voice was smooth and seductive, like the snake speaking to Eve. "That's an interesting new look. Less feminine, but I imagine it's easier to maintain."

Her hair. She'd forgotten he hadn't seen her drastic cut. That he didn't like it thrilled her as much as the fact that Rocky had. But she wasn't stupid enough to please him by reacting to his thinly veiled criticism. "I came to ask you about some jewelry you bought."

"Ah, yes. The Pellinni necklace." At her startled look, he gave a condescending smile. "You didn't think I'd find out about your aborted attempt to sell it? I do watch TV and read the newspapers, you know."

"I hadn't really thought about what you might have heard, but it's nice to know you're not totally isolated," she countered.

His smile faded, and the skin tightened the tiniest bit around his eyes. *Score.* It was probably juvenile to admit, but it felt good.

"Did you purchase the rest of the Pellinni Jewels?" she asked, getting right to the point.

"I'm afraid not," he said, looking regretful. His demeanor alone made his answer suspicious. "Of course, I didn't know the necklace was stolen or I never would have bought it."

"Of course." *Liar.* She smiled, an insincere token to match her words. "But you must have seen the rest of the collection. Didn't you want it?" Just knowing whether Sleazy had the whole collection to begin with would help. If they were broken up before they got to him, then maybe it hadn't been a recent, local job after all.

He managed a genuinely puzzled expression. "I'm sorry, I don't recall seeing them. But I looked at so many pieces trying to find the perfect gift for my new wife that it's all a bit fuzzy."

It sounded as rehearsed as it undoubtedly was. Banner and his lawyers were ready to refute any evidence related to money laundering. He'd only been buying a gift for his wife. Yeah, right—a priceless stolen necklace and a handful of loose diamonds.

"You don't remember them, and yet you're sure you didn't buy them?"

"The necklace wasn't exactly inexpensive, my dear. I think I'd remember if I spent money on anything else."

"Like the diamonds."

She noted the small hesitation before he rallied and drew his brows together in a decent imitation of confusion. "Diamonds?"

"The ones you bought with the necklace. Or the ones you bought from the same guy after that—take your pick."

His eyes betrayed a flicker of surprise, and she took satisfaction in scoring a second hit before his calculating look was back. "I see my brother's little friend has been helping you again. He did have some questionable connections as I recall. What was that ridiculous nickname he used—Rocky? A rather low-class image, isn't it? But then, Jack never had sophisticated taste."

He was fishing, and Rocky was another piece of bait she refused to take.

"The diamonds," she reminded him.

He shook his head. "I don't know anything about any diamonds. Perhaps you have a receipt from the purchase that would refresh my memory?"

She flashed a tight smile. "No, no receipt."

"Then I regret I can't help you." His eyebrows rose hopefully. "But there is something you can help me with."

"I doubt that."

He clicked his tongue in mock disappointment. "Really, Janet, there's no need for attitude. It's a small thing. I've gone over the list of items from our divorce that were put into storage. It seems not everything is accounted for."

She frowned. "I gave you all you asked for, which is far more than you deserved."

"But along with the dining room set, I should have

received the china and crystal from the antique break-front, and according to the list my lawyers received, I didn't get everything."

She gave him an incredulous look. "I don't want your dishes, Banner. They're at your mother's. Send someone to get them."

"Thank you, I will," he said. He was the epitome of fake courtesy. Folding his hands on the shelf, he cocked his head and said, "You made a special request to see me. Is that what you came to ask me, whether I bought the rest of the Pellinni Jewels?"

"Yes."

"Hmm." His days must be incredibly boring if he was actually this interested in her problems. "Did the FBI ask you to find out?"

"No, I'm sure they would ask you themselves."

"Yes, I believe you're right." His thoughtful stare made her uncomfortable. "So why *are* you asking? Surely you aren't simply doing a good deed by tracking down the missing jewels for them?"

"Unfortunately, I don't have that sort of time to waste. I have enough to do salvaging the company you nearly destroyed."

He stroked his jaw. "I can't help but wonder why the whereabouts of the remaining pieces of jewelry would be of any concern to you, though."

She'd used no more than five of her thirty minutes, but they were done. "Thanks for your time. Have a nice day." Even telemarketers sounded more sincere.

"Unless the authorities think you have them," he mused, then lifted his eyebrow as another thought occurred to him. "Or a thief does." Her closed expression was all the verification he needed. "Oh, dear, have you been bothered by break-ins, Janet? Is someone looking for the remaining Pellinni Jewels?" A benevolent smile touched his mouth, as frightening on him as it would be on the devil himself. "I do believe my little purchase is having an unexpected payoff."

She didn't have to listen to him gloat. She turned away, intending to tell the guard at the desk that her visit was over.

"And I thought it would only be the diamonds that would cause you problems."

She spun around, arching an eyebrow. "The diamonds you didn't buy?"

"True, I can't seem to remember acquiring them. Still, you aren't the only one who assumes I've been buying diamonds." His voice dropped, enticing her back toward the screen. "The FBI seems to be under the same mistaken impression. Curious. And I hear my former business associates are looking for a certain cache of diamonds I allegedly purchased. They're quite persistent."

A detached part of her was surprised she could still have underestimated his evilness. "You purposely withheld hundreds of thousands of dollars from drug dealers knowing they'd come after me?"

"What an appalling thought." Even as he said it, his wide eyes narrowed and his lips slid into a smirk. This was the real Banner, the one she hadn't seen until after she'd married him, and watching the facade drop still sent goose bumps dancing up her arms. "I believe that sum is closer to a million, Janet. And lucky me, having them go after you wasn't planned, it just worked out that way. You see, darling"—he played with the word, savoring it, reminding her that she'd once believed he'd meant it—"you owe me something. Once you ruined my carefully constructed operation, I decided I needed the money more than they did. I was planning on being out of the country by the time anyone came looking for the diamonds, but as it turns out, I've been slightly delayed. So I'm here to watch events unfold as my former associates search for their stones. I see that's happened." He closed his eyes with a blissful smile. "Thank you for sharing this information with me. You could not have given me a better present."

There was a time when Banner could intimidate her, but no more, she decided. She let him have his moment of satisfaction, knowing it would be all the sweeter when she ripped it away. If she'd learned anything from him, it was that sometimes you had to meet threats with threats.

Smiling coolly, she mirrored his folded hands, looking her most composed. "Those business associates of yours really *are* persistent, aren't they? Vengeful, too. I imagine they'd go to great lengths to find what they wanted."

His momentary hesitation was the only evidence of his suspicion. "Exactly. I find myself worried for you, Janet."

"How sweet. But don't be, I've taken care of it."

Feigning as little interest as possible, he asked, "How did you do that?"

"Why, I simply talked to the two gentlemen from Colombia who have been looking for the diamonds. I explained that you still have them, or at least you know where to find them. I was sure you'd want to complete your last business deal and keep your reputation intact."

His smile was condescending. "Don't you think that sounds a little naïve, Janet? They aren't thrown off that easily."

"Oh, I know. That's why I gave them one of your gold-plated commemorative golf balls. You know, the hollow ones?" She kept her voice light, but it was difficult not to gloat when his smile slipped away and his eyes showed the first touch of worry. "I told them the mementos had been in your possession when you went to jail, but that they were deemed insignificant as evidence and were returned to us by the police." She leaned close and dropped her voice. "It seems the Colombians don't fully understand our legal system, so they think that could really happen." She winked and stepped back, noting happily that Banner's worry had edged into panic. "Anyway, I told them I was sure the diamonds had been in there, ready for delivery, and, of course, they believed me because that's how you've delivered them in that past, right? Very clever."

He swallowed, visibly trying to remain calm. "That's ridiculous, Janet. They would know the police wouldn't allow me to keep a cache of diamonds in jail."

"You're absolutely right, Banner." The story she was making up sounded so plausible she almost wished it had happened. "And being familiar with the legal system in *their* country, I knew exactly what they would think. They would assume the police were corrupt enough to keep the diamonds for themselves. And we wouldn't want to mislead them like that, would we? So I explained that you obviously did the same thing any good drug mule would do—you swallowed them." She brightened. "And you know what? I think they'll leave me alone now and work on making a few contacts inside the jail."

Banner's face had gone pale. "Nice try, Janet. But I'm kept in isolation here. No one could get to me if they tried."

She nodded. "I hear that sometimes works, especially if the guards actually like you." She gave him an encouraging smile and rapped a knuckle on the shelf. "You might want to work on those people skills, Banner."

Walking away was much more satisfying knowing she'd disturbed that studied calm. She imagined Banner eyeing the guards nervously until he was able to place an agitated call to his lawyers, pleading for more protection. Too bad she couldn't stick around to see that.

Putting a dent in Banner's confidence was enough to make it a successful visit in itself, but she'd achieved more. She'd bet anything that Banner had at least seen the rest of the Pellinni Jewels, meaning Sleazy must have had them all at one time. So they were likely still in the area. That should help her and Rocky track them down.

One thing puzzled her, though—his reaction when she mentioned the golf balls. She could understand him being worried about the Colombians thinking he had the diamonds, but beads of sweat had popped out on his forehead, at the first mention of the golf balls. She'd expected a smirk, some arrogant acknowledgment of his clever idea, but he'd been visibly worried. If he had more diamond-filled golf balls lying around, she could understand his fear, but she'd gone through

every single one. If there was another place he could
have stashed more of them, she couldn't believe she
hadn't already searched it. She just couldn't shake the
feeling that Banner had been terrified when she'd figured out the hollow golf balls.

But there were more important things to worry
about right now. Despite what she'd told Banner, the
Colombians were stalking *her*. And so was the thief
who wanted the rest of the Pellinni Jewels. Both were
intent on their goal, and both seemed willing to sacrifice her to get it.

She tried to put Banner out of her mind for the rest of
the day. Rocky was on his way over and asked if she
could meet him and his friend at the door. He wouldn't
say why, only that he wasn't sure Mr. Peters or Elizabeth would let him in. As soon as she saw him coming
up the walk with a familiar German shepherd puppy
hugging his heels she understood.

Unfortunately, Elizabeth must have spotted Rocky
and the pup from the living room window.

They were two steps inside the foyer when Elizabeth
came up behind Janet, her face stern and hands on her
hips. "Roberto, perhaps I have given you the wrong
impression. This is not an animal shelter."

"Yes ma'am, I know." Janet watched him throw
a dismissive glance at the puppy that sat huddled by
his feet, clearly intimidated by all the people staring
at him. She didn't buy that suck-up attitude for one
second, but maybe Elizabeth did. "I wouldn't dream
of imposing on you, I just stopped by to see if Janet
wanted to accompany me to the pound."

Janet would have choked if she didn't know what a

load of bullshit that was. There was no way that sad little puppy was going to the pound, not if Rocky had any say.

Elizabeth appeared unmoved. "Yes, I'm sure they can place him in a good home."

Rocky lifted his eyebrows as if the thought hadn't occurred to him. "They might," he said as if offering hope that he didn't believe himself.

At the implication that the dog might not survive the placement process, Elizabeth's cool gaze cracked the tiniest bit. She looked from the pup to Rocky. "Where did you get it?"

"Some young punk I ran into. He didn't seem to care about the dog much, and I thought he deserved a better home."

Elizabeth pondered the cleaned-up version of Adolf's history. "Why don't you keep it?"

He shrugged. "Guess I'm just a cat person. Besides, I'm not home much, and he needs more attention than I can give him."

Janet raised her eyebrows skeptically but Rocky looked away from her. Thinking she'd help by showing how friendly the puppy was, she squatted down and tapped the floor. "Hey guy, come here."

The puppy wound himself around Rocky's legs but wagged his tail and tipped his head toward Janet. His floppy ear straightened momentarily to give him two large rabbit ears, then fell again.

She looked up at Rocky. "He's even more shy than yesterday."

"Yeah, he was scared to come out of the cage. You know how Sleazy was with him. He probably got kicked around a bit."

Janet doubted that. Sleazy wasn't affectionate toward the dog, but he probably knew enough to value his investment. Elizabeth, however, became indignant. "Kicked? That's unconscionable! What sort of man would abuse an innocent little puppy?"

"Maybe kicking's not unusual when they train attack dogs."

Attack dogs? Janet stole a glance upward at the loaded word. He caught her eyes with a desperate "I have no idea what I'm talking about" look. But judging by Elizabeth's frown, it didn't matter. Holding her silk dress to her legs with one hand, she squatted next to Janet and reached a hand toward the puppy, allowing him to sniff. "Poor little thing," she murmured. The dog wagged his tail harder and licked her fingers. Janet hid a smile.

"What's his name?" Elizabeth asked.

"The guy called him Adolf. As in Hitler," he added helpfully.

Elizabeth's scowl was outraged. "That's disgusting."

"Probably not for an attack dog." Janet saw him give the pup a gentle nudge with his foot toward Elizabeth. Adolf crept toward her, pushing his head under her hand.

"No, no, Adolf," Rocky said, his gentle tone making the reprimand unconvincing. "Don't get hairs on the nice lady."

"Don't be silly. He's not shedding," Elizabeth corrected. "And don't call him by that awful name."

"It's all he knows. I imagine his new owner can rename him. If anyone adopts him, that is."

Elizabeth stood, annoyance plain in the narrowed

gaze she aimed at Rocky. "Stop patronizing me, Roberto. I'm not a simpleton."

His face fell. "Yes, ma'am. Sorry."

"And give me that." She snatched the leash from his hand and glared as if he'd forced it on her. "I don't suppose you have a dog crate in the back of your car?"

He bit his lip, eyes sparkling. "In fact, I do."

"Well, go get it. Any fool can see the animal is scared and would be happier if he had a safe place to hide for a while."

Rocky darted out the door. Janet smiled at Elizabeth. "He is kind of sweet, isn't he?"

"Oh, definitely." Mischief twinkled behind Elizabeth's eyes. "You did mean the dog, didn't you?"

Janet decided not to touch that one.

Elizabeth leaned over to pat the dog's head. "He reminds me of a boy I knew in fifth grade named Freddie. He had big ears, too." She smiled. "Come along, Freddie. I have the perfect place for your crate."

Janet grinned as the two headed toward the kitchen, Elizabeth's heels and Freddie's nails making matching clicks against the tile floor. When Rocky came back carrying the big, collapsible dog crate she grabbed him and kissed him soundly. "Bonus points for you," she told him.

He grinned back. "I intend to collect them as soon as I can. Don't go anywhere."

"Wouldn't dream of it."

The man got more intriguing every day—and more attractive. Not in the model-handsome way Banner was attractive, where physical beauty merely disguised what was missing on the inside. Rocky's good qualities went beyond his toned body and devastating smile, even though she had to admit that simply watching him was a treat. He was smart, attentive, and considerate. He liked kids, rescued helpless animals, and made her laugh. She shook her head, hardly believing she'd rejected him for so long—and he'd waited for her. Bonus points, indeed.

He came back, throwing an arm around her and sweeping her out the door without stopping. "I told Elizabeth I was stealing you for the day, and Libby discovered the dog, so no one's going to miss you here. You're all mine. Where do you want to go?"

"Uh . . . your place?" She looked at the sky as some nasty storm clouds threatened to turn into a downpour. "Any place with a roof."

"Gotta love your enthusiasm," he laughed, keeping her close as they went down the long flight of steps. "My place eventually, but not yet."

There was that bad boy smile again, stirring up all sorts of desires. "Why not?"

"Because you're not the sort of woman a man rushes into bed."

She was pretty sure she wanted to be that sort of woman, at least today. "What sort of woman am I?"

"The sort who deserves to be romanced."

That devilish look was hard to argue with, but she tried. "I'm easy. Really."

"Since when?" He opened the passenger door for her. "I dropped hints for six months without results. It's too late to call yourself easy, lady. You get the full-on date treatment or nada."

She let him get behind the wheel before voicing her other concern. "What about whoever's after the

Pellinni Jewels? And those two guys you beat up? Won't they follow us?"

His smile turned grim. "I didn't see our Colombian friends when I cruised the neighborhood before pulling in, but that doesn't mean they aren't simply hiding well. And whoever wants the Pellinni Jewels doesn't want *you*, he wants you to lead him to *them*. We know that's not gonna happen. I don't want you to feel like a prisoner, but we'll be safe if we stick to public areas."

She focused on the part that concerned her most. "Public areas? I thought you said this was going to be romantic."

"Janet, Janet, Janet." He shook his head with feigned disappointment. "I'm seriously hurt that you underestimate me so. I can be romantic anywhere." In demonstration, he moved his finger in a tingly trail around her ear and down her neck, ending behind her head where he spread his fingers through her hair and leaned close. Her lips parted in anticipation as he rubbed his nose against hers before placing a soft kiss on her mouth.

He was off to a good start right here in the car. But it wouldn't do to feed his overinflated ego. "Whatever you say. I'm just surprised you insist on going through the motions. I thought every man wanted a sure thing," she mused.

His brows furrowed, his mood shifting. "I don't believe you were ever anyone's sure thing."

"No, but I'm trying to be," she muttered.

The gaze that scraped over her was hot and possessive. "Sweetheart," he said, his voice as low as the thunder starting outside. "We both know where this is going. But you were right when you said you didn't really know me, and I imagine there's a lot I don't know about you. So we're going on a date because that's how couples get to know each other. Okay?" He turned away to start the car, switching the wipers on against the quickening rain.

"Okay. Except we're not a couple."

"Yes, we are."

She felt a slight unease at how permanent that sounded. "We're just having sex."

"Sex is called coupling. I win." He smiled as he started down the drive.

She could get annoyed, but what would be the point? He was going to make sure that she was entertained and fed—at least she hoped there was food involved—plus shower her with great sex. If he wanted to play semantics with the event, why should she care?

She settled back, content to let him deal with the sheeting rain and the congested Friday afternoon traffic. The car was quiet, save for the slapping of the wipers and the hiss of tires on wet pavement.

"So talk. Tell me how you became a jewel thief."

He smiled, keeping his eyes on the road but obviously happy that she'd finally asked. "Short or long version?"

"Short." She didn't need the dirty details of his life of crime, just the reasons behind it. "Mostly, why did you do it? Misspent youth? Rebellious years and bad influences? A fascination with shiny, sparkly things?"

At least he looked amused. "I guess you could say I was righting a wrong."

"What was the wrong?"

"My grandparents had lost some heirloom jewelry pieces and gold coins in a burglary. The police said they'd never get them back. So, I dropped out of college, learned a few new skills, and tracked down every piece. Of course, the new owners weren't interested in giving them back, so I stole them. I got careless at the end and spent a year in jail. End of story."

Okay, maybe his reasons were a slight deviation from the norm. "Like Robin Hood?"

"I prefer the Zorro analogy myself. It's more appropriate with my Spanish roots."

She had to agree. He was dark and charming, and far more dangerous than he looked on the surface. Like now—from his placid expression, he might have just admitted to a typical youth spent selling popcorn for the Boy Scouts. Nothing about Rocky was typical or expected, and she berated herself for not having known better. But family heirloom jewelry? Quitting college to track down stolen pieces? The short version of this story wasn't going to do.

"I'd like the long version," she decided. "Please."

"Anything you want." He favored her with a sexy smile that made it obvious he was referring to more than stories of his past. Despite her determination to keep the upper hand, fireworks exploded in her pelvis.

"Just your criminal history for now." She tried to sound cool and collected, but knew she'd been a little too breathless to pull it off.

He winked at her. "I love it when you find me irresistible."

She said, "I'm resisting just fine, Zorro. Go on."

One more of those smiles and she'd make him pull over so she could have her way with him. Fortunately, he returned his attention to his driving and began.

"Think of a Spanish version of the *Mayflower*. My

father's family history goes back to the early Spanish settlers in California."

"I thought that was mainly monks or priests or something—setting up missions and converting the so-called heathens."

"And some wealthy land owners who stole their land. The important part here is that there was some rather good jewelry that came from Spain, along with some gold doubloons, and it all got passed down in the family. When a California museum did an exhibit on their early settlers, my grandmother loaned them the coins and three pieces of jewelry to put on display. When the exhibit was robbed, all of my grandparents' pieces were taken. They were valuable, but the sentimental value was even higher. It was irreplaceable family history. The police had their suspicions but no solid evidence. My grandmother was devastated."

"So you dropped out of school, confident you could solve the case."

"Of course."

"Very macho. Why not hire a private detective?"

"They did. No luck."

"What made you think you could do any better?"

He laughed. "That's pretty much what my grandparents said. And my parents. But I had a roommate who knew security systems, and I had a plan to work with the fences. I'd bring them what they wanted in return for information on my family's jewelry." He shrugged. "It worked."

"Somehow I doubt it was that easy."

"Actually, it was, but I had to work with some scary people to do it. They got the leads I needed in return for me picking up a few items on their shopping lists. The last two pieces led me to Detroit."

"So you really were a thief."

He conceded with a nod. "I like to think I was a thief with principles. I had one rule: I'd only take previously stolen items. Anyone who bought from legitimate dealers or artists was safe. I'd only steal from other thieves."

She supposed it was an important moral distinction, but not a safe one. "You must have made enemies."

"I would have if they'd known who I was. There's a member of the Russian Mafia in Detroit who taught me a lot of stuff I shouldn't know, and who keeps my secret. In turn, I don't tell anyone about the jewelry that ended up in his hands as a result of the tips he gave me. I stole for him, and he helped me find my family's possessions."

Something clicked in her memory. "Is that how you knew about the Pellinni Jewels? Because you were tracking down other valuable old jewelry?" He nodded. "So what did your grandmother lose? The Hernandez Jewels?"

He laughed. "Nothing exalted enough to have a name, but valuable enough to be attractive to their collectors. Being knowledgeable let me pose as a buyer and they gave me access to their collections. I found one of my grandmother's necklaces that way. The guy actually invited me in and showed it to me. I robbed him later."

She wondered if his family knew how much he'd gone through to find their jewelry. "Sounds like a dangerous life."

"It was." He gave her a hard look. "That's why I

want to keep you out of it. Exposing you to Sleazy was bad enough, and he was just the scum on the surface of a very deep, very dirty pond. There's only one good thing I got out of those years—an appreciation for art and culture. Which is why I like coming to this place." He tilted his head toward the window.

She peered through the slackening rain at the creamy stone facade of the Detroit Institute of Arts just before the car dipped into the underground parking structure. "The DIA?" She smiled. "Not a bad date, Hernandez. Plus they have a good cafeteria."

He nodded sagely. "Eat now, work it off later."

"Wow, such a smooth talker. You're sweeping me right off my feet." The embarrassing part was, it was true. It had been easier to pretend she didn't like him when she avoided him. These past few days had been more about pretending she wasn't constantly thinking about what it would be like to get naked with him.

He made sure she didn't stop thinking about it, too. He held her hand as they walked through the museum, occasionally stroking it with his thumb while pointing out the bright colors in a Van Gogh or the sense of movement in a Degas, as if he had no idea what he was doing to her. He didn't fool her, though. It was hours of foreplay, keeping her mind on physical sensations, and it worked. By the time they carried their trays to a table, she was so focused on him she barely noticed the people around them. She thought he was just as focused on her, so she was surprised to see him scanning the crowded tables in the cafeteria.

"Looking for someone you know?"

His gaze darted back to her. "No one important, just a couple old friends I noticed earlier."

"Really? Do you want to go say hello? I don't mind."

He smiled. "Perhaps friend is the wrong term. I recognized them, that's all. How's your lunch?"

His eyes searched the room again, settling on a table behind her. She lowered her sandwich, watching as something hard crept into his gaze. She didn't want to be obvious by turning to follow his stare, but something was up. She considered it: two people he knew but didn't want to talk to. And obviously didn't trust. In an art museum.

She inhaled sharply, nearly choking on her chicken salad. His brow creased with concern. "Are you okay?"

She nodded, and leaned across the table so he'd hear her whisper. "Are they art thieves?"

His long, dark lashes blinked in surprise. "Who?"

"The guys you're watching. Do you think they're planning a robbery?"

His lips curved upward. "You're talking about the big leagues, honey. I don't even know those kinds of people."

"Then why do you keep looking at them?"

His expression was nonchalant as he made a dismissive gesture. "It's nothing, just your self-appointed Colombian groupies. Guess they got that flat tire fixed."

Her throat tightened again and all that carefully constructed sexual tension drained away. "They followed us here?"

"Apparently. I couldn't be sure in the rain, but don't worry, I'll lose them once we leave." He stroked her cheek. "Hey, you can trust me. They won't be a problem."

It had to be a sign of how far they'd come, because something made her believe him. "Okay."

He beamed at her confidence, a sexy, riveting smile which pretty much restored most of her naughty thoughts.

Except for a few casual glances to keep track of their tail, she had his undivided attention as they toured the rest of the museum. Who knew a man's hand lightly rubbing the back of her neck could be erotic? The old woman who stood next to her as Janet stared at a contemporary painting and moaned softly must have wondered what she was missing in the splatters of paint.

By the time they left the museum she was ready to suggest the nearest hotel, but he was still following some master plan of his own as he pulled back into the early evening traffic.

"We can have dessert at the house, as soon as I lose those goons behind us." He drove with half his attention on the rearview mirror.

She decided he could handle the Colombians, and tried to concentrate on the rest of their evening. "I don't need dessert."

"I think you'll want this dessert."

If he'd planned it, this had to be something more than cake and ice cream. "What kind of dessert?"

"Whipped cream."

A fluffy pile of calories she usually preferred to skip. "On what?"

"You." He gave her a sly grin. "And me."

"Oh." She had to admit, it was intriguing. "I've never had that kind of dessert before."

"I'm not surprised. That husband of yours looked a bit stiff—and I don't mean where it counted."

She held back a laugh, choosing to sound indignant instead. "Banner wasn't the first man in my life. I have had some experience, you know."

"I see. With whipped cream?"

"Well, no—"

"What? Handcuffs and whips?"

"No! I just meant I'm not, you know, naïve." She thought about what he'd said and bit her cheek. Maybe she *was* naïve. "You aren't into stuff like bondage, are you?"

He leered, making her heart skid in her chest. "Scared?"

"No." She shifted in the bucket seat, considering how far she should trust him in this. According to Ellie, he'd dated a lot of women and was undoubtedly more experienced than she was. "Maybe."

He reached over to squeeze her hand. "Just whipped cream, sweetheart. Nothing kinky. Unless you call licking it off your breasts kinky. Or following a line up your thigh, licking slowly until I get to the top. Don't worry, I'll make sure I get every last bit of cream—everywhere." He turned his hot gaze on her.

Her heart nearly beat through her ribs. She swallowed and licked her lips, and swore her thighs were parting in anticipation. "I think I could eat a lot of dessert tonight."

His slow, crooked smile made her want to take him right there in the car.

She was suddenly in a hurry. "Have we lost our friends yet?"

"Not yet." He signaled his exit from the expressway, giving anyone who cared plenty of time to follow them.

"I hate to tell you, but that's not gonna do it." She watched the traffic behind them in the passenger's side mirror. "Which car, the black one behind us?"

"White SUV, four cars back." He made several more turns through a light industrial area, signaling each one in advance. The SUV was half a block behind them when they pulled into a lot and stopped at a tall chain-link fence topped with razor wire. Behind it she saw nothing but haphazardly parked rows of cars, most of them pretty disreputable looking.

"What is this place, a prison for cars?"

"Exactly. It's an impound lot." He rolled his window down and waved at a man behind the fence.

The man squinted, then broke into a smile. "Hey, Rocky!" He pushed a button on the fence and a gate slid open. Rocky rolled forward, meeting him halfway.

"Hey, Danny. I want you to meet Janet Aims."

"Hi." She leaned forward to see him better, smiling, like stopping by police impound lots was something she did every day.

Danny ducked his head and looked her over. "Hey, Janet. Nice to meet you." As he straightened she caught the nudge he gave Rocky's shoulder.

"Got a favor to ask you, Danny."

"You aren't here to pick up a car?"

"Nope, just passing through. That okay?"

"No problem." Danny raised his head and looked up and down the street. "That white Caddy?"

"Yup. Bad people, don't mess with them."

"Don't worry, I just work here. I don't know nothin'."

"Thanks, buddy." Rocky eased the car forward as the gate closed behind them. Waving, he headed down a row of cars that looked like the sloppy overflow from an outdoor concert.

She saw nothing ahead but more cars and another razor-topped chain-link fence. "I don't get it."

"Let's hope they don't, either. There's a back gate that lets out on another street. By the time they figure it out, we'll be long gone." He waved at a gangly kid with an earpiece who'd apparently just gotten orders to open the back gate for them. They cruised through, hit the street, and sped back toward the major roads.

"Won't they just wait for us at home?"

"I'm sure they will. But whose home? Mine? Yours? Elizabeth's?"

"So we've reduced the odds of them finding us."

"Better than that. We've got a place they don't know about—Jack and Ellie's house."

Safe, but a little weird. She really didn't want to make love in the same bed Ellie and Jack used. A big sexual buzzkill. "Um . . . I don't really want to have sex in my best friend's bed."

"Neither do I. They have a guest room."

"Oh." She smiled. "Not bad. And you need to water those plants."

"Then this is a necessary stop, isn't it?"

"Vital. Ellie loves that fern."

He parked in the empty spot in the garage, ensuring no one would see their car. All it took was one kiss and they stumbled into the house, kicking off shoes as they tried to kiss and walk at the same time.

"Wait," he said against her lips, sucking the lower one into his mouth before pulling away. "Refrigerator."

"Not again. I've already done the refrigerator thing. I want a bed."

He chuckled as he opened the door and pulled out a spray can. "Whipped cream."

"Oh." She was salivating already, picturing where she wanted to spread it on that hard body of his.

He yanked her back against him, kissing her hard and deep. She came up gasping for air and more than ready to play his game. "You asked for it, buddy." Grabbing his shirt in both hands, she jerked it open, sending buttons flying across the kitchen floor and parting the blue hibiscus flowers and green palm fronds to reveal a plane of tanned chest. She smiled.

"I hope you know how to sew."

"Give me that can. I'm feeling inspired."

Something sparked in his eyes and he didn't stop to ask questions. Giving it a shake, he held the aerosol can between them.

Holding up two fingers, she allowed him to spray them with a glob of the silky cold confection. She studied his chest like a master studying a blank canvas, then smeared a line of cream across his right nipple. Beneath the cold white stuff, his nipple tightened into a hard bud. She paused to admire it, then leaned in and ran her tongue over it, lapping at the tight nipple and savoring the sweetness in her mouth. Savoring, too, the warm yearning that blossomed below her stomach. "Ooh, I'm gonna like this."

"Jesus," he breathed. The can hit the counter. The next second her shirt came over her head and his hand pushed at her bra, bypassing the hooks and simply shoving it down to release an eager breast. "Perfect," he murmured, touching with one hand while the other reached blindly for the whipped cream and found it. He spritzed a dollop over her nipple.

She gasped at its cold touch. It quickly turned warm from the heat of her breast, and she burned as his mouth settled over her nipple and sucked hard. Fierce jolts of pleasure shot through her, settling between her legs in a pool of heat. She moaned, pushing into him, one hand holding his head to her while he suckled before releasing her and raising his eyes to hers in a smoldering gaze. "This is the best idea I ever had."

"I have a better one."

He treated her to a devilish smile, grabbed the whipped cream, and took her hand as he headed for the hallway. Seconds later she was standing in Ellie's guest room, one breast exposed, taking in the clean lines of dark furniture while he set the container on a night stand and flung aside a comforter. Without hesitating, he turned her around, unfastened her bra, flung it aside, and gently pushed her onto the bed.

She caught her breath and smiled up at him as he settled astride her. "Nice technique, Hernandez. Primitive but effective."

"Glad you approve."

She ran her hands up his chest and over his shoulders, appreciating his lean muscles. She could watch him with his shirt off all day and never get tired of the view.

"Hey, what's the tattoo on your shoulder mean?"

"Claw marks, because I was a cat burglar. Get it? I did it right before I embarked on my life of crime. It's embarrassing, but I used to be a bit cocky."

She laughed. "So what are you now?"

He held her gaze, something blazing deep within his eyes. "Confident. And incredibly competent."

He sprayed a dab of cream on one finger and held it in front of her.

She closed her mouth over it, making a show of sucking the cream off, then licking her lips. "Yum."

His dark eyes went black. "You're playing with fire, lady."

"Prove it." Not waiting for him, she reached out to unbutton his jeans and lower the zipper. The material stretched across his hips where he straddled her, effectively trapping the part she most wanted to set free. "You'll have to move for the next step. Oh, and I'll be needing that can."

His smile met hers. "You catch on quickly."

"I'm a fast learner."

"Uh-huh." His mind seemed to be elsewhere as he scanned her shoulders and bare breasts. His fingers followed, palms softly molding the sides while his thumbs brushed the tops of her nipples. She drew a sharp breath and closed her eyes, riding the wave of pleasure that built inside her. His hands continued downward, unfastening her jeans. "But I'm on top so it looks like I get to go first."

She arched her hips, allowing him to strip off her pants and panties in one tug. "Darn." She didn't even pretend to sound sincere.

He laughed, but the dark desire in his eyes banished any thoughts of boyishness in his expression. He was pure man. His hair was mussed from her fingers, arms corded as he held himself over her, chest hard, and the line below his open zipper even harder. She ran her hand along its length, just to remind him that she had plans, too.

His eyes turned to shadowed slits as he reached for the whipped cream. Hooking an arm beneath her knee, he spread her thighs apart, sprayed a blob of whipped cream on two fingers, and smeared a line from her knee to the edge of her dark curls. He looked at the cream left on his fingers as if it were the most interesting part of what he'd done. She bit her lip and watched, mesmerized. Just when she was certain he was going to offer it to her to lick clean, he lowered his hand and stroked it up her center.

Flares shot off between her legs and she struggled to keep her voice steady. "I hope you plan to do more than tease me with that."

"Sweetheart, that's not teasing. That's a promise."

She knew it as well as he did, and she loved how he made her feel like she was melting into the bed.

"Promises, *shmomis*—" She broke off on a gasp as his tongue licked along the whipped cream trail from her knee upward. Without pausing, he followed it to its sweet end. She couldn't think; all she could do was feel.

Her fingers grabbed for purchase, fisting first into the sheet, then his shoulders, as fireworks danced behind her closed eyes. She thought she might scream from the pleasure, but her throat closed up and all she could manage was a tiny squeak of delight as he pushed her legs open and drove every nerve ending to shattering ecstasy. Muscles clenched all the way down to her toes, rigid with delight, then went limp.

He raised his head, looking pleased with himself. "I keep my promises."

"No argument here," she managed. Raising a limp hand, she wiggled her fingers as if testing for nerve damage. "I believe I've momentarily lost my fine motor skills, so would you mind taking off those jeans and boxers for me?"

He laughed and got right to it. Before tossing the jeans, he pulled a string of three condoms out of his pocket.

"Not yet. I haven't had my dessert," she purred.

"I can't tell you how glad I am that you aren't on a diet."

Even if she were, she would have given it up on the spot. Pulling him down beside her, she raised to one elbow and took her turn with the whipped cream, first applying it with gentle strokes, then licking it off. He shuddered once, choked on an expletive, then groaned in surrender. Less than a minute later, he lifted her head and flipped her onto her back. "You're done."

"I was just getting into it."

"You're done or else I'll be done. And I have other plans." Since he was reaching for a condom, she wasn't about to argue the point.

She was more than ready, making room for him between her legs, gripping the headboard behind her in anticipation of the same energetic pace he'd set so far. Her breaths were already coming fast, her body impatient with need, aching to clench around him. He settled over her, took her mouth in a deep kiss, then slid inside her with one slow easy stroke.

And stopped. She felt hot and full, and whimpered with pleasure.

"God, you feel good," he groaned.

She gave him a another kiss. "I've heard it's even better if you move."

"Funny. You in a hurry?" He took one leisurely stroke, pushing hard against her, watching her.

She caught her breath in the rush of desire. "Yes!"

But then it would be over too fast. "I mean, no." But if he didn't move soon she'd die from sheer longing.

"Not thinking clearly?" He took another slow stroke and rubbed against her.

She moaned happily. "Guess not."

"Poor baby. How about if I drive this time and you don't have to think. But next time you're in charge."

"I can deal with that." Considering the liquid heat he ignited with each thrust, she'd agree to anything he suggested right now.

His lips curled into a cocky smile as he began a slow rhythm. Dipping his head, he nuzzled her neck with feathery kisses as he moved.

It was quite possibly heaven. She trembled as the first few jolts of pleasure shot through her. Surprise flickered at the intensity, and she could have sworn she saw the same glimmer of wonder in his eyes, but she quickly dismissed it. There was nothing mysterious about enjoying sex after going for so long without it. Especially if it was good sex. Very good sex. She refused to be distracted.

He moved faster and she followed his rhythm, allowing the mind-blowing sensations to drown any emotions beneath them. When he moved his hand between them and touched her, her last shred of coherent thought was gone. She tipped her head back as desire built to frantic purpose.

His ragged breaths matched hers. Tension showed in his jaw as he held back, waiting for her need to catch up with his. In the next breathless moment it did, and somehow he knew. He drove into her with the force she craved. She came hard, releasing a startled exclamation before wrapping him in a tight embrace as he shuddered and dropped his head into the cradle of her neck.

A contented groan vibrated against her. "That was definitely worth waiting for."

The dreamy haze cleared as a sliver of concern pierced her languor. Worth waiting for? She ran his comment past her dulled brain one more time. "We just did it yesterday."

"Not that, we didn't."

She didn't want to ask him what he meant, because she was afraid it had something to do with that moment when physical pleasure got tangled up with emotion, and everything had suddenly felt brighter, and warmer, and *more right* than it ever had before.

It was more than she had expected.

And she was still shaking.

Chapter
Eleven

F ive hours later Janet was pleasantly sore, exhausted, and more pleased with her life than at any time in the past eighteen months. Rocky was a passionate and experienced lover, better than she could have imagined, even if he did have a few misguided ideas about her. Like his notion that marrying a psychopathic liar said nothing about her ability to choose men. He obviously gave her too much credit. But since that seemed to be his only major flaw, she was willing to overlook it.

Rocky dropped her off at the Westfield mansion with still-damp tresses after a hasty shower at Ellie's house. She'd done a half-assed job drying it, what with putting the freshly laundered sheets back on the bed and still being a bit foggy after he'd blown her mind. As they stood at the front door, he reached up to rearrange a few tendrils near her face, like a fussy hair dresser making final adjustments.

She raised a self-conscious hand to her hair. "Does it look awful? Do you think Libby will know that my night out ended with a shower? That kid notices every-thing, especially if it has to do with sex."

"It's fine," he told her, fluffing a spot over her ear and smiling at the results. "I've developed an affection for that tousled look. Makes it look like you just got out of bed." His smile turned roguish. "With me."

She slapped his hand away. "Grow up." But she couldn't help indulging a thrill of delight at his smug and very masculine look of conquest. She was feeling a bit smug herself, like the plain Jane high school girl who somehow snagged the popular quarterback.

"Thanks for taking me out, Rocky. The DIA was fun."

"Anytime."

"Good." She gave him a warm kiss. "See you in the morning?"

"Except then."

She blinked, surprised at how quickly she'd been rejected.

"I have to work tomorrow," he explained. "I've been putting off clients all week, and I need to get a few security jobs done. Maybe tomorrow night?"

"Sure."

He drew her in for a long, soulful kiss that probably curled a few more hairs on her head. "I'll call you, babe. 'Night."

"Good night." Damn, she really had to get over this feeling that her day wouldn't be as much fun unless he was with her. Surely she wasn't *that* far gone.

Janet slipped in the front door as quietly as possible, careful not to draw attention to her arrival. She'd prefer to get to her room without having to answer a dozen well-intentioned questions about her evening. She'd nearly made it when Libby came around the corner of the upstairs hall, rushing forward as she spotted her.

"Janet! You're finally home!"

Great, the girl had been lying in wait. Maybe she could plead exhaustion and make a quick escape. "Hey, Lib. How's it going?"

"Awful." Her huge brown eyes expressed her misery, wide and worried.

Janet paused. It wasn't the reaction she'd expected from the perpetually bubbly teenager. "I'm sorry to hear that." She took a closer look as Libby stopped in front of her, with her hands tucked deep in her jean pockets and her shoulders hunched beneath her glossy brown hair. Concern showed in her eyes and the pinched corners of her mouth. The kid was obviously miserable. And worse, she looked scared.

"Come here." Janet grabbed Libby's arm and pulled her into the bedroom, closing the door behind them. Turning the girl to face her, she dipped her head down to force eye contact from Libby. "What's wrong?"

Libby shrugged and bit her lip. A dozen possible fears ran through Janet's mind and chilled her to the bone. Was something wrong with Elizabeth? No, she would have gotten a call. Bad news from Jack and Ellie? Traveling through Europe by car, train, and who knew what else exposed them to a frightening list of possible accidents. A tragic encounter between the cats and the young dog? They'd left Elizabeth with a menagerie of pets perfectly primed to explode. Janet's mind invented disaster after disaster and her stomach clenched nervously as she waited.

The girl finally pushed aside her curtain of hair and peered at Janet. "Did you hear them when you came in?" Libby's near whisper made the question seem almost sinister.

"Hear who?" Janet had snuck through the foyer and up the stairs as fast as she could. "I didn't hear anyone."

Libby's lips pressed together before she spit out the answer. "Grandma and Grandpa B. They've been fighting for *hours*."

"Oh." Rocky had mentioned a disagreement between them, and Elizabeth had seemed a bit more edgy the past couple days. She doubted they'd literally been arguing for hours, but it definitely had been long enough to upset their granddaughter. "All couples have disagreements," she told Libby. "It doesn't mean they don't love each other."

As soon as she'd said it, she realized what a weak platitude it was for a girl with Libby's background. Starting life abandoned by a drug-addicted mother had been just her first disadvantage. She had grown up with maternal grandparents who didn't have the money or inclination to raise another child, leaving Libby with a ton of insecurities. If her mother's younger sister hadn't shouldered the responsibility of raising the girl no one else wanted, Janet didn't want to think about what path Libby's life could have taken. Finding Jack had been lucky. Not all birth fathers would have offered the unconditional love and security she'd found with him, and Libby knew it. People couldn't always be trusted to do the right thing. This kid had seen the worst life could offer; she wasn't going to buy into hearts and rainbows.

She rubbed Libby's arms, hoping the physical contact would be reassuring. "Come on, let's sit down. Tell me why you're so worried." She led the way to the bed, thinking they could settle against the headboard for an intimate chat, but Libby dropped to the floor instead, legs folded and back propped against the bed. Janet smiled to herself; she'd forgotten that floors were the same as furniture for thirteen-year-olds. She sat down, too.

"So what's going on? Are they yelling at each other?" As hard as it was to imagine Elizabeth Westfield raising her voice, she knew it would be scary for Libby if she overheard something like that.

"My grandmother doesn't yell," Libby stated flatly.

So much for that theory. "Is Ben yelling at her?" That was a little easier to picture, even though she'd never seen it happen. But she had seen him get furious over some of the things Banner had done, and knew he could be intimidating.

"Not exactly. He doesn't have to yell. You can tell he's mad."

She could believe that. "Do you know what they're mad about?"

"Yeah, I listened for a long time." She said it without a trace of shame, as if she had every right to eavesdrop. "Grandpa Ben wants them to get married, but he won't live in this house. He says it's pretentious—I looked it up, and I guess he's right. Plus it's Banner's house, so he says it's a conflict of interest for the chief of police to live here. He wants Grandma to sell it and buy something smaller so they can start fresh."

It was hard to imagine Elizabeth selling the Westfield mansion. Janet knew the elaborate house and grounds had been Banner's idea, but Elizabeth had always seemed to belong here. Maybe because she'd grown up with wealth it was difficult to imagine her living without all the trappings, right down to the butler and the koi pond.

"I guess your grandmother likes it here," Janet said.

Libby shrugged. "Maybe."

The indifferent response surprised her. "Isn't that why she doesn't want to sell the house?"

"No." Libby's voice grew more miserable. "It's because of me."

She would have refused to believe it, but Libby was more perceptive than the average kid. And the crushed look on her face wasn't due to some imagined problem. She almost hated to ask. "What did you hear?"

Libby picked at the carpet as she talked. "Grandma thinks people might hate me for my background. 'Cause I lived in Detroit and 'cause my dad was in jail, and mostly 'cause Uncle Banner did all those things and will probably go to prison for the rest of his life. Everyone at the club whispers about her and says our family lost all its money because of Banner, and we might lose the company, too."

"That's not true, Libby."

She shrugged. "That's what people think."

"It doesn't matter what people think."

"It does to Grandma." Janet couldn't argue with that. "She grew up here and she says appearances are everything. And now our lives are a train wreck, and everyone in Bloomfield Hills is watching."

Janet could see how that would mortify Elizabeth. "How does that affect you?"

"Grandma said I won't get invited to the right places or meet the right people. I don't even care about that stuff, Janet! But she said I don't realize how people think, and it's more important than I know."

Shit. That sounded just like Elizabeth Payton West-field. Libby hadn't been kidding when she said it was because of her. And the hell of it was, Elizabeth had a point.

Janet hadn't thought about it before, but she'd been raised in a well-to-do community, too, and knew what Elizabeth said was true. For many people, money equaled status. And for a kid with Libby's question-able background to fit in and be accepted, it took a lot of money. It wasn't right and it wasn't fair, but it was a fact. Libby shouldn't suffer because her earlier life had been less than perfect, or because she had the misfor-tune of being related to Banner—but she would.

Though not with everyone. Janet had no doubt some shallow and vain people would reject Libby, but Janet had lived in this town long enough to know there were plenty of open-minded people who would never judge Libby by those standards. Elizabeth had to know that, too. So, her reasons for not wanting to sell the house went deeper than her granddaughter's social life. Startling as it seemed, beneath that confident exterior, Elizabeth buried a lot of insecurity.

Libby raised suddenly watery eyes and asked, "Do you think Ginny's parents won't like me if Grandma sells the house?"

Janet's heart nearly broke. She didn't have the first clue who Ginny's parents were and what they were like, but she put an arm around Libby's shoulder and reassured her. "Oh, honey, of course not. They know you're a good person, and they'd never be that mean."

Libby chewed the inside of her cheek, considering. "Grandma thinks so."

As much as Janet wanted to stay out of it, she was

going to have to have a talk with Elizabeth. "I guarantee that your grandma is exaggerating. She's just worried about you and wants to be sure no one talks trash about her precious granddaughter."

A reluctant smile touched Libby's mouth. "I don't think Grandma knows what that means."

She faked a shocked expression. "Are you kidding me? She and her girls are always sittin' around the club, givin' props and dissin' the bitches. Don't tell me Elizabeth Westfield isn't down with the talk."

Libby giggled and Janet relaxed at the small concession. Sighing, she got to her feet. "It's been a long day, kiddo, and I'm going to get ready for bed. How about you go get into your PJs and come back here? We can have a sleepover and talk about boys."

That one earned her a grateful smile. "Okay."

Libby was almost out the door when it occurred to Janet that the room was a little too quiet. "Hey, Lib. Have you seen Jingles?"

"He and Fluff are watching Freddie in the kitchen. I think they're all going to be friends 'cause Freddie wags his tail and barks at them, but Grandma said he has to sleep in the cage tonight. The cats keep walking by to check him out."

Flaunting their freedom. She winced. Between the competitive cats, the clueless dog, and the feuding grandparents, tomorrow was going to be interesting.

Interesting wasn't how Rocky would have described the next morning. "Fucked up" was more like it. He stared at his four flat tires and ground his teeth.

He knew who was responsible for the deep slashes and that there was nothing he could do about it. The message was clear: what you do to us, you get back—times four. No doubt Rocky's security system had restricted their efforts to his car. Thank God Janet was beyond their reach.

Getting new tires set his schedule back two hours. By the time he finished the backlog of Red Rose Security jobs and headed over to see Janet, it was already dark out.

He ran up the front steps to the Westfield mansion, then stopped midway as the door opened and noise poured out, a rolling mixture of laughter, barks, and excited squeals, followed by Ben Thatcher's heavy footsteps. Slamming the door behind him, the police chief stomped toward Rocky.

One look at Ben's expression and he stepped aside, leaving far more room than necessary for the chief to pass on the wide stairway. Instead, Ben stopped one step above Rocky, hands on hips, ready for a confrontation, and leveled a stare that had surely intimidated many a criminal. Rocky swore under his breath, realizing that he was about to catch the backlash of another lover's quarrel between Elizabeth and Ben.

"I hear you're the one I have to thank for bringing another goddamned animal into that house," Ben snapped.

Rocky took a judicious step back, determining how much evasion he could get away with. Not much, probably, since Ben was glaring at him like he was smuggling gerbils in his pockets. He held up both hands, palms out. "Hey, it's just one homeless puppy. And it's temporary."

"That's what animal shelters are for. Ever hear of them?"

"Um—"

Ben stabbed at his chest with a blunt finger. "You might want to think of that next time some sorry little dog rolls its eyes at you, instead of running right over here to the Elizabeth Westfield Animal Shelter."

Rocky knew he should keep his mouth shut and let Ben vent, but it was an unfair accusation. "Weren't you the one who suggested bringing over more animals?" he challenged.

Ben stopped mid-rant, head cocked and one eye squinting a laser beam at him. *Damn.* Rocky hoped the man wasn't carrying his gun. "That's right, I did." Ben nodded. "My mistake. So you know what? Why don't you just find a few more cats and dogs in need of homes and bring 'em on over. The mangier the better. Introduce them to the good life. I'm sure if you cruise the alleys you can find plenty." His finger jabbed back toward the front door. "Let her see that turning that house into a goddamned zoo won't make any difference. She'll be doing our granddaughter more harm than good by hanging on to Banner's house."

Rocky couldn't think of a single safe thing to say, so he tried a tight smile.

Ben shook his head in disgust and started down the steps. But before Rocky could breathe a sigh of relief, the police chief turned back.

"Hey." He barked it like a drill sergeant. "You happen to see Janet's Colombian shadows last night?"

"No. They followed us from the DIA, but we dodged them." And he hadn't given them another thought, with all the fun distractions that followed.

"Huh. I figured."

That pricked his curiosity. "Why?"

"I suspect they're the ones responsible for a couple smash and grabs at jewelry stores last night. One in Troy, one in Novi. Made off with about fifty grand altogether. They either got tired of waiting for Janet to lead them to what they want, or they had a little temper tantrum over you two shaking their tail. Maybe a little of both."

He knew Ben wouldn't hold him responsible for what the Colombians did, so it must be the man's generally nasty mood that made it sound accusatory. "Was anyone hurt?"

"A store manager got beaten up by one of the guys. The asshole seemed to go out of his way to do it, too."

"Strange," he muttered, hoping like hell it wasn't some sort of skewed revenge for what he'd done, but suspecting it was.

Ben looked him up and down. "I'd strongly advise against taking that girl anywhere right now. If these guys are getting impatient, I want to know she's in a safe place."

"Good idea." Janet was going to hate it.

"You just remember, Hernandez, I'm counting on you to keep her safe." Ben drilled him with a hard look, then stomped off.

Ben was right; Janet's safety came first. If they couldn't sneak off to Jack and Ellie's house again, at least he could spend a few hours with her here. His attraction to her had never been all about sex, anyway. He'd admired her spirit since the day they'd met. She'd escaped an attempt on her life, then fought back. Not against the paid Colombian hitmen, which would probably be suicidal, but against her crazy husband who had orchestrated the plot. The smart thing probably would have been to let the DEA and FBI and God knows how many other alphabet agencies try to prove Banner's guilt. They might have even succeeded after a few years. Instead, she went after him herself with nothing more than a bumbling, well-intentioned friend and a whole lot of anger. She'd succeeded, too, and Rocky had fallen for her on the spot.

But now he was determined to keep her safe. As long as the Colombians were stalking her and someone was still looking for the rest of the Pellinni Jewels, his sex life was on hiatus.

Rocky half expected Mr. Peters to answer the door armed with a water rifle and packing a spare tank on his back. The boring black suit was almost a disappointment.

"Good evening, Roberto." Elizabeth appeared from the direction of the living room. If she'd been upset by her conversation with Ben, she'd regained her composure nicely. "Should I have you frisked for kittens?"

"No ma'am, no kittens. Not even a flea."

"Then I believe you're welcome. Janet is downstairs with Libby."

"I guess that means you're rejecting me."

She shook her head. "Ah, Roberto, you have a remarkable talent for flirting."

He grinned, recognizing *flirting* as a euphemism for *bullshit*. "It's a gift," he agreed. "But sadly underappreciated. Maybe Janet and Libby will fall for it."

"Oh, I think they already have."

He smiled, not sure if that was good or bad, and headed for the staircase.

The spa, bar, and rec room on the lower level were deserted, but the door to the home theater was closed.

He opened it into a dark room with a movie playing on the large TV screen. From the center of three rows of reclining chairs, Janet raised a hand and waved him over, while Libby called out, "Close the door!"

On the screen, a pretty red-haired actress hugged a stuffed animal and whined to her friend, "But he said he loved me. How am I supposed to know if he's lying?" Chick flick—he should have guessed.

He walked down the inclined floor to the middle row, where he was nearly knocked over by the furry critter that lunged toward him, dancing on hind legs and whining.

"Hey there, Adolf buddy." He pushed the pup down and gave him some friendly thumps on the shoulder.

"His name's Freddie," Libby offered without taking her eyes off the screen.

"Much better. Hi, Freddie."

"Shhh," Libby hissed. "Sit down."

He slid obediently into the seat next to Janet, whispered, "Hi," and leaned over to kiss her before settling back in the plush chair.

On the other side of Janet, Libby bent forward, eyes wide with surprise. "You kissed her."

He gave her a blank look. "Did not."

"Yes, you did. I saw it."

"Hush," he told her. "This is my favorite part of the movie. I always cry."

She raised her eyebrows and gave Janet a look that said, *You will tell me all about this later.* Since Janet seemed amused, he took her hand and conspicuously held it.

They watched in silence for several minutes, during

which Libby checked out the handholding with furtive glances. She finally turned to them with a sly smile. "You want me to leave so you guys can make out?"

"Sure, would you?"

"As if."

Janet nudged his arm and gave him a "what the hell are you doing" stare. He wasn't sure, but he thought he was trying out the idea of them as a couple, bouncing it off Libby's dependably honest personality. He liked the result. Libby's only objection seemed to be that she hadn't been told directly. He smiled to himself, convinced they could take this thing public. If Janet agreed. It was a big "if."

He tried to follow the movie, even though the only good part was being able to hold Janet's hand while the clueless redhead made one bad decision after another. He was actually relieved twenty minutes later when his cell phone rang.

"Outside," Libby and Janet said together without taking their eyes off the screen.

Gladly. He looked at the caller ID as the theater door closed behind him. "Hi, Ben. What's up?"

"Thought you'd like some good news. We picked up the two guys who've been tailing Janet. Got enough to hold 'em for forty-eight hours."

"Great!" Without the Colombians watching for an opportune moment to strike, he'd have Janet out of here within a minute of hanging up the phone.

"Yeah. That's the good news."

Suspicion clouded the happy scenarios that were already running through his mind. "What's the bad news?"

"The gun you took off them wasn't the one used in

the pawnshop murder in Detroit. Neither was the gun we found in their car."

Shit. "That was pretty fast for ballistics results."

"Didn't need to do 'em. They're carrying forty-fives. The kid was shot with a thirty-two. It was a long shot anyway; guns aren't their style. The feds say these guys like to be a little more hands-on. Besides, we had 'em under surveillance during the probable hours when the pawnshop kid was murdered."

Damn. Someone else had killed Sleazy. It wasn't hard to imagine that Sleazy had another shady customer, but it was unlikely both would come back to bite him at the same time. If his deal with Banner had stirred up the Colombians, then most likely it had stirred up someone else, too. The Colombians would be looking for diamonds, their usual method of laundering money. Which meant, just as he'd expected, someone else was looking for the Pellinni Jewels. Which meant—

"Janet is still in danger," Ben stated for him. "She had the necklace, so they're going to assume she has the rest of the collection. And this guy is willing to kill to get it. Didn't think the damn things were that impressive myself."

"Trust me, they are to collectors."

"Well, if someone is that desperate to get them, he won't give up just because he didn't find them the first time he searched her home."

"I know."

"We're releasing her place as a crime scene, but you can't let her move back in."

"I know."

"They might even be looking for a way to get into Liz's place, as long as she's staying there."

"I know, Ben. The house is pretty secure already, but I'll talk to Elizabeth about it and make sure she increases the security." He doubted she'd be open to any suggestions coming from Ben right now.

Ben grumbled, "Thanks," before saying good-bye. Rocky closed the phone as Janet and Libby walked out, Freddie bounding after them. Libby clapped her hands and chased the dog around the rec room. Rocky sensed she'd had a sudden attack of self-consciousness and was now avoiding him and Janet.

He watched Libby while saying in a low voice to Janet, "Your Colombians are in temporary police custody. Want to get out of here for a while?" He skipped mentioning the mysterious jewel thief. If the guy was watching Janet, he'd be interested in breaking into places when she wasn't there, not when she was. In Rocky's experience, most thieves would prefer to obtain their pieces without ever seeing, much less threatening, the owners. If the guy still didn't find what he was looking for—well, they'd worry about that later.

The idea of freedom lit up Janet's face, with an added sparkle of what he hoped was lust. "Yes!"

He smiled and called out to Libby, "Janet and I are going for a drive. We'll see you later."

"Okay." She didn't look up from playing with Freddie.

He didn't believe her; it wasn't okay.

Janet caught his worried look. "Three's company," she murmured, confirming his thoughts.

He nodded and held up a finger. "One minute." Crossing the room, he stopped beside Libby as she bent over, petting Freddie and acting as if she didn't know he was there.

"Hey, Lib."

"What?" She straightened, looking a little flushed.

Most of the time he felt like an uncle to his best friend's daughter, but right now she seemed more in need of a big brother. "Come here." When she hesitated he forced the issue and tugged her toward him and wrapped her in a hug. For a couple seconds she remained stiff, then softened and hugged him back.

"What's that for?" she said against his chest.

Setting her back, he waited for her eyes to meet his. "For being cool about me and Janet."

She shrugged. "Yeah, well, it was bound to happen."

The resignation in her voice made his smile slip. "What do you mean?"

"You know. She's so pretty and nice, and you're always dating pretty girls, so it figures you'd add her to the list."

Alarm bells rang in his head. He hadn't seen that one coming, but he should have. He couldn't even remember how many times he'd gone to Jack and Ellie's house for a backyard barbeque with a casual date, or stopped by to pick something up while a woman waited in the car. More than he cared to count. Even if they hadn't meant much to him, he should have realized showing up with a different woman so often would make an impression on a highly observant teenage girl—especially when he was aware that her friendship bordered on a semicrush she was still learning how to handle.

God, he was dense. And Libby was more mature than he'd given her credit for. She wasn't feeling rejected. She was worried about *Janet* eventually being rejected. By him.

Deliberately turning his back on Janet, he wrapped

an arm around Libby's shoulder and put his head near hers. "Lib, I have to tell you something, but I don't want you to tell anyone else. Not yet."

She looked suspicious. "Maybe. Tell me first."

He couldn't help smiling at her caution. "I know you're worried about Janet, but you don't have to be. She's not like anyone else I've been out with. Janet's different."

"No kidding. She's way better."

"Yes, she is. I'm not about to screw it up."

She gave him a skeptical look. "Promise?"

"Promise."

"Good." Her stern expression could have come from his own mother. She folded her arms, a younger version of her authoritative grandmother. "But why should I believe you?"

He looked back at Janet, who stood with hands in her pockets, waiting, a hesitant smile on her beautiful face, wondering what he was saying to Libby.

The truth hit him—because he loved her.

He actually wasn't that surprised. He'd never been so infatuated with a woman before, and Janet Aims had more than lived up to his fantasies. But fantasies were just part of the chase. In the light of the morning after, they tended to wear off. Not this time, though. That didn't surprise him either. With Janet he only wanted more. What *did* surprise him was the urge to rip apart any man who stood in his way. He hadn't known he could love that quickly or that deeply. And he knew telling her would risk scaring her off forever.

He couldn't tell Libby. Not yet, not before he'd told Janet. He understood that on a cellular level. Janet would *not* appreciate having someone else hear it first. Actually, she wouldn't appreciate hearing it at all.

"Because she means a lot to me." He put as much sincerity in it as he could. Libby searched his face, her narrow gaze unnervingly mature. He had the feeling she already understood men all too well, and could categorize them by acceptable and unacceptable behaviors. He very much wanted to be one of the good ones.

Her expression gradually softened to something kind and gentle. "Good luck," she told him. "I hope she feels the same way."

A tiny quiver of panic shot down his back, shaking his confidence. Libby knew Janet well. "You think she might not?"

Libby shrugged, unconcerned with the possibility of his future heartbreak. "It's always a risk, isn't it?"

He looked at her as if she'd suddenly grown a tail. "God, you're tough. I think I feel sorry for the man who falls in love with you."

As if he'd complimented her, she said, "Really?"

"Definitely. Poor bastard." He tousled her hair lightly to counteract the joking insult, even though she didn't seem to take it as one. She couldn't have looked more satisfied as they left. His last glimpse was of Libby firmly instructing Freddie to "sit," while pushing his bottom into place. The pup wriggled but stayed, adoring eyes on Libby's face.

Rocky couldn't help but wonder how many men would be in Freddie's position before Libby found one who would ignore her orders, then choose to stay on his own initiative. Probably more than he cared to know. "Poor bastard" was right.

Chapter
Twelve

Janet thought the day would never end. After chaperoning nose-to-nose introductions, she and Libby had spent the afternoon refereeing Freddie's exuberant pursuit of kitty friendship. The outcome was still pending. And Elizabeth had conveniently found reasons to leave the house, so Janet hadn't been able to corner her about Libby's insecurities. It'd been her primary concern right up until Rocky walked into the room and kissed her, wiping all thought from her mind. She was pathetic, like an addict getting her fix.

He probably wouldn't mean so much to her if he didn't represent her only chance to get out of the house, she told herself. It was a bonus that he was fun to be with and, as Libby's friend said, cute in a bad way. *Oh hell, who was she kidding?* He was downright dangerous, and any woman with hormones knew it. But the real danger with Rocky was an emotional attachment that would just get her hurt in the end.

That danger was especially high tonight, judging by the hooded looks he kept shooting her way as he drove. She smiled, recognizing the route he was taking. "Jack and Ellie's house?"

"Of course. I'm really worried about that fern being lonely while they're gone."

"Oh, me, too," she assured him.

"But if you don't mind, I'd like to stop at my place first, just to make sure nothing happened today. I'd like to think Easy Joey would give up on breaking in, but when the guy thinks he has a point to prove, nothing will dissuade him."

"Okay." She was content to let him lead tonight.

She watched him as he drove, not even trying to hide her interest. She noticed the way his hands held the wheel and imagined them touching her with the same casual competence. Then she noticed his legs, recalling the hard muscles of his thighs as he knelt between hers. It nearly made her blush, but it was impossible to ignore. She was obsessed, completely tuned in to his body and how he felt. Beside her, on top of her, inside her.

"If you keep looking at me like that, I'm going to pull over right here."

"Just watch the road. I can watch whatever I want."

His look promised payback.

Rocky kept Janet close as he checked out his alarm and the first floor. She let him check the upstairs alone while she poked through his CD collection and bookshelves. The man certainly had a broad range of interests. She wandered back to the kitchen, where memories hit her. Not visions of the miniature explosion in the sink, but the thrill of being pressed against his refrigerator while he drove her crazy with desire.

She remembered every touch, her body burning again as she did. She glanced at the kitchen counters, distracted by what he'd promised to do on them. Or on the floor.

She stood next to the countertop, stroking the granite, gauging the height. *Nah, it could never work.*

"Interesting thoughts?" He stood behind her with his arms crossed, his hip cocked against the stove.

She smiled. If he didn't already know what she was thinking, he hadn't been paying attention. "It's too high."

"Maybe you're just not creative enough."

"Whoa. Is that a challenge?"

"Could be." He moved toward her, looking her over. His gaze changed as she watched, becoming hypnotic, his body moving as stealthily as a cat on the prowl.

She waited until he stood in front of her, so close she could feel the heat of his body inches from her own. She licked her lips. "I don't know what you're thinking, but if you lead, I'll bet I can follow."

"Bet you can," he agreed, bending to nip at the delicate skin beneath her ear, sending shivers all the way down to her fingertips.

She tried to replicate the maneuver, but he moved his head and her lips hit air. "Uh-uh," he said, giving her a thoughtful smile. "You don't get to play this time." Before she could protest, he slipped his hands around her waist and boosted her onto the corner of the counter above the lazy Susan. He pushed between her legs and leaned into her, holding her hands to the countertop. Her heart sped up a few dozen beats.

He leaned closer, his chest touching hers. "I know

you said you hate me, but I'm starting to think you lied."

"That's just the pheromones." She dismissed the subject. "Are you planning to have your way with me or not?"

His smile was tolerant. "It's more than pheromones."

Because it felt dangerous, she hedged. "What makes you think so?"

"I can feel your heart pounding."

No kidding. She was surprised the whole counter wasn't vibrating. "That's because you're so annoying. You gonna make a move here?"

He clicked his tongue disparagingly. "You're too impatient. Making love is an art."

She was tempted to correct him, to say they were having sex, not making love, but he was kissing her neck and unbuttoning her top. She didn't want to interrupt. Besides, if the man was willing to put enough dedication and focus into sex to call it an art, she wasn't about to argue.

He popped the front closure of her bra with a smile. "Easy access. Were you planning ahead?"

"Darn right," she managed before sucking in her breath as his mouth explored. His hands did, too, holding, caressing, and finally drifting down to her waistband. She arched back, doing her bit to help. While he opened the snap at her waist, she ran her hands through his hair. Desire and affection and need mixed together in hot waves. She tipped her head against the cabinet and moaned. As if it was a signal, his mouth came back to hers and he took the sound into himself. She opened to every touch, feeling as if he was peeling back layer after layer until she was laid bare.

Bare. Only one of them was bare. With urgent whimpers she pulled at his shirt, needing to feel his chest against hers. He understood, and tugged it off, her tender nipples against his chest.

"Oh, yes," she groaned.

"Hold onto me." He pulled her closer and she held his shoulders, not knowing what he wanted. In the next second his hands slipped beneath her bottom, taking her unfastened shorts with them. He set her back on the counter as he dropped them to the floor.

His fingers were on her, probing and stroking, while his gaze held hers. "I love when your eyes get all soft and hazy like that," he murmured.

She caught a few panting breaths while she worked at his belt and zipper. "Glad to oblige your sexual quirks."

He pulled her forward, fitting her against him. The important parts were evident even through his pants, and still a couple inches off. "You're right, this doesn't work," he told her.

She clamped her legs around him, throbbing and desperate for relief. "I gotta tell you, that's an even bigger disappointment now than it was a few minutes ago."

"Hang on."

She clung to him as he pulled her off the counter and walked a few short steps to the kitchen table. The smooth wood pressed against her bottom as he set her down, feet dangling over the edge.

She fixed startled eyes on him. "On the table?"

"Why not?" He was making quick work of stripping

off his pants and shoes, and putting on the condom he pulled from his pocket.

She giggled nervously. "Because you eat here?"

He gave her an appreciative look from head to toe. "Believe me, dinner will never be the same again." He pressed her back as he said it, propping one leg on a chair and hovering over her. "In fact, maybe kitchen tables were made for this. I think we've found the right height."

She didn't have to look to know he was right; she could feel him hot and hard and poised at just the right spot between her thighs. She circled him with her hand just to watch his eyes grow dark as they closed halfway.

"You know what I love about you?"

He was suddenly still. "What?"

"Your eyelashes. I'm a sucker for long lashes."

She thought he'd smile, but he didn't, simply watching her as his hands spread her thighs. "The curse of the Hernandez genes. Dreamy eyes." He pushed against her.

"Mmm," she said, appreciating the pressure and wanting more. Moving her hand aside, he rubbed himself against her while she closed her eyes and fisted her hands, lost in the sensation.

"Rocky."

She opened her eyes. "Please," she whispered. "Now."

His gaze steady on her own, he slipped inside her.

Warmth filled her, flowing to every limb, followed by a deep restlessness.

She had to move, but her damp skin stuck to the table. He moved for them, turning the vague, restless feeling into something tighter and heavier, an energy that burned until it was nothing but raw urgency beating in time with her pulse. Every stroke was too much and not enough. His arms were braced on the table beside her, and she gripped his wrists, using the leverage to increase the force of each stroke, and urge him to pump harder.

She gasped as the first spasms hit, then gave in to the mindless bliss, riding her orgasm as he pushed harder and faster until he reached the same mindblowing peak. With one final thrust, he went still. She could feel his breath on her neck, and she went limp on the table.

"I can't believe we just did that." She reached up to stroke his face affectionately, feeling the stubble on his cheek. "But I'm definitely accepting any future dinner invitations from you."

He smiled. "You're the only one on the guest list."

"I think you mean on the menu."

His lopsided smile was back. "Even better." He licked her neck until she was helpless with laughter.

"Get off and help me up! No, wait," she ordered, pulling him back for a long kiss. "Okay. Go slowly; I don't want to leave too much skin behind."

He did, grinning. "I guess we don't need to go to Jack and Ellie's house after all. Unless you'd like to use me again."

She'd been the one to insist that she was only using him for sex, so it shouldn't have struck her the way it did. But what he'd said made the past fifteen minutes sound crude and dirty. That wasn't at all the way it had felt. She wasn't sure what it was, but she no longer wanted Rocky to think she was using him.

"Don't say that."

"Say what?"

"That I'm using you. It doesn't sound right."

"But you were the one—"

"I know. Just don't. Please."

"Okay." He pulled her close, her breasts pressed against his hard chest, his arms holding her tight. His kiss was tender, and she knew he meant it to soothe her even though he didn't say so.

She kissed him back, wondering how everything had turned upside down in such a short time. Words that hadn't bothered her before sounded different now. What had begun with strict boundaries seemed to have crossed them when she wasn't looking. An uneasy flutter in her chest made her pull away. Stepping out of the circle of his arms, she put some distance between them.

"I want to wash up."

"Use the upstairs bathroom; it's bigger."

Checking to see that the window blinds were drawn, she scampered upstairs, well aware that his gaze followed every jiggle and bounce. Typical Rocky—he'd always been open about his attraction to her. It used to make her uncomfortable, but she had to admit it gave her a little thrill of power to catch his appreciative stares. And there was nothing wrong with that.

Except there was. In fact, it was in complete conflict with the code she'd sworn to follow ever since her narrow escape from Banner: Never trust her feelings. They'd led her astray before, into a marriage to an emotionally detached, calculating man who was most likely a psychopath.

She tried to block her thoughts, but they kept

battering her, insisting on being heard. Spying a radio on the bathroom counter, she turned it on, bouncing loud rock music off the tiled walls while she turned the shower on full blast, drowning out the little voice inside her head.

He nearly missed the alarm. The rush of water upstairs had covered up the tiny, intermittent beep from the security box. If he hadn't walked into the laundry room to drop a washcloth and hand towel into the laundry basket, he never would have noticed the blinking red light. Even then, he double-checked the circuits before coming back to that one alarm, forced to admit that only one circuit had been broken—the one for the skylight in the upstairs bathroom.

It could be a short. With all the steam that must be billowing up there, some of it might have seeped into a loose connection and tripped the alarm. He might have even talked himself into believing the light had been blinking all day with no one there to see it, except he'd checked the box when they first came in less than an hour ago. The sentry light had been off. And he'd bet his life it had been off when Janet walked upstairs, naked and flushed from making love, and closed herself in the bathroom.

The acid deep in his gut began a steady burn. From upstairs he heard water beating down and music blaring; it was more than enough to drown out the sound of a skylight being forced open.

The knob squealed as she shut the water off. Condensation dripped down the frosted glass of the shower door. Sliding it open, she wiped the water from her eyes and groped for the towel she'd left on the bar outside the door. Her searching hand found a bare, hairy arm.

She inhaled a scream. It tried to come out, but the hand covering her mouth wouldn't let it. With another frantic swipe at her eyes, she blinked.

"Rocky!" It came out muffled behind his hand.

"*Shhh.*" He held a finger to his lips. With the other hand he reached for the radio and turned it off. In the sudden silence she could hear the last tiny gurgle of water going down the drain.

"What the hell are doing? You scared me to death." She whispered harshly, resenting that she didn't know why she had to. The sound barely seemed to carry through the heavy steam anyway.

Instead of answering, he wrapped her in the big bath towel he had ready, tucking it snuggly around her and ushering her out of the bathroom. He closed the door behind them.

The hallway was about twenty degrees cooler than the bathroom, and she shivered, water running down her legs and dripping onto the carpet. She held the towel together at her breasts with one hand and planted the other one firmly on her hip. "What—"

His fingers went to his lips, repeating the mime to stay silent. Her voice changed to an irritated whisper. "What's going on?"

"Nothing yet," he said softly. "I just want you to stay out here. Did you hear anything unusual while you were in there?"

"A bad David Bowie cover. I don't know why they find it necessary to ruin a perfectly good song."

He was so preoccupied with his thoughts, she didn't

even get a smile. "Any scratching sounds or grating noises from the ceiling?"

"No. Rocky, will you please—"

"Shhh!"

She mouthed the rest: "—tell me what's going on?"

He held up a finger while cocking his head toward the bathroom door, listening. "Just being cautious."

Cautious, her butt. He was whispering so quietly she could barely hear him. He was worried. Then his body froze and his eyes narrowed. He'd heard something on the other side of the door.

She copied his stance, completely still, head tipped attentively to the side, the only sound a soft splat of water that dripped from her bangs onto the back of her hand where it held the towel together.

Scritch.

The small sound came from up high, behind the door. Seconds later it was followed by a creak.

Before she could ask questions, Rocky jerked back to life, taking her by the shoulders. "Wait in the bedroom," he mouthed, nudging her in that direction.

She understood immediately that someone was in the bathroom. Someone had been breaking in through the skylight above the bathtub while she showered.

She didn't have to guess who the weasely little pervert was—Easy Joey.

A prickly feeling slid down her spine as she replayed her actions. She'd stood in front of the sink and in the shower, but not close to the bathtub. Could he have seen her from the deeply recessed skylight, even at that angle? Seen her standing there naked?

Anger snapped like a rubber band, stronger than her fear.

"Rocky," she called loudly. "Are you in the bedroom? I'll be right there." She took a few steps in that direction, then stopped to see what Rocky would to do.

He nodded his encouragement and flattened himself to the wall beside the bathroom door, motioning her down the hall. She shook her head. She might not be able to kick Easy's ass herself, but if Rocky intended to, she wanted to see it.

He looked ready to argue, but something turned his attention back to the bathroom door. He crouched, with one hand on the knob, as if waiting for a signal. Ten feet away, she waited with him, not daring to breathe. Wondering if their burglar intended to search the house for valuables first or if he'd be tempted by whatever his perverted little imagination thought they might be doing in the bedroom. *Come on, Easy.* Having been his victim once, she was eager to see him get what he had coming.

They stood still.

Rocky must have heard whatever he was waiting for on the other side of the door. Without warning, he threw it open and dove into the bathroom. She heard the crash of bodies and a startled cry, followed by the sharp smack of a fist on flesh. Then it was quiet. A cloud of steam billowed into the hallway and dissipated.

Keeping a firm grip on her towel, she approached the open bathroom door. Inside, Rocky crouched on the tile over the spread-eagled body of Easy Joey. While Easy moaned, Rocky rooted through a small knapsack. He tossed it aside, returning his attention to the man on the floor.

"Easy!" Rocky slapped him, none too gently.

Easy blinked several times. She knew the second full consciousness returned, because he scrambled into reverse, a half crawl propelled by elbows and feet, until he backed into the toilet bowl. "Don't touch me!"

"Then don't move." Rocky stood, kicking the knapsack further away as he turned to look at Janet. "Hey, babe, could you call nine-one-one and tell them to come pick up this piece of garbage?"

"No, wait!" Easy yelled. She did, even though he directed his plea at Rocky. She didn't want to miss anything. "We had a deal. You said I could try to break in. You can't call the cops now."

"Why, because that would be just like what you did to me when you set me up?"

Beneath the red circle on his cheek bone, Easy's face went pale.

"I warned you, Easy. I said you could try, and I told you what would happen if you got caught." He looked at Janet again. "Police," he reminded her.

She ran for the bedroom, made her report, and returned to the hallway with the cordless phone, hoping to take out her anger on Easy before the cops hauled him away. But Rocky had it covered.

He knelt beside Easy, who was trapped with the commode at his back. Rocky ran a hand over each side and down his legs, checking for weapons. "Have you taken on a new sideline, Easy?"

"What do you mean?"

"Are you a Peeping Tom now? Watching women in the shower?"

Easy's gaze flew to Janet, then back to Rocky as he shrank back farther. "No! I wasn't watching her. I was just breaking in."

"While she was in here. A coincidence, then."

"Yes! I don't give a fuck about your girlfriend, man."

"I see." She'd expected to hear anger, but Rocky's voice was surprisingly calm—unnaturally so. She didn't blame Easy for being nervous. "You didn't know she was in here?"

"No! How would I know that?"

"Oh, you couldn't. Unless you heard the water running," Rocky suggested. "That would be hard to miss. Or saw all the steam fogging up the skylight."

Easy tried to squeeze between the toilet and the vanity, but only managed to wedge himself against the toilet paper roll. Panic made him blink faster as he kept his eyes on Rocky. "I didn't see her."

"You mentioned that. I'm just not sure I believe you." Rocky rose to his feet, taking a few steps toward the tub and casting a casual glance toward the open skylight. Easy didn't even try to make a break for it as he followed every move with his darting eyes. Rocky considered the opening above his head. "I guess you can't see much with the skylight set so far in like that. Unless she was in the bathtub." He looked to where she hovered in the doorway. "Did you stand by the bathtub, honey?"

She shook her head no, scattering water droplets from the spiky, short ends of her hair. She was nearly as fascinated by his manner as Easy.

"No? Well, that's good. Because then we know he didn't see anything. Maybe he really *wasn't* trying to spy on you." He wandered back to Easy and squatted in front of him, making direct eye contact. "But then again, maybe he was." Before either Janet or Easy could react, Rocky pulled back a fist and slammed it into Easy's jaw. Easy slumped against the base of the toilet, unconscious.

Rocky stood, shrugging. "I guess we'll never know." He eyed Janet's towel where it showed a good bit of cleavage. "Honey, maybe you could get dressed before the cops get here and I have to beat them up, too."

She nearly forgot she'd been standing there dripping wet. She trotted downstairs and collected her clothes, using the downstairs bathroom to dry off and get dressed. She finished just as Rocky let two police officers in the front door and escorted them upstairs. She followed.

Easy was just coming around. One officer stepped forward to cuff him before he was alert enough to resist.

"Don't usually find burglars in bathrooms," he said, eyeing the room as if looking for a hidden doorway.

Rocky pointed at the recessed area in the ceiling above the tub. "He came in through the skylight here. I think he must have hit his head on the toilet when he jumped down. Stupid criminals, eh?"

She couldn't help feeling a small thrill about the whole thing. They were all fine, and Rocky'd had the situation under control the whole time. So she didn't understand why he acted so withdrawn. He hardly spoke to her, staring straight ahead as he drove, his face expressionless.

She supposed he felt responsible because he'd practically dared Easy Joey to do it. Rocky was good at taking responsibility for things—whether he should or not. He took it on himself to reclaim his family's lost jewelry and coins. He kept her safe from an elusive jewel thief, not to mention a couple of angry Colombians, while trying to track down the Pellinni Jewels. Ben had told her that even the FBI probably couldn't have traced the jewelry to Sleazy's pawnshop.

He even tried to protect her heart. She'd known it when he'd joked about letting her use him again. The phrase had been useful for establishing an emotional distance between them. But now it grated against her happiness, making it feel vaguely salacious.

The reason why was obvious—she liked him. A lot. The intimacy and the connection she felt now were things she'd never had with Banner. Being with Rocky was comfortable, but it was also new and unexpected so she needed to move slowly. She knew now it was time to take the plunge, though, and talk about how this had turned into something more, something with the potential for a relationship.

Saying it out loud would be the perfect way to punch through that preoccupied frown that made him look so grim. She smiled as she imagined his reaction.

She waited until they stood before the huge double doors of the Westfield mansion. In the porch light he looked even more serious. Her heart skipped like a kid's on Christmas morning. Just when he was feeling dejected about her lack of commitment, she would tell him exactly what he'd waited to hear, that he meant something to her.

"Janet—"

"Rocky—"

They spoke at the same time, and she laughed. "You go first." She hugged her confession to herself a little longer, her excitement building.

He didn't look happy about going first, but he gave her a brief nod and went on. "I can't see you anymore."

For one stunned moment her ears buzzed like a swarm of hornets in her head. "You can't—what?"

The look on his face said it all. She'd heard him right.

He touched her face, a tender caress that brushed her cheek and gave him an excuse to avoid eye contact as he watched his own hand. "We can't see each other anymore, at least not for now. Being with me is putting you in more danger. I won't allow it."

"You won't *allow* it?" He was tossing her aside, and she had no say in it.

"I thought I was keeping you safe, but it's just the opposite. Twice now you've been in my house and been right in harm's way. The first time you ended up in the emergency room. This time I don't even want to think about what Easy might have done if I hadn't caught him."

She forced herself to stay rational, trying not to give in to the frustration bubbling inside her. "You *did* catch him. He's not a problem any more."

"He's not a problem *tonight*. In a couple days he'll post bail and be out looking for revenge."

Annoyance seeped around the edges of her cool facade. She dodged his fingers as he smoothed a lock of her hair, causing him to drop his hand in confusion.

She spoke slowly, forcing herself to stay calm. "So, you can't see me because of Easy Joey."

"Yes. And because of the Colombians who have followed us everywhere and slashed my tires to show they don't appreciate my presence. *And* because of the thief who wants the Pellinni Jewels so badly he followed us to Sleazy's and killed him. Don't forget that part."

She folded her arms and pressed them against the painful knot in her stomach. "If the thief still thinks I might have the jewels, how does not seeing you keep me safe?"

"It's worse because of me, and you know it. I never even told you about the Detroit Barber Shop and the scarier-than-hell Russian who thinks he's my best friend. Or God knows how many more disgruntled thieves besides Easy who have a score to settle with me. I don't want any part of that world to touch you, Janet, and it has. If I leave, it goes with me. I'll still try to track down the Pellinni Jewels and figure out who is after them, but I need you safely out of it. Safely away from me."

She stated the obvious because it seemed to have escaped him. "You don't think I might worry about your safety, too?"

"There's no need to. I know these people, Janet. You don't." He darted an annoyed glance at her tightly pressed lips. "I don't understand why you're mad that I want to keep you safe."

She lifted an eyebrow. "Maybe because you aren't giving me much credit here. What happened to all that stuff about how competent I was when I escaped the drug dealers in Colombia and when I went after Banner?"

He ran a hand through his hair, looking thoroughly frustrated. "You *were* competent. And *lucky*, Janet. I'm not willing to count on luck this time. I had—still have—connections to an underworld that is both illegal and violent. The closer I get to finding the jewels, the more danger it puts you in. Easy is only a small part of it. God knows how many other cockroaches will come crawling out of the woodwork, looking for the jewels, thinking they're on the right track because they recognize me." He touched her arm tentatively. "Please try to understand, Janet."

The anguish behind his words softened her anger a bit, but not enough. "I resent being stashed away when I could be helping."

"Or getting yourself killed."

"Not likely."

"I'm not willing to take that chance." His voice was hard and unequivocal.

She wasn't going to win this argument. "Fine," she ground out, as if conceding to being locked away. "We won't see each other."

Saying it out loud made it suddenly real. The anger drained away, leaving her feeling hollow. A couple hours ago his lovemaking had warmed both her body and her soul, making her think maybe she wasn't irreparably damaged from her sick relationship with Banner.

"I'll miss you," she admitted, the tightness in her throat making it barely more than a whisper. Before she could get too emotional about it, she turned to leave.

He grabbed her arm, spinning her back so close she felt the heat of his body and had to tip her head back to meet his gaze.

"Nothing's changed between us." His words vibrated into her, deep and strong. "Not the way I feel about you and not what we have together." His gaze burned into her for several seconds before his mouth came down over hers in a searing kiss that took her breath away. She clung to his shoulders until he pulled back, leaving her staring and confused.

He ran a gentle hand over her cheek. "Good night."

She swallowed. "'Night." Slowly this time, she turned to unlock the massive front door and slipped inside without looking back.

She leaned against the closed door. She had seriously underestimated Rocky when she'd thought she could have a safe, easy relationship with him. Whatever they had—and she wasn't ready to use the scary "L" word—was too powerful to be casual.

And too incredible to be put on hold. If he thought she would agree to that, then he'd underestimated her, too.

Not seeing Rocky until the remaining Pellinni Jewels and the diamonds were found wasn't going to work. There was only one solution—she'd just have to find them herself. And quickly.

Chapter Thirteen

Rocky wasn't happy with his decision, but at least Janet would be safe. That was all that mattered.

All that *should* matter, anyway. The ache in the center of his heart mattered, and that would take a long time to get used to. He missed her already. He drove home, trying to keep his mind on traffic and only partially succeeding. He couldn't get her stricken look—or the anger beneath it—out of his mind. He hoped like hell it wouldn't take long to track down the jewels and diamonds.

He would find the jewels, but his priority was getting the criminals off her back. It was no less important to him than when he'd given up three years of his life to track down his grandparents' stolen heirlooms. With one exception—their lives hadn't been in danger if he failed.

The Colombians would only be patient for so long before they came for revenge. Drug dealers weren't the forgiving sort. Neither was the thief who was after the Pellinni Jewels. He was already desperate enough to kill Sleazy. It was damned inconvenient, too, since Sleazy was the only tie they'd had to the stolen jewels. No one else knew anything except Banner, who would rather see Janet die than give her information.

Finding the diamonds might not even be possible—they were untraceable and easily converted into cash. The Pellinni Jewels would be easier to find, if someone were dumb enough to brag about having them. But who would advertise the purchase of the hottest cache of jewelry to hit the black market in years? The thief might as well call up the FBI and surrender. Or hold an auction, since every thief in the world would be targeting him, waiting for their chance to—

The idea hit Rocky with such force that he missed the light change to red and nearly rear-ended the guy in front of him. As soon as it turned green, he pulled his Lexus into a deserted strip mall, letting his pulse return to normal while his mind created a plan.

It would be dangerous. It would mean taking another dip into the local underworld cesspool of thieves and killers. It would mean dealing with Vasili and the Russian Mafia.

But it just might work.

Vasili raised one bushy eyebrow high enough to make it disappear under the wild tangle of hair at his forehead. "You want me play trick on customers? You crazy man." He leaned over the glass countertop, staring into Rocky's eyes. "I run business. You want ruin my reputation? I work hard, earn respect."

There was no way Rocky would tell a member of the Russian Mafia that he was full of shit, even if he was.

"Your reputation won't be ruined." How do you

ruin a reputation as a brutal, conniving mob boss? It's not like Rocky was asking him to buy Girl Scout cookies. "In fact, it might be improved. You'd be the envy of every other"—he searched for a polite euphemism for Vasili's particular criminal activities—"dealer in used jewelry. Who wouldn't want to host a bidding war on the Pellinni Jewels? How often do you get an opportunity like that?"

"Never. Is not my business." The Russian straightened, crossing his burly arms across his chest. "I buy jewelry. I export jewelry. Simple. What you think this is, Sotheby's? You think I sell to highest bidder? *Pfft.* You know better." Vasili's scowl said Rocky should at any rate. "Someone want buy from me, they pay my price. No auction." He made a cutting motion with the side of his hand, a visual aid more convincing than his blunt words. "No deal. Bad what you call it— example?"

"Bad precedent?"

"Precedent." He thrust a finger at Rocky. "Right."

He'd known Vasili wouldn't like the idea, but it was the only way Rocky could think to draw out the thief who had trashed Janet's place. As much as he wanted to believe the guy wouldn't hurt her, he knew it wasn't true. This guy had already killed once looking for the Pellinni Jewels. He would do it again.

"It wouldn't be an auction, Vasili. You'd just pretend it was in order to lure the guy in. It's like a sting. You put out the word that you have the rest of the Pellinni Jewels and that you'll make them available for the right price. He'll contact you."

Vasili snorted. "Him and ten others."

"No, I don't think so. Most of them don't want

something they might have to hold onto for a long time before they find the right buyer. I wouldn't have. They want a fast turnaround, the faster the better." He was telling Vasili what he already knew, but he needed to be persuaded. "But one guy out there will be interested, because he already has a buyer. I figure it's the person they were stolen from in the first place, but it doesn't matter who, it only matters that someone wants to get their hands on the rest of the Pellinni Jewels."

"And if he comes here, so what? I got no jewels."

"If he comes here, he's mine." Rocky wasn't sure what he would do with the thief, but it would probably include some persuasive martial arts. He couldn't involve the police or FBI in their sting, and not just because Vasili would have him sliced and diced and lost at sea. Their mark wouldn't be breaking any laws; expressing an interest in stolen jewelry wasn't a crime.

Vasili looked intrigued with his answer. "You want beat crap out of this guy?"

"Yes." That, and give his name to Ben and the FBI. A little unofficial harassment couldn't hurt.

"Sounds personal."

"It is."

"Huh." Angling his head, he contemplated Rocky before speaking. "I heard about guy at Treasures store." Another lift of his bushy eyebrow. "Shot dead."

"Yeah, I know. I found him."

"Yeah?" His interest rose. "That personal, too? You do him?"

"Hell no!"

Vasili gave a dismissive snort. "No loss to human race if you did."

"I didn't."

"Okay, I believe you." He patted Rocky's cheek as if he were a small child. "You good boy now, eh? Obey laws?"

"Absolutely." Especially the ones about murder, which he'd never considered breaking. Maybe Vasili couldn't conceive of refraining from killing someone simply because it was illegal.

"So who did him?"

Rocky shrugged. "Whoever wants the rest of the jewels. The same guy I expect will contact you if you put out the word that you have them."

"So I should try get murdering, scum-sucking bastard to come here? This is your great plan?"

He gave him a hard look. "Why not? This guy murdered a fence."

"Like I said, no big loss."

"You don't want to know who he is?"

Vasili shrugged. "Why I care? He knocks off my competition. Plus I got plenty protection. No one stupid enough to try kill me."

No one without a death wish, which was why Rocky needed to arouse the Russian's pride. "So this guy looking for the jewels gets to decide who lives and dies? I don't know . . . seems bad for business, Vasili. Intruding on your turf, deciding he can eliminate someone if he wants to." He shrugged. "Sets a bad precedent."

Vasili squinted at him over his fat cheeks, his eyes calculating pools of darkness amid acne-scarred skin. Rocky tried to look unconcerned.

"You do this because of girl, eh?"

Where'd that come from? "Like I told you last time, she's a friend and she got dragged into this."

"More than friend, maybe?"

Vasili's hard look said this was important, although Rocky couldn't tell if it was good or bad. Either way, he preferred to keep Janet out of it—and far away from anything to do with Vasili. "Maybe."

"Maybe you got hots for this girl, eh? Got it bad."

The crudeness of it irritated him, making him respond a little too abruptly. "Hey, what do you care? That's my concern, not yours."

He expected to see Vasili's eyes go cold, ruining his only chance to lure the man who was after Janet into the open. Instead, Rocky was startled by a burst of laughter.

"Yes! I am right!" Vasili grinned, his caterpillar eyebrows wiggling up and down. "Girl is special, eh? She have you by balls." He reached over the counter to slug Rocky's shoulder with a beefy paw. "Admit it."

Rocky sighed, knowing he was backed into a corner. "I love her, okay? I admit it. Does that make a difference?" It sounded belligerent, even to his own ears. He must be out of his mind, allowing his frustration to get the better of him around Vasili. The man could make people disappear forever—*had* made them disappear— just because he didn't like what they said. If Rocky didn't get a grip, he'd be of no help to Janet at all.

"Yes. Makes difference," Vasili intoned, suddenly serious. "You take risk, try to catch criminal, because you love this girl. Makes very big difference."

Rocky rubbed at the spot on his temple that seemed to be the source of a perpetual throbbing pain lately.

"Look Vasili, I swear my judgment hasn't been compromised. Just because—"

"I do it."

He paused, unsure he'd heard correctly. "You will?"

"I help you by doing sting. We trick thief into coming here to buy Pellinni Jewels. That what you want, yes?"

"Yes. But . . . why?"

Vasili's heavy hand landed on Rocky's shoulder, drawing him closer to the counter. "Rocky, I tell you important truth. Russians very romantic people. Money, jewels, power . . . all good. Very good. But nothing without love, eh?" The hand lifted from his shoulder, then pounded him in a friendly slug. "You must have Russian blood, my friend. You take big risk for love."

Rocky would do whatever it took to keep Janet safe. Risk hardly factored into it.

"Just promise Vasili one thing."

"Uh, sure. What is it?"

"I meet this girl who wins heart of my friend. You bring her here after."

Rocky didn't like the idea, but if Vasili would help him catch the asshole, how could he say no? He didn't have a choice. "Sure. You can meet her." For a quick hello. God help him if Ben and Elizabeth ever found out.

Vasili beamed. "Good." He added a nod and a sly smile. "She is beautiful, yes?"

"Yes." Rocky smiled back.

"Sexy?"

The smile slipped. "Yes."

Vasili was looking at the ceiling, deep in thought, and didn't notice Rocky's discomfort. "Long blonde hair?"

"No. Short and brown."

He clicked his tongue. "Too bad."

"Works for me."

Vasili's sudden laugh nearly made Rocky jump. "That's all that matters, yes?" Another punch landed on his bruised shoulder. "Yes," Vasili answered his own question. "Now. We talk details. You tell to me what you need. We catch little fucker and teach him lesson, so I can meet your girl."

Rocky exhaled, releasing the tension that had built up. "Yes, first we catch him. Then—" heaven help him "—you meet her."

He sincerely hoped Janet was speaking to him by then.

The Westfield mansion was huge—twenty-two rooms by Janet's count, not including bathrooms. Janet had torn apart each one today. Just like in her previous searches, she found no trace of Banner's diamonds. There had to be someplace she hadn't looked.

She was allowed to go wherever she wanted around the house and yard, but everyone got twitchy whenever she went outside. She could almost hear red alert sirens as the two security guards suddenly popped out of the bushes, keeping a vigilant eye on the perimeter while she batted tennis balls or swam. It was easier on everyone if she stayed indoors.

She had no idea where else to look, though. Frustrated, she'd asked to go back to her condo, if only to clean the place up, but Ben had uttered such a forceful

"No!" she didn't press the issue. There was already enough tension in the house when it came to him.

It had Elizabeth on edge, too. Janet had never seen her composure slip so often, even when Banner's crimes had been exposed. She'd held her head up through the public embarrassment and handled her grief in private. But the continual friction with Ben left her jumpy and irritable—and so self-absorbed she didn't seem to notice Libby's manipulations.

"Can I call Grandpa Ben and invite him over for dinner?" Libby asked from her lotus position on the ottoman in front of Elizabeth. Janet paused in the doorway where she'd overheard the question, waiting to see what excuse Elizabeth would come up with this time.

"May I," Elizabeth corrected.

"May I ask him?"

Her grandmother lowered her book. "I think he's busy tonight, honey."

It sounded weak to Janet, and Libby was equally unimpressed. "But I could ask, couldn't I?"

"Not while he's at work. Being chief of police is an important job, and you can't interrupt him just to ask him to dinner. I'm sorry."

Slam. End of discussion.

Or it should have been. But the threat of being a pest has never deterred a thirteen-year-old.

Libby waved the argument aside. "That's okay. Grandpa Ben said I can call his cell anytime. It'll go to voice mail and he'll call me back as soon as he gets a chance." When the tight lines around Elizabeth's mouth didn't soften, she rushed to add, "Pretty please, Grandma? With Dad and Ellie in Europe, I really miss having family around."

Janet stepped closer, astonished. Libby must be off her game; Elizabeth would never fall for that "poor me" shtick.

Libby appeared suddenly shy beneath her lowered lashes. "It's all still kind of new to me, you know. Having a family." She actually looked slightly embarrassed as her shoulders trembled with an apparent shiver of delight over so many newly discovered relatives. Janet imagined teenagers everywhere gagging in response.

It shouldn't have worked, but Libby's vulnerable eyes hit her grandmother's guilt dead center.

Elizabeth's resistance crumbled. Janet knew her soft gaze was seeing the semiorphaned waif of eighteen months ago, unwanted by one set of grandparents, unaware of the existence of her father and his parents. Never mind that the waif had been a tough kid well in touch with her self-sufficient Payton genes. To Elizabeth, Libby had been a child without the all-important benefit of a stable family, a family with connections to the best schools and opportunities. In Elizabeth's privileged world, those advantages were Libby's birthright. And here she was, depriving the poor girl of that very love and support by preventing her from seeing her grandfather.

Keeping Libby from spending time with Ben was only part of it. Libby's touching plea had no doubt reminded Elizabeth of all the years she'd deprived Jack of a family, never telling him that Ben was his father. Tons of guilt to tap into there.

Double whammy. The kid was good.

Elizabeth smiled in defeat. "Fine, give him a call. Tell him dinner is at seven."

Libby unfolded her legs in one fast move and bounced

to her feet, giving Elizabeth a quick hug. "Thanks, Grandma. He knows when dinner is, but I'll ask him to come early so I can spend more time with him, okay?"

Elizabeth gave a helpless nod before Libby raced off to call Ben. From the floor beside the ottoman, Freddie jumped up and bounded after her.

Janet's chuckle from the doorway caught Elizabeth's attention. "You are such a sucker for that kid," she said, walking over and dropping onto the couch beside her. "It's kind of cute."

To her surprise, Elizabeth set her book aside and turned concerned eyes on her. "I've been wanting to ask you something. Do you think Libby seems different lately? Rather . . . needy? She always seems to want Ben around, and I don't know if it's because Jack has been away. Do you suppose it's some sort of phase teenage girls go through, needing a constant father figure?"

Janet laughed. "You're asking the wrong person about teenagers and father figures. Libby's the family expert on psychology." She paused, knowing she couldn't pass up this chance to talk to Elizabeth. "But I can tell you that's not what's on Libby's mind."

"It's not?"

"No." Any remaining shred of amusement faded at Elizabeth's confused look. The poor woman was so distracted by her own emotions she really didn't see what was going on. "Libby's matchmaking, Elizabeth. She's getting you and Ben back together."

Mild irritation mixed with her puzzlement. "What do you mean? We've been together for years. Libby knows that."

"Not really." She reached out to squeeze Elizabeth's hand, reminding her of the affection behind the words she was about to say. "You and Ben have been fighting for the past few days, and Libby's scared."

She didn't deny the fighting part. "Scared?"

"She's probably afraid she'll lose one or both of you if you don't resolve this issue about selling the house."

"That's nonsense," Elizabeth recovered, dismissing the thought with a shake of her head. "It's a temporary disagreement, and we'll work it out. Libby's a smart girl; I would expect her to know that couples don't always agree."

This was the hard part. "She does. She's just not used to being the cause of it."

"She—" surprise made her falter for a moment. "She's not the cause. Why would you think that? Why would *she* think that?"

"Because she heard you say it." Hesitation tugged at Janet's heart; she couldn't imagine how much it was going to hurt Elizabeth to hear this. "She overheard part of an argument," she began, editing out the part about Libby eavesdropping on the whole thing. "Apparently you told Ben that selling the house would hurt Libby, that her friends' parents might think less of her if she didn't come from this wealthy family with its incredibly expensive mansion."

Elizabeth's mouth dropped, and she raised a hand to cover it. "I . . . I didn't mean it like that. Oh, God, she heard that?"

Janet nodded. "Now she's afraid you think the Payton-Westfield money is buying her friends." Before Elizabeth could respond, Janet hurried to add, "I told her that's not true, that her friends would like her no matter where she lived." She wished she could say Libby believed her, but she wasn't sure. Teenage girls could be incredibly insecure, and she promised herself to reinforce that lesson later. Right now she had to worry about correcting Elizabeth's impressions. "But she thinks you believe it, and that it's keeping you from selling the house. And because Ben refuses to live here, Libby thinks *she's* keeping the two of you apart."

"That's not true!"

"It's not true that Ben doesn't want to live here?"

She sighed. "No, that's true. He said the house was Banner's idea, not mine, which is accurate. And that it's inappropriate for the chief of police to live in a huge mansion on the salary of a public servant."

Janet could see his point but kept quiet.

Elizabeth stood suddenly, too agitated to sit still. Pacing the Oriental rug, she wrung her hands. "It's true I don't want to sell the house, but it's not because of Libby. I just told Ben that because I thought it would convince him. It's because—" her voice caught, the words coming out hoarse and whispery. "It's me. I'm the one who's afraid of what people will think."

Janet breathed a sigh of relief that she didn't have to point that one out. "I know."

That earned her a sharp look. "I'm not a snob." Elizabeth rolled her eyes and corrected herself. "Okay, yes, I am. I admit I've been a spoiled princess my entire life, and I like it. I prefer to live in luxury." She stood straighter, eyes hard and unflinching. "But I don't judge others by where they live or what they do for a living, or where their kids go to school."

Janet smiled, as much to reassure Elizabeth as at the absurdity of the statement. "I know that, too."

"And I wouldn't want anyone to do that to Libby."

"Do they? Do they treat her differently?"

"I don't know," she hedged, then tightened her lips, forcing the truth out. "No, not that I know of. She's had no problems at school or at the club. But how do I know it's not because they're afraid of offending *me*?"

"I guess you don't." Janet avoided eye contact, absorbed in examining her cuticles. Making the next question sound as nonthreatening as possible. "Do you care if Libby has friends like that, people who are nice to her just because her grandmother is superrich and owns the biggest house in town?"

The silence finally got to her, and she looked up to meet Elizabeth's steely gaze, wondering if she'd just crossed the line.

Janet wasn't sure until something flickered in the gray-blue depths of Elizabeth's eyes as she drew a deep breath. "Yes." Stiffness seeped out of her body like air escaping a blow-up pool toy. "Yes," she repeated, nodding her head for emphasis. "I care deeply. I don't want her to have superficial friends. I tried to pretend this thing about selling the house was because of Libby, about protecting her way of life, but I'm the one who's insecure about how others will perceive me."

Elizabeth was talking to herself as much as to Janet, so Janet kept her mouth shut. Some things had to be said out loud, and this seemed to be one of them.

"I made mistakes before, but they were my own business. I didn't love Leonard Westfield but I stayed with him anyway. That was my bad decision. But then Banner—" Janet didn't expect her to list Banner's sins, since they were too numerous to name. "You know what happened as well as I do, Janet, as much as I wish you didn't. Smuggling drugs, laundering money, and having his own brother sent to jail for a crime he didn't commit. And—my God, I still can't believe it—he and Leonard are somehow responsible for murdering Joe Benton. The police may never prove it, but I know they did it, and so does everyone else in this town. My husband was a murderer. And my son . . . my own son is one of the worst criminals this town has ever seen. It's—" her voice dropped to a whisper "—it's shameful."

"He's sick, Elizabeth. It's not your fault." It didn't excuse anything he'd done, but she couldn't bear to see her ex–mother-in-law suffering for what her son had done.

"Yes, he is. But it hasn't stopped me from being embarrassed. And that's the problem. I'd given up everything to marry Leonard Westfield, to give my children a name and a family with prestige—I gave up *Ben*. I was a fool, and I paid a steep price. I thought I was past that, but now I've been even more foolish. I—" As if she no longer had the energy to hold herself up, she dropped into a brocade wing chair, staring at nothing for several seconds before turning her desperate gaze on Janet. "I can't believe it. I've taught my own granddaughter that people's perceptions are more important than who she is. That having money and keeping up appearances matters more than anything else." She let her head fall into her hands. "I'm such a hypocrite. What have I done to Libby?"

"Nothing!" Janet hurried over to kneel in front of her, clasping Elizabeth's clenched hands in her own. "Libby is the nicest, most well-adjusted kid I've ever known. Her friends like her for who she is, not for where she lives." At least, she prayed they did. "You just need to let her know that you aren't staying here because of her."

"No," Elizabeth admitted. "I'm staying because of me. Because I'm shallow and afraid to face the world without the protection of my fancy house and all the trappings of wealth. What a great example for my granddaughter."

"That's a bit harsh."

"No. It's embarrassing, but it's true."

She should have known Elizabeth would be as unflinchingly honest with herself as she was with others. And as cathartic as their conversation might have been for her, only one thing mattered. "As long as Libby knows that whatever differences you and Ben have, it's not because of her, or because of what you want for her."

She nodded, deep in thought. "You're absolutely right. I have to fix this as soon as possible."

It was typical Elizabeth: Identify the problem, take control, and fix it. Janet smiled to herself. "I think Libby understands, but she'll be glad to hear it from you."

Elizabeth stood, her gaze focused and clear, and smoothed her skirt. "Thank you, Janet. Will you excuse me? I don't think I should wait any longer."

"Sure thing."

She refrained from adding, *And for God's sake, work it out with Ben while you're at it.* She hoped it was possible, but no one knew better than she did that some issues couldn't be worked out, no matter how you felt about the other person. No matter how much you cared or how wrong your world felt without him. Sometimes it was out of your hands.

Unless you refused to concede.

Janet was more determined now than ever to resolve the issues that were keeping Rocky from her. There had to be a logical way to figure out what Banner had done with the stones.

The diamonds had been close by when he'd been arrested at the house—he told her he'd planned to take them—but they weren't here now. They must have been moved after that. Yet she couldn't think of anyone he'd trust to keep them safe. Hell, no one would even talk to him these days except his lawyers, and they were paid well for that dubious honor.

She grew still as her mind suddenly raced. How *were* his lawyers paid?

Banner had hired the most expensive criminal lawyers in the state, and she'd seen his financial statements during the divorce. She was sure there were no attorney fees noted. Seabrook wouldn't do this pro bono. With all Banner's money tied up in lawsuits and pending charges, he had to have come up with a retainer somehow.

Her jaw dropped as the realization hit. He must've paid with the diamonds.

She ran through the house, checking rooms, until she finally found Elizabeth in the solarium.

"Janet! What's the problem?"

She held onto the back of a chair, catching her breath. "This is awkward, Elizabeth, but I need to ask you a personal question."

Her ex–mother-in-law shook her head with a look of infinite patience. "You're family, Janet. I wish you would stop making me remind you."

She smiled. "I'm sorry. It's just . . . it's really not my business anymore, but trust me, it could be important." When Elizabeth simply waited, she asked, "Are you paying for Banner's legal defense?"

The kindness left her eyes. "Not a cent," she said, her voice tempered steel.

Janet nodded. "I didn't think so. So how *is* he paying for it?"

"I have no idea. Nor do I care."

Rising excitement kept her heartbeat from slowing its mad gallop. "You had to deliver some papers to his attorney's office soon after his arrest, though, right? Did that include a key to a safe deposit box by any chance?"

Elizabeth's brow quirked the tiniest bit with curiosity. "No. Just papers and a couple personal items." Seeing Janet's disappointment, she added helpfully, "He asked for some financial papers, the cash he had in his bedroom, and a list of phone numbers."

She couldn't hide her disappointment. "That's all?"

"I'm afraid so. Oh, and some stupid commemorative golf ball. He said he forgot to give it to . . ." Her vice trailed off as she noticed Janet's excitement. "What?"

"A gold-plated ball from the Wesfield-Benton Classic?"

"Yes. Why?"

"That's it!" She laughed. "That's where the diamonds went!"

Elizabeth looked stunned. "The diamonds those Colombian thugs are looking for? They were in the golf ball?"

"Yes! We have to call Ben."

A faint smile pulled at the corners of Elizabeth's mouth. Laying a hand on Janet's arm, she steered her toward the doorway. "As it happens, I already did. He said he'll be here in about an hour. I think this will be quite an eventful visit for him."

Chapter Fourteen

"Can't talk now, I'm driving," Ben said. In the background Rocky heard the Tigers' baseball game on the car radio, the same one he'd been listening to. He figured *can't talk* meant *I don't want to talk while the game is in extra innings.*

"Okay, I'll call you back later."

"No, I'm on my way to Liz's house. Why don't you meet me there? We can talk before dinner."

He must have assumed Rocky would be showing up there anyway, or at least be welcome. Neither was true. He didn't want to say it, then have to explain to Ben why the woman who was practically like a daughter to him wouldn't want to see Rocky's sorry ass anymore. At least, not without kicking it.

He hesitated, trying to come up with an excuse not to meet him at the Westfield mansion, but Ben's impatient voice interrupted his thoughts.

"I'll be there in ten minutes. Just—damn it! Fuckin' bullpen's gonna give away this game. Talk to you later." The line went dead.

He had no choice but to drive to Elizabeth's place if he wanted to talk to Ben. But he was probably closer than Ben was. Maybe he could intercept him in the driveway.

Naturally, traffic on Woodward was a nightmare. He turned onto Elizabeth's street fifteen minutes later, certain he'd have to ring the doorbell and suffer poisonous looks from all three females, who undoubtedly would stand together in their resentment. But Ben's car was right in front of him, pulled onto the grassy verge at the side of the street just before the driveway. Ben sat stiffly behind the wheel.

Rocky's first thought was that he'd pulled over to hear the end of the ballgame before driving up to the house. But Baltimore had scored the winning run just as Rocky turned onto the shady side street, and instead of smashing a fist into the dash and switching off the radio, Ben didn't move. Not so much as a twitch.

Something was wrong. Rocky threw the car into park and jumped out. He ran toward Ben, his mind racing ahead of him, envisioning the gray face and clutching hands of a heart attack victim. Or even more frightening, the round, bloody hole of a bullet neatly centered on Ben's chest. It was a crazy thought, yet he couldn't help scanning the street for any sign of the Colombians. *As if they'd shoot someone and stick around.*

Every sense went on full alert, heightened by the fear of what he might find. They hit him in a confusing collage, the scent of fresh-cut grass, the sound of a basketball bouncing on a driveway behind him, the hot feel of metal as he smacked his hand onto the sun-warmed roof of the car. He braced to jerk open the driver's door when the hum of the window lowering stopped him. Rocky straightened, puzzled, as Ben turned toward him, face flushed with health and chest devoid of bullet holes.

Ben's blank gaze gave nothing away. "Did you know about this?" he asked.

He followed Ben's pointed finger, turning his gaze toward Elizabeth's front yard beyond the open gates. Less than a hundred square feet of grass lay between the gates and the dense screen of lilac bushes, rhododendron, and pine trees that shielded the property. Yesterday it had been bare, an open piece of green offering a glimpse of the mansion beyond. Now a large black sign was standing in the clearing, carrying the logo of a local real estate company. Big gold letters at the top proclaimed, "For Sale."

Rocky's jaw dropped for several seconds before he found the words. "She's selling the house?"

"Apparently. So I take it you didn't know?"

"No. Didn't you?"

"No."

They both turned to stare at the sign. "What made her decide to move out?" Rocky hoped it wasn't something to do with all the animals he'd dumped on her lately.

Ben rubbed his chin. "Don't know."

He glanced at the other luxury homes nearby. "I don't think the neighbors will appreciate the sign. Not very classy."

"I think it's for my benefit."

"Oh. Where's she moving to?"

A small smirk touched Ben's mouth. "That part I might know." Suddenly animated, Ben put the car in gear.

"Hey, wait!" Rocky put both hands on the open window frame, as if he could stop the car from moving. "I need to talk with you about an idea I had to catch whoever is after the Pellinni Jewels. It's important."

"Not as important as this." Ben must have given his rash statement a second thought because he paused and said, "Call Detective Furley. I'll catch up with you later." He hit the gas, spraying grass and bits of gravel.

Rocky stepped back and watched him speed up the winding driveway. He preferred talking to Ben, but there was no way he wanted to go in the house, especially while Ben was asking Elizabeth to marry him or move in with him or whatever happy ending he'd seen on the man's face. Rocky was pretty sure his presence would kill the mood.

Turning, he walked back toward his car, head down, eyes watching the ground.

"Hey!"

He jerked around, recognizing the voice even when it barked at drill sergeant volume. "Hi, Libby."

She stood at the edge of the driveway, beside one of the tall black gates, Freddie at her side. The dog leapt forward to greet him, then fell back at Libby's sharp tug on his leash. Rocky felt the correction as much as if the leash had been attached to his neck. This was not going to be a friendly encounter.

Freddie settled for wagging his tail and whining as Libby folded her arms and thrust out her jaw. Her fiery glare was as intimidating as her grandmother's. "You promised."

She didn't have to say anymore. He'd promised not

to hurt Janet, and as far as Libby was concerned, he'd broken that promise.

It also seemed to have hurt Libby, shutting down the open, loving part of her and teaching her at the tender age of thirteen that men couldn't be trusted. *Nice going, Hernandez.*

He stepped toward her, then stopped, deciding it was safer to heed her rigid body language and keep his distance. Holding his palms up to ward off a lecture, he said, "I know what you think, but I didn't dump her."

"I know, you just don't want to see her anymore."

He scowled. "Who said anymore? It's just until I finish this business dealing with some people who aren't nice enough to meet Janet. I'm trying to keep her safe."

"That's a new one."

With anyone else he might have told them to mind their own business, but Libby's feelings were important to him. "I'm not making it up, and it's not like I don't want to see her."

"Then see her."

It sounded so logical. But he shouldn't spend time sitting around with Janet when he could be doing something about getting rid of at least one of her problems. He stuck his hands in his pockets, more than a little uncomfortable with trying to explain himself to a thirteen-year-old. "It's not that easy, Libby."

She kicked at the ground and muttered, "Seems easy enough to me."

He squinted cautiously. "What did Janet tell you?"

"Nothing, just that you won't see her. But I like Janet—a lot. Ellie and I have been hoping she'd find a boyfriend, and it seemed like she did, except now you went and made her unhappy. And that makes me mad." In case he didn't find that part significant, she added an icy glare. "You have to fix it."

"I will."

"You better."

He couldn't agree more, not only for the sake of his precarious future with Janet, but to erase that heart-wrenching look of betrayal from Libby's face.

God, when he screwed up, he went all out, pissing off two women at once. He didn't even want to imagine what Elizabeth thought of him, because he had a bad feeling she would be angry female number three.

"Janet, sit down and relax." Ben indicated the patio chair across from the glider where he sat with Elizabeth. "They'll call me as soon as they know anything."

"I can't. I'm too nervous." She stopped pacing the flagstones long enough to ask, "How can you just sit there while your officers might be recovering a fortune in hot diamonds at this very moment?"

"They know how to do their jobs without me looking over their shoulders." Turning a page in the real estate booklet, he showed it to Elizabeth who sat next to him on the glider. "What do you think of this one, Liz?"

She looked at the listing. "It has a tennis court. If I keep my club membership, we don't need that."

He looked concerned. "You don't have to give up everything."

"It's my choice, Ben." She laid a hand over his. "And you know it makes sense. Libby's the one who takes lessons, and she doesn't even live with us. We don't need a tennis court."

He nodded, but worry lines still etched his face. "I just don't want you to feel like I'm making you change your lifestyle when you change houses."

"You're not," she assured him quickly. "I'll still have my clubs and charitable organizations. I just won't have this enormous house. People will have to accept me for who I am and what I do, not for what I have." She allowed a sly smile. "It should be quite interesting to see if anyone disappears from my circle of friends."

"Good riddance if they do," Ben snorted.

Janet agreed, but didn't think it would happen; Elizabeth's friends weren't that superficial.

Her gaze wandered over the property, a bit amazed that the magnificent estate might soon belong to someone else. The imposing mansion had seemed synonymous with the Elizabeth Payton Westfield she'd first met when she married Banner. Of course, that hadn't been the real Elizabeth. She had still been secretive about her renewed love affair with Ben Thatcher, and had not yet known that her older son's jail sentence was unjust—and arranged by her youngest son. The changes in the family over the past two years were mirrored in Elizabeth's relaxed demeanor and easy smile. Janet supposed the grand estate didn't suit the new Elizabeth Payton Westfield. Or—she smiled at the news Elizabeth had shared at dinner—the future Elizabeth Payton Thatcher.

Elizabeth seemed to be pondering other changes as she watched her granddaughter across the lawn, trying to convince Freddie to give up a ball.

"Libby will be losing something, too, in a way. After all, she used my pool and tennis courts more than anyone else. She should have something to make up for it."

Ben's hand stilled where it had been kneading her shoulder. "Liz, I can't afford the kind of luxuries you've had here, and you know Jack and Ellie don't want to spoil her."

"I was thinking of a dog," Elizabeth said, unruffled.

"A dog." Ben's frown turned into a slow smile.

"You know, it's amazing that Jack and Ellie haven't noticed the gaping hole in their daughter's life. I think Freddie would fill it wonderfully."

Ben chuckled. "I can't wait to tell them when they get home. What would they do without grandparents to figure these things out?"

Elizabeth leaned contentedly into the curve of his arm, both of them looking so satisfied Janet felt like she should tiptoe away and give them some privacy. She was about to excuse herself when Ben's cell phone rang. She froze as he dug it out of his pocket.

"Yeah," Ben said. Then nothing else while Janet fidgeted. She tried to catch his eye as he repeated, "Uh-huh, uh-huh," but he studiously avoided her. Finally, he chuckled and said, "Fantastic!"

"What?" she demanded.

He hung up and grinned at her. "You were right. As soon as they told Seabrook the search warrant specifically named a commemorative gold-plated golf ball, he handed it over."

"Yes!" she said, pumping her fist.

"They still had the diamonds in a safe, and couldn't

wait to get rid of them once we said Jarod Davis—
that's the guy you called Sleazy—had receipts for their
sale to Banner. It probably didn't hurt that we implied
a couple guys from Colombia were very interested in
learning their whereabouts." Tucking the phone in
his pocket, he said, "We owe you a big thanks for this
one, Janet."

"My pleasure, believe me."

"My guys said Seabrook acted surprised and outraged by the possibility that the diamonds might have
been connected to drug money. They're pointing the
finger back at Banner, and it looks like there'll be a few
counter lawsuits flying back and forth. The upshot is
Banner's going to need some new lawyers. And some
money."

Elizabeth huffed and folded her arms, which Janet
took to mean Banner wouldn't be getting any from her.

Finding the diamonds gave Janet a rush as big as if she
had handled the bust herself. Adrenaline flowed through
her, ricocheting around with no outlet. She needed to *do*
something. Nearly bouncing on her toes, she asked Ben,
"What do we do about the Colombians?"

"*We*? *You* don't do anything. The detectives will
let them know the diamonds have been confiscated,
and my bet is they won't hang around long enough to
say good-bye. I'm not sure Banner can quit worrying
about them, though." He slid a glance at Elizabeth.
"Drug runners are big believers in vengeance, and they
lost a lot of money today."

With a grim look, Elizabeth gave a small shrug. Apparently Banner's fate was his own problem.

It couldn't happen to a more deserving guy, Janet
thought.

Still brimming with energy, she shifted her focus—
one threat down and one to go. As soon as she located
the rest of the Pellinni Jewels, she and Rocky could
resume their very hot, very promising relationship. She
wouldn't fool herself anymore either—she had fallen
for him far more than she wanted to admit. She'd
fallen for all of him, from his stupid Hawaiian shirts
and his easy grin to the way his eyes crinkled when
he laughed. The way he looked at her with so much
warmth when he stroked her cheek . . . and kissed
her . . . and cupped his hand under her breast . . . and
pushed inside her . . .

She flushed with heat. Maybe she'd even fallen in
love. Surprisingly, the word no longer made her want
to run and hide; in fact, she was eager to explore just
how deep her feelings were. But she couldn't do that if
Rocky refused to see her.

She could fix that. If she was able to find the
diamonds, she could find the Pellinni Jewels. She just
needed to decide where to start. Rocky's shady connections were probably the perfect place, but the only
ones she knew were Sleazy, who was dead, and Easy,
who was in jail, and in any case not disposed toward
helping her.

There was one other possibility. Rocky had mentioned a scarier than hell Russian with a fondness for
him—*perfect*. Since he hadn't mentioned the man's
name, her only clue was his innocuous-sounding place
of business, the Detroit Barber Shop. Surely a place of
business would have a listed phone number and address.

Rocky wouldn't like it, but he didn't have to
know until it was all over. It didn't require a criminal

background to handle his former associates. Wits and courage had been enough for her to escape Banner's Colombian friends. How could a Russian barber be any worse?

She cruised by the address several times, unsure where to park. Certainly not by the boarded-up building at the end of the block—the two men loitering in front of it stared each time she drove past, making her nervous. This probably wasn't the best time to have gotten her BMW back from the body shop. It stood out in this neighborhood. The safest place might be the unkempt parking lot across the street from the barber shop. The crumbled pavement was half covered by weeds, but there were three other cars there, snuggled close to the brick wall of the bar next door. Possibly employees— the neighborhood didn't look like it attracted much business. She parked near the other vehicles and walked across the street.

No bell tinkled to announce a new customer coming through the door, but it wasn't necessary. The two burly men in white jackets were staring at her before she cleared the threshold. Barbers, apparently. Big barbers, with hairy forearms and humorless expressions. They might have been Mr. Universe contestants if they'd consent to a full-body wax. There was no way she'd let either of them near her with a pair of scissors.

They sat in the only two barber's chairs, silently watching her.

She cleared her throat, wishing she'd thought this out a little better. "Hello. I'd like to talk to the owner, please."

The man in the first chair got to his feet and approached her slowly. "You want haircut?"

She shook her head. Could this be the guy who considered himself Rocky's friend? The heavy accent was Russian, and if she had to describe him, scary would have been one of the first adjectives that leapt to her mind. All the more reason to act unconcerned.

The man looked her over, ending with a glance at her hair. "You don't need haircut, is short enough. Maybe just little trim."

She folded her arms. "I don't want a haircut. I want to talk to the owner."

"Talk." He took another long look up and down, probably intended to intimidate or at least creep her out. He succeeded at both. "About what?"

He probably screened visitors. The other man hadn't moved, and she didn't see a sign of anyone else. "About selling some jewelry." She'd decided ahead of time that that had to be why Rocky knew him. "I'll save the specifics for your boss."

The last part had been intended to remind him of his place, but it didn't seem to bother him. "Jewelry," he repeated. This called for another up and down scan, maybe to determine if she was wearing any of the merchandise. He gestured at the chair he'd vacated. "Sit."

So he could pin her in place while he intimidated her, or worse? "No, thanks. I'll stand."

His eyes narrowed for a second, like a nervous tic, as he sized her up. He didn't look the least bit impressed. She glanced at the man who still occupied the other chair. He was a bit swarthier, and he stared back at her before giving her a small smile. He looked nicer when he wasn't smiling. The first man moved closer, the smell of onions on his breath mingling with a heavy dose of aftershave. She held her ground.

"No jewelry here. Cut hair." He leaned closer to examine the ends of her hair where they lay beneath her ears, and she forced herself not to flinch. "Could make shorter on neck."

He was either testing her or teasing his prey before eating it. "I like it the way it is." She nodded over his shoulder at the other living tribute to steroids. "Why don't you practice on your friend, there? He could use a trim. But first, call your boss. I don't have all day."

A humorless smirk pulled at his mouth. "Boss busy. You wait." He lifted his hand slowly toward her hair. "We find something to occupy us . . ."

"Don't touch me," she snapped. His hand stopped, inches from her head. "You touch one hair and I promise you'll be sorry."

In silence, he looked her up and down. Giving a derisive snort, he curled his upper lip. "Puny thing. Not worried."

She could see that was true. And she was letting him distract her from her goal. "Look, I came to make a deal. But if you don't want my business, I'll go elsewhere."

He didn't look impressed. "We cut hair. Who tell you we make deals?"

Progress—he'd asked her for information. Since it seemed he needed a name, she gave him one, hoping it wasn't the wrong thing to say. "Rocky told me."

She couldn't tell if the name registered with him, but it must have meant something to the other man because he pulled a cell phone from his pocket and dialed, watching her. They all waited in silence until he finally uttered a rapid monologue in Russian. Then listened. Then pocketed the phone.

"*Da.*"

She didn't know Russian, but she understood that much, especially when accompanied by the head jerk toward the back of the store. Someone wanted her taken back there. She just couldn't tell if it was a good or bad thing.

Muscle Man nodded toward the back of the store. "That way." At least he didn't touch her, which seemed sort of like respect.

She took a few steps, then turned to speak to him as she walked slowly toward the back. "Where are we going?" Not that it would make a difference, but it might quiet the wild fluttering in her chest.

"See Vasili." He leered at her. "Talk."

She was pretty sure that by *talk* he meant something other than talk.

If this was the dangerous element Rocky had wanted to keep her away from, she was ready to agree. They were heading for a door at the back of the shop, an interior room away from the big front window, away from witnesses. She fingered her car keys until one protruded from her closed fist. If she needed to defend herself, it would have to do.

The Neanderthal in the barber's coat opened the door. Taking a deep breath, she stepped inside a dim room. The door closed at her back.

An overhead light blazed to life and she shielded her face. A second later the blinding glare was eclipsed by the body of a man even larger than the two out front, but softer, his muscles comfortably hidden under a layer of fat. This had to be the guy she was looking for, even though he looked less scary than she'd expected; he was more like a dark version of Santa Claus.

The man settled his hands on his hips. "So. You know my friend Rocky."

She squinted. "Yes. Are you Vasili?"

As if her voice had set it off, she heard wild scrambling behind Vasili. He turned, too, eyebrows lifting in surprise as someone shoved him aside.

"Janet!"

Her heart pounded. "Rocky?"

"What the hell are you doing here? Never mind, you're leaving right now."

Emotions swirled like a whirlpool inside her—surprise at seeing him, curiosity about his visit, and most of all, annoyance at being caught. In order to cover up the latter, she tried to distract him. "How did you get here? I didn't see your car."

"You weren't supposed to. I parked in an alley three blocks down. You shouldn't be here." His clipped tone told her he was being more civil than he felt. "Come on, I'll walk you out."

He took her arm, but she shook him off. "No, thanks. I came on business, and I haven't had a chance to conduct it yet."

Vasili smiled with dawning understanding. "Ah! This short dark-hair girl?"

Rocky scowled. "Yeah, that's her."

The Russian drew himself up. "Introduce, please."

He gave an exaggerated sigh. "Janet, this is Vasili. Vasili, meet Janet Aims, the most contrary woman on the planet."

Vasili beamed and lifted her hand, placing a kiss on her knuckles. "My big pleasure."

She gave him a hesitant smile. "My pleasure, too." If Rocky thought Vasili was dangerous, she believed him, but at least the big Russian acted friendly. She was willing to go with that.

"What 'contrary' mean?" Vasili asked Rocky.

"Disobedient," she answered for him, broadening her smile and winking. "I don't like him telling me what to do."

Vasili chuckled, causing a full-body jiggle in the flabby parts. "Women not so good at taking orders, this I know." Casting a pitying look on Rocky, he said, "Sometimes you not so smart."

"Ha-ha," Rocky muttered. He directed a suspicious look at Janet. "How did you find this place?"

She shrugged. "You told me the name. I looked in the phone book."

He was obviously unhappy that he'd made it that simple for her. "Well, you wasted a trip. What you're looking for isn't here."

"How you know?" Vasili interrupted. "Don't interfere with customer. She say she come to do business. Maybe your Janet looking for jewelry, eh?"

"I am," she agreed.

"See?" He beamed. "I give good deal on many kinds jewelry. What you want, bracelet? Necklace?" His furry eyebrows wiggled upward. "Diamond ring, maybe?"

Rocky folded his arms. "She's looking for the rest of the Pellinni Jewels."

Vasili's expression became cautious and he glanced at Rocky before telling her, "I might have them."

"You don't have them," Rocky said.

"I don't have them," he corrected himself. Leaning toward Rocky, he said, "I thought I had them."

"If anyone besides Janet asks, you have them."

"Okay." He held his hands out helplessly as he looked at her. "Honest, I don't have them. But I have other jewelry. Better jewelry, not so much illegal."

Ignoring Vasili's equivocation on degrees of legality, she faced Rocky, hands on hips. "You two already planned something. I want in."

He said nothing, and his stubborn expression didn't change.

"Is no big deal," Vasili told her. "We make believe I have—" Rocky elbowed him. "No plan," Vasili shook his head. "Big nothing."

She narrowed her eyes at Rocky, which didn't affect his even stare one bit. Sensing Vasili was her only ally here, she told him, "You don't have to do what he says, you know. He just thinks it's his job to keep me safe."

Vasili hesitated, gaze darting from one to the other. "Is not bad thing."

"Is not fun, either."

"Maybe dangerous for you." One eyebrow lifted in warning.

She made a guess at his weak spot. "Sometimes there's no joy in life without a little risk."

"Ah! Is true," he affirmed. "You maybe little bit Russian, eh?"

"Maybe," she agreed, ignoring a snort from Rocky and saying a silent apology to her English and French ancestors.

Vasili beamed. "I knew this!" he said, shoving Rocky's shoulder.

"Oh, please." Rocky closed his eyes, as if in pain.

"But my friend Rocky is right about this thing," Vasili added.

Rocky looked as surprised as she did.

"Bad men in this business," Vasili went on. "Is no place for classy woman like you. Rocky is right to protect you. He is good man."

She didn't have an argument for that, since stubborn or not, Rocky was possibly the best man she'd ever known.

"You like him, yes?" Vasili prodded.

She darted a glance at Rocky before answering. "Yes."

In a low voice, Rocky said, "Stay out of this, Vasili."

"Maybe you love him, too."

"Vasili . . ." Rocky warned.

Something inside her went soft and mushy. She couldn't lie. "Maybe I do."

Rocky froze.

Vasili declared, "He should buy you jewelry. I give good price."

"He doesn't have to buy me anything." She met Rocky's startled gaze. "He just has to let me be part of his life."

"I have," he protested. "I mean . . ." He smiled and squinted as if he'd heard wrong. "Could you say that first part again?"

"I want to be part of your life."

"That's good, too, but I meant the other part."

"You lucky man!" Vasili slapped Rocky's back, although he'd looked so stunned to begin with she wasn't sure he even noticed. "Janet is good woman, better than you deserve."

"Thank you." She gave Vasili her best smile. "But I think Rocky deserves a good woman."

The Russian considered it. "If you say so."

"You just said I was a good man," Rocky reminded him.

"Not that good." He turned back to Janet. "Go on."

She'd given this some thought in the past twenty-four hours. "I think he deserves more than some casual affair with no real emotional connection."

Rocky cocked an eyebrow in obvious interest.

"Eh," Vasili said, dismissing his friend's love life. "Even good man can make do with bimbos. Woman like you deserves fine Russian man with romantic soul, who treat you like princess."

"You're very sweet, Mr. . . . Excuse me, I didn't get your last name."

"He just goes by Vasili," Rocky said.

"Petrovich. But you good friend, you call me Vasili."

Rocky rolled his eyes.

"Vasili, let me ask you something." She stepped closer and laid a hand on the Russian's beefy arm as he leaned toward her attentively. "Suppose a woman really cares for you—"

He nodded vigorously. "Do I care back?"

"I hope so."

"Let's say yes." Rocky smiled. "For the sake of your story."

"Okay," she said to Vasili. "This woman cares for you enough to want a real relationship. She's brave and clever in a crisis—she's proved this before."

"Good qualities," Vasili agreed.

"And she's smart enough to discover that her ex-husband was paying his lawyers with stolen diamonds, and she tells the police in time to recover them."

"No shit?" Rocky grinned. "Good job."

"Thank you."

"*Hmm*," Vasili rumbled as he frowned. "Police always a problem."

"Yes, well, this capable, smart woman wants to share every part of your life, even the slightly dangerous ones, because that's how much she cares about you. Do you let her?"

Vasili rubbed his chin. "Good question."

"Yes, it is." She spoke to Vasili, but her gaze was locked on Rocky. If she stood here much longer she might fall right into those feverish brown eyes. Before she could, she said, "You think about it and let me know."

"I will," Vasili called as she walked out the door.

She strode past the two burly barbers without glancing at them, yanking the outer door open without even a pause in her step. A feeling of power surged through her, a sense that she could take on the world. She nearly skipped across the street to the abandoned parking lot, elated with the way she'd laid her argument out, and even more elated with the way Rocky had reacted. It had been a long time since a man's smile had made her tingle, and his had shot jolts down to her toes.

She was reaching for the door handle of her BMW when a hand slipped around her neck and covered her mouth and nose, pulling her back against a hard body. Another hand chopped at her wrist, sending her keys flying from her suddenly numb fingers. She opened her mouth to scream, but a cloth muffled the sound. It smelled funny, too.

Oh, shit, not again. One deep gulp made her realize she should hold her breath, but it was too late. The already dusky sky went pitch black and the sound of heavy breathing in her ear faded to nothing as she slumped into unconsciousness.

Chapter Fifteen

Rocky grinned. "Damn, I love that woman."

Vasili nudged him with a his elbow. "Good! I have perfect ring for you!" He hustled around the counter, fumbling with his keys.

He laughed. "I'm not getting engaged, Vasili." He shot a thoughtful look toward the closed door. "At least not yet."

Vasili straightened. "Of course you marry Janet. You love her. Very beautiful girl. Fire in eyes." He gave a knowing wink. "You know what that mean."

He narrowed his eyes at the Russian, wondering what in the hell had happened to the Mafia boss who used to threaten to cut his fingers off if one single gemstone was missing from a heist he'd ordered. Romance seemed to have turned his aggressive tendencies to mush. The big guy was a sap—who knew?

"What you think, two carats? Three?"

"I'm not giving Janet a stolen ring."

"Not stolen." Vasili looked offended. "Loose stone.

Get band at store, all legit. Three maybe too much for little fingers, eh? I have nice two and a half."

Great, a hot diamond, probably stolen from some upscale suburban home and pried from its setting. "I already have a stone, Vasili." Anything to keep Janet from walking around the rest of her life with a stolen diamond on her finger.

What was he thinking? She wasn't talking about marriage, and one thing he knew about Janet was not to rush her. But she wanted a relationship, and that was good enough for now.

"Gotta go," he told Vasili, reaching for the door.

"Wait! We got business."

The sting. They'd had word that someone was interested in buying the remaining Pellinni Jewels and might show tonight. The response had been so fast, they were sure they'd hooked the right thief. When he showed, Rocky wanted an up-close look at the bastard who had searched Janet's condo and killed Sleazy. When he was done with him, Ben could have him.

"I'll probably be back before he shows. And I decided I'm bringing Janet, because she's right: We make one hell of a team, and I'm not going to risk losing that. If he stalls on closing the deal, you'll have it on tape, right? You have cameras hidden in here?"

Vasili stared under lowered brows. "I look stupid to you?"

He had cameras. "Not in the least. I'll be back."

"No hurry, she said let her know, she didn't say deadline," Vasili called after him, but Rocky didn't stop. He didn't want her to think he was hesitating, weighing the decision.

Rocky scanned the street, squinting through the

growing darkness as he looked for her rental car. Gone. Not surprising, since she'd had that purposeful look about her. He didn't want to chase her all the way back to Bloomfield Hills, then drive back here to wait for their thief to show up. If he could get her to pull over, he'd meet her somewhere. It might even be romantic.

He smiled to himself as he stood on the cracked sidewalk outside the barber shop and dialed her number. His gaze wandered along the street as he listened, idly noting the kids loitering outside the convenience store down the block. One ring. Up the street in the other direction, a resale store closed up for the night with a clang of metal bars shutting over the front window. Two rings. She was driving, so she might have to dig the phone out of her purse. Three rings. Four rings. He frowned and looked around again, doing a double take when he saw a BMW in the lot across the street.

He snapped the phone shut and jogged toward the car. The bar's neon sign cast the only light in the sheltered lot, but he could already tell that it was a dark colored BMW—not the usual car for this neighborhood.

An old man smoking on the sidewalk glanced at Rocky as he dashed by, tossed his cigarette in the gutter, and ducked into the bar. Probably avoiding whatever trouble had Rocky sprinting.

He reached the car and rounded it quickly, examining it. Dark blue, just like Janet's. There were no marks on the body, but it had been recently repaired. Nothing inside to give him a clue about the owner, and he didn't know her license plate number. He circled the car again, trying to remain calm, but something inside him was edging toward panic. He ran his hand over the smooth metal, peered through the windows, and stepped on something hard in the process.

He bent down. Keys—with a large, silver rectangle bearing a company emblem and black letters. He held it up to catch the light. Aims Air Freight.

A cold jolt of fear hit him in the gut. She hadn't left here on her own.

His gaze darted around the parking lot, though he knew there was nothing to find. She'd been taken. There was no other possibility.

Questions tumbled through his mind as the fear inside him thrashed and twisted like a wounded snake. This *had* to do with the Pellinni Jewels. Had he been followed again? Had his sting been turned back on him?

He couldn't think clearly; instinct took over. With frantic fingers, he called Ben. The Detroit police would take a call about a missing woman more seriously from Ben than from Rocky. Then Ben could help him search for Janet.

Rocky winced, remembering how the police chief had ordered him to keep Janet safe. His ass was grass, but he didn't care. Nothing Ben could do or say would be worse than what he already felt. If he didn't find Janet . . .

He would. He refused to think about any other possibility.

Ben was terse, snapping out questions and ordering him to stay put before hanging up. Rocky closed his phone, breathing as heavily as if he'd run a mile. His heart thundered even faster. He was torn, anxiety telling him to move, to search for her, and reality telling him he had no idea where to start. He paced the lot while he waited for the police.

There could be witnesses. The idea made him look frantically up and down the street. The group of kids was gone from the corner, but someone from the bar might have noticed her. She was pretty and had been in enough of a huff to be memorable, even without the expensive car.

Yanking open the door to the bar, he stopped just inside, scanning the small room. Dim yellow lamps hung over a banged-up pool table and several booths, but no one occupied them. At the bar, three old men looked up, faintly curious. The bartender who'd been slouched over the bar talking to them straightened up but said nothing.

The closest man was the smoker Rocky had seen earlier. All three seemed well past their first beer. The bartender was younger and far more clear-eyed. Rocky included him in his hard stare as he spoke. "Anyone see a young woman in the parking lot next door? White girl, pretty, short dark hair. It would have been just a few minutes ago."

The old guys looked at each other as if checking to see who knew the correct answer before shaking their heads. The bartender offered, "Ain't been outside."

The smoker waved a thumb in the direction of the parking lot on the other side of the wall. "She the one drivin' that fancy BMW?"

Excitement cracked through him like electricity, but he held perfectly still, as if his anxiety might leap across the room and shock the old guy. "Yes! You saw her?"

The guy tipped his beer and took a swig. "Nope. Nice ride, though." He looked at the guy next to him. "Tol' ya someone had a Beemer out there."

The fraying feeling inside Rocky intensified in a rapid unraveling of patience. Keeping his voice calm and even was the hardest thing he'd done in a long time. "Did you see anyone out there at all? Anyone passing by or hanging around? It's important. Someone may have abducted this woman."

The old men shook their heads and the bartender said, "Sorry, man." Two seconds later, they casually went back to their conversation. Just another missing woman, nothing worth getting excited about. Rocky turned and banged out the door, stalking back to the lot as the first police cruiser pulled up.

Ben arrived minutes later, and Rocky couldn't tell him any more than he told the Detroit cops. Janet hadn't received any threats that he knew of and had only been out of his sight for a few minutes. He did his best to leave Vasili out of it, admitting that he'd been at the barber shop, claiming he'd come for a haircut. Ben gave his overlong hair a skeptical glance, but when asked, Vasili backed up his claim, fairly demanding that the police officers admire Rocky's artistically trimmed ends. There was no way he'd mention the sting they had planned, and no way it would ever net them a thief now with three cop cars parked outside the door. The plan might be ruined for good. And Vasili looked torn between worry over Janet and a strong desire to string Rocky up by his tender parts and put his barber's shears to use on something other than his hair.

It was hard to care. If anything happened to Janet, it wouldn't matter what Vasili did to him. Nothing mattered to him as much as she did, not even his own life.

As soon as he could, Rocky snuck away. He didn't know where he was going, but he had to do *something*. If he stood around simply listening to theories he'd go crazy. He was at his car when his cell phone rang, and he dug it out of his pocket, half-annoyed at the interruption and half-hopeful it would be Janet.

He looked down and there was her name, solid and reassuring, on the caller ID. He flipped it open, plastering it to his ear. "Janet! Where are you? Are you okay? Holy shit, you scared the hell out of me!"

"Really? Good to know."

The voice was wrong—male, cocky, familiar. Anger tore through him. "Easy! Where's Janet?"

"Well, duh, where do you think? Your pretty little girlfriend is right here, keeping me company."

Fury churned in his chest, gripping his heart like a vise. He had to clamp his lips together to keep from sputtering profanities and threats. Caution was required, and he fought down the crazy part of him that longed to throttle the little weasel. His free hand plugged one ear to dull the city sounds and he lowered his head to growl into the phone. "What did you do to her? If you hurt her, I swear I'll kill you."

It was too rash; he knew it as soon as he said it.

"Hey! I'd watch the threats if I were you. Understand?" The sharp edge that jumped into Easy's voice convinced him to back off.

Rocky repeated the pertinent part. "What did you do to her?"

"Why? Are you worried? Mad?" Easy taunted. He almost expected to hear a childish *"Na-na-na-na-na."* If the man were standing in front of him, Rocky's hands would be around Easy's neck, choking the life out of him. "How does it feel when someone takes the thing you care about most? Yeah, I finally figured out what it was, Hernandez. Or rather, who."

Rocky didn't think taking Janet came close to the few gold doubloons he'd reclaimed from Easy, but he knew better than to say it. If Easy considered this a game of getting even, then it should be over now.

"So what do you want from me, Easy? You did what you said you were going to do. Congratulations. Now let her go."

"Does that sound fair to you?" The voice on the phone sounded unperturbed, even friendly. "I don't remember getting my gold coins back. Seems like that would be more fair, don't ya think?"

He wanted to make a trade? "I told you, those coins belonged to my grandmother. I gave them back."

"Oh, that's okay, 'cause I changed my mind," he said conversationally. "It turns out you have something I want more—the Pellinni Jewels."

He nearly held the phone out and stared at it. "*You* want the Pellinni Jewels?"

"Surprised? Did you think they were out of my league? I'm hurt, Hernandez."

That was exactly what he'd thought, but he revised it quickly. If Easy was the Pellinni thief, the man was also far more dangerous than he'd ever imagined. "You were the one who was coming to make a deal with Vasili?"

"Yeah, and imagine how surprised I was to see your girlfriend come skipping out of Vasili's place."

"She has nothing to do with this."

"I don't care." The smooth voice had become irritated. "I don't care if she's your partner or if you just bring your girlfriend along on jobs. What I care about is getting what I want. I want the Pellinni Jewels; I have a buyer waiting."

Now was not the time to say he'd never had the jewels. "You want to trade Janet for the jewels?"

"You get your valuables, so to speak, and I get mine."

All he could think was *stall*. "Vasili won't give them to me."

"Your problem. Meantime, sweet little Janet and I will get better acquainted."

Rocky responded exactly as Easy knew he would— with revulsion and rage—and used every bit of will-power he had to keep from screaming and swearing into the phone. He wouldn't give him the satisfaction. He also didn't want to imagine Easy laying one finger on Janet, much less doing whatever else came to the little asshole's mind. And the longer it took to get Janet back, the greater the chance that something would happen.

"Oh, and Hernandez? If you even think of calling the cops, you'll never see your cute little girlfriend again. You won't even find her body."

Rocky tried to think. Easy and Janet had to be somewhere nearby, no more than a half hour from where he stood, and yet he had no idea how to find them. The cell call could only be traced to a tower, which still left a million possible hiding places in a city this dark and dense. They could be anywhere. Even Canada, which was only fifteen minutes away by bridge or tunnel. Or boat. Security on the Detroit River between Canada and Michigan was lax enough for a criminal like Easy to bypass.

The possibilities made Rocky sick. Waiting even a day was too much. He didn't trust Easy to keep his hands off Janet, and Rocky didn't even know if she'd been hurt when he took her.

"Okay." He rubbed his forehead and took deep, slow breaths, inhaling damp night air. He had to sound like he intended to do what Easy asked. "I'll get the jewels, even if I have to buy them," he lied. "But I have to know that Janet is okay. You're not getting them until I talk to her."

"Of course. Call me when you get them, you know the number."

"Wait!" He relaxed marginally when Easy didn't hang up. "That's not good enough. How do I know she's not already dead?" He didn't think Easy would go that far, but he hadn't been terribly competent with the gas bomb. Rocky had no idea how Janet had been abducted. Hit on the head? Injected with drugs? The possibilities had him breaking out in a cold sweat. "You have to let me talk to her."

No answer. "Easy?"

"Hang on," Easy snapped.

It was simple to play weak and helpless when you were puking your guts out on a cold cement floor. Whatever had been used to knock her out had a brief but nasty effect on her stomach. And whoever had done it had bound her wrists and ankles with duct tape, connecting them with a string of tape that wasn't long enough for comfort, forcing her to keep her hands between her knees even while she was sprawled on the floor. It made being sick pretty damned awkward.

She'd wiggled as far away as she could from the mess on the floor. She was still bleary-eyed and groggy when Easy Joey crouched in front of her, holding out a cell phone and demanding she tell Rocky she was okay. Like she could make it sound believable.

Easy was giving her instructions she barely understood as she struggled to clear her head. She blinked as he talked, trying to make her eyes focus. Where was she? A dark doorway loomed to her right and a long hallway lay behind Easy's squatting form, a bare bulb on its ceiling the only source of light. "Where am I?" she mumbled.

"Never mind. Just tell him you're okay," he ordered. She was pretty sure it was the second or third time he'd said it. "But nothing else."

Speaking into a cell phone, he said, "Shut up and listen, Hernandez. I'm lettin' her talk so you know she's okay. But she's not answering any questions and I'll hear anything you say. Got it?"

Her mind was clearing, and she finally realized who Easy was talking to. "Rocky?"

"Yeah. Here, talk." He pressed the phone to her ear.

She cleared her throat and spoke hesitantly. "Rocky?" It still came out scratchy and weak.

"Janet!" His voice was edged with something she'd never heard from him before—fear. "Are you okay?"

"I'm . . . okay." Not really, but she knew being alive was all that mattered.

"I'll come get you as soon as I can, babe."

"I know."

"Okay, that's it." Easy pulled the phone away.

"Wait! I have to tell him something!" She didn't know what, but something that would help him figure out where she was. It was going to be hard, considering she didn't know that herself.

"You think I'm stupid? You're done. He knows you're alive. If I were you, I'd just hope I stayed that way."

"Please! It's important."

Her gaze darted around, looking for something that would give Rocky a clue. Squinting around Easy, she peered down the dimly lit hallway where a metallic flash caught her eye. If he noticed, he probably thought she was still woozy, leaning over like that and scrunching her forehead. But something looked familiar. It took several seconds, but she got it: She was looking at the edge of the barred window in Sleazy's pawnshop. They must be in the back of the shop, looking toward the front. And the metal winking at her from the floor beyond was the edge of Freddie's cage.

Her thoughts scrambled as she raised pleading eyes to Easy. "I left my dog locked up. Just let me tell him to feed my dog."

"I don't give a shit about your dog."

But he did look annoyed by her pleas. "But my poor puppy," she whined, making it sound as obnoxious as possible. "He must be so anxious and hungry, and his water is probably gone, too."

"Shut up!"

"I'm just so worried about him!" Desperation made a tear slip out, and she added some sniffles for effect. "Please let me tell him! I can't stand the thought of little Freddie suffering all night, maybe even longer."

Easy flinched from her grating whine, looking as

uncomfortable as if someone had dragged fingernails down a chalkboard. She cranked up the volume and added an hysterical edge. "Oh, God, what if no one finds me? What if I never get home and poor little Freddie—"

"Okay! Christ, just shut up. I can't stand that whining. Just tell him to feed the dog. Nothing else."

She sniffed and nodded. "I promise."

He held the phone back to her ear. "Rocky?"

"Janet!" His voice was pure panic. "What's going on? Has he hurt you?"

She wanted to talk to him forever, but Easy's cold stare drilled into her, reminding her that his patience was nearly gone. With her gaze locked on Easy's, she spoke over Rocky's frantic questions.

"Rocky, just listen. Remember to feed my dog, okay?"

"What?"

She opened her mouth to repeat it, but Easy pulled the phone away, disconnecting before she could say another word. "There, little Fido's safe. But you're not, so shut the fuck up."

She did. She just hoped Rocky figured out her message.

Rocky lowered the phone slowly. Feed her dog? Freddie didn't belong to Janet, but he was the only dog they both knew. Dog food was her clue? It seemed an unlikely stretch. Or had feeding him just been an excuse to bring up the dog. Because she hoped he'd connect Freddie to—

Damn, he loved that woman. He was in the car

and laying rubber within seconds. When he got there he could figure out if he'd guessed right and call Ben.

Or not. Some things were best left to the thieves.

Janet figured Easy probably had an aversion to distraught females and gave in just to get her to shut up. She hoped that meant he didn't have enough duct tape left to cover her mouth.

Just in case, she pretended to gag again, which at least got him to take a couple steps back. "Sorry about the ether," he mumbled, looking slightly ill himself. "That should wear off soon."

It *was* wearing off, but she wasn't sure she wanted him to know. She studied his face in the dim light, trying to figure out the best way to play it. He was keeping a cautious distance and casting disgusted glances at the pool of vomit to her right. Clearly not the grit and fortitude type. And since he'd trussed her like a roped calf, he probably feared any sort of aggression. Meek and cooperative was probably the way to go, to keep his defenses down. She might even catch him off guard if she could play on his sympathy.

"Can I clean up?" She kept her voice soft and a little whiney.

"No."

So much for mercy. "Please?" She tried again, adding a helpless, pleading look. It had worked before. "Just a drink of water to wash my mouth out?"

His lips pulled into a grimace as if tasting sickness in his own mouth. With a sudden pivot, he disappeared into the darkened room across the hall, reappearing with a paper cup. He thrust it toward her mouth. "Here."

She leaned toward it, swishing the first mouthful and spitting it on the floor, then eagerly swallowing the next. He pulled the cup back as she tried for more. "You'll get sick again."

He was probably right about that. The water had stirred up a feeling of nausea and she leaned against the wall, willing it to pass. The fact that he seemed to be familiar with the effects of ether didn't make her feel any better. While she concentrated on quieting her stomach, Easy laid about a mile of paper toweling over the puddle of puke, taking care to cover every drop. *Just a little neurotic?*

He stepped back and stared at her. She had the creepy feeling he'd do the same thing on a date. Apparently it was up to her to carry the conversation.

Best to start with the obvious. "Why did you bring me here?"

"I'm holding you for ransom."

"For the Pellinni Jewels—yeah, I heard." She'd barely been conscious, but that much had sunk in. It was a dead-end topic, since she didn't plan to stick around long enough to be traded. The duct tape was going to make escape difficult, though. Maybe she could get him to release her if it were for something a bit more serious than a drink of water.

She squirmed. "I have to use the bathroom."

"Hold it."

"I don't think I can."

He thought, then nudged her foot with his. "You got some slack between your wrists and ankles. You could stand if you stay hunched over. If you take baby steps you'll eventually get to the bathroom. Might be entertaining to watch."

That was an awkward picture. "Uh . . . and how do I use it when I get there? You'll still have to untie my hands."

He grinned, a slow, challenging leer. "I'll be glad to unfasten your pants for you and pull them down."

Talk about revolting. "Thanks, I think I'll hold it."

He still smiled. "Suit yourself."

If Rocky didn't come soon, the bathroom trip would become more than hypothetical, and the gleam in Easy's eyes told her he was still stuck on that particular fantasy. She needed a new topic of conversation, but the choices were limited. "Rocky doesn't have them, you know. The Pellinni Jewels."

Easy shrugged. "He'll get 'em if he wants you back."

"What if he can't?"

He tilted his head, sizing her up. "Then I guess you become disposable. A liability, like the last guy I talked to right in this very building. He didn't have the jewels, either. Guess you don't know about that, do you?"

But she did. Cold sliced through her, bringing the nausea back with a rush.

Rocky had acted like Easy was harmless, and she'd thought so, too, from the way he cringed or ran away when confronted. Apparently a gun made him bolder.

Her gaze darted to his pockets and she looked for a bulge under his shirt. She saw nothing, but that didn't mean he didn't have a gun somewhere. She licked her lips and didn't have to pretend to be scared. "You killed someone?"

"Shit happens." A sliver of interest shone in his eyes. "Worried your boyfriend won't come through?"

"No."

They stared at each other for another minute. "So, you done being sick now?"

Was there an advantage one way or the other? "Maybe."

"Let's hope so." He reached into a backpack that had been in the shadows, pulled out a roll of duct tape, and ripped off a six-inch piece.

Oh, no. "What are you—"

He pressed the tape over her mouth.

Shit.

Chapter Sixteen

Easy wanted to move her. For whatever reason, he preferred the darkness of the room across the hall. It was better for hiding, but Janet thought the uncomfortable looks he kept throwing at the pile of paper towels were part of it, too.

She didn't want him touching her but the shuffling gait he'd described proved impossible to perform. He grabbed her under the arms as she stood bent at a ninety-degree angle, and half carried, half dragged her into the room. Once there, she saw that it wasn't completely dark—a wedge of light slipped through from the hallway bulb, gradually allowing her eyes to adjust.

Skeletal metal shelves filled the room in rows. He'd dumped her unceremoniously against a wall at the far end of one shelf. Struggling into a sitting position, she spotted another door to the side, opening into a bathroom. White lines caught the light—the chalk outline of a body covered most of the bathroom floor. She looked away quickly.

Easy sat on the cement near her, playing with the gun he'd pulled out of his bag of tricks. Loading it. Polishing it with his shirt. Pointing it at her while making a soft click with his tongue. Fun for everyone.

She sat quietly, hands dangling between her bent knees as she picked at the twisted length of tape connecting her wrists to her ankles. At this rate she'd be able to rip through it in about another two months.

Progress with the tape on her mouth was more encouraging. For the past hour she'd forced every bit of spit she could muster through her lips, gradually wetting the skin around her mouth and chin. The tape was starting to feel loose. At least if Rocky broke in she'd be able to brush it off with her arm and yell a warning.

That wouldn't be good enough, though. Even if he could break into this fortress of a store, she doubted he could do it without making a sound.

More than an hour passed, and the cold from the cement floor was spreading through her, stiffening her muscles. Keeping her hands hidden behind her knees, she picked at the tape, irrationally encouraged by the miniscule bit she nicked off as she watched Easy fondle his gun. She was about to give up on being rescued when she heard a small sound from the front of the store.

She immediately shuffled her feet and cleared her throat, but Easy had heard it, too. "Shut up," he ordered. Just in case she didn't want to, he touched the gun barrel to her temple. She froze.

Seconds ticked by while her heart hammered in her chest. Her ears strained to hear. Finally, it came again—a clicking sound, like a door closing.

Her heart soared. She rubbed her face on her sleeve, trying to start the edge of the tape to peel away from her mouth. The only way she could help Rocky would be to call out, letting him know where they were.

"Don't move." Easy's harsh whisper was next to her ear, his face touching the side of her head as he spoke. "If you do, I'll shoot you. He'll want you even more if you're wounded, so it makes no difference to me. Understand?"

She nodded, frozen in place.

He stood and crept soundlessly toward the door, gun pointing forward and leading the way. He reached one hand around the corner, flicking a switch. The hall light went out, leaving the storage room in pitch darkness. She could no longer see him—which meant he couldn't see her. Ducking her head down to meet her hands, she found the edge of the tape and pulled. A few hairs above her lip pulled off with it, but the rest fell away easily. She wiped her mouth on her sleeve and paused to listen.

Nothing. Easy had to be creeping toward the front office. If Rocky was out there, she should warn him that Easy had a gun. But if he wasn't there, she might get herself shot for nothing.

From above her a shadow moved. She couldn't see anything, but heard something drop through a hole in the ceiling to the steel shelf unit beside her, and from there to the floor. The figure landed at her feet with barely a sound. She gasped and drew back, only Easy's previous warning keeping her from screaming.

A pencil-thin beam of light swept the room, landed on her, then flicked off. "Shhh!" A hand covered her mouth while the warm body moved closer to her. A familiar scent encompassed her. Behind the hand, she breathed a barely-audible, "Rocky!"

His cheek touched hers as he whispered in her ear, similar to what Easy had done but far nicer to experience. "Don't talk. Stand up."

"Can't. Duct tape."

He didn't say anything, but one hand trailed down her arm to her hands and the light shone on the silvery tape for two seconds, then went out. Moments later she felt something cool and hard slip past her hands. With a soft ripping sound, the tape parted. She yanked at it as he slit the tape on her ankles, gritting her teeth as the tape performed as well as a wax, pulling hairs out by the roots.

Rocky tugged on her hands, helping her to her feet. "Okay?" he whispered.

She took it to mean, *Can you walk?* She nodded and grasped his arm, eager to get out of there even if she had to limp and hobble.

An explosion of sound ripped from the doorway and something rang against a metal shelf above her head.

"Down!"

Rocky didn't wait for her to follow his order. He shoved her to the floor, shielding her body with his own. She tried to flatten herself against the floor, but he pushed her toward the cold edge of a bottom shelf "Go!"

It was tight, but she did, ducking into the open metal shelving and pushing through to the next row as another bullet blasted into the shelf not far from where she'd rolled through, zinging as it ricocheted and sending a vibration through the metal. Easy was aiming low, which meant he must have heard her—or Rocky.

Where had Rocky gone?

She crouched on the cement floor, every instinct telling her to run. But in a pitch black room that plan didn't seem so smart. Plus, Easy was standing in the only doorway. He'd stopped shooting, but she heard him there, slapping at the wall searching for the light switch. If the lights came on, she was dead. Wounded, anyway. According to Easy, she just had to be alive to be useful, not necessarily whole.

If she stayed calm she might escape. Fortunately, she'd had some self-defense training, thanks to Rocky and the Bloomfield Hills Lady Sparks. A few deep breaths did nothing to calm her racing pulse, but at least it cleared her mind. Concentrate: What had Rocky said about an attacker with a gun? Oh yeah—that he wouldn't tell them how to defend themselves in that situation because it was too dangerous to try. Great. Scream and run, he'd said. Except no one was around to hear her scream, and there was no place to run.

A flare of light interrupted her thoughts as Easy found the switch. Fluorescent bulbs flickered and caught, illuminating the rows of bare shelves. She ducked from the sudden glare, then shielded her eyes and squinted through the empty metal framework. Rocky, her phantom rescuer, was gone. She staggered to her feet, gaze darting toward the doorway. Easy stood just inside the door, gun pointed outward as his anxious gaze scanned the empty rows. Probably looking for Rocky, too. But Easy's eyes found hers, and his lip twisted into the semblance of a smile. Through the shelves, the gun aligned with her heart.

She couldn't look away. Even the flicker of movement in the corner of her eye couldn't tear her gaze from the gun. Then the flicker turned into a blur as Rocky dropped through an open ceiling tile onto a top shelf, before hurtling outward. Arcing out like a diver in freefall, he slammed into Easy.

Easy yelled in surprise as they crashed to the floor and rolled apart. Easy skidded toward her, while Rocky rolled in the opposite direction. The gun hit the floor with a clatter and slid toward Rocky. She saw him spot it as he got to his feet. If she acted quickly she could get to him, passing Easy before he got up.

She ran. Easy scrambled to intercept. Her leap almost cleared him, but her muscles were stiff and he snagged her foot, throwing her off balance and slamming her into the nearest shelves. She felt like the dummy in an impact test as steel rammed into her hip and shoulder. Bruised, if not broken, she clung to the shelf. An arm snaked around her neck, pulling her backward as Easy put her in a choke hold. He swung her toward the doorway, and she saw why.

Rocky pointed the gun at them. At her. The way he held it with two hands and a braced stance made her think he knew how to use it, but she had no idea how good his aim was. Maybe it didn't matter; Easy hid every vital part of himself behind her. His hold tightened on her neck, forcing her to gag as her airway constricted.

"Shoot him," she croaked.

"Go ahead," Easy agreed, nearly lifting her off her toes as his arm tightened further. "Or drop it and she gets to live."

On second thought, living would be nice. She tried

to amend her choice, but couldn't get any words out. It took all her effort just to inhale a raspy breath.

Rocky didn't answer and didn't move.

Easy did, circling the two of them around Rocky toward the doorway. Rocky backed away, letting Easy drag her along. When they reached the hallway, he finally spoke. "I can't let you leave, Easy."

"I don't see you stoppin' me. Thing is, I want my gun back. And I'll bet you want the bitch. So toss it here and I'll trade you."

Janet pulled at the arm that cut off her air, fighting to breathe.

"Not much of a choice," Rocky said in a tone she found altogether too thoughtful. "Could I have a third alternative? There must be something else we can do."

His steady gaze met hers. As if his last words had been meant for her, she fought to calm herself and focus on the problem. He'd held her like this once, without the constricted airway and the flood of adrenaline that made it so hard to concentrate.

Easy was losing his patience. "You've got three seconds to drop it, Hernandez, or I'll—goddamn son of a bitch!" The exclamation nearly broke her eardrum. She flinched but didn't release the fingernails she'd dug into his arm or the hunk of flesh she grabbed between her teeth as soon as his grip relaxed enough for her to move her jaw.

"*Aiyeee!*" Easy screamed. His free hand batted at her head and connected. As the blow stunned her into letting go, Rocky darted forward. His fist connected with Easy's face and he fell back, releasing her. She crumpled to her knees, hands on her throat, wheezing painful, wonderful gulps of air into her lungs. Rocky crouched in front of her and she glimpsed his concerned expression before she was distracted by Easy stumbling toward the back door. Unable to shout a warning, she pointed.

Rocky turned. With an almost casual move, he raised his right arm and fired the gun. Easy screamed and staggered. Limping away, he slipped on the pile of paper towels covering her puddle of vomit. Feet flying out from under him, he crashed onto the cement floor and lay still.

Rocky pulled Janet to her feet. "Are you okay? Let me see."

She nodded and pushed his hands away from her neck. It hurt with every breath, but his concerned look tore at her heart. Fighting off the trembling aftershocks of adrenaline, she stared from Easy's still form back to Rocky.

"You shot him," she whispered hoarsely.

He threw a dismissive glance at Easy before taking her by the shoulders. "Just in the foot. Now hold still and let me see your neck."

She did, her incredulous gaze shifting between him and Easy until he seemed satisfied that she was unhurt. Then he hugged her hard and kissed her, nearly distracting her from the fact that her abductor and almost killer lay on the floor less than twenty feet away. She kissed him back with a bit more passion, then motioned toward Easy. "We should check," she said, asking as little of her larynx as possible. Easy still hadn't moved, and Rocky didn't seem to care.

He sighed and followed as she cautiously approached Easy's body. Rocky knelt and felt his neck for a pulse, then pulled back an eyelid. "He's out.

He hit his head pretty hard." Wrinkling his nose, he looked around. "What smells?"

She pointed to the paper towels scattered over the floor. "Whatever he used to knock me out made me sick. I threw up, and he piled paper towels on top of it. Must have been slippery."

"You took him down with puke?"

She shrugged, not nearly as amused as he was. "Shooting him would have been more satisfying."

He smiled. "You did exactly the right thing."

She pursed her lips and sighed, grumbling, "I guess so." But just for good measure, she kicked Easy's foot. The one with the neat hole through the center.

Chapter
Seventeen

A ringing sound woke her up. Janet slapped the alarm on her nightstand several times, before realizing it was the phone. Eyes still closed, she fumbled for it, pulling it under the covers. " 'Lo?"

"You have a collect call from an inmate at the Oakland County Jail. Will you accept the charges?"

Huh? She scooted up on her pillow, brushing hair off her forehead while trying to think. She must have forgotten to shut off the service that allowed her to receive calls from inmates, or Banner's call wouldn't even have gotten this far. Who else could it be?

She didn't want to talk to him. She opened her mouth to refuse the call when curiosity made her pause. Banner hated her; there was no way he would want to talk to her. What was so important that he'd swallowed his pride and called?

"Yes, I'll accept the charges."

Rocky rolled over and slid his arm around her waist. Nuzzling against her breast, he murmured, "Who's that? Jack and Ellie? Was their plane delayed?"

"Banner."

"What?" His head popped up, eyes narrow and alert. "Why?"

She shrugged and held up a finger as Banner came on the line. "Good morning, Janet."

Was that warmth she heard? "What do you want, Banner?"

"I apologize for the early call; I don't have much latitude on the times that I'm permitted to use the phone."

An apology? She must be dreaming. That or something really bad was coming. If Banner thought one little apology would soften her heart, he was sorely mistaken. "Get to the point."

"Of course. You undoubtedly have things to do."

Rocky sat up, throwing the sheet back with annoyance. "What's he saying?"

She covered the speaker. "*Shhh.*"

"I'll be brief," Banner said. "As you know, my attorneys sent someone on my behalf to collect the crystal and china we spoke of."

"Yes, I know." Elizabeth had monitored the process, making sure none of her own pieces were taken.

"Well, apparently"—he chuckled, a disturbingly artificial sound—"it seems he neglected to take one bowl."

Banner had called her from jail to ask about china? She couldn't keep the incredulity from her voice. "A bowl? You want a *bowl*?"

"A serving bowl from the blue-and-white stoneware set. Do you remember it?"

"It sounds familiar, but I don't know anything about a missing serving bowl."

"It must be mixed in with your dishes, Janet. Will you look for it?"

She stared at the phone, then shifted her puzzled gaze to Rocky. "He says I have one of his blue-and-white stoneware dishes," she whispered.

He snorted. "And he needs it right now? Why, are they having a potluck on cellblock D?"

Laughter bubbled in her throat, and she muffled the phone against her stomach while she choked it back.

"Janet, are you there?"

She cleared her throat and elbowed Rocky. "Yes, I'm here."

"I'm sorry to bother you with this, but I would really like the set to be complete. I ordered it from a local artisan to match the upholstery of our dining room suite, remember? It's become a memento of . . . happier times. Would you mind looking for it?"

Something was up. Banner was being friendly, polite, and downright maudlin—about a serving bowl! As if he would ever use it again. "Okay, I'll look."

"Thank you. If you find it, you can call Nathan Eiger. He's the attorney handling my case. I switched firms."

That can happen when you try to pay your legal team with stolen diamonds. "Nathan Eiger, got it." She hung up before Banner's good-bye was even out of his mouth.

Rocky frowned. "What's that about Nathan Eiger?"

"Banner's new attorney. I'm supposed to call him if I find his precious bowl."

"Figures. The guy makes a career out of representing slime." He studied her. "Banner and Eiger are not what you should wake up to. I think I need to get them out of your mind." He grabbed her and fell back, holding her on top of him.

"Excellent idea." She kicked the tangle of blankets away from her legs. Skin touched skin all the way down her body—much better. A lingering kiss made it better yet. "Hang on," she said, leaning sideways and groping over the edge of the bed.

"What are you doing?"

"Getting a condom out of your jeans. They're right here on the floor, and the nightstand is all the way across the bed. I think I can reach—"

With a yelp of surprise she fell back as he flipped her over and rolled on top. "No problem, I've got it."

He leaned to his left as he straddled her, reaching for her nightstand.

"I've already got them." Yanking the jeans onto the bed, she pulled the small packet out of his pocket and found her hand tangled with his as he tried to take it from her. "You don't have to be so eager, I know how to—" she took a look at the small plastic bag in her hand. "This isn't a condom."

He sighed and released her hand. "No. It's a surprise. On me. Just like every time I think I can keep you out of something."

She scooted into a sitting position and dangled the bag in a ray of sunshine, examining the object inside. A white gold band held a diamond that sparkled in the morning light. She sucked in a breath.

"What is . . . um . . ." She licked her lips. "Whose is it?"

"It's for my fiancée."

He grew still, watching her. She couldn't meet his

eyes, overcome by a sudden shyness, which felt all the more ridiculous when she was sitting there naked in front of the man who'd kissed every inch of her body.

But neither of them had ever mentioned marriage.

She lowered the baggie and stared at it—anything to avoid looking at him—while her mind scrambled to sort out her feelings.

"Janet."

She bit her lip. "Hmm?" The emotions zipping through her were surprisingly pleasant.

He reached out and tilted her chin up. He looked so gentle and concerned that she wondered just how vulnerable he thought she was, because she wasn't anymore. Her confidence had returned, and he was a big part of why.

"Janet, you know I love you."

She nodded, feeling the familiar warm rush. "I love you, too."

He brushed back her hair, reminding her of the unkempt mess he was no doubt looking at. Great, possibly the most significant emotional moment in her life, and she was sitting there with bedhead, not wearing a stitch of clothes.

"It's a comfortable place to be, loving each other, learning how well we work as a couple. And by the way, I think we work pretty damn well."

"I do, too." She swallowed audibly. Even though comfortable was nice, she didn't want to settle for that anymore. She wanted marriage, kids, and all the excitement that went with them.

"I wanted to give you some time to get used to us being together."

"I don't need time." She knew it in her bones and

felt it in every cell of her body. "I've wasted too much already."

He grinned in the lopsided way that always tugged at her heart. She was such a sucker for that smile.

"Are you sure? Because I was going to wait. . . ." His voice trailed off as he plucked the little plastic bag from her hands. "Before asking for anything more."

She raised an eyebrow and tried not to throw a longing look at the ring and everything it represented. "I'm not so fragile, you know."

He cocked his head thoughtfully. "No you aren't. I think I'm still learning how strong you are." He fingered the bag. "So maybe you'd be willing to consider something more?"

Tingles crept up her spine. "Maybe I would."

He pulled the ring out of the bag but didn't offer it to her. "There's a story that goes with this ring. Not as historically significant as the story behind the Pellinni Jewels, but one far more important to me."

She hadn't cared about the Pellinni Jewels, but this ring captured her attention the way Rocky had captured her heart.

"This diamond didn't originally belong on this band."

Disbelief crept in. "You didn't get it from Vasili, did you?"

He chuckled. "No, although he offered. And before you ask, it isn't from Banner's private collection, either."

Good to know.

"It was originally set in a heavy gold band made in Spain a few hundred years ago. It was intended to be worn by a man. It's one of the pieces I recovered for my grandmother. She repaid me by giving me this heavy, ostentatious ring that hadn't been in style since the time of the Conquistadors. I didn't want it. I tried to give it back, but she told me I was meant to have it. It had traveled thousands of miles and had been passed down through generations of my family, and so it was a symbol of strength and endurance. She told me to keep it for the day when I met the woman with those same qualities, the woman I wanted to spend the rest of my life with."

"Oh." No other sound could get past the tight knot in her throat.

"And I did. I took it to a jeweler and asked him to reset the stone in a new band, something suitable for a woman who surpasses the strength and beauty of my grandmother's diamond."

She blinked back a tear. "You didn't really say that."

He smiled. "Yes, I did. And it was in my pocket because I just picked it up yesterday and I didn't want to put it back in a box when I'd already found the woman it should belong to." He held out. "Will you marry me, Janet?"

They locked eyes. "Yes," she whispered. "Oh, yes."

She sniffled as he slipped the band on her finger, then laughed as she marveled at how well it fit. "It's beautiful! And the perfect size."

He shrugged modestly. "I know a little about jewelry."

Laughing again, she threw her arms around him. "I love you so much."

He smiled and pulled her down beside him for a kiss. A long kiss, one that turned into soft touches and tender nibbles, and ended, predictably and happily, where it usually did.

It wasn't just sex; it never had been. It was so much more. Physical sensations blended so seamlessly with emotion that she couldn't separate the love from the lovemaking. It was just the way it was supposed to be.

Exhausted and content, she fell back on the bed, breathing hard. A white ball of fur landed beside her, offered a dignified strut across her stomach, and sat on Rocky's chest, staring him down. She propped herself up to confirm what she already suspected—Jingles sat on the floor beside her, delivering the same telepathic message. "I think we're being tag teamed."

Rocky stroked the cat before setting her aside. "I can take a hint." He sat up, casually running a hand down Janet's bare thigh, a gesture that elicited the same rumbling purr from her as it had from Fluff. "Are you coming down for breakfast, babe?"

"Mmm. Right after a shower." She smiled and watched as he walked out the door.

She tried to hurry but kept getting distracted by the ring on her finger. The irony hadn't escaped her. She'd successfully avoided Rocky for months, until hocking Banner's engagement ring. Less than two weeks later, she was wearing Rocky's ring. It sounded impulsive and rash. Except it was an impulse she'd been resisting for a year, and she had no doubt it was the smartest, sanest, most *right* thing she'd ever done.

Janet dried off, dressed, and skipped down the stairs, then pulled up short at the kitchen doorway. Rocky stood shirtless, wearing nothing but jeans, his delectable butt propped against the counter and a thoughtful expression on his face. It was a sight worth savoring, so she did, even as she wondered what was so fascinating about watching their cats eat.

Fluff and Jingles crunched cat food as Rocky watched intently. She smiled. "Are you considering kibble instead of cereal? If so, I may have just lost my appetite."

"Hey." He grinned like he hadn't just seen her twenty minutes ago, then nodded at the cats. "That bowl they're eating out of looks exactly like the one you said Banner is looking for."

She stared at the twelve-inch shallow blue serving bowl with a white ring around its outer edge. "Huh. I think you're right. No wonder it wasn't with the rest of his stuff. Damn, I suppose this means I should wash it and give it to his lawyer. The sooner I get rid of the last reminder of Banner, the better."

She pulled the dish from under the offended noses of the two cats, who meowed their distress. Dumping the cat food into another bowl, she returned it to the floor and rinsed out the heavy blue dish.

"Now I remember why I decided to use this bowl," she told Rocky. "Besides the fact that it would piss him off if he knew, which naturally was a factor, it's heavy. Jingles used to shove his bowl around the floor, and I'd trip over it. He can't move this one an inch."

She held it up. "See, it has this thick base even though the inside isn't very deep." She paused, scrunching her brows as she took a closer look.

"It doesn't look that special," Rocky said. "Not Banner's style. I can't imagine why he wants it."

Holding the bowl higher, she examined it from all angles as she talked. "He had the set of dishes made to match the dining room furniture. He consulted on the design and everything," she said absently, turning the bowl over in her hands. Her mouth fell open as the realization hit her. Looking up, she said, "I know why he wants it."

He gave her a puzzled look.

She held the bowl out. "Look. There's a good inch between the inside of the bowl and the base. And it's *heavy*." She handed it to him.

Rocky hefted it and handed it back. "So? Stoneware's supposed to be heavy."

"If that's what it is."

"What else would—" his eyes widened as he got it. "You think?"

She lifted her eyebrows, excitement growing. "Why not? He had it made to order. And he seems awfully interested in getting it back." Her excited gaze left the bowl and darted around the kitchen, finally landing on the back door. Meeting Rocky's eyes, she said, "The patio."

He nodded and followed her out the back door to the small square of flagstones and grass that passed as a backyard.

If she was right, this warranted a pause for dramatic effect. She raised the bowl up, then hurled it to the ground. The stoneware smashed loudly enough to wake the neighbors. She hopped backward as ceramic shards flew in all directions, scattering across the yard. At the point of impact, several large chunks of crockery lay in splintered ruins. She peered closer and caught her breath. Amid the chipped pieces of blue-and-white pottery were bits of cotton padding; a brooch, a ring, and two earrings gleamed in the sunlight.

Rocky stepped carefully through the shards, shoving a few pieces aside with his bare feet. Bending over the shattered base, he held up the filigreed gold earrings with their dark red stones. He laid them in his palm along with a pearl- and ruby-encrusted broach and a matching ring.

He presented them to her with a triumphant grin. "The Pellinni Jewels."

She examined the pieces in his hand and wrinkled her nose. "They're as ugly as the necklace."

"And just as valuable."

That part still amazed her. "And just as stolen. I can't believe I had them all along." She drew her eyebrows together. "What was Banner going to do with them, pay off another lawyer?"

"Eiger? I wouldn't be surprised. It's not like Banner could turn them in to the FBI. It'd prove he had them all along."

"But I can."

Rocky dumped the priceless pieces of jewelry into Janet's open hands. "Thank God," he said with feeling. "And then it'll all be over."

She fondled the jewels, distracted by the thought that she might be holding a million dollars in the palm of her hand.

He watched, arms folded. "You know, I think this is the first time since I've known you that I finally don't have to worry about some dangerous, disreputable man wanting something from you." He cocked his head, considering her with a smile. "How will I stand the tedium?"

She had to tell him sometime. "Well—"

Suspicion replaced his smile with tightly pressed lips. "What?"

"It's just that I got a call yesterday. From Vasili."

"He *called* you? *You*?" His brows lowered as he demanded, "Why?"

"He wanted to know when we're getting married."

He ground his molars hard enough to crack enamel. "He can't come to our wedding. Please tell me you didn't say he could."

"I didn't even know we were getting married. But—" she shrugged meekly. "He said we would, and he sort of invited himself. How could I tell him no?"

"Bluntly. Forcefully. Like this: *No*."

"But he's always so charming and effusive. We can't hurt his feelings."

Rocky nodded firmly. "Yes, we can."

She winced and delivered the bad news as quickly as possible. "It's too late; I sort of promised to invite him."

Resignation mingled with despair on his face.

Rushing to make him feel better, she asked, "How bad can it be?" She wasn't sure she wanted an answer.

He raised one eyebrow. "Vasili in the same room with Elizabeth and Ben?" His expression grew more bleak. "With my mother? With your mother?"

She swallowed. "What do we do?"

He sighed and wrapped an arm around her shoulder. "It'll be okay. We'll be married, and that's all that matters." He gave her a reassuring squeeze, then added a pained afterthought. "But I think we should warn all our guests not to wear jewelry."

Epilogue

In the gathering dusk, the Westfield grounds were a fairyland of lights and ribbons. Janet couldn't believe their luck in getting to hold the wedding and reception there. It had taken a year to sell the mansion, and in another month Elizabeth would sign the papers and turn it over to a new family. Janet and Rocky's wedding marked the end of an era, Elizabeth claimed, and she wanted to end it in typical Westfield style. The fact that she was a Thatcher now didn't seem to matter.

Janet meant to enjoy every last second of it. At the moment, that meant taking a break from dancing and socializing to steal a kiss in the shadows with her new husband.

Rocky kept one arm around her waist as they sipped their drinks inside the shelter of the gazebo and watched their guests across the lawn. Nearly two hundred people gathered on the patio and the adjoining dance floor—a modest celebration by Westfield standards. She scanned the crowd, looking for her maid of honor.

"Where's Ellie?"

"Inside with Jack, checking on little Ben. For being only a month old, that baby sure knows how to wrap his parents around his tiny fingers."

"I'm just surprised his grandparents and big sister aren't inside the house cooing over him, too."

"I don't know about Ben and Elizabeth, but Libby's busy with her best friend."

They had a clear view of Libby standing beside the cake table. She appeared to be cutting slices and setting them out for guests, but every so often they could see a hand slip below the table as she snuck crumbs to Freddie. The dog snatched them with a quick lick before looking away, as innocent as if he were guarding the cake rather than eating it. In fact, he might be guarding it, whether he meant to or not. Freddie had grown into a striking dog, and the flowers around his neck from his role as their ring bearer didn't do a thing to soften the watchful pose of an adult German shepherd.

Considering the amount of cake left, maybe he was too intimidating. "Do you think Elizabeth and Ben are okay with letting Libby keep Freddie here for the reception? Some of the guests might be too afraid of him to get a piece of cake."

"Are you kidding? That's exactly why Ben loves the idea. Watch this." He grinned in anticipation and nodded to the right of Libby.

Janet followed his gaze. A young man slowly made his way around the dance floor, smiling and exchanging hellos, but never stopping as he worked his way toward the cake table.

Janet frowned. The boy looked to be about sixteen or seventeen, far too old for Libby. Of course, he might not realize that. Jack and Ellie's daughter looked frighteningly mature in her pale blue bridesmaid's gown.

Libby finally noticed him as Freddie finished a smear of frosting off her finger. Janet smiled. A mixture of pride and panic clutched her heart as she realized how close her friend's daughter was to womanhood and how many boys would soon be making this same approach, testing their luck.

The boy stepped closer, smiling and cocking his head in the manner every man used when checking out a woman. Janet tensed as she watched.

She wasn't the only one.

At knee level, Freddie's body bumped the young man as the dog inserted himself between them. The boy took a step back, looking down to meet the direct stare of two unblinking canine eyes. Every muscle on Freddie was alert, from his sharply pricked ears to his stiffly planted hind legs.

Libby smiled, dropping her hand to Freddie's head in an obvious introduction. The boy's gaze flicked between Libby's casual smile and Freddie's hard stare. Although they couldn't hear what was said, Janet imagined his words must have become as tentative as his posture as he inched backward again. Finally giving in to his discomfort, he turned and walked away. Libby leaned sideways, watching him with casual interest until he blended into the crowd before scratching Freddie behind the ears and offering another bit of cake.

Rocky chuckled.

Janet hummed a noncommittal sound. "One of these days some boy won't be scared off so easily. Or she'll leave Freddie at home. Then what?"

"Then she'd better be ready to shoot her father with a tranquilizer gun."

Janet suspected he was right. "Are you going to be like that if we have a daughter?"

"Damn right. Especially if she's half as pretty as her mom." He nuzzled her ear, sending delightful shivers across her shoulders. "Is it too early to ditch this party?"

"I'm afraid so."

"Then dance with me again. I need to have you in my arms."

"Well, when you put it like that . . ." She was such a sucker for this guy. He had her wrapped around his finger every bit as much as little Ben did his parents.

She let him lead her across the lawn and onto the dance floor. Leaning against her husband's firm shoulder, she closed her eyes and swayed to the live orchestra music, thinking she could stay like that all night.

It only lasted a minute before a large hand tapped Rocky's shoulder. "Cut, please."

Rocky frowned but before he could protest, Vasili wrapped Janet's hand in his own and inserted himself between her and Rocky. With a wink, she mouthed " 'Bye" at Rocky and let the big Russian sweep her away.

He was surprisingly nimble and held her with a light touch as though she might break if he squeezed too hard. She probably would. "You look fantastic in a tux, Vasili."

"I'm handsome, no? And you are perfect gorgeous bride." She beamed, allowing fondness for the big

Russian to mix with a healthy caution. "We make beautiful couple, better than you and Rocky. Too bad you have to settle for second best."

"My rotten luck."

"I get nice present for newlyweds, too."

"Thank you." Without faltering, she added, "You included a gift receipt, right?"

"*Pfft*. You think I give you stolen merchandise? Such sticklers for law, you two." He shook his head over her hopeless moral standards. Looking around the yard and its hanging lanterns and strings of lights, Vasili nodded to himself, as though approving of the ostentatious wealth. His gaze lingered on the house. "Nice place."

"Yes, it is."

"Lots of money here."

"Lots of burglar alarms, too."

He gave her a sly smile. "You funny girl."

She smiled. "Dead serious."

"Maybe you and Rocky make good couple, after all. You too uptight for me."

"You think so? Rocky thinks he needs to protect me from myself and my reckless tendencies."

Vasili puffed up with feigned outrage. "What he know? He think I am dangerous person. Me! Can you believe this?"

"Outrageous. Anyone can see you're a pussycat."

He had to know she didn't believe it, but he preened anyway, fond of the image. "See? You smarter than Rocky. Maybe I give you back to him before he spreads more nasty lies about me."

She looked across the dance floor to where Rocky

watched them with folded arms and a steely gaze. He was still prickly about Vasili's affection for her, and became more possessive of her after every encounter.

"In a minute," she told Vasili, her voice calm despite the excitement already building inside her. "Let him wait. My husband needs to remember that he's married to a reckless, dangerous woman."

He eyed her suspiciously. "You use me for sexy, jealous purpose?"

"Yes," she admitted.

Vasili nodded his approval. "Excellent! Rocky get what he deserve."

Janet smiled. He certainly would.

Turn the page for a sneak peek
at the first book in a new trilogy by

STARR
AMBROSE

featuring the feisty and beautiful Larkin sisters

Coming Soon from Pocket Books

Rafael DeLuca had his hand on Maggie's ass. Again.

If they'd been at Del Tanner's bar in Barringer's Pass, she would have planted a vicious elbow jab in his wonderfully ripped midsection and told him to get lost. But they weren't in the valley. They were in the Aerie, the posh Colorado nightclub at the Alpine Sky resort on Two Bears Mountain. People came here to play and be seen, especially if they were rich or famous.

Rafael DeLuca was both. Anything Maggie did to him would be seen by the hordes of his fellow vacationing Hollywood glitterati. Plus, management frowned on pissing off the guests, especially the famous ones. Since management included her sister Zoe, Maggie spared Rafael's pretty rib cage and settled for grinding her three-inch heel into his toes as she turned to leave.

The star jerked his hand away. "Ow! Shit, baby, watch where you step."

"I did." She leaned close so the reporter lurking by the crowded bar wouldn't hear. "Time to go play with someone else."

Rafael's lip curled in a cynical smile. "After buying you drinks for the past hour? I don't think so, baby." He slipped his arm around her waist and pulled her close.

Maggie stiffened, but reminded herself that she should have seen this coming. She should have blown him off five minutes after he hit on her, when he'd scanned the room, then sauntered over with his smoky-hot gaze and confident opening line: "I always like to meet the most beautiful woman in the room first." He'd flashed his TV smile. "I'm Rafe. And you are. . . ?"

Despite the lame line, Rafael and his reality show costars had been fun to joke around with for an hour. But she preferred men with more depth, and an hour of Rafe and the cast of *Trust Fund Brats* was enough for her, especially after the unwanted ass grab.

Her toe-crunching move should have worked, but all those drinks he'd been buying had gone down *his* throat, not hers. His extremities were probably half numb by now. Unfortunately, it didn't affect the strength of his grip as he held her against him.

For Zoe's sake, Maggie gathered some restraint and didn't slug the drunken jerk. But she did put her fists on his chest, holding him at a slight distance. "Get your hands off me before I hurt you," she hissed through clenched teeth.

To her surprise, he released her. Laughing, he growled like a tiger. "*Rowr!* Maggie." He clawed the air playfully.

She took a step back while she could. "Look, Rafe, it's been fun, but I'm going to go mingle."

"Perfect. Mingling's what I had in mind, too." He

snagged a lock of her long strawberry blonde hair, twirling it between his fingers. "I hear redheads are hot."

"That's hot-*tempered*, genius." She hated to prove the cliché, but he was pushing her limits. Maggie turned to the man next to her. He had biceps like twin picnic hams and had hovered around Rafael DeLuca all evening like he might be a bodyguard. "You want to help me out here?"

The guy sipped his drink—not his first one—and gave her a dispassionate glance. "Nope."

Rafe smirked. "Baby," he crooned, "be sensible. I'm about to change your life. See that reporter over there from *The Hollywood Scene*? If I give the signal, your picture will be all over the country by tomorrow, and that little store of yours will be flooded with more customers than you can handle. My name is magic." He fingered the lock of hair, making sure his hand rubbed against her bare skin at the opening of her blouse.

Her flesh crawled and she brushed his hand away. "My store's doing just fine already. And if you don't move right now, I'll give your paparazzi friend an even better picture to splash across the tabloids."

He stroked her arm thoughtfully, and she checked to make sure he wasn't leaving a trail of slime. "You really have to learn to recognize an opportunity when it's handed to you. Especially when it comes in such a *big* package." He winked. "I'd think one of the Larkin girls would know all about that."

Maggie froze. Slowly, she lifted her gaze.

A hard edge touched his smile. "Oh, yeah. People talk, babe. But don't worry, I can spice up those rumors for you, make you more popular than ever." His hand slid up her side and found her breast. "I know exactly what you want."

Rafe's cool gaze cut into her like a knife, slicing right through the frayed bonds of her temper. She could almost hear them snap.

Cal set his beer down with a thunk. Pretty Boy DeLuca had just put his hand on her again. Damn it, this was not going to end well.

The redhead had captured Cal's attention even before Rafe DeLuca had hit on her. She was the type who always drew looks, with a smile that sparkled and the kind of lilting laugh that made others smile when they hadn't even heard the joke. She was certainly a distraction he didn't need. But, fortunately, DeLuca zeroed in on her, making it easy for him to watch them both.

Cal had to give the woman credit. Her engaging smile had grown stiff within minutes of talking to DeLuca. If that other woman from the *Trust Fund Brats* crew hadn't claimed Red's attention, she probably would have slipped away. But instead she got stuck next to DeLuca long enough for the man to feel *possessive*.

Even from across the room, Cal could see the woman didn't like it. She didn't look like the type to bow to fame or fortune, either. DeLuca didn't have much experience with that, so he wouldn't see it, but Cal did, and in another thirty seconds the whole bar would, too, including the reporters that swarmed after DeLuca like flies around manure.

The last thing Cal wanted to do was draw attention to himself, but he couldn't stand by and watch another woman be victimized. Red had no idea what she was getting herself into.

Abandoning his beer, Cal shoved through the throng of mostly women who loitered three deep around the bar. The damn reality stars attracted them like magnets.

"Hey, watch it!" A drink sloshed and someone swore. Cal mumbled an apology but didn't pause. A man grabbed his arm with an angry, "Hey, buddy!" but Cal shook it off, cursing under his breath because he wasn't going to make it in time. Twenty feet away, Red's eyes narrowed with icy determination. Maybe DeLuca was too smashed to recognize it, though a ten-year-old could have seen it coming.

Cal watched it happen like a slow-motion accident. The woman raised her left hand to DeLuca's shoulder. The gesture looked friendly, even to Cal, who knew better, and DeLuca actually smiled. He hadn't even noticed her right hand drop, taking aim. DeLuca's lips curved in smug confidence.

She drove her palm upward, smashing into De-Luca's nose with an audible crunch.

His scream was instantaneous. Reeling backward, he covered his nose with both hands as blood seeped through his fingers.

Shocked silence hung in the air for a second, then pandemonium erupted. People turned, reporters shoved, and a couple of women screamed. A dozen cameras flashed, held high and pointed toward the center of the action, while DeLuca yelled obscenities, blood dripping onto his sparkling white shirt.

Red hadn't moved. Cal noted the satisfaction in her eyes as he pushed through the onlookers and finally reached her side. He also noted the angrily contorted face of DeLuca's bodyguard as the man threw his drink aside and lunged at the woman.

Introductions would have to wait. Grabbing her arm, he spun her aside, putting himself in the guard's path. The man plowed into him like a linebacker. Cal barely had time to turn his shoulder into the blow, and the impact staggered him. It luckily also knocked the wind out of the guard. Muscle Man doubled over, confused and breathing hard.

Behind Cal, Red's furious yell pierced the bedlam. "Hey, what the hell do you think you're— Oh, shit!" Her objection broke off and he knew she'd seen the even more furious behemoth glaring like a bull ready to charge.

"Get out of here! Now," Cal ordered without taking his eyes off the guard.

She was smart enough to see the danger. Cal braced himself, ready to deflect DeLuca's lackey long enough for her to get away. Instead, she pushed around Cal, shoving him aside as she planted her feet and stood ramrod straight, jabbing her finger at DeLuca's bodyguard.

"Don't you dare touch me, you incompetent Neanderthal! If you had half a brain you'd take that mentally stunted, oversexed drunk you work for and lock him up in his room until he learns to act civilized!"

Cal felt as stunned as the guard looked. Red was either oblivious or too enraged to notice. Taking a step forward, she balled her fists. "In case you haven't heard, women aren't submissive playthings, put on earth to stroke your feeble male egos!"

Cal squinted as two cameras flashed in sync, flaring like a nova. Among the raised cell phones, several professional cameras clicked furiously, recording frame after frame of Red's tirade and DeLuca's bloody rant on the sidelines. They'd also probably captured clear photos of Cal. Shit! Grabbing Red's hand he hissed, "Lady, are you nuts?"

She shook him off, apparently just hitting her stride. She continued her lecture. "Do you even understand what sexual harassment is? Because it's obviously your job to keep the little pervert in line, and his behavior was beyond inappropriate. No one gets to treat me like that and—"

"Red!" Cal yelled loudly enough to cut through her fury.

"What!?" She whirled on him. "Someone has to tell these superficial morons—"

She couldn't see the crazed look on the guard's face, but Cal did. He also heard Muscles snarl, "Bitch," as he reached into his coat pocket.

Adrenaline shot through Cal. He'd hoped to get out of this without more violence, but that option just evaporated. Bloody noses and barroom tackles were one thing; guns were a whole new set of rules.

"Move! Now!" Grabbing Red's arm, he yanked hard. She staggered as he released her, but he couldn't watch to see if she stayed on her feet. The bodyguard extended his arm to the side, the anticipated black metal visible in his hand.

It was Cal's only chance. In that one moment, while the guard stood with his body wide open and unprotected, Cal jumped forward, throwing a kick directly at the guard's midsection.

His foot hit flesh, hard. The guard went wide-eyed, grunted, and crumpled. In one continuous move, Cal spun, his gaze finding Red's. "Go!" he ordered. And because he no longer trusted her to do the sensible thing, he grabbed her hand and charged forward. They dodged through the confusion into the resort's elegant lobby and through the main doors, out into the cool Rocky Mountain night.

Red clutched his hand and ran with him, finally agreeing with his agenda. She slowed and would have stopped under the front portico, but he tugged her to the right without skipping a beat. They followed the driveway until it split toward the parking lot. He hopped the low flowerbed border, landing on thick, well-manicured grass. She hesitated before making a cautious jump, and he realized she'd been running in high heels. Slowing to accommodate her strides, he rounded the corner of the hotel and drew her into the shadows against the brick wall.

Voices faded. Panting, they listened to a few running footsteps and shouted questions as people dashed outside, looking for them. Paparazzi, if they were lucky; DeLuca's hired guns, if they weren't. When Cal was sure they were alone, he finally released her hand. She leaned against the wall, eyes closed, catching her breath.

After several seconds, her breath evened and her eyes opened. She finger-combed her hair and shook it back behind her shoulders. He tried not to notice its silkiness. It was the kind of hair that tempted a man to run his hands up under it to cradle her head when he kissed her.

"Are you okay?" he asked.

She nodded, taking a deep breath and blowing it out. "Yeah. Thanks."

"You're welcome." That was the end of the niceties. He gritted his teeth. "You want to tell me just what the fuck you were doing back there?" he snapped.

Fire shot into her eyes as she moved away from the wall faster than he expected.

"I was defending myself." Her voice was low and controlled, but already seething with fury. "I thought that was obvious. Isn't that why you jumped into the middle of things in the first place?" She stuck her hands on her hips. "And who the hell are *you*, anyway?"

"I'm the guy who saved your ass."

They faced off for a long moment until Cal muttered, "Oh, hell. Come on, let's get out of here before they find us." He took a few steps toward the parking lot before he realized she wasn't following him. "What's the problem now?"

"What makes you think I would go anywhere with you?"

He might have smiled at her attitude if he'd been in a better mood. Unfortunately for them both, he was feeling pretty tense and irritable. "How about because you sure as hell can't go back in there without causing a bloodbath. And because I'm going to explain to you how you just ruined both our lives. Is that okay with you?"

She stared him down. "No. Give me your phone."

"What?"

"Mine's in my purse, in my sister's office. She's the assistant manager here. I can guarantee she'll want an explanation for that little scene, and you're going to help me convince her I was provoked and doing nothing wrong in defending myself."

That might be hard to do, considering she'd thrown the first punch. But she was holding out her hand, fingers wiggling impatiently, and damned if he wasn't curious to see how this played out. Besides, he couldn't leave her alone until she understood just how much danger she was in.

He pulled his phone from his pocket and she snatched it away. Dialing rapidly, she tapped her foot while she waited. Finally, she straightened. "Hi, Zoe, it's me."

She winced, and he bit back a smile. Apparently he wasn't the only one who found her aggravating. "I'll explain, just let me in the door by the kitchen. I don't want anyone to see us." When her eyes flicked up to his, Cal knew her sister had asked who was with her. "The guy who kicked Mr. Universe in the nuts."

Smiling sweetly, she snapped the phone shut and handed it back. "Follow me."

She marched off without a backward glance. He narrowed his eyes at the swing of her hips under her black skirt and weighed his options. His cover was blown. Red had just jumped into more danger than she knew and—taking a wild guess—she was bound to make it worse.

Shoving the phone in his pocket, he marched after her.

Her name was Maggie. He gathered that much during the enraged tirade from the highly polished, younger version of her that was her sister Zoe. To be fair, it was probably the official hotel management duds that made Zoe look so prim and proper—navy blue skirt and blazer, white blouse, and strawberry blonde hair identical to her sister's but pulled into a neat bun. Maggie's loose waves went a long way toward erasing any hint of propriety.

So did her attitude.

"I tried not to start something, I swear," she

claimed, brushing by her sister to head down the hall. Cal trailed them to what was apparently Zoe's office. Maggie paced before the desk, hands alternately combing hair off her neck and gesturing as she spoke. "I told him to get lost several times, but the little perv wouldn't take no for an answer."

Since Zoe didn't ask who the perv was, he figured she'd already heard some version of the incident.

"He kept *touching* me." Maggie glared, looking like she'd like to smack DeLuca again. "And even then I controlled myself, Zoe. I didn't want to cause you any trouble."

"But you did." Zoe stood with arms crossed, unmoved by her sister's anger.

"Yes, and you know why?" Maggie put her hands on her hips, her pretty pink lips pressed into a tight line. "He said he could give me what I wanted, and he knew I'd like it because—get this—I'm one of *the Larkin girls*."

Zoe's arms dropped. "Oh." Pain crossed her face. Cal definitely had to look into the significance of their supposed last name.

With all the energy sucked out of her anger, Zoe's gaze finally shifted toward Cal. "Who are you?"

"Cal Drummond. I hauled your sister's ass out of there before it got really ugly."

Maggie lifted a hand from her hip. "I was handling it."

"Bullshit," he scoffed. "You were asking to get killed. Rafe DeLuca is a dangerous man."

Her eyes narrowed, a look he was getting used to. "Thanks a lot. I brought you along to back me up, not throw me under the bus."

"It happened just like she said," he confirmed to

Zoe, then turned a hard look on Maggie. "And it was incredibly stupid."

"Hey, at least I stood up for myself. I was brave, damn it," she seethed.

Brave . . . and reckless. The words hit him like an icy splash of water. He'd been attracted to that mix once before and knew how deadly it could be—and how devastating. It was something he never wanted to go through again. He pushed the memory of Diane into the deep well where he kept it and spoke through gritted teeth. "There's a fine line between brave and stupid, and you plowed right over it."

Zoe looked ready to side with him. "Couldn't you have been a little more diplomatic? I've got half my staff out there trying to soothe some very powerful, very pissed-off customers. I'll probably have to comp their meals and rooms for several days, just to keep them from suing the hotel."

"I wouldn't go that far," Cal said.

She arched a condescending eyebrow. "Oh, really? Why not?"

"Because you shouldn't let the DeLucas put you on the defensive. And when I say the DeLucas, I mean their lawyers, because that's who you'll be hearing from. You could have easily called the cops on their precious boy and his hired ape, but you didn't. Be sure to point that out. Forget the sexual harassment part—"

"Sure, that's not important at all," Maggie muttered.

Cal ignored her and kept talking. "It's too hard to prove and you'll only get conflicting accounts. But the big guy they employ pulled a gun in a crowded room. Maybe he only planned to scare your sister with it, although I wouldn't bet on it. He had two drinks while I was there—seriously unprofessional for a bodyguard. He'll probably get fired anyway for letting something happen in the first place, but if I were you, I'd point out what you *didn't* do. You didn't call the cops and make an official report, you didn't have their gun-wielding bodyguard Breathalyzed, and you didn't have Rafe held on charges of harassment. Maybe none of it would stick, but it wouldn't matter because it would already be headlines, and not the kind they want. You know it, and they know it. *You* minimized the damage."

Zoe stared at him for several seconds, then gave a curt nod. "You're right. Thanks."

Maggie peered at him. "Who *are* you?"

"I'm a cop."

"Where?"

"Oklahoma City. I'm on leave."

"And you just happened to be at an exclusive resort in the Colorado Rockies watching me?"

He uttered a short laugh. "You? I was watching De-Luca." And Maggie, which still irritated him enough to make him deny it. He refused to be seen as one more poor sucker panting after her when he was sure there must be dozens. "I've been following him for three weeks."

Zoe tilted her head, puzzling it out. "Not because you're a fan, I imagine."

"Hardly," Cal scoffed. "Flexing and posing for the camera is only one of the things that sorry excuse for a man does. The other is much less pretty." He flicked a glance at Maggie. "He's a killer."

Cal watched their mouths open and their eyes go

wide before Maggie blurted, "Rafe DeLuca? Star of tabloids and reality TV? Famous for being rich and obnoxious?" She looked at him like he'd lost his mind. "The man can't even go into Starbucks without causing a media alert. How could he possibly get away with murder?"

He noted that she hadn't objected to the idea that he'd do it, just that he'd get away with it. At least she had no trouble reading the man's character. "If I'm right, he's gotten away with it several times. He has a violent temper, a lust for power, and a family that will go to any lengths to protect the reputation of their only son."

"You're kidding." Zoe sank into her chair, staring at him in disbelief.

"I wish I were."

Maggie seemed less shocked than skeptical. He didn't know if that was due to his claim or to the fact that it came from him. "You can prove it?"

"Not yet." It was a sore spot, since he wasn't sure how he ever would, short of finding the bodies on Rafe's property. He figured the odds of that were greatest right here, where the DeLuca family had a huge estate and where at least two of the young women in question had last been seen.

"But you're building a case? I can't believe the Oklahoma City cops would let you trail him to Colorado. Are you working in conjunction with the FBI?"

She was sharper than he'd thought. "No," he admitted. "I took a leave of absence, like I said. I'm doing this on my own."

Maggie took several seconds to absorb the information, rubbing a finger over her lower lip, which he found distracting all over again. "Why?"

He dragged his focus away from her mouth. With the way her eyes had softened, he knew she'd already guessed it was personal. "His last victim was my half sister, Julie." The corners of her mouth tightened, but she said nothing. "She lived in L.A. Her body was dumped in the hills. She'd been tied, then had her throat cut."

"Oh my God," Zoe breathed.

"I'm sorry," Maggie murmured.

"Me, too." He heard the gruffness in his voice and hardened his expression to match it. Anything to keep the vise grip of guilt from immobilizing him now that he'd finally started making progress. When it came down to it, he hadn't known Julie well, but her death had taught him an uncomfortable truth—guilt could be just as crippling as grief.

Scowling at the unwanted emotions, he said, "Once I starting looking into it, I saw a pattern of missing women leading back to Rafe. I don't want to see it happen again. I took a personal leave after Julie's funeral, and I'm not going back until I stop the son of a bitch for good."

Maggie nodded once, as if approving of his plan. "But he's not going to do that to me." The aggression was gone, but the naïve, stubborn confidence was still there. "It would be a stupid move—there were too many witnesses. He'd be the first suspect."

Cal heard a sigh, his exasperation with her returning. "You don't get it. You made him look bad in public, and the DeLucas never look bad. He's going to fix it one way or another." He stepped closer, making sure Maggie's golden-brown eyes couldn't look away from him. He needed her to understand, to fear like Diane hadn't. "Don't underestimate what just happened. Rafe's family is probably already huddling with lawyers, trying to figure out the best way to put a positive spin on your little incident."

"You act like it's headline news."

"It is! Didn't you see the cameras flashing? That place was full of paparazzi."

"But they don't know who I am."

"By tomorrow morning, they will. I guarantee it." A flicker of discomfort touched her eyes, and he went after it, ruthlessly driving home his point. "You're going to be tabloid headlines, Maggie. They'll have your name, and they'll be digging hard to find mine. The incident will be blown out of proportion and so will the theories they come up with for why it happened. Have you ever read those papers? You're in the shark tank, and they smell blood."

Worry lines creased her forehead. "I don't have to talk to them."

"That's your best move, but it won't be enough."

She blinked, staring, and he saw real apprehension finally settle in. She licked her lips nervously. "Then how can I stop it?"

"You can't. Rafe DeLuca's coming after you, and there's nothing you can do but try to survive it."